Pledge

D1737942

Eleanor Rose

finch benson

For Chase and August,

For being an incredible inspiration for romance, intimacy, and
friendship between two men.
This book is for you and everyone who strives for a love like
yours.

"All along there was an invisible string tying you to me…"
Taylor Swift

SCAN THE CODE IN YOUR SPOTIFY APP TO ACCESS THE OFFICIAL
OLLIE AND GABE APPROVED PLAYLIST FOR:

Pledge

Table of Contents

Chapter One
Gabe

"Aren't you the guy whose parents died in the plane crash?"

The audacity of this douchebag nearly made me choke on my beer.

"Yeah, I am," I replied, plastering my face with a manic grin. "Did you hear they found my mom's head in a field a mile away?"

The guy got a greenish hue to his face, and a horrified expression crossed his eyes.

As well, it should.

I had only been on campus for six weeks, and I'd lost count of the number of people who had asked me about the untimely demise of my parents. It wasn't really the kind of thing a civilized person brings up in conversation, but it's weird how desensitized people can get when it's all New York high society has been talking about.

Martin and Elizabeth Hoffstet, also known as the billionaire movie producers, had died when their plane engine caught on fire over the Hamptons. Apparently the crash cost nearly twenty six million dollars in damages to homes and, of course, cost me my parents.

They were sort of like the real life version of a certain superhero billionaire and his girlfriend played by Gwenyth Paltrow. So when their lawyer sat me down to read me the will—three days after I turned nineteen—I wasn't surprised they left me everything. Of course, it wasn't without strings. They'd left me a letter emotionally blackmailing me to go get a degree, and they'd always wanted me to be some kind of scientist. Me. The guy who'd only managed to squeak a C minus in biology and failed chemistry.

Twice.

But after a generous two million dollar donation to the science center, my application for Columbia was graciously approved.

The one shining beacon of hope was that going to college meant I had the opportunity to join a fraternity. It was the single thing in the world I could imagine myself being good at. All you had to do was drink and not die doing it. I wasn't super into the idea of the weird rituals fraternities usually did, but I figured it would be worth it.

I also learned pretty quickly that having money didn't make me much of a standout here—all the "brothers" were from well-off families. But apparently being questionably bi-curious and having no shame was the fastest way to become popular with everyone.

In particular, one guy, Alex Kessinger, who was closeted as shit, had already throat-fucked me twice in the bathrooms, then bought me a Rolex. Not that I couldn't buy my own Rolex, but I liked the power it gave me to know this guy was frothing at the mouth over what I could do with mine and still had the balls to introduce me to his girlfriend.

Tonight was my official initiation into the fraternity I'd chosen—well, the one that had chosen me. My dad had been president of the chapter when he was in college, and when the board found out I was matriculating, they sent me a personal invite to rush.

2

I was lucky I had my inheritance, because I had never worked a job, and this particular frat had a minimum account balance rule. Before initiation, all of the pledges had been forced to hand over their debit cards to the upperclassman, and they would be drawn out of a hat for party expenses. If your debit card didn't have enough to pay for the expense, you would be forced to take a harsher punishment.

Once we arrived at the party—not knowing if our bank accounts had been emptied—our hands were duct taped to two forty ounces of Olde English 800, and we weren't allowed to take them off until they were empty. I had been drinking since I was about thirteen, so it was no surprise when I was the first pledge done.

The house went wild as my brothers tore the bottles from my hands, jumping up and down around me, throwing beer and sweat everywhere. I had never been more grossed out or happier. It almost made me forget I was an orphan.

Almost.

Alex caught my eye from across the party and dipped his gaze before staring at me harder. I knew what he wanted. But the chase was half the fun.

I walked over to where he was standing, grabbing a shot of tequila and downing it as I approached.

"Great party," I said as he eye fucked me. I'd been watching him slowly get closer all evening and was pretty sure where this was headed. Why not get it there faster?

"Yeah," he replied, ruffling his hair. "We throw the best ones on campus."

"Any idea if they used my debit card for this?" I asked, hoping his obsession with me would give me an in on what to expect tomorrow.

"Oh, yeah," he said slowly with an exaggerated nod. "Not sure they used anyone else's, to be honest."

"Amazing," I said with an irritated smile. I could have seen that coming a damn mile away.

I was forced to lean in closer as the bass dropped, and I decided to let my playboy swagger flex. "You wanna go somewhere quieter to talk?" I asked, pretending the music was making me uncomfortable.

"Sure," he said with an expectant grin. "Where?"

"Bathroom?" I asked, and he nodded in agreement. That was where we'd met both times before, and I found it to be a relatively private location for the… transaction.

Up a flight of stairs we went, and into the multi-stall toilets, slamming and locking the door behind us. Almost immediately, Alex grabbed me by the throat and pushed me hard into the door in what I assume was meant to be a sexy, dominating way.

In reality, I was pretty sure he gave me a concussion, and I let out a whimper I didn't mean to.

"You good, dude?" Alex asked, taking a step back as if he was freaked out.

"Yeah, I'm great," I replied, rubbing the back of my head. "So, what's the offer?"

Alex stuffed his hands into his pockets sheepishly. "Well, I only have one thing, but it's pretty fucking good," he said.

"Go on…"

"I can get you the one unoccupied bedroom for an underclassman in the upperclassman hallway," he said, like he was telling me a secret.

"Sweet," I said. "Do I have to share it with anyone else?" If I was doing this for something I couldn't buy, I wanted to make sure it was worth it.

Alex shook his head, no, and I bit my lip in a way I'd noticed he liked. He took that as my consent, which for all practical purposes it was, and grabbed me by the hair, pushing me to my knees.

"Steady there, Champ," I said, looking up at him as he frantically undid his jeans and pulled forth a—frankly—unimpressive cock. He looked at me expectantly, and I only realized what he wanted a second later. "Oh, uh… it's so big…"

Fairly quickly, he grabbed hold of the back of my hair with one hand and pressed the head to my lips with the other. It smelled like ball sweat and cheap body spray. But having my own room freshman year was unheard of, so I took it.

Alex had already proven twice before that he wasn't a marathoner—no, this guy was definitely more for a sprint. So with a few well-placed tongue flicks along the underside of his length and a gentle massage of his balls, he was spilling onto my mouth in minutes.

I grumbled as a thick splotch dripped off my chin and onto my shirt. The worst part about messing around with guys was the mess. I wasn't even sure if I was into dudes or if I just had a lot of childhood trauma, which resulted in me constantly needing praise.

Thanks Mom and Dad.

Rest in peace and shit, I guess.

"Fuck, you're good at that," Alex groaned, letting his quickly softening cock flop in my face.

"You came on my shirt, dick," I said with irritation that lacked conviction.

"Oh," he said, finally tucking his junk away. "Sorry. Want me to pay for it?"

I scoffed. "Is paying for it gonna get me something new to wear the rest of the party?"

Alex shrugged. "What do you want me to do, Gabe?" He started to fix his hair, then indicated to the door. He wanted to leave, and he was willing to say anything to make that happen.

"Nothing," I said, knowing he wouldn't do anything even if I did ask. "But this room better have a phenomenal view."

I turned and unlocked the door, stepping out while studying the creamy glob sitting on my chest. I might have been a dick at times, but I would have been more careful than that on an important night.

I made my way back into the party, rubbing the white spot furiously, when suddenly, I bumped into someone.

"Sorry, man."

"No worries," the other guy replied. I turned to find Ollie, one of the brothers who I met first, but spent as little time with as possible. He was tall as shit and had these weird, yellowish, feline-esque irises that made me feel like he was scanning my brain.

"Well, uh…" I mumbled, looking around. "I think I'm supposed to see, uh, one of the board members to tell them I'm done with my forties." Ollie was making me nervous with the intensity of his stare, and I was eager to find an exit.

"Alex couldn't take care of that for you?" he asked with a smirk, but it was hard in a way that made me think he wasn't as amused as he seemed.

"What?" I replied. Fuck. He'd seen the white mark on my shirt. "I'm, uh, not sure what you're talking about, man. But I'll catch you later."

I had never power walked away from someone faster, and all I could do was hope that if he had seen me with Alex, he was more interested in a rendezvous of his own than spreading the dirty news.

I looked back at where he was standing and found him still watching me. A chill ran down my arms and across my back, causing me to shudder. I'd be fucked if he ended up being my big. Having a guy who looked at me like I was either a viper or a steak didn't sound like a particularly positive mentor/mentee relationship.

My attention was drawn away by some other pledges nearby, throwing up in the bushes with half empty forties still on their hands.

I shook my head with a giggle. "Amateurs."

In fact, it would have been difficult for them to reply with the volume of kick back they were currently watering the bushes with.

"More shots for me, then," I said, tipping my Solo cup toward them. "Good luck, gentlemen."

And with that, I marched off to the bar to try and push my luck with all the toxic things I could swallow in one night.

You know, a typical Tuesday.

Chapter Two
Olympio

After nearly twenty years of celibacy, continuing to practice restraint was nothing short of heroic.

The party was in full force when Gabriel was in the midst of the "game" intended to get the pledges drunk as fast as possible. He finished first, downing one of the bottles without taking a breath, then letting out a belch which made his lower lip tremble.

I watched him from across the room and tried to make my way through the crowd to be the first to congratulate him, but he walked in the other direction. He grabbed a cup of weak ale as he went, which he used to chase down a shot of something someone handed him when he walked past. With every step he took away from me, it felt like my soul itself was being yanked by the flowing, shimmering purple magic that connected me to him. It was insistent, compelling me to follow, to take him, to finally have him for my own.

But I couldn't. Not yet.

It was no easy task to spend almost two decades with only my hand to keep me company, either. From the time Gabriel was an infant to the moment his parents died, thrusting him into adulthood, it had been a compulsion for me to keep him safe. It wasn't until the day in the convenience store where he nearly collapsed after his parents' demise that I had even felt the first stirrings of romantic interest. The bond prevented me from coming into any kind of physical contact with him prior to that, which had made the disquieting number of times I'd had to intervene to save Gabriel's life before then a challenge.

But I had sworn to myself and to him, the day he was born and the soulmate bond had formed between us, that I would let him know me, to want and need me the way I wanted and needed him, before making my move. Before telling him about the bond.

But now I was stuck in this "fraternal" hellscape where I couldn't get drunk, couldn't sleep with anyone, and couldn't make my soulmate interested in spending time with me.

As much as I hated watching Gabriel destroy his body and mind like this, being able to be near him in the open was more intoxicating than anything, regardless. Even whatever he'd been drinking that was causing him to stumble around the room—something I knew because I could *feel* the drunkenness within him through our bond.

I could also feel a hunger in him, which had nothing to do with the large tray of fried items and crispy snacks he was currently picking at while speaking to a boy I'd met on my first day in the house. One who had made an enemy of me without even knowing why.

Alex Kessinger.

Alex had a girlfriend, but he barely hid that he was interested in Gabriel. Anyone who was sober would have been able to see Alex stalking him around like a predator. He had my soulmate wrapped around his finger and disgustingly got what he wanted by bribing him.

9

I had seen him watching Gabriel—*my* Gabriel—all night, even with his girlfriend at his side. He paid just enough attention to her to keep her from noticing, but it was obvious he was shaking with the anticipation of getting my soulmate alone.

The very sight of it sent a white-hot rage through me.

Sharing Gabriel's affection wasn't something I'd prepared for, even after spending most of his life as a living shadow, so I could stay close, keeping watch over him.

It was my family's magical lineage which allowed me to do it, and it had come in handy more than once during Gabriel's life. My sister Ariadne could summon weapons from shadow, but I had the ability to move hundreds of feet in a second, entirely unseen to those around me as I became the shadow itself.

I had always known my need to keep Gabriel from harm's way would eventually override my good sense. Which was how I ended up in the bathroom on the second floor of the fraternity house, blending into the shadows as easily as a mortal might cover themself with a blanket. They found security in being wrapped in fabric, somehow feeling guarded against whatever evil may lurk in their darkness, while I found mine in *being* the darkness.

There I was unseen. There, I could work my magic without having to come into contact with people, which was preferable here in the mortal realm, where I was just another face in the crowd rather than a prince.

I nearly lost my composure within the first few seconds when Kessinger grabbed Gabriel by the throat and slammed him against a door. I felt the impact of his head as though it was my own, our bond

10

granting me unfettered access to his emotional and physical state, giving me the tools I needed to keep him happy and safe.

Siphoning away some of the pain through the bond into myself, I ensured Kessinger's blow was tempered just enough to keep Gabriel standing, not that he remained so for long. After a halfhearted attempt to "check on him," Kessinger put his hand on Gabriel's head and pushed him to his knees before pulling out his cock and pushing it past my soulmate's lips.

I hovered around the edges of the room, pacing, listening to the sounds of Gabriel—*my* Gabriel—servicing this boy who had sworn to provide him with a better room in exchange for the act. And it wasn't the first time. They'd made deals like this before, and every time, I grew less and less tolerant of seeing something—someone—of mine in such a position.

Alex finished quickly, as boys with no real skill for sex are inclined to do, and I slipped from the room, knowing they would be coming out. I wanted the opportunity to confront Gabriel about the situation, to try to convince him this standing agreement with Kessinger was a poor choice. But I had no idea as to how I would bring it up or convince him when, to my great distaste, Gabriel seemed to trust this miscreant more than he did me.

My soulmate left the bathroom first, fixing his hair, his lips flushed from their engagement. I stared at them, pink and swollen, from halfway across the room, wishing it had been me who had managed to undo him like that. Alex left the bathroom right behind him with a smug look on his face. His zipper was still open, and the slight dampness from Gabriel's lips and his own fluids clung to the exposed fabric of his underwear. Not that anyone but me would notice. The rest of the house was already drunk, with most too intoxicated to even stand up properly.

But not me. And not Gabriel. Not when I could siphon away just enough of his drunkenness to keep him from falling too deeply into his intoxication. I'd hoped to give him a better resistance to the advances of people like Kessinger, but, unfortunately, I could see that my Gabriel needed no inebriation to be inclined toward trading his body for meaningless mortal possessions and privileges.

After Alex went back to the party and to his girlfriend, who was none the wiser about her boyfriend's bathroom activities, Gabriel began to meander the room, which was when I allowed myself to run into him.

"Sorry, man," Gabriel said.

"No worries," I said, trying to smile but feeling my rage bubbling up within me. It must have shown on my face, because Gabriel's own grin faltered.

"Well, uh…" he said, looking around. "I think I'm supposed to see, uh, one of the board members to tell them I'm done with my forties."

I was going to let him go, but I saw a shining white spot on his shirt where some of Kessinger's seed had dripped free of my Gabriel's mouth, and my possessiveness took over.

"Alex couldn't take care of that for you?" I asked, immediately regretting the way I spoke in anger, especially considering there was no way he could know I'd been watching the entire event in the bathroom.

"What?" Gabriel said, and I could feel from him that he was no longer slightly uncomfortable but had progressed to a mild distress at my reaction. "I'm, uh, not sure what you're talking about, man. But I'll catch you later."

He walked away, and I felt the pull of our bond tug at my heart, demanding I follow, but I knew I had to be patient. Gabriel needed to be willing. He had to need me as badly as I needed him, or the consummation of our bond wouldn't work.

And he wasn't ready yet.

I lost track of him after that, my own thoughts cloudy with jealousy. Thankfully, I had avoided having a target on my back by using magic to transfer in as an upperclassman. It came with the lie that I had been involved in the same fraternity at my former university, so when I vanished upstairs to my own room, it went unnoticed.

I paced the floor, feeling Gabriel's defensiveness wane in my absence, and I cursed myself for coming at him with such dominance. He would need to be eased in, not cornered and forced into this. If I was going to convince him to come with me, I would need to try a different tactic. I would have to be charming, friendly, seductive. All things which came as naturally to me as breathing.

Except when it came to my Gabriel.

In the two and a half thousand years I'd been alive, I could count on one hand the number of times I'd failed to seduce someone I wanted. I was certain at least a small part of that was due to my title, but I also knew I was gifted at getting someone, anyone, to spend a night of endless debauchery with me. And faced with my soulmate, someone fate had chosen just for me to be my other half, I couldn't even get him to talk to me for five minutes.

I threw myself onto my bed, looking out the window at the night sky. The moon here was so small, so dim compared to the moons in Sefaera. The stars simply sat in the sky, not sparkling and sharing their gleam with the people below in the form of shimmering rain.

I missed home greatly but knew this time to let Gabriel know me and earn his trust would be worth it when we returned.

I reached into my pants where I felt my already rock hard cock. Simply thinking about Gabriel—*my* Gabriel—in Sefaeran finery, laying on the ceremonial bed, ready for me to take him, was enough to have me throbbing. I unbuttoned the jeans I wore—a horrible, inflexible garment, which was the standard among young men of the age I appeared to be to these mortals. My underwear, an excessive and redundant layer, came next, pulled down to reveal my thick, stiff member.

I gripped it in my hand, feeling it pulse immediately as I thought about Gabriel on that bathroom floor. Kessinger was rough, which I was no stranger to myself, but he was rough because he had no grace or concept of others, and was willing to injure in pursuit of his own pleasure.

It was my responsibility to care for Gabriel, which is why I would never allow him to be truly hurt, unlike the little bastard downstairs, who would be lucky every day he survived after I had to witness the way he treated my soulmate.

I stroked myself, shadows unfurling from my fist as I moaned softly into the dark of my room.

"Gabriel… *my* Gabriel…"

No reply came. I could feel him still enjoying the party, but he was only human and couldn't feel the bond himself—at least, not in a way that would let him know what I was doing or feeling.

Not yet.

But as I came, spilling my own seed across my belly, I reminded myself it would not be forever that he couldn't access our bond. Soon he would be mine. We would belong to each other.

And then we would be eternally bound.

Chapter Three
Gabe

I woke up the next morning wishing I had died in my sleep.

My face was practically stuck to the sofa, and I was genuinely concerned the vomit that was acting as the glue wasn't mine.

No, if I'd barfed, I'd almost certainly feel a lot better.

I could smell bacon from where I lay, and even though the scent nearly made me paint the couch with my own special color, I knew food and water was the only thing that could really combat this terrible feeling.

I sat up, and the room spun around me. It really had me second guessing my alcohol tolerance I'd previously been so goddamn sure of.

Stumbling to my feet, I trudged down the stairs, half-tripping three or four times. I would have been embarrassed, but I frankly didn't give a shit what any of the other boys thought of me. They all already had their own opinions of who I was—good or bad.

The scintillating and nauseating smell of the roasted meat led me to the dining hall where a dozen or so boys sat already, most looking like shit warmed over themselves. I knew a few of them by face but not by name yet, so once I'd filled a plate with way more food than I intended to consume, I sat at an empty table and began to eat.

I'd only made it through three strips of bacon, two sausage links, one piece of toast, and some eggs when I suddenly felt the shifting and tilting of the world that only the very drunk and the very hungover experience, and I laid my head down on the table to make it stop.

I engaged in some focused breathing as I sat there, willing my body to keep it all down—alcohol included. There was nothing that would make me look like more of a bitch than barfing up my initiation night booze.

It says a lot that I was feeling bad enough to not hear someone pull up a chair and sit down.

"You look like hell."

I looked up to find Ollie staring at me from a little too close for my comfort. Most dudes would sit across the table from you. Ollie was sitting in the chair next to me.

"Thanks a lot, man." I met his eyes and saw he was giving me that weird, judgy, slightly evaluating look he had started to use whenever he saw me. "What?"

Ollie's lips quirked up just slightly on one side, giving his expression a cocky look to it. "Nothing, I suppose," he said in the strange cadence he used. "I mean, I knew you liked meat, but that wasn't really what I thought you meant..."

"Oh, haha," I replied, amused but unwilling to let him see it when he was making fun of me. Had I not felt like I'd been hit by a truck, I probably would have giggled.

"I would have thought you'd had your fill after I saw Alex Kessinger spilling out of your mouth last night, but clearly you're still working toward a heart attack."

"Did you have a point of coming over here? Or is this just a sprinkle of salt into the open wound that is my life choices leading up to now?"

He chuckled quietl and reached into his pocket. He held up something that glinted in the fluorescent lights, then set it down in front of me. "I'd say you've had enough sprinklings of salt lately. This is for you." He tapped on the little object, and once my eyes stopped unfocusing, I saw it was a little pin with the fraternity letters on it. "Congratulations. You survived initiation."

I took the pin in my hands and turned it over a few times. This was the moment my dad had wanted for so long—though I don't suppose he imagined I'd be this hungover. "Thanks," I said. "It would have really meant a lot to my parents."

Ollie's smile never faltered, but his eyes shifted just a little. I worried he was about to say something pitying, which might have made me hurl once and for all. But instead, he said, "Not to you, though?"

I almost laughed, but the thought of that much pressure on my stomach...

"I didn't have any plans for my future in place when my parents died, so it felt like the least I could do was make their plans for me happen instead." I paused for a moment, thinking about what I might have done if I hadn't come to Columbia. "I guess if I wasn't doing this, I would have probably gone on one of those world tours where you like, drink in every country and make a checklist about banging one chick of every flavor."

God, I sounded like a frat boy from a movie, and I almost barfed from cringing at myself.

Ollie reached over to take a strip of bacon from my plate. He took a bite and chewed slowly, his eyes never leaving mine. A yellow color with flecks of… purple? I'd never noticed *that* before. Weird.

"That's… something," he said once he'd swallowed. "Expanding your horizons, then. I've always found traveling to be really enlightening. After all, I wouldn't have ended up here if I'd just stayed home forever, would I?"

I shrugged. "Where are you from, exactly? And what's with the hardcore nineties name? Skater parents?"

He smiled at me in that weird, enigmatic way, like he was trying to decide if he was going to answer or not. "More like… ancient civilization enthusiasts. It's short for Olympio."

I cringed at the moniker. That was a hell of a name to be strapped with for the rest of your life. "Thanks, Mom and Dad." I laughed before realizing doing so made my head hurt and my stomach churn.

But honestly, at that moment, everything did, and I was back to wishing I was dead.

I suddenly saw Ollie clutch his stomach, and I raised an eyebrow. "You okay, man?"

He blinked, then refocused his eyes on me. "Yeah. Just, uh…" He shook his head and chuckled. "I'm not sure the bacon is good. But enjoy your breakfast. You'll need your strength for Big/Little night tonight." He stood up, still looking a little out of sorts, and walked away, his shoulders tense, not looking back at me once.

Ollie had barely left when I saw Alex attempting to catch my eye from across the room. He crooked a finger at me, biting his lip, and I gave him an apprehensive look. He nodded, and I decided it might be worth my time to at least see what he wanted.

He looked really fresh for someone who'd been drinking like he had last night, and I had to admit, he smelled like an Abercrombie Model.

"Hey," he said quietly as I slid into the seat next to him.

I felt his hand slide down my thigh and give my knee a squeeze, which my cock promptly replied to. "How do you look so... unfucked?"

"Good genes." His fingertips brushed the inside of my thighs, and I shuddered against him, my hips pressing forward so he was forced to stop teasing me. "I wanted to give you this personally," he said, pressing a small piece of metal into my palm.

I looked down to find a key in lime green, my favorite color. "Is this...?"

Alex nodded. "I hope you'll find the view suitable. We could go check it out right now, if you like."

As he spoke, he pressed his fingers flat against my junk and gave it a gentle squeeze. Everything south of my belly button tensed, and I nodded with enthusiasm. "Sounds good."

We both stood, and I nearly ran into someone as I did. A tall, broody someone.

"Oh, sorry, man. I didn't see you there." I looked to where Alex had gone and realized he had only just noticed I wasn't following. He hovered near the bottom of the stairs, barely trying to hide his hard on.

Ollie put out a hand like he was trying to steady me so I didn't fall, but I didn't need the help. He seemed to realize this halfway through and ran it through his hair instead.

"Have you seen Kessinger?" he asked, his eyes narrowed in a way that made me think he knew I not only had *seen* Alex, but he also knew exactly how much I'd *felt* him.

"He…" I mumbled. "He was just… surely you saw him here."

Ollie always had this weird way of posturing, so it felt like he was towering over me. It simultaneously made me feel uneasy and curious. And I'm not sure what I was smelling, but every time he got this close to me, I could feel my senses clouded with this amazing scent.

"Mm," Ollie said with a tight-lipped smile and a half-nod. "I thought that was him. I was just coming to get him. They need the upperclassmen upstairs in five for a meeting. Mandatory. No excuses."

He spoke to me, and I felt like he was looking at me, but his eyes seemed to be going just past my ear to where I knew Alex was waiting.

I could feel the weight of my decision in my chest. I was hard as fuck even though I'd adjusted in an attempt to hide it, and the only thing I wanted to do was find out precisely what Alex had in mind for the raging boner he'd given me.

On the other hand, if the two of us disappeared together, and anyone noticed, our cover would be blown.

I shifted sideways, crossing my legs in a way I hoped looked casual.

"Uh… I mean, I'm not in charge of him. Why would I know where he went?"

I swear Ollie's eyes flashed entirely violet for a second, but it was gone as fast as I thought I saw it. He put his hands deep in his pockets with a knowing smile and leaned in, his head over my shoulder, to speak directly into my ear.

"Maybe because your cock is pointed directly at him like a compass."

"My wha—" I looked down to see my shit had shifted and was about as hidden as a fire engine in a haystack. "Oh, uh… nah. It's just…" I looked for Alex once more, but he had disappeared.

Fucking bastard.

"You hoping Alex is your big?" Ollie said, seemingly oblivious to my distracted nature. "Might be the only thing 'big' about him, if rumors are true."

I jerked my head back to him and found myself trapped in his eyes, wondering what kind of scientific wonder made someone's irises swirl like a bottle of cheap shiny liquor.

"Your eyes…"

I could feel myself gaping, yet somehow, I was totally transfixed.

Ollie raised an eyebrow, giving me the hint of a smirk as he did. "What about them?"

"They… They… is that purple?"

He suddenly looked like he'd won some kind of prize, but the expression vanished before I could be sure. "Oh," he said with an overabundance of nonchalance. "You can see it? Not everyone can."

My head felt fuzzy as I tried to understand what he meant, but just then, I spotted Alex leaning back down the stairs.

"Oh," I said before I'd really thought it through. "There's Kessinger."

Ollie's eyes lingered on me for just a couple seconds too long before he slowly, casually looked over his shoulder at Alex. "So he is," he said as he turned back to me. "Thanks for your help." He glanced down to where my cock had thankfully stopped pointing at Alex. "Sorry for keeping him from you. But mandatory means mandatory."

He didn't sound sorry in the least.

"He's not waiting for me. I mean he's not… I'm not…"

But Ollie walked away from me without allowing me to finish the thought, leaving me even more desperate to try and explain myself.

I didn't know why it felt like torture to have him make the assumption, even if he was right. All I did know was Ollie had my number, and if he could figure it out—it wouldn't be much longer before everyone else did, too.

Chapter Four
Olympio

There were few parties involving the nobility of Sefaera I was not invited to, and even fewer where I did not manage to make myself the center of attention. Even as the ruler, in practice, if not title yet, I was never one to turn down a good time. Truthfully, dealing with the Council—with that absolute bastard Typhir—day in and day out would drive anyone to drink and let loose at the end of the day.

But here in the human realm, I needed to keep a low profile, and I couldn't get drunk even if I wanted to. The spirits available here had no effect on demon blood, and even if they did, I needed to keep an eye on Gabriel and that little shit stain Kessinger to keep them apart as much as I could.

It was the day of Big/Little Night for the fraternity, the event where the pledges were paired with upperclassmen who would mentor them as they made their way through school until they were upperclassmen themselves. As a "transfer," I had no little brothers under my wing, so I was one of the first to be offered my choice of littles, much to Kessinger's distaste. He even tried to corner me during the meeting where we had made the selections to convince me to give up my claim on Gabriel so he could have him, instead.

"Why?" I asked, crossing my arms and giving him a look that has made hundreds of powerful beings shrink away from my challenge.

But not Alex. He was either very brave or very stupid, and he attempted to rise up to my level, something impossible since he was at least half a foot shorter than I. He stood toe to toe with me and stared me directly in the eyes, challenging me, something few have ever done and not wished for death afterward.

"Because we're already bros," he said, stubbornness radiating from him. "Why mess with success? Let the kid have the big brother he wants. Not someone who doesn't even know the school that well."

I stared at him silently for a moment, then looked down at the little paper in my hand as though I was contemplating it hard.

"You know…" I said, tapping Alex twice on the arm with it. "As much as I think you have a point, maybe it's better if Gabriel's big brother doesn't take sexual advantage of him every other night. In fact," I pressed the tip of my finger into his chest, the paper tucked into my fist, "I bet if there was a little distance between the two of you, your girlfriend might not feel so abandoned that she has to keep spending the night over at Phi Kap."

Alex looked as stunned as if I'd beaten him over the head with a mallet. His mouth went slack and his eyes unfocused for a second before he shook his head and regained his composure. Of course, he had no idea what I was saying was entirely true. Christine had been cheating on him with one of our rival brothers as surely as he'd been cheating on her with Gabriel and anyone else he could convince to touch his unimpressive excuse for a cock.

"Don't fucking touch me," he sneered, batting my hand away. He looked and sounded like a caricature of a bully that might be in a movie Gabriel watched when he was younger. "You want to be careful who you piss off. I don't give a fuck who you thought you were back wherever you came from, but here, I'm in charge."

"And yet," I said with a patronizing smile, "I'm the one holding Gabriel's card."

I turned and left him fuming as I went to sit on one of the couches. The board went through the rest of what we needed to know for the night, including where each of us would be stationed once the underclassmen were good and drunk. It seemed to be a common theme at these events—getting the freshmen as drunk as possible to test their resolve or constitution, I supposed, since the end result was never orgies of beautiful people, but piles of vomiting young men who were too inebriated to get it up.

As the rest of the upperclassmen chose their little brothers, I watched them negotiate and needle each other about their choices, as if every single name on that table hadn't been extensively vetted to fit in with the rest of the house. Alex shot me furtive looks every few minutes as he held onto the name he'd selected, a boy called Thompson, as if he was denied a first name at birth. He was cut from the same mold as Kessinger himself—an over-inflated ego and nothing but bravado to back it up.

A few hours later, all of the upperclassmen and the pledges were gathered in the common room of the house. Two kegs of beer were already empty, with two more being rapidly depleted, as though it was a race against time to finish them all—which, I supposed, it was. Everyone tossed ping-pong balls into cups or flipped their cups on the edges of tables to determine who had to drink too much too fast. And that wasn't even taking into account the massive display of liquor being emptied into shot glasses and, subsequently, into open mouths.

And my Gabriel's was no exception.

As I watched him from the edges of the room, I saw Kessinger pull him into several games and encourage him to take far too many shots of various alcohols. I felt the unsteadiness coming over him as he grew more and more inebriated. I tried my best to siphon away some of his drunkenness, allowing him to be a bit more clearheaded, but all I succeeded in doing was making *myself* drunk—something I hadn't experienced once since coming to the human world. And to make matters worse, the more I took from him, the more he drank to make up for it, so it was a lost cause all around.

Suddenly the music cut out, and the house lights came back up. Everyone looked around in mild disorientation, even me. I was just intoxicated enough that it took me a couple of seconds to understand what was happening.

"Alright, pledges!" the president of the fraternity said into a megaphone, standing at the top of the staircase and looking down at everyone. "You are all to stay right here and keep drinking while the upperclassmen head out. Me and Gary will be staying here to hand out your first clues once we think you're all good to go. Upperclassmen... to your stations!"

I turned to the door and started to make my way over there, and found myself running into the door frame as someone bumped past me.

"Sorry, man," Kessinger said in a slimy, insincere voice. "Didn't see you there. You feeling okay? You don't usually get this drunk. Why don't you head to bed? I'll make sure Gabe is taken care of."

The implication that he would be willing to go against the fraternity rules was nothing to the rage I felt at this human child once more thinking I was going to be intimidated or otherwise coerced into conceding this unspoken war over my soulmate.

Little did this insignificant speck know who he was dealing with.

"While I appreciate the generous offer…" I said, reaching out and putting a hand on his shoulder. He tried to pull away, but I dug my fingers in just enough that he would have to make a scene to get me off of him. "… I think it would be more appropriate for Gabriel to find his big brother at the end of the hunt, instead of someone who's only there to get his cock serviced. Because he deserves a lot better, and I think you know it. That's why you're so intent on sleeping with him. You think it will prove you're not totally worthless." I shrugged and removed my hand before leaning in to show him he posed no threat to me. "But nothing can do that, Alex. Only *not* being worthless can have that power."

Once again, I left Alex standing with his mouth open as I walked out into the cool fall air. I wanted to glance back, just to marvel for a moment at how his low brain cell count made it far too easy to leave him dumbfounded, but I wasn't going to give him another ounce of thought. Tonight was going to be a big step toward earning Gabriel's trust. I had waited a thousand years for a soulmate, for him. I was

28

willing to wait a while longer until he wanted me as much as I wanted him—as much as I needed him—before I exposed him to the truth of his existence and the majesty of his future.

And if that meant ignoring scum like Kessinger instead of destroying him like he deserved, so be it.

I walked with a couple of the other upperclassmen toward the athletic fields, where we all finally dispersed into our own hiding spots. Mine was in the dugout of the baseball field, about as far away from the house as you could get. A vague memory surfaced beneath the rapidly fading haze of intoxication of Alex being delegated to assigning our hiding spots.

I suppose he could have chosen somewhere riddled with sewage or garbage, but this was still clearly a power move.

The slow motion of the cosmos overhead was soothing in an odd way. Even though the stars were dimmed and difficult to see through the light pollution of the city, the patterns of stars, never changing their positions, simply slid across the sky as if on a track, lulling me nearly to sleep before I jerked awake. After a moment of disorientation, I realized it had been half an hour, and Gabriel still wasn't here. I wasn't entirely sure of the length of time I was expected to wait, but after leaving Kessinger seething back at the house, I didn't trust him to not somehow sabotage Gabriel's path to me and direct it to himself, instead.

I reached out along the soulmate bond, feeling for Gabriel and where he was. He wasn't far, but he certainly wasn't heading in my direction. Not knowing if that was part of the scavenger hunt or if he had been misled, any patience I had evaporated.

With a swirl of darkness, I shifted into the shadows, smoke-like wings propelling me along the line of buildings and beneath large trees, following the beautiful, shimmering, purple line of magic that joined us.

Moons and rivers, if Gabriel could see me like this, in my true, demonic form, he'd never agree to come with me willingly.

It took me nearly a mile away to one of the academic buildings, which was surprisingly unlocked—probably a favor from a bribed security guard.

Up the stairs and down a hall, I found Gabriel and two other brothers standing uneasily outside of a heavy metal door.

"This can't be right," one of the others said.

"Light and sound, all around, but the source of it all could lead to a bad fall," Gabriel read off a piece of paper. Each of them was holding an identical sheet with their name on the back of the one they held. "Sounds like the catwalk over the theater to me."

"I, uh…" a boy I thought was called Tyler said, his voice clearly shaking. "I'm afraid of heights."

The other boy began to ridicule him for being a "bitch" and a "pussy." But to my delight, Gabriel turned to them both with an irritated look on his face.

"You're afraid of crossing the street without the walk signal on, Thompson," he said. "We live in New York—if you're afraid of traffic, you need to go somewhere else. Don't make fun of people for shit you don't want to come around and bite your own ass."

Thompson promptly shut his mouth, looking put out. I knew Gabriel's intoxication had loosened his normally soft-spoken tongue a bit, but the sentiment made me proud.

30

They continued to discuss the likelihood that they were in the right place when I heard movement on the other side of the door. It pulled my attention away from *my* Gabriel's display of at least one of the reasons why fate would have chosen him to be my soulmate. Justice, fairness, and protection of the weak were all things which he would one day be in charge of in Sefaera.

As long as I could keep Kessinger from driving a wedge between us.

And speaking of Kessinger, whoever was moving on the other side of the door gave off an aura I thought I recognized. I drifted away from Gabriel and through the crack below the door, keeping to the shadows of the metal walkway that hovered over the stage and rows of seats below. I wish I could say I was surprised to find Alex Kessinger shuffling through the envelopes of clues. As I watched, he swapped Gabriel's clue with Thompson's.

Was he hoping the official records would be changed if Gabriel found the wrong upperclassman? It seemed so, as the door began to rattle, and Alex scampered off in the opposite direction.

Thankfully, in my shadow form, I could move faster than any human, and I switched the clues back to the proper envelopes. As the other boys entered and found their clues, I smiled, knowing I'd managed to once more undermine Kessinger's attempts to create a divide between *my* Gabriel and me.

I followed him through the rest of the scavenger hunt, which lasted nearly another hour, until finally, Gabriel was alone and walking across the baseball diamond toward the dugout. I rushed ahead and took my place, reclining back on the bench with my feet up and my hands behind my head, like I had been casually waiting there for him the entire time.

"Surprise," I said smoothly, raising my arms up in a 'y.'

"Ollie?" Gabriel said, looking confused. He glanced down at his clue, then around the dugout.

"In the flesh," I said, chuckling to myself at my little joke, since I hadn't been flesh most of the night.

"You're…" he said slowly, not entering the dugout. "You're my big brother?"

I stood up and walked to him, hands in my pockets. "I am," I said, smiling down at him.

He bit his lip, and a jolt of pain shot through my chest as I saw the disappointment flash across his face before he recovered and gave me an empty smile.

"Cool," he said.

A long, uncomfortable silence blossomed between us, and it was filled with the unspoken fact that, to my disappointment, Gabriel clearly had been hoping for someone else—Kessinger. And for perhaps the first time in my life, I was at a loss for words. I stared at my soulmate, standing in front of me, and was forced to confront the knowledge that, given the choice, he wouldn't choose me.

A steely resolve hardened within me. I had been playing this as though there wasn't any room for competition. I had no intention of risking losing my soulmate to some mortal—certainly not one as worthless and intellectually bankrupt as Alex Kessinger.

I reached out to embrace him, feeling Gabriel's resistance to the gesture. But all it took was a small suggestion sent along the shining purple bond for him to open his own arms and hug me back.

I felt guilty for doing it. I had wanted Gabriel to choose me of his own volition and had expected he would. But things had gotten complicated. The door to our future together was closed with a rusty hinge, and if using my influence on Gabriel in small, innocuous pushes could work as an oil to loosen the hinge…

So be it.

Chapter Five
Gabe

I sat on my bed the next day reading through a mind numbingly complex textbook, Alex laying at the foot of my bed like a dog and tossing a tennis ball at the ceiling. We were passing a flask back and forth and discussing the events from last night.

Vodka. Cheap.

"I swear to god, dude," he said to me, trying to explain how I got Ollie as my big. "I did everything I could. The guy is just one of those alpha douchebags."

I looked up from the text to nod in agreement. "He's weird as fuck. Like he might be hot if he wasn't such a future serial killer."

Alex nodded in agreement, turning on his side to watch me. "You know, spending time with you is the best part of my day," he said. "I got you a present."

Now the textbook was set aside, and I gave the senior my full attention.

"A present?" I asked suspiciously. "For what?"

"Just because you have the best smile I've ever seen——"

"Does your girlfriend know you feel that way?" I asked.

Alex got red in the face but tried to play it off with a fake little chuckle. "Come on... you know that she's just... an obligation. Gotta keep the *Kessinger legacy* intact."

"So glad I can do my part," I snorted, taking another swig from the flask and waiting for this supposed gift.

"Don't be like that," he said, scooting toward me so he could run his hand along the inside of my thigh. "I swear to God, Gabe—if you wanna drop out of school, I will pay for your entire livelihood."

I gave Alex the most scathing look I had in me. "You are aware that I'm a billionaire, right? I don't need *anyone* to take care of me."

He held up his hands in surrender. "Okay, okay. Here."

He handed me a small box, and I took it, wondering what in the world Alex would have gotten me to further garner the affection I was already giving willingly.

Alex was a hobby, as much something to do as attending Columbia. But it was nice to pretend like there was something there, even if it was only for a little bit each day.

As I pulled the lid aside, I found myself looking down at a vintage class ring from 1988—the year my dad graduated. On one side of the ring there was a scale of justice, and on the other...

"Dad?"

Alex was wearing a terribly smug grin as my eyes filled with tears. "Do you like it?" he asked.

I nodded. "How did you get this?" I asked him, choking slightly.

Alex bit down on his lower lip, the grin shifting to a look of victory. "This past summer, I heard about an estate sale for a deceased billionaire. I went looking for a Lambo but saw this with our letters on it and thought maybe they would want to display it here or something. I had no idea Hoffstet's son would end up pledging. Once I made the connection…"

I felt like I couldn't breathe.

Watches, corner rooms—all nice but meaningless. Totally worthy of a transactional relationship.

But this was personal.

I leaned forward, pushing the wrapping and box to the side and slipping the ring on my right ring finger. Then I placed my hands on either side of Alex's face and pressed my lips to his in a simple, grateful kiss.

At first, Alex seemed like he was going to pull away. But then he deepened the exchange, his tongue crossing my lips and caressing my own.

His mouth tasted like vodka and chapstick, and it was delicious in a dizzying way. Or maybe I was dizzy from the booze.

Suddenly there was a knock on my door, and Alex fell the fuck off the bed as I jumped.

"Gabe," he hissed, having clearly hit his head on my bedside table.

I mouthed the word sorry to him, then turned my face to the door. "Just a—"

It opened before I could finish, and Ollie's head came into view.

"Hey," he said, smiling at me. Then, with an exaggerated glance at Alex, he said, "I didn't think you'd be here, Kessinger. Especially since your girlfriend was downstairs asking for you about fifteen minutes ago, and no one knew where you were."

"Mind your own fucking business," Alex grumbled with a little too much defensiveness to not be completely transparent about what had been happening.

"Do you frequently barge into people's rooms?" I asked with a heavy tone of annoyance. I could hear my words slur, but the more I tried to control them, the messier they got.

Ollie stood with his hands in his pockets in the doorway, looking almost sheepish, if that was even an expression he was capable of. "Sorry about that. I had no idea I'd be interrupting anything... important. But tonight's the Greek night at Amity Hall, and as your big brother, I was just coming to see if you had any questions about what to expect."

"Nah, I'm good man," I said, suddenly aware my breath reeked of booze. "Alex was just telling me what it's gonna be like."

Alex looked from me to Ollie, then back to me. "I'm just as capable of filling him in as you."

Ollie looked down at Alex where he still was on the floor, and, to my surprise, extended a hand to him. "Of course you are," he said. "Like I said, I wasn't aware you'd be here. But I'm glad you're filling him in. I have homework to do, anyway."

Alex took his hand, but gave him a firm tug as he stood, slightly knocking Ollie off balance.

"Bye, then," I said with more vitriol than I intended. "I mean, obviously, I'll see you later."

Great recovery, Gabriel. Now you sound like more of a douche than he does.

"Looking forward to it," he said, patting Alex on the shoulder like they were best buddies. "I'll come by around eight to walk over with you."

"Oh, you don't need—"

"I want to," he said, interrupting me. "I didn't get a little brother at my old school because I transferred before I could. I've been waiting for this for a long time."

Clearly, this was something I wasn't getting out of.

"Yeah," I said stiffly. "See you then."

Ollie left the room without looking back and closed the door behind him.

I looked up at Alex, feeling my heart pounding in my ears, amplified by the vodka I'd so readily consumed. The intervals at which it was beating were accelerating, and suddenly I couldn't think. I couldn't breathe.

Alex looked me in the eyes, then sat back on the bed next to me, pulling me into a hug that quickly morphed into a kiss.

It was the best feeling in the world, having his strong arms embracing me, his fingers toying with my hair as he attempted to kiss away my panic. If I hadn't drank as much as I did, I would be hard as hell right now and begging him to fuck me.

Nothing made sense and everything did all at once, and I felt like I didn't know which way was up or down, or whether I should have been kissing him at all.

All I knew was I felt moments away from a panic attack, and his lips seemed to be fixing it.

Alex pulled away and reached for his bag about a foot away across the floor. He set it on the bed in front of us and reached inside, pulling out a bottle of pills.

"Here," he said in a gentle tone. "This should help with the anxiety."

He handed me the pills and the flask, and, in hindsight, I should have thought about the combination a lot longer than I did. But I was so desperate for the pain to stop, I would have done anything.

The pill went down easy—they always did—but the burn of the vodka on my throat was still intense. I took a second drink for good measure, then laid back on the bed.

Alex leaned forward and hovered over top of me, dipping down for another kiss. "Feeling better?"

Actually, I was. In fact, I was feeling so good I couldn't even feel the bed beneath me anymore. I was floating. Floating away from the emotional weight I couldn't bear and from Alex, who was shaking me.

"Dude, are you asleep?" he asked.

I tried to reply, but I couldn't. My mouth felt heavy, like it was filled with peanut butter, and the world around me was closing in.

Everything was fine.

Everything was going to be just fine.

Chapter Six
Olympio

It was only the third time I'd ever felt pain of that magnitude, and each of the times before, it had been for the same reason.

I watched Kessinger get up after breakfast and less than subtly make his way to Gabriel's room, and almost immediately, I felt a slight burning in my chest. At first, I didn't notice it, but within minutes of Alex's departure and presumed meeting with my soulmate, the bond began to shift and change as it had done only twice before—the morning of the plane crash that had taken his parents from him, and one other time. The once shimmering purple magic had become opaque and the color of human blood, like a trail of it leading to a murder scene.

Each time, this had happened because Gabriel was in danger of dying. That couldn't possibly be the case now, could it? Kessinger was a cunt, but overall harmless to anything except for my future with my soulmate and my kingdom.

But as the red color deepened and boldened, the pain in my chest intensified to the point that I had to excuse myself to prevent doubling over in front of the other members of the fraternity.

"You good, man?" asked one of the members whose name I hadn't bothered to remember. "You look like that jungle juice from last night is about to reappear to decorate the table."

"Yeah," I said with a forced laugh, putting my hand on my stomach to sell the facade. "I think I'm a little more hungover than I realized. I should go get some rest before Greek Night."

"Good idea," he said. "The board are hardasses about attendance at shit like this since it makes us look good to the Greek Life admins."

"Noted," I said. "Thanks."

I turned and left the dining room, escaping to the hallway upstairs where the bedrooms belonging to the upperclassmen were.

Well, the upperclassmen and Gabriel, thanks to Kessinger throwing his weight around.

My room was only three doors down from Gabriel's, and being this close, I was able to attune to some of what he was feeling, even through the agony. He was drunk and mildly annoyed, but then a wave of something different overtook it. Something deep and emotional, and I began to tear up as though whatever was happening had touched me that deeply.

What the hell was going on in there? What was Kessinger up to?

My question was answered almost immediately when I felt Gabriel's arousal pique. Whatever had started it, the intent was obvious now. Alex was seducing my soulmate, and Gabriel's response was strong enough to be a threat to the bond between us.

Was he falling in love with Kessinger? With the idiot human who I once heard tell a dehydrated Gabriel he should drink some vodka? Who frequently forgot to zip his pants after urinating? Who wore sunglasses inside and at night? It was unfathomable that my soulmate would prefer him over me. What was it about Kessinger that had Gabriel so enthralled?

The questions burned within me, but for the moment, I couldn't dwell on them. I had to get in there. Fast. I needed to put a stop to whatever was about to happen, not only because of the raging jealousy within me, but for the sake of my kingdom.

Pulling myself together enough to seem unbothered, I knocked. A heavy thud sounded beyond the door, and I smiled as the bond began to return to its usual state. I let myself in, and after making sure I'd well and ruined the moment, retreated to my own room.

But it wasn't over.

The bond twisted and tightened inside of me, immediately turning deep red again, and I knew I had minutes at best to prevent whatever was about to happen.

Fading into the shadows, I rushed back to Gabriel's room, slipping in through the crack below the door and moving to the corner to watch, ready to step in and do whatever I needed to in order to keep the pulsing, aching bond from breaking.

But I was already too late.

I was helpless to stop it as Gabriel washed down some kind of pills with whatever was in the flask Kessinger had brought. I watched as he gave Gabriel, who had quickly fallen unconscious, a gentle shake. "Dude, are you asleep?" he asked. When no answer came, he looked

42

down at the bottle of pills and the flask, sighed, and tucked them into his pocket before leaving the room without bothering to even check if Gabriel was breathing. He was, but barely, and his heart was fluttering weakly and quickly.

Red-hot pain exploded in my chest, and I was transported back two years earlier to one of the most terrifying nights of my life.

Gabriel and his parents had attended a movie premier, and Gabriel was just starting to be recognizable in the Hollywood scene. After the screening, Gabriel had gone back to the hotel while his parents attended an after party.

"You sure you'll be okay?" his mother asked as he crawled into bed.

"Yeah, Mom," he said, smiling. "Tonight was fun. Thanks for bringing me."

She kissed his forehead, and his father said, "Good night," as they exited the room, leaving Gabriel alone.

Thinking he was safe for the night, I'd let my guard down. I booked myself into the room next to his in order to get some sleep, exhausted after following him through the shadows all day. It required a high level of physical and mental stamina to maintain that form, but it was worth it to keep an eye on Gabriel, especially in a city where danger and temptation lurked around every corner.

And that night, as I slept, *my* Gabriel had managed to find both.

I had woken up shortly after two in the morning with that same agonizing pain in my chest, where the bond connected my soul to his. It had never happened before, but it could not have been more apparent something was wrong. With only the slightest effort, I felt Gabriel was no longer in the room beside mine, but had traveled halfway across town.

It took me a matter of minutes to get there, to the house on the edge of the cliff, where dozens of young celebrities and trust fund recipients had gathered in a haze of pounding bass and smoke from various drugs. I rushed inside, looking for Gabriel, and if I didn't have the bond, crimson and throbbing, I wouldn't have been able to find him.

Behind a locked door, in a bedroom at the end of a relatively empty and quiet hallway, I managed to slip inside and take up my post in the shadows.

And just like in his room at the fraternity house, I was seconds too late.

"What is this shit?" Gabriel asked the four other adolescents in the room, swallowing the pill and washing it down with a swig from a bottle of hard liquor.

"Just a little dance fever," said a boy I recognized from the film earlier that night.

"How fucked up am I about to be?" Gabriel asked, a disturbing excitement bubbling up beneath the agony of the threatened bond.

He had dabbled in other substances before, but none of them had ever been dangerous like this.

"Whoa…" he said, his voice weak. "That's… that's…"

Gabriel smiled, laid down, and passed out as the other youths in the room just laughed.

"Should have figured billionaire baby was a bitch," one of them said.

"Too bad," said one of the girls who was snorting some white substance off a credit card.

As they all continued to talk, drinking and swallowing pills, they slowly forgot Gabriel was even there.

Until I was forced to watch in horror as he started to shake.

"Shit," said the one who'd given him the drugs. "He OD'd." He sounded no more upset than if he'd ordered a sandwich missing the sauce and not like someone was dying next to him.

"Should someone call 911?" said another, shrugging and taking a huge sip from the bottle they were passing around.

"And have the party busted? Fuck, no."

And that had been enough for me.

For the first and only time since entering the mortal realm, I emerged from the shadows in my full demon form, knowing these idiots probably wouldn't even remember this tomorrow.

"Get out!" I bellowed, my horns brushing the ceiling and my wings spreading wide to fill the length of the room.

They began to panic and scream, scrambling from the room, climbing over each other in their haste.

Once we were alone, I'd locked the door behind them and allowed myself to return to my human-esque appearance. I knelt by Gabriel's side, unable to touch him since the bond prevented it, helpless to do anything but watch as he continued to seize, foaming at the mouth, his eyes rolling back into his head.

"No, no, no," I moaned, my hands unable to make contact to roll him to the side, to hold him, to comfort him, if he was even conscious of what was happening, which didn't seem likely.

The bond twisted and clenched harder with every passing second, mirroring the emotional agony of knowing Gabriel, whom I truly loved with my entire being, was fading away before me.

Tears began to fall as the thought of Gabriel ceasing to be overtook my mind. I had lived two and a half thousand years without ever even knowing he would exist, and now that he did, I knew to live without him would be impossible. He couldn't die. I wouldn't let him. I couldn't.

I closed my eyes, reaching along the bond to Gabriel, feeling the drug coursing through his veins. His systems were already beginning to shut down. I had been too late to stop him from taking it, but I wasn't too late to stop *it* from taking *him*.

On countless occasions where Gabriel had overindulged and ended up at the point of blacking out, I'd used a skill unique to those with a soulmate bond to siphon away some of his drunkenness, taking it into myself to keep him from suffering the effects of alcohol poisoning. That night, I used the same skill to reach through the bond with my mind, searching his body for signs of the drug. I pulled the poisonous effects into myself instead, knowing it would hurt, but, unlike Gabriel, I would survive it.

It took nearly an hour of nonstop focus, fighting through the toxins now coursing through my own blood, but when I was finished, Gabriel was no more intoxicated than if he'd had a little too much to drink. I, on the other hand, could feel my body struggling to cope with the poison.

I managed to send a message from Gabriel's phone to his parents, letting them know where he was, then used the shadows to get back to the hotel only seconds before losing consciousness. I woke up days later, my entire body aching like I'd never felt in my whole two and a half millennia.

And here I was again, watching Gabriel fighting for his life, and I knew he was losing. The agony in the bond left no doubt as to how dire the situation was. Except this time, instead of him knowingly taking something that could be dangerous, he'd been given the drug by someone he trusted.

This time, however, I could touch him. Instead of kneeling helplessly by the bed, I sat near his head and pulled it into my lap, turning him so when the inevitable vomit began to bubble up from his throat, he didn't choke.

"I'm here," I said, stroking his hair. Once more, my magic pulsed along the bond and into *my* Gabriel, pulling out the toxins Kessinger had given him. The "dance fever" had the same effect the second time around, shutting down his systems one by one, but this time, I knew what to do. And touching him, holding him in my arms, it made the process easier, as though being in contact with my soulmate made the connection deeper, stronger.

"I promised you…" I whispered, the poison already going to my head, making me drowsy, causing my limbs to feel heavy. "I promised you… I would always protect you… No matter what. And I'm not going to fail you. Not now… not ever."

The bond slowly returned to the familiar shimmering purple as Gabriel's breathing evened out, and the pallor on his face faded, replaced by the usual gentle blush of his cheeks. I ran my thumb over them, feeling his warmth, knowing my consciousness was limited, but not wanting to waste this moment. I didn't know when the next time I might get to hold him like this would be. It could be weeks, months... more, if I didn't find a way to earn his trust and affection.

The edges of my vision began to blacken, and I knew I had to go. I laid him down on his pillow and pressed a fleeting kiss to his forehead. That alone, in any other circumstance, would have been enough to break any restraint I had left. But with the drugs pulling me under and the all too recent threat to Gabriel's life, my departure was swift.

Pulling myself away, I shifted into the shadows to get back to my room quickly. I fell into my bed once I'd regained my solid form, knowing I was seconds from blacking out.

But in those seconds, with the immediate threat to Gabriel's life over, my mind went back to what I'd seen when I walked in.

Gabriel had taken a pill. Kessinger had a pill bottle when he left. Had he... had he drugged Gabriel on purpose? If so, he was deliberately trying to harm my soulmate, or worse. If it was a mistake, he had just nearly killed someone through sheer stupidity.

Either way, he was dangerous. I had clearly underestimated the impact a simple mortal could have on my future.

But for now, I couldn't dwell on it. I couldn't even thread two thoughts together anymore. All I could do was succumb to sleep.

And sleep, I did.

Chapter Seven
Gabe

I woke up in my bed, not really remembering falling asleep at all. I remembered the ring and the panic attack, and I remember Alex giving me a Xanny. But the rest was…

I guess it was a big Xanny.

I rolled out of bed, allowing my body to bend casually like I was part Jello until my feet touched the floor. Then I forced my bones to support my body again as I hobbled over to my dresser and pulled out the clothes I'd planned to wear tonight.

Who was I kidding? They were the clothes that were clean. Even at the height of my access to fashion, I never once planned an outfit.

When I finished the longest part of my "get ready" routine—my hair—I left my room and locked the door behind me, stuffing my key into the pocket of my jeans.

"Hoffstet," a voice called from behind me.

I turned around to see one of my fraternity brothers, Kaleb, running up to me with a huge grin on his face. Kaleb looked like he belonged in a science lab rather than a frat house, but he'd pulled a different girl every night since we'd all moved in.

"Hey," I said, starting to walk backwards to converse with him. "Sup?"

Kaleb slowed to join me, and I went back to walking forward as we headed for the house. "You wanna come to a party tonight? Off campus... east village... upperclass girls..."

I looked at him with what I hoped was a casually interested look and knew I was failing at. "Aren't we all supposed to go to Greek night?" I asked.

Kaleb shrugged. "Only if they catch us."

I thought about Alex promising to see me later, and the fact that Ollie would definitely be looking for me. "Sure. I don't have anything better going on. Older girls sounds fun."

"Nice," he said, patting me on the chest. "You gonna ask your big if he wants to come with?"

I scoffed. "Fuck, no. Ollie's a weirdo."

Kaleb giggled, and it made me feel a little too pleased with myself. I was really enjoying the realization other people found me funny. I'd never felt like the funny guy in my life before.

But then again, with everything that had occurred the last six months, I wasn't the same person I was. No, that Gabe would have shied away from the kind of attention I got on a regular basis now. I'd gone from broody kid in the corner of the party to some kind of closet bait.

"Well, I'm heading out at about eight. Wanna take a cab together?"

"Sure," I said, carefully planning how I was going to avoid Ollie til then. "Eight it is."

A night without Ollie, and even a night without Alex, sounded more than relaxing. And maybe, for the first time since I'd gotten here, I'd get to figure out who I was all on my own. I certainly wasn't going to figure it out with the two of them hovering.

And hovering was all they seemed capable of doing.

Chapter Eight
Olympio

Every inch of me hurt, and my eyelids felt like they were made of lead. I forced them open anyway, my mouth feeling like it was full of cotton.

Night had fallen, leaving my room in darkness, and I turned over, ready to allow myself the chance to sleep more.

But then I remembered I'd told Gabriel I would meet him to walk over to Greek Night. I shot up, and I suddenly understood the human expression of feeling like I'd been hit by a truck.

I wasn't sure if it was even the same day, and if it was, I didn't know if I'd pulled enough of the drug from Gabriel to allow him to be functional already. But if he was, and I was late to meet him, there was no way Kessinger wouldn't take advantage of that.

Fighting the ache, I crawled out of the bed and rushed to Gabriel's room. I knocked as calmly as I could, cognizant of others around and not wanting to make a scene, but he didn't answer. Once the hallway had cleared out a few seconds later, I shifted into shadow and moved into his room to find it empty.

"Damn it!" I said, my frustration getting the better of me. I needed to pull myself together. I was a prince, one who could go about his daily duties even while suffering the effects of a hangover from the strongest Sefaeran liquor. I wasn't going to let weak mortal substances bring me down, not with my soulmate's future, the future of our bond, and my kingdom on the line.

Drawing on the deepest well of strength I had, I assumed my shadow form, fighting the fatigue that overcame me immediately. I could rest when I knew I hadn't lost, when I knew Kessinger hadn't managed to take Gabriel from me forever. I moved silently through the darkness, coming upon Kessinger first, but he wasn't with Gabriel either. In fact, as the members of the fraternity moved en masse toward Amity Hall, my soulmate was nowhere to be seen.

Alex, however, was walking behind the others, that obnoxiously smug look on his face. Gabriel might have died by his hand earlier, and he didn't even seem to notice he was missing. I was about to go off on a hunt of my own when Kessinger's phone rang.

"Gabe?" he said, as if he wasn't sure who was calling, but then, with a shake of his head, his face fell into that disgusting smirk he always wore. "Where you at, man?" There was a pause, then he laughed. "One fifty East Third? The hell are you doing there?" Another pause. "Oh, man, you're already so fucked up, aren't you…? You need me to *what?*" His eyes lit up, and he turned, walking resolutely in the other direction toward the address Gabriel had given. "About time. I'll be there as soon as I can. No way I'm gonna miss *that*. I've been waiting weeks for you to want it as bad as I do."

The meaning of what was being said hit me like a blow to the chest. My jaw tightened, clenching my teeth together as my eyes began to throb, and a burning feeling took root in my gut. Gabriel had called him in a drunken state, asking Kessinger to fuck him.

Not as long as I drew breath.

Still fighting against the effects of the drug Kessinger had given Gabriel, my temper was shorter than usual. Knowing the very person Gabriel wanted at his side in his most vulnerable moments was the same one who had nearly killed him just hours ago was enough to make me murderous. And if he hadn't been in a public space, surrounded by people, I might have ended Alex Kessinger right then and there, once and for all.

I had to make Gabriel see that he couldn't fuck Kessinger. That he couldn't fall in love with him. I had to give Gabriel a reason to see that he belonged with me, which meant that I had to get there first.

Thankfully, I found him rather quickly, navigating the miles in seconds. I could feel how drunk he was, losing consciousness by the second, and it was a wonder he was even standing. Sure enough, as I watched from the edge of the party, he suddenly bent over to vomit into a houseplant.

Several people backed away in disgust, and I watched Gabriel tip forward.

"Whoa," I said in what I hoped was a reassuring way, giving him a friendly smile as I caught him. "Careful. You hit your head when you're this drunk, you may not wake up."

Gabriel looked up at me, squinting like he was trying to see something in the distance. "What... what are you doing here?" His words slurred together like some cheap drunk in the city streets outside.

"You called me," I lied, putting his arm around my shoulder. "Don't you remember? You asked me to come. I thought I was coming to party, but I guess you needed my help." I began to move toward the edges of the party, bringing Gabriel with me until I found an open, empty bedroom.

"Oh..." he said with a tone like he'd just had the meaning of the universe explained to him, *and* he understood it. "Yo... that is so nice of you, man. What a good brother you are."

"That's me," I said sardonically as I closed and locked the door behind us. I lifted Gabriel and carried him to the bed and laid him on top of it. Then I started to move to the chair in the corner, but Gabriel's voice stopped me.

"No..." he said, the words long and drawn out. "Don't go." He grabbed onto the collar of my shirt, and I turned back to look at him. His eyes were half-closed as they tried to focus on me, and he pulled me closer. And while my mind told me I needed to resist, my body obeyed his silent request.

I was still weak from the poison, and I stumbled, my hands falling on either side of Gabriel's head. I looked down at him, where he lay beneath me. For the first time ever, I found myself hovering over my soulmate, our bodies so close a pin wouldn't have fit between us.

My heart pounded as I fought every urge in my body to take him, to rip his clothes off and finally have him. But now was not the time, nor was this the place. He was drunk, and I wanted him sober and able to consent when we came together. I wanted it to be because he wanted me, not because he was intoxicated and aroused.

But before I could pull away, not wanting my rapidly stiffening cock to press into him and make him aware of my desire, he wrapped his hands around my neck and pulled me into him, kissing me fully on the mouth.

And the self control I'd been exercising every second since he came of age, when the bond shifted from a protective desire to a romantic one, broke into a million little pieces.

As his tongue slipped past my lips, I was overcome with need for him. I knew I shouldn't even allow the kiss—he was too inebriated to make reasoned choices. But the bond lit up like fireworks, and my entire body and soul cried out in ecstasy.

Gabriel's hands were all over me, pulling me close, holding me against him. We were both hard, and I felt like I couldn't get close enough to him.

"Gabriel…" I moaned as my lips traveled down his neck. "I've waited so long for you. *My* Gabriel… my soulmate."

There was only a single second after I said it where it seemed like Gabriel's drunken mind might not have caught my slip. But then he froze and pulled his lips away from mine, shoving me away.

"What did you say?"

Somehow, he seemed instantly sober, as though his drunkenness had all been an act, despite the fact that I knew through our bond it was genuine.

He scrambled backward and out from under me, and my heart sank. I had slipped. I had said too much, and now Gabriel was farther away from me than ever.

"I—"

I didn't get a chance to speak. Right then, someone began pounding on the door, and I turned, the frustration of the ruined moment combined with my still aching body and pounding head making my temper flare up at whoever it was who dared to interrupt us.

I opened the door and began to tell the knocker to go away, but my eyes fell on Alex Kessinger, who looked into the room, then shoved past me to where Gabriel was looking shell-shocked and unsteady.

"The fuck are you doing?" Kessinger said, putting his hands—his filthy, unworthy human hands—on *my* Gabriel's face, then turned to me, slowly moving toward me until he could press a finger to my chest. "Gabe doesn't want you, bro, and taking advantage of him when he's wasted just shows that you're a fucking predator. Get the fuck out. Tomorrow we're going to the dean—maybe even the cops. You're done at Columbia, and you're never going near Gabe again."

The idea that I had planned to take advantage of Gabriel in this state, knowing that had been Kessinger's entire intention in coming here, would have been enough to put me over the edge on its own. But the fact that he couldn't hide the victorious smirk on his lips sealed his fate.

I took a single step back, and triumph blossomed over Kessinger's face, but it only lasted for a second—exactly as long as it took for me to say, "Big mistake, Kessinger," and then to close my fist and bring it up under his jaw.

I ached to unleash my demon form, to use my full strength, but I felt like transforming into something Gabriel would only see as a monster and then killing Kessinger in front of him might have not gone over well in earning his trust. So, I settled for knocking him immediately unconscious.

Suddenly, Gabriel was rushing at me, his arms swinging wildly as he made unintelligible threats at me for hurting Alex.

And that was enough. It had been months of taking it slow and giving my soulmate the space he needed to come to me, only to always be second choice to an idiot with no true care for Gabriel. I had grown tired of playing by these human rules and losing.

Because I was not a human.

I was so much more.

As Gabriel's hand came directly at my face, I grabbed him by the wrist, stopping the blow in its tracks. He was still unsteady on his feet, the brief sobriety caused by Kessinger's entrance and the ensuing fight already waning. But he was still just aware enough that his eyes went wide as he realized the disparity in our strengths, something I'd kept well hidden until now.

"Sleep," I said, breathing the command into his ear and along our bond.

He immediately crumpled into my arms. I lifted him easily, his slim frame cradled against me.

In the brief moment of silence and calm, I looked down at him. Despite knowing the distress I'd just put him through, something I had never wanted or intended, he looked peaceful in my arms. It felt right to have him there, like I'd finally found a puzzle piece that had been missing, and holding him made me whole for the first time.

I had made a promise. I had pledged to him that I would give him time. He would know and trust me and come with me willingly. But the game had changed. I had underestimated the challenge mere humans would pose to my ability to win over my soulmate. I had thought it would be easy, that watching over him his whole life, saving him several times over, would somehow translate into things being easy with him. I'd thought the bond would have more of an effect on him, the way it did on me—that he would feel the need for me, the way I did for him.

But I was wrong, and in my oversight, I'd fallen into a trap I could only see one way out of.

And there was only one way to get there.

I focused on the empty space in the center of the room, and in seconds, shadows began to swirl and coalesce, the void forming a portal. I looked at Gabriel again, then leaned down to speak in his ear.

"This will hurt," I said, knowing he couldn't hear me and not caring. "And I know I had to break my promise. But I will not break this one. You will not face this alone. I will be with you. I will always be with you. Until my heart no longer beats."

And with a final look at my defeated rival on the floor, I bent my face to bestow what may have been the final kiss I would give my soulmate for who knows how long. When I pulled away, I took a deep breath and stepped into the darkness, letting it take me and Gabriel.

Letting it send us home.

Chapter Nine
Gabe

As the first moments of consciousness washed over me, a screaming pain ripped through my skull, and a wave of nausea consumed me. It felt like I'd been out all night partying, and the main entertainment had been hard Hollywood drugs. I hadn't done them often, but even once was enough to remember a feeling like this.

I attempted to open my eyes but failed. Even the light coming through my eyelids caused me tremendous discomfort. I was sweating—nauseous and sweating. It felt like someone had dropped me off a building, and I'd landed in hell. I had to force myself to even roll over, leading to me tumbling down off whatever kind of surface I'd been perched on.

I had no idea where the hell I was, and I wouldn't have admitted it to anyone, but I was moments from crying out for my mom. The fear was disorienting in a way that nothing I'd ever felt before had been.

I forced my eyes open to evaluate my surroundings and immediately vomited all over the marble floor below me. I attempted to raise my head, but my neck might as well have had no spine at all for how heavy it felt.

"Careful," a familiar voice said in a low, reassuring tone with a hint of amusement. "That journey isn't made for humans. You probably needed another day of rest, but there's just no convincing you to do anything you don't want to, is there?"

My eyes watered and burned like they were filled with chlorine as I desperately clawed for something that would get me to my feet. I couldn't tell where he was, and my heart pounding in my ears made that even more difficult.

"You fucking bastard," I growled, which likely was a lot less intimidating than I wanted because I was sobbing from the pain. "I swear to god, I'm gonna fucking kill you."

I stumbled forward in the direction of his voice, arms outstretched. I was determined to get him by the neck and make him take me back to my room. I was certain I had never hated him as much as I did at that moment.

"Gabriel," his voice said. The amusement was still present, but there was an element of being scolded to it as well. "You need to lie down. Your body is recovering from a trip most people will never make, and even fewer would survive."

Then I felt his hands close around my outstretched wrists, holding me firmly and trying to guide me back to the bed.

"No," I screamed, flailing and trying to create distance between us. "Don't touch me."

In my panicked state, I felt my calf make contact with something painfully sharp. The sting of the new injury was almost as excruciating as the burn that lingered in my eyes and the ache in my bones.

Seconds later, I felt myself tumble backwards, and with a heavy thunk, smack into the floor. I really was going to kill myself if I didn't stop moving.

"What do you want from me?" I asked, whimpering and running my hands across the blood that I could now feel dripping from the injury on my leg.

Ollie was kneeling at my feet, his outline all I could make out, as he ran his hands quickly over the cut before turning his head and calling over his shoulder.

"Fetch Perla," he said in a stern but calm voice.

I didn't know who the fuck Perla was, or if that was even a person at all. But what I did know was that—regretfully—I was at the mercy of this prick.

"That was my fault," he said quietly, his hand still lingering on my leg. "I should have made sure that all weapons were put away, not leaning against your footboard."

"Weapons?" I asked, my voice cracking. "The hell do you mean weapons?"

For the first time, my thoughts slowed enough to feel properly scared. I didn't really know Ollie all that well. Did I really know anyone all that well if I thought about it?

"Are you trying to hold me for ransom?" I asked. "Cause I hate to tell you... my parents aren't gonna pay up."

62

There was a moment of silence, and I felt Ollie's fingers tense on my skin.

"You're not being held for ransom," he said even more quietly than before. "I recall quite well about your parents, and while I cannot begin to express my sympathy for your loss, I will never stop being grateful that you chose to stay home that day."

I rubbed my eyes furiously, wanting to look the dickhead in the eyes, and when I finally cleared them, I nearly passed out once more from my shock.

Ollie was kneeling before me, his chest bare except for the leather strap spanning the length of it, wrapping under one arm and over the opposite shoulder, where it disappeared beneath some kind of elaborate decoration of small spikes on a rough surface. A black flowy fabric that I guess could only be described as a cloak cascaded down his back from that one shoulder. A gold chain hung low across his hips, revealing muscles he'd hidden really well beneath other clothes, and a knee-length skirt in the same deep black as the cloak was attached to the chain. On his feet were sandals that looked like they were made of gold, themselves.

"You're... you're wearing a skirt," was all I could manage from the state of my shock.

Ollie raised an eyebrow, his amusement clear.

"Have you not looked down at yourself?"

I peered down in dread at what could be so unusual that it would entertain this jackass and, to my horror, found myself dressed in a fucking toga like we wore to parties sometimes.

"Oh, fuck, no," I said, pulling it off over my head and tossing it across the room.

Then, to my dismay, I found the white silk garment had been the only scrap of clothing on me, and I now sat ass-naked in front of the guy who'd been trying to get with me for months.

"What the hell, Ollie?" I said with acceptance. "What is all this?"

In my mind, I was envisioning ritualistic frat hazing, or even just a wild prank gone wrong. But I was really hurt, and even the air didn't smell like home. Something was horribly off.

Ollie took a deep breath and stood up. "Gabriel... I tried to tell you—"

Just then, a smallish woman with dusky purple skin and—I shit you not—*horns* on her head came in carrying a basket, which she set by my feet and opened. She pulled out bottles that had shimmering, smoking, and glowing liquids. Finally, she smiled and held up a bright yellow one, which she opened, poured onto a piece of cloth, and pressed to my cut before I could stop her.

And even if I wanted to, I couldn't move.

I wouldn't have been surprised if my paralyzation was Ollie's doing, because at this point, I was convinced he was a wizard or something. Luckily for me, whatever elixir was being administered didn't hurt—not that much could, following my various injuries related to stumbling around the room.

I watched the healer with curiosity, then caught Ollie looking at me the same way. I glared at him, folding my arms.

"I want fucking answers, man."

Ollie sighed and said, "Thank you, Perla," his eyes never leaving mine. The creepy little woman smiled, bowed at both of us, and left just as fast as she entered. He took a few steps from side to side, pacing a small section of floor before leaning his shoulder onto one of the tall bedposts.

It was only then that I noticed the odd decor of the place. It was like a garden come to life in the form of a bedroom. Everywhere I looked, there were dozens of pale blue flowers dripping off every surface, and past the luxurious sleigh bed there was a tub that looked like it was made of rose quartz or something, filled with aquamarine water.

Ollie didn't seem to notice my gaping, and instead, launched into his explanation.

"Alright," he finally said. "I tried to tell you back at that... party." His lip curled up in a derisive sneer on the word, as though he was disgusted by it. "I told you that you're my soulmate. And it's true. I've been waiting for you for a long time—over a thousand years, in fact. From the moment you were born, you were destined to be my consort, my partner, ruling Sefaera at my side."

My mouth went dry, and I suddenly began to wonder if maybe, just maybe, this was real.

"I know what you said," I interrupted. "But what I want to know is the truth."

His expression shifted from one of gentle understanding to one of mild annoyance, and as it did, I swear his eyes flashed that weird purple color. You know, because yellow wasn't weird enough.

"I have told it to you," he said, a bite to the words, but then his expression softened to one that was fully neutral. "Come with me." He turned and walked across the room, and my body followed him, moving without me giving it a command to.

"What are you doing?" I whimpered in fear. "Why am I walking when I want to stay in the bed? You have to be doing something… freak."

He paused, took a visibly deep breath, then looked at me over his shoulder.

"Our bond grants me an ability to… nudge you into doing things in order to keep you safe. I've used it many times in your life without you knowing, and it has saved your life more than once."

He'd been near me my whole life? "So, you thought you could just manipulate me with magic into wanting you? That's sick, man."

"Hardly," he replied, still not fully facing me. "I would never presume to—"

"This can't be real," I gasped, bending in half and clutching my chest. "None of this can be real. What the hell are you?"

Suddenly, my feet began moving forward again as Ollie walked to the long, shimmering, silvery gossamer curtains on the wall, and with a glance at me, he pulled them aside and stepped out onto a balcony.

Two moons, larger than any full moon I'd ever seen, one pink and one aqua, were both sitting just at the horizon. Behind and around them, what I guessed were stars sparkled like glitter.

"This can't be real," I said again.

Then I felt his body press against mine from behind, his hot breath eliciting goosebumps across my skin.

66

"It's very real," he said in a low, sultry purr right next to my ear. He reached his arm over my shoulder, pointing to the pink moon. "That is Coricas, the southern moon. She represents good fortune and prosperity for Sefaera." He moved to indicate to the other. "That's Talaea, the western moon. She represents health, not only for the individual, but for our world." He chuckled. "Of course, that's all folklore and myth. The bond you and I share? It's nothing of the sort. It's real. You were made for me—quite literally." His hands moved to my waist, pulling me closer.

"But who the fuck are you? *What* are you?"

Ollie tilted his head to the side, and, right before my eyes, his body began to darken and shift. It happened so fast that I only just made out what looked like wings coming from his back before he dissolved into a dark gray mist that moved into the shadows and vanished. A second later, I felt a tap on my shoulder and turned to see him with his arms crossed, looking annoyed again.

"I'm Olympio, crown prince of Sefaera. I am what humans would call a demon, though the way your people think about that word isn't exactly true to what I am. You are now a member of my kingdom. And even though you will be my consort and fellow ruler one day, you are not either of those things yet. Our bond has not been consummated, which means I am still your prince, and you will obey me. And because we are connected, I can make sure you do, but I'd rather you choose to cooperate on your own."

Like hell I would. I'd go down kicking and screaming to the death if I had to.

Every nerve in my body went haywire, and I quickly shoved him away. "Don't fucking touch me," I growled. "I'm not *your* anything. Now take me home."

I ducked under his arm and ran back inside. Near the fire was an array of tools, and I grabbed a poker but immediately dropped it. My hand froze up like I was suffering from arthritis, and no matter how I tried to force it to move, I couldn't.

"Traitor," I spat. "You befriended me. I trusted you—you—" I struggled to think of the right word. "Predator."

I felt every inch of my body grow hot, and in moments, his hand was on my throat.

I didn't hesitate—not even for a second.

With all the training childhood martial arts classes had given me, I pulled back and slammed my forehead into his, finally knocking him back from me with a shocked look on his face. My body was still screaming in pain, but I took my chance where I had one.

I ran for the nearest door, not caring that I was in a state of undress, and bolted out of it, into a hallway that was extremely contrasting to the room I'd woken up in. This one was open to the outside, with massive white marble pillars. Between them, there was a lush courtyard filled with hedges in the green I would expect, but also blues, pinks, and yellows. I used every ounce of stamina I had to round a corner, then cover my mouth to keep from panting, not wanting to reveal my location.

But as I faced the empty corridor, Ollie suddenly appeared, solidifying out of the shadows, and my entire body seized up. I began to tip over, but he caught me and helped me upright again, and now, there was no tenderness in his eyes.

"You will *not* do that again," he said, beckoning someone behind me. "Yes, I befriended you. I had hoped to gain your trust enough to tell you all of this and have things progress naturally, but I can see you've chosen the more difficult road." He sighed and shook his head slightly. "No matter. I've waited for you for over fifteen hundred years. I can wait weeks... months... years, if that's what it takes. But fate has chosen you. You are mine, and I will not lose you. Not now, not ever."

A pair of guards in bronze armor that definitely looked like it belonged in a museum came up on either side of me.

"Your Highness?" they asked in unison, and I could hear a slight hiss in the voice of the one to my left, almost as if... yes, that was a forked tongue sticking out between his lips.

"Take him to his quarters and lock him in," Ollie said. "The usual enchantments on the windows and balcony to keep him in, and double blood magic seals on the door."

"Yes, Your Highness," the guards said, lifting me and carrying me away, still facing backward at Ollie.

"Fuck you," I spat. "Fuck you forever. I will never give you what you want, and I will never stop trying to get away."

I could have sworn I saw something that looked like pain flicker across his face, but it was gone as fast as it had appeared, and I had bigger problems to worry about as the two brutes tossed me unceremoniously back into the garden room, then bolted the door behind me.

I fell to my knees and vomited once more, then broke down into tears.

"Stop being a bitch, Gabe," I said, hitting myself round the head. "Man up and fix this."

But the abuse on myself didn't help one bit, and at least for then, the only thing I could manage was to cry myself to sleep.

Chapter Ten
Olympio

"Gryfian," I said, addressing one of my personal guards. He stepped forward, and I handed him my curved obsidian blade. "Seal it."

I stood outside of Gabriel's door, where I heard crashes and other noises of destruction. I wasn't happy about it, but anything in there could be fixed or replaced. Our bond, if broken, could not.

Gryfian ran the blade across his palm, drawing a dripping line of emerald green blood. Then he pressed his hand to the first sigil I'd placed on the door and handed me back the sickle, which I used to cut my own palm, freeing my own shimmering golden blood. The color all of the royal family of Sefaera had, including those who were bound to us by fate, once their bonds were consummated.

I pressed my hand to the second sigil and watched them both glow before vanishing completely. They were still there, just unseen, and no one except for me and Gryfian would be able to enter or leave, and even we would have to be there together to unlock the blood seal.

I set a pair of guards at the door, just for extra protection, sending Gryfian into an adjacent hallway so I could fetch him if needed, but he wasn't directly near the door. I didn't believe we had any enemies on the inside, but I also had never thought Alex Kessinger would have posed such a threat, so I was taking no chances with Gabriel's safety—from himself or anyone else.

I smoothed out my clothes, unwilling to go anywhere in the palace looking less than the prince I was. It had been nineteen years since I'd done this. Well, nineteen for me. Every day I spent in the human world saw three days pass here. My people had been without their prince all that time, having to deal with the Council overseeing things. But now it was time to shed the frat boy Ollie and return to myself—to Olympio.

I wasn't sure where to go at first, but my feet seemed to know the way before my mind did. I was already in the hallway I had decided to go to by the time I had made the decision. It wasn't surprising, considering that, other than my own room, my feet made this journey more than any other within the palace. It was muscle memory.

And I tried desperately to convince myself there was no reason other than that.

With a bit of a smile, I made my way to the large silver doors and stood outside of them. I nodded toward the door, and my guard reached out and knocked for me.

Several seconds went by before a tiny imp of a man answered the door. Just as with demons, the human idea of them was informed by legends and myths rather than reality. This imp, Hiram, looked like any mortal human—except that he stood three feet tall and had skin the color of flames.

"Your Highness!" Hiram said, sinking into a bow. "It has been too long."

"Olympio?" said a familiar voice on the other side of the door. I heard the patter of feet all but running, and the door flew open, revealing my most trusted advisor and oldest friend, Vassenia. No one else, outside of my family, would ever get away with using my given name.

"Hello, Vass," I said, my face relaxing into the first true smile I'd worn in Coricas knew how long at the sight of her bronze skin and dark tresses hanging over her shoulders. "Can I come in?"

She grinned and stepped aside, allowing me to enter. Following the protocol which had been set thousands of years ago, my guards and Hiram remained outside as Vass closed the door.

I walked around her room, smiling at the familiarity. While my chambers were decorated in black marble with gold accents, representative of my family line, Vass had chosen a deep, sanguine red theme. It was equally luxe, but with a decidedly different effect.

I turned back to her, not quite sure how I would begin to explain where I'd been, but I didn't have to. My lips were occupied as Vass jumped into my arms, wrapping her hands around the back of my neck and her legs around my waist, and she consumed my mouth in a deep, loving kiss.

I kissed her back, the feeling of her as familiar to me as any other part of my home. I carried her to her bed and laid her down, my hands moving across her body, tracing the familiar planes I'd sorely missed. Her own hands wasted no time in finding their way between us to stroke me beneath my toga, lighting my insides on fire instantly, making me hard. It had been nearly two decades since anyone else had touched me, and she was warm and soft.

And after the day I'd had, I was eager to lose myself in her.

But I couldn't.

With gentle, careful motions, I pulled away from her kiss and her embrace, standing up and taking a deep breath, trying to convince the raging erection her very presence had caused to end. I took a step back, putting space between us.

She looked up at me in hurt and confusion. We had been casual lovers since our youth, and we always said it was no more than that, especially after my brother died and I became the heir to the throne. We'd known a day might come where my soulmate was born, and we knew if that happened, everything would change.

"What's wrong?" Vass asked.

She didn't know. When I'd felt the bond, only my mother and sister knew it had happened, and I was leaving to find Gabriel. I knew seeing Vass before I left would present a temptation I couldn't afford.

I couldn't repeat my brother's mistakes.

I crossed my arms, guarding myself from the emotional tension between us. I looked away, not wanting to meet her eyes.

"I found him," I told her.

She shook her head, still not understanding, and I knew I should explain, but I didn't know how. How do you tell the person who has been your companion for thousands of years you can no longer continue your relationship as it has always been?

Instead of speaking, I motioned for her to come with me. After a brief hesitation, she fell into step behind me, Hiram and the guards keeping several paces behind us. We made our way to Gabriel's door, and I sent Hiram to fetch Gryfian.

74

"What's going—" Vass started, but then she noticed the room we were standing outside of. It was the room belonging to the king's consort—to the Hand of Justice of Sefaera. "Your soulmate? You found... *him?*"

Gryfian arrived, and we both sliced our palms to unlock the door. Vass had barely glanced inside when she turned to me, appalled.

"A human?" she said, her jaw hanging as she looked back at me.

I followed where she'd been looking and saw Gabriel, sound asleep in the center of the floor on top of a pile of feathers from torn pillows, cheeks pinked from where he'd clearly been crying. I'd been watching him sleep like this since he was an infant, always crying himself to sleep.

It pained me to know I was now the cause of these exhaustive fits. He now cried because of me.

I nodded to Vass. "For now." We both looked back at Gabriel, knowing once we were bonded, he would be immortal as well.

Gabriel stirred in his sleep and turned over, revealing his beautiful, naked body. Vass wasted no time evaluating him from a distance. Her judgment didn't need to be spoken. I knew she was forming one.

She scoffed, motioning to the destruction he'd caused in just a short time. "Don't you think you'd be better off without a soulmate at all than this—?"

"Be careful what you say," I interrupted her in a dangerous voice.

She looked stunned. She'd heard that tone hundreds and thousands of times, but never toward her. It pained me to use it, but she had known for a long time it might come to this. My heart ached to see the look on her face, to know, even now, I wanted to hold her and apologize, to take her to my bed and fuck the sadness out of her.

But even putting aside my devotion to Gabriel, something so strong I still couldn't believe it was real at times, my kingdom needed me to fulfill my duty. And that meant my sexual adventures with anyone other than Gabriel had come to an end.

"Olympio…" Vass said softly.

"Vassenia," I said, using her full name rather than the familiar moniker I'd used our entire friendship. I forced the words out, knowing I needed to be firm and set down the boundary now, before there was any room for confusion or discussion. "That young man is my soulmate. He is the other half of me. He is scared, and he is angry, and he is confused. But I have watched him his entire life, waiting for him to be ready. He is kind, and intelligent, and just. And if you wish to remain my friend and advisor, you will remember your place as my subject first, and anything else second, meaning that you will recognize his value to me and the kingdom and will treat him as the precious asset he is."

Vass's eyebrows drew close together in the center, the pain evident on her face, but then she bowed and, in a painfully flat voice, said, "Yes, Your Highness."

I reached out and pulled her face up by placing a finger under her chin. Her emerald eyes met mine, and I tried to convey to her anything I could about the way I felt for her.

"Thank you," I said. "I need you through this. Gabriel is… a challenge. And I trust no one else the way I trust you."

She nodded and sighed. "What do we need to do?" she asked, resigned. I was relieved she had come around so quickly, but I knew she was still hurting, and a part of me wanted to hold her and make the pain go away.

"He needs to be readied for his first appearance," I said, taking a step away from Vass, needing to put physical distance between us before I made a mistake. "I wish I had more time to help him settle in and feel comfortable, but news of my return has already spread, and I need to address the court with the reason for my absence."

Vass nodded tightly, her face shifting into the same mask she wore when we were working. She turned to Hiram and said, "We need the royal presentation preparation teams."

Hiram nodded and scurried away, leaving me alone with only Vass and my guards. I turned to her, wishing there was something I could say, but her eyes were resolutely fixed on Gabriel, refusing to meet mine. She would need time to come to terms with this, I knew. But I couldn't care for Gabriel, to help him to adjust to life in Sefaera, *and* nurse Vassenia's feelings about the shift in our relationship. Gabriel's plight would be short-lived in comparison to the lives Vass and I had already lived. Even if it was years, decades, it was nothing compared to the millennia of life we'd experienced so far.

Uncomfortable silence stretched between us, but thankfully, Hiram was quick in returning with nearly a dozen servants, all clad in white with the royal gold accents and emblems on their clothing.

"You all know the situation," I said calmly, gesturing inside for them to look at my Gabriel. One of them let out a tiny gasp at his disheveled appearance. "My soulmate is struggling to adjust to his new life, and has taken to fits of panic." It was true, but greatly underscored the severity of his resistance. "I will be here to ensure everything goes accordingly. Now, follow me."

I strode past Vass, who fell into step behind me, leading the team into the room, where they immediately began to fan out, taking their stations and preparing garments and paints and bath oils. As they got to work, I moved to Gabriel's side and sat beside his prone form, gently pulling him toward me to rest his head on my lap.

I knew once he awoke, we would be back to the same tug of war, the same conflict he was intent on maintaining. But right now, looking down at him, touching his face, running my hands through his silken brown hair, it was easy to imagine we were already past that. That he had embraced our bond and his role, and he would open his eyes into mine with love.

A loud clatter echoed behind me, and I saw Vass looking embarrassed. She had accidentally kicked a metal vase that Gabriel had obviously cast onto the floor at some point during his tantrum.

The noise was enough. I felt Gabriel beginning to stir, and it took all of my willpower to keep from losing myself in the hope that he would have softened to me in his sleep.

My fingers brushed through his hair as his eyes began to twitch, still not opening. A gentle smile crossed his lips, and my heart yearned to kiss them. But as quickly as the expression appeared, it began to fade, and within seconds, his eyes shot open, finding mine.

"Get the hell away from me," he grunted, swatting at my hands and writhing fitfully until he rolled off of my lap onto the hard marble floor. "Don't touch me."

"Gabriel," I said calmly, getting to my feet and extending a hand to him to help him stand, too. He ignored my hand, choosing to remain on the floor. "Being difficult won't change your fate, nor will it change the traditions you are a part of." I nodded around the room to the servants. "These are your attendants. They have long served the royal family, but they have all been granted the honor of being your own personal team. Orma and Frine will be in charge of bathing you," I pointed to the large rose-colored bath, filled with the stunning blue-green water. "Let's start there."

Gabriel remained still, glaring at me, and I could feel the desperation he was experiencing through our bond as he tried to figure out some kind of escape. It was staggering, but I had to keep things moving with him. Not only for us, but for my kingdom.

"This is kidnapping," he hissed. "I will get a hold of the police and have you arrested. I know big names—"

It was clear he was floundering, rejecting the reality of his situation for something that felt safer to his mind. My heart ached from the fear I could see in his eyes, could feel in our bond. This wasn't like *my* Gabriel—making threats and throwing his weight around. He was always soft-spoken and kind. But now, he was a dog backed into a corner and was ready to strike at any point.

"The police don't exist here," I told him, my voice still calm, expression neutral. "You have already seen enough to know you are not in the world you've always known. You're where you belong—with me—and it's time for you to accept that."

I hated having to force him to act. I hated how he wouldn't just trust me. I had done everything I could to show him I was an ally, someone who cared for him. But I'd failed, and now I had to use my influence to make him stand and walk to the tub.

"First, you need a bath," I said, hoping to convey reassurance, but knowing by the terror in his eyes that I was unsuccessful. "No one will hurt you. They're just going to bathe you."

I'd put my entire will into making him move to the tub, but had left his mouth uncontrolled. It felt cruel to at least not let him speak.

"You fucking bastard," he snarled, his voice breaking like he might cry. I could feel his body tiring from the fight already, and his jerking movements slowed as he lowered himself into the tub, panting from the effort. "You said you love me, right?"

"More than anything," I confessed to him, and I heard a soft noise from behind me. Vass. I wanted to comfort her, but she would have to wait. Gabriel was my priority. "You have no idea what it's like to spend two and a half thousand years thinking you understood love, only to realize how wrong you'd been. When I saw you for the first time, everything else fell away, and there was only you. The first time we touched, the feeling of you remained with me so fully that I can still show you exactly where your body met mine. And when you kissed me at that party, I knew then I would die without you. I need you like you need air to breathe, Gabriel. Yes. I love you."

Gabriel's face softened, like he had heard me properly for the first time. "If you truly love me," he said. "Love me like nothing ever before—"

My heart was pounding. Was that all it took? A declaration of devotion?

"—then you wouldn't keep me somewhere against my will. I know enough about love to know that."

And just like that, I knew it had been too easy.

"Someday…" I said, hearing the growl of frustration in my voice and knowing I couldn't disguise it. "Someday you will understand why I did this. You will understand why your freedom in the world you came from could destroy the one you truly belong to. I don't want you to be my prisoner. I want you to be the person I trust with my own life. And someday you will be. Fate has never been wrong when choosing soulmates. If you were born to be mine, and I was born to be yours, there was a reason. And I trust the reason will reveal itself once you accept who you were meant to be. Once you accept *me*."

I took a deep breath and moved to stand against the wall, arms crossed, as Gabriel was washed from head to toe and rubbed down with various oils that made his skin almost glow with a dewy shine.

I couldn't blame Gabriel for not wanting this. I hadn't wanted it myself, when Vasileios had died and left me with this responsibility. But this was where we had both come to, and there was no point in wishing for things to be different when they never could be.

Two more servants came with towels to dry him off before leading him to a team who had several garments prepared. They settled on a stunning piece—gold with black accents. The silken straps came up on both shoulders and hung to his waist, where it was cinched with an obsidian chain, then fell to the floor, swirling around his feet. Sheer gossamer strips of fabric flowed down his arms like open sleeves so that his skin was still visible, making him look ethereally beautiful.

The ensemble was finished with golden sandals that criss-crossed over his feet and wound up his legs to his knees. He wore delicate golden jewelry, including the thinnest chain necklace, wrapped around his neck five times, with each loop reaching down to his waist. His ears weren't pierced, so that had to be done in order for the golden leaves to be applied. I could see the fear in his eyes as Sulie approached with the pin, so I braced myself and took every bit of the pain, so he felt nothing.

Finally, he was stood in front of a long mirror as three attendants oiled his hair so his natural waves stood out in loose cascades, which were sprinkled with gold leaf. Golden paint was applied to his face, highlighting his cheekbones and brow. Intricate curling designs were painted along his exposed skin, giving him the appearance of a walking work of art.

Which he always had been, even without the adornments.

Chapter Eleven
Gabe

The deep bass of the drums being pounded in the hall as we made our entrance reverberated in my bones. The heat coming off the torches summoned forth a dewy sweat on my brow, but I doubted I was at liberty to wipe it away. I doubted I was at liberty to do anything right now.

Olympio walked ahead of me, the way at least a dozen people had explained to me was proper for our first appearance. He didn't look at me once, but his power thrummed through me like it was my own heartbeat.

With every step I was forced to take, I could hear his voice willing me to be silent. He knew better than to leave me to my own will. I would certainly make good on my promise to escape.

My cheek suddenly itched, and I had to resist the urge to scratch it in order to avoid smearing the gold flakes that were placed so delicately you'd have thought they were diamonds.

But the more I resisted, the more it bothered me, until Ollie turned around and put a gentle hand on the side of my face. I was beginning to understand he could feel what I felt—and it was just as creepy as it sounded.

"Where?" he asked.

"Where, what?" I asked through gritted teeth, my volume forcefully controlled.

"Where is the itch?" he asked, looking at me as though he could see it. "I can scratch it for you."

He looked at me like he was the most benevolent son of a bitch in the world. Like scratching my itchy cheek would make up for kidnapping me and keeping me prisoner.

"It doesn't," I grumbled. Of course, the sensation intensified the more I tried to ignore it. "Can we just get this over with?"

Ollie looked at me with this expression I was starting to recognize as well as I did my own face. A disappointed, semi-hurt determination that always appeared when he tried to take care of me and I rejected him.

He seemed to wrestle with himself for a moment, maybe deciding whether or not to demand I tell him, but instead, his face melted into a neutral expression.

"If you insist," he said evenly before turning toward a massive golden curtain and waiting.

I was not prepared for what was on the other side. I could have been expertly schooled about what a consort presentation looked like, and I *still* wouldn't have been prepared for what was on the other side.

As soon as the curtain was pulled, Ollie walked through, throwing his hands up in a victorious pose, and the people inside roared to life with applause and cheering. The smile that rested comfortably on the prince's face looked real, yet simultaneously unnatural there. Perhaps it was because he was my captor, or maybe it was the fact that I'd been making his life so hard.

At this thought, I grinned to myself, causing him to turn and look at me.

"My dear friends," he said, his voice booming almost unnaturally over the crowd. "It has been decades since I have seen your faces and since I have had the pleasure of addressing you." He paused, and the room broke into applause. "I know many of you wondered where I had gone, and my mother had agreed to say nothing." Another pause, though now the room was silent enough that you could hear a pin drop. "I have been in the human world." A murmur went through the room, but Ollie put his hand up, and they fell silent again. "And I return to you with great news." He stepped aside, so I was visible. "My soulmate has been found."

The crowd went wild once again, and the din was enough that I wished I had control of my hands so I could plug my ears.

Ollie turned to me, still on the other side of the doorway, and extended a hand I was clearly supposed to take. But I gripped my sheer sleeve so hard I poked through it with my fingers in an attempt to refuse him what he wanted.

"Please don't make me force you," he said in a soft, frustrated tone. "This is all for you, Gabriel."

"No," I sneered, fighting so hard against his will that my nose began to bleed. "This is all for *you*."

Ollie's lips tightened into a scowl.

"You know nothing," he hissed through his teeth. "You do not understand what a gift you are being given. You are angry and obstinate, and while I can be sympathetic to what you are feeling, I cannot allow it to interfere with my duties or with my ability to govern my kingdom."

I was becoming rapidly aware that my window to act was closing in, and I clenched my throat, spitting on his face.

His head snapped back in shock. With a frighteningly calm motion, Ollie reached up and wiped away my spit.

"I'm sorry it came to this," he said, and suddenly my body no longer belonged to me. I placed my hand in his and smiled as I walked through the curtain.

It was agony, every second of it. I was the picture of grace and devotion, and yet inside, my body was burning pain—the result of Ollie controlling every breath I took and every muscle I moved.

I felt a tear forming in the corner of my eye and wondered if Ollie would permit me to wipe it away or force me to cry before his people. But before I could wonder long, he began to speak once more.

"While I would love to spend the day allowing you all to meet your future Justice," he said with a tight smile, "I do believe we have a dinner to attend. We appreciate you all, as well as your support." He turned to me and placed a hand under my chin in what would have been an affectionate gesture if I had any affection for him. "My Gabriel and I are ever in your debt."

Without another word, Ollie turned and walked through the crowd, with people bowing as we passed on our way to a second chamber which contained a massive table running along each wall of the room with chairs facing the center of it. The walls were white marble, the ceiling nonexistent, so the room was bathed in natural light. The table seemed to be made of solid gold, but as I took my seat at the head of the table with Ollie, I realized it was warm to the touch.

"My Gabriel..." It rang in my head like a fire alarm. *"My Gabriel."* It made me feel sick every time he said it.

I felt my body sit, totally uncontrolled by me, the painful smile still canvassing my face.

Much to my dismay, my stomach grumbled the second I smelled the food, and I knew it was going to be murder to resist his attempts to feed me.

Servers dressed in white surrounded us, putting beautiful plates down for us to eat from. The food looked foreign but utterly delicious, and I became suddenly aware it had been days since I'd eaten.

Ollie stood, raising a glass of what I assumed was wine, but it was a glimmering blue color.

"To my friends and subjects, to Sefaera, and to *my* Gabriel, future Justice and royal consort!"

Everyone in the room echoed it back at him, though they left out the horrible "*my*" before my name.

Ollie sat back down, placing a hand on my thigh that I couldn't swat away.

"I will have you know," he said, leaning into me like he was telling me an intimate secret, "I hate having to do this to you. I would much rather have you at my side as a willing and eager partner. You could be here enjoying yourself instead of fighting me." He paused, patting my leg before removing his hand. "You will get there. I'm certain of it."

Dinner began, and joviality echoed through every inch of the chambers. I couldn't help but notice people—at least, I think they were people—gazing at me with looks of adoration. I quickly diverted my eyes and stared a hole in my plate, avoiding conversation with everyone—especially Ollie.

By the time the second course came, then the third, *his highness* picked up on the fact that I wasn't eating.

He leaned in, once again speaking quietly enough that only I could hear him.

"Eat," he said.

My hand shot out to grab the beautiful looking bread-type food sitting in the top right corner of my plate. I took it against my will and began to bring it to my mouth. But before I could consume it, I took the pain of fighting him and threw the bread across the room.

Which subsequently went dead silent.

Once again, I felt my nose begin to bleed from the effort of fighting his commands as a whisper broke out through the other diners.

Ollie froze, staring at the bread where it had fallen. Then, smooth as anyone I'd ever seen, he rose, the room following suit.

"Thank you all for joining us," he said, his voice tight. "It has been a turbulent few days for my soulmate. He still has not fully recovered from the journey from the human realm, and he needs to be tended to and offered rest."

He held out his hand for me to take it, and I felt the control he had over me swell to the highest intensity it had been yet. My hand went right into his, and he slowly led me from the room, his other hand placed gently on the small of my back like we were truly soulmates. Like we both wanted to be there.

We passed by guards and other servants, many of whom looked human, like they'd been brought here like me, but just as many had skin in every color of the rainbow and features that would be considered monstrous.

Horns, tails, and scales. Wings, forked tongues, and clawed feet. It was so much to take in, and I felt myself growing faint, even as my body obeyed Ollie.

He brought me to my door, which I almost didn't realize, having only seen it once as I was leaving it earlier. He called for one of his guards, and they both sliced into their palms before placing them flat on the door. Symbols I hadn't seen before appeared and began to glow, and the door swung open.

I walked inside and sat down on the bed as Ollie moved to stand in front of me. He was furious. Even if I couldn't see his face, he was radiating rage.

"Do you have any idea," he said quietly, "what your little outburst could have done?"

I had never in my life been tazed, but the way the electric pain moved through me had to feel close. It was like a physical manifestation of Ollie's rage, like the prince no longer had the desire to temper himself.

I shook as he seethed, the pain exhausting me. "Then let me go home," I begged.

Ollie opened his mouth, and I was surprised to see him suck in a breath like he was in pain himself.

"This is your home now," he said, clutching his middle. "I would love nothing more than to give you anything and everything you want. But I have a duty, and so do you, even if you never knew it until now." He straightened up, his jaw set. "I'm going to lock you in with the blood seal. You won't be able to get out, but no one will be able to get in either." He paused, a hopeful look crossing his face. "Unless…"

"Unless?" I asked.

"Unless you'd rather join me in my chambers. Unless you'd rather give me a chance to show you what you would be missing if you went back to that place."

The grinding of my empty stomach was nothing like the emotional pain his flippant request sent through me. I struggled to my feet, breathing heavy as the shared pain rebounded between us like a fucked up game of Pong.

I took a few tentative steps forward, and Ollie held out his arms, ready to receive me.

I felt his power go slack, and I stepped into his embrace. He brought me into his chest, and I leaned into his ear, breathing for what felt like the first time since I woke up this morning.

"Ollie," I sighed, pressing my lips to his ear. "I would rather die."

His guard was down, and I knew it, so I kneed him in the groin and ran for the balcony. I was ready to die. Whatever it took to stop this monster from keeping me here.

I didn't even break my stride. I put my hands on the ledge, launched myself up, and vaulted over—

Ollie was faster. In that fucking shadow cloud thing he turned into, he could move in one second what would take me at least ten. And even as I soared through the air, I felt his arms close around my waist, pulling me back to the balcony.

I hit the stone floor with a painful thud, the wind knocked out of me. I got a small bit of vindication seeing Ollie was also struggling to breathe and stand. But once he was on his feet, he reached out and grabbed a stone from a nearby decoration.

He tossed it into the air once, like he was testing its weight. Not looking away from me, he threw it over the edge of the balcony. Or he tried to. It didn't go further than the railing before it bounced back like a tennis ball on a stone wall.

"I thought," he said, still breathing a bit heavy, "that it would hurt less if I broke your fall rather than letting you be thrown back without a cushion." He shook his head, sadness changing to resignation. "Locked in it is. I'll see you in the morning. Goodnight, *my* Gabriel."

He turned and walked out the door. I was certain he was doing that weird magic again to seal it.

This was far from over. I would figure out an escape one way or another. And after that last, "*My Gabriel*," I had half a mind to take him with me.

Chapter Twelve
Olympio

The effort to maintain an even stride as I moved through the halls was monumental. My jaw was tight to the point of twitching, my arms and legs tense and wooden in their movements. I didn't want to have to be the prince right now. I just wanted to be able to be Olympio—Ollie, even—and to have time and space to mourn the rejection from my soulmate. Or, if I could have what I truly wanted, to have the freedom to win Gabriel over the way he needed, rather than the way *I* needed.

But that was a freedom I was not granted. And I did love Gabriel enough to let him go, as he'd asked. If I only had myself to worry about, I wouldn't have brought him here this soon. If our bond hadn't been at risk, I'd have been willing to spend years building the relationship he deserved.

But I'd ruined any chance of that when I lost my temper and brought him here. I was too close to losing Gabriel to Kessinger, either because they were in love or because Kessinger's stupidity would get my soulmate killed, destroying my line's connection to the ancient magic that protected the throne. Not that I think the little bastard would have cared if he did. What did the future of my kingdom matter to a mortal narcissist who didn't even know Sefaera existed? And, if I was perfectly honest, I doubted Gabriel's life would matter to him, either.

I stood outside the large, opulent doors to my chambers, looking up to where they towered over me, nearly four times my height. They were cast in gold, with obsidian inlaid in intricate designs with a smooth, flat area where a handle or knob would usually be. These doors had been made generations ago, by my grandfather's grandfather, or possibly even farther back. They were made to open only for the monarch of Sefaera and those they deemed worthy of entering.

I sighed and hung my head, allowing a single moment of weakness in the relative solitude of the hallway, with only the two guards who stood as my sentinels at all times to witness it. I had been granted these quarters the very day of my brother's passing. It had been a blow to the kingdom when he'd died. It was only hours after that I found myself being moved into the quarters, alone, as my mother took the suite that had been mine.

That was over a thousand years ago, and I still hadn't been crowned king. And that left Sefaera open to usurpers, because having a bonded monarchical pair on the throne offered protection formed in deep, ancient magic that prevented the royal line from being overthrown.

But now there was Gabriel. And even looking past that same deep, ancient magic weaving our souls together so thoroughly that I knew losing him would destroy me, body and soul, I had grown to love and care for him. I wanted him by my side for eternity, not only because fate had chosen him, but because, knowing him as I did, I would have chosen him myself if given the chance.

And I couldn't give him the things I wanted to, because I had to maintain the image of control, even when I felt like I was spiraling out of it, like now.

I placed my hand on the smooth metal and felt warmth blossom beneath my fingers as the doors swung open for me. The second I was inside, my guards turned to face outward, and the doors shut with a dull *clunk*, sealing me inside.

I walked over to the large sofa in front of my already roaring fireplace and leaned forward, elbows on my knees and face in my hands. I took a deep, shuddering breath, ready to let go and finally feel everything that had happened, when a voice rang out behind me—from my bed.

"You look terrible."

I was startled, but the weight of my current struggles was so great I didn't even move. Of course, she would be here. She was one of three people—besides my guards—who had access to this room. I heard Vass climb out of my bed and walk over to stand in front of me, her arms crossed, her face haughty and cold, and her body entirely naked.

"I need to talk to you," she said, a quiver in her voice that belied the stony demeanor she was presenting.

"Now isn't a good time," I said with a quick glance up at her before looking into the fire, watching the blue and pink flames dance rather than allowing my eyes to linger on her form.

"It seems like your time is a bit occupied lately," she said. "So, I have to take what I can get."

"I have nothing to say to you, Vassenia," I said wearily, sitting up, so I was leaning on the back of the couch.

94

"No?" she said, stepping forward. "You don't want to apologize for the way you spoke to me earlier?"

"No, I don't," I said, wishing she would just leave me to my desolation.

That was until she moved even closer, until she was standing over me, and then put her legs on either side of my hips, straddling me. She took my face in her hands and kissed me deeply.

It was warm and familiar. For thousands of years, this was our tradition, our ritual. When one of us—usually me—was overcome by life, we would lose ourselves in each other. And in that moment, when I needed comfort as badly as I did, I was weak to her.

I grabbed her by the waist, pulling her against me and deepening the kiss, and she rotated her hips against mine, stirring my arousal. I growled with need and stood, carrying her with me to my bed, where I laid her down and positioned myself between her legs. I pressed my lips to the side of her neck, and she arched up into me.

"I knew you hadn't forgotten about me," she moaned, and I claimed her lips again, needing her. Her hands were everywhere, the feeling of her fingers on my skin drawing my breath from me in short, rough bursts.

"I could never," I breathed, and I cupped one of her breasts in my hand as I grabbed her hip with my other, pulling her up more tightly against me. My hardness pressed into her thigh, and I moved my fingers to her sex, groaning when I felt how wet she was for me.

And if Vass hadn't uttered her next words, I might have destroyed everything in a moment of weakness and passion.

"I love you," she said into my ear.

I don't know why that was what brought me to a sudden halt. It was no secret, from either of us or anyone else, that what we had was certainly love. But we'd never said it, not once in two and a half thousand years. Back when we thought I would never have to worry about the throne or a soulmate, it hadn't seemed to matter, because we both knew what we had. And once I was the heir, I worried that to say it would only make things harder if—when—my soulmate came along.

And I was right.

I stood up, taking a step back and wiping my lips, trying to rid them of the feeling of her to keep from being sucked back in. I shook my head and walked to the fire, leaning against the mantle.

"What the fuck just happened?" Vass asked. I looked back at her, and she was still on my bed, propped up on her elbows.

"I can't," I said, trying to form more words but struggling.

"Why not?" she demanded, getting up and beginning to walk over to me.

"You know why not," I snapped. Didn't she know this was just as painful for me? Loving her didn't just end because of Gabriel. But it did change. "You know that the second Gabriel was born, I was bound to him, body and soul. You know if I were to give in to this, that bond would break."

"Would that really be the worst thing?" she asked, scoffing at me.

"How can you even ask that, Vassenia? After everything we—I—went through with Vasileios?"

"He doesn't even want to be here—"

"Because he doesn't understand!" I shouted, cutting her off. "But he will. It will take time, but he will. And I won't give up on him."

96

"But you'll give up on *us*?" Her words were quiet and filled with emotion as she pulled on a robe, no longer wishing to be exposed. And it hurt, because I did love her. But I loved Gabriel and my family and my kingdom, too.

And the choice, while hard, was clear.

"There is no us, Vass," I said as gently as I could. "We've always known I might one day be bound to someone, and now that he's here…" I took a deep breath, "… our affair is over."

She pursed her lips, and I prepared for her to rage at me. I wouldn't have blamed her. But she didn't. She turned her back on me, hunching her shoulders.

She was crying.

My strong, intelligent, compelling friend and advisor Vassenia was in pain, and it was because of me. Because we'd fallen into something we never should have—love.

"I'm sorry," I said, taking a step toward her, reaching out to comfort her.

But my hand never made contact, because at that very moment, I felt the slightest shift in the air behind me. No one else should be in here. This room was the best protected in the entire palace.

But there was no mistaking the *swish* of a knife slicing through the air.

I spun, but I was a breath too slow. I hissed sharply as a stinging pain ripped across my forearm when I attempted to disarm the intruder.

A lithe figure clothed in black fighting leathers and a mask sprang backward, brandishing a dagger. An assassin.

There was absolutely no chance I was letting this person get another mark on me with her knife. Wasting not one single second, I shifted into the shadows and moved behind her before solidifying once more. I couldn't risk allowing her to hurt Vass or kill me. If I was assassinated now, Gabriel's existence would be in grave jeopardy as a human no longer under my protection.

I grabbed her wrist from behind, twisting it until she dropped her blade, then walked forward, pressing her into the wall to restrain her. It didn't take much to hold her there—it couldn't have been more obvious that her deadliness lay in her speed and stealth. I'd heard her approach, taking away the element of surprise.

And with the shadows on my side, I would always be faster.

"Fetch the guards," I barked at Vass, and it was a mark of the seriousness of the moment that she didn't hesitate or question my tone.

Instead, she scrambled to her feet and ran to the door, yanking it open and saying, "His Highness needs you," in a rushed voice.

I was still facing the wall with my attacker pinned there as the sound of booted feet came pounding into the room.

"Your Highness!" Gryfian said, coming to a stop just behind me.

I turned my head over my shoulder to look at him. He was with my other guard, their swords drawn, with Vassenia behind them, looking horrified.

"We have had an assassination attempt," I said, my voice shockingly calm, given the circumstances. A small part of me wondered if I was in shock. "I need the intruder apprehended and thrown into a cell to await a trial."

There was only a single beat of a pause before the guards stepped to either side of me and reached forward to grab the assassin by her wrists. She didn't even struggle as they restrained her, allowing me to back away. They spun her to face me, forcing her to her knees while they shackled her hands behind her back. I reached down and pulled off her mask, hoping for some kind of enlightenment, but I didn't recognize her.

"Who are you?" I asked, but she simply stared straight ahead, refusing to meet my eyes. "Why did you do this?"

She remained silent, and, in the aftermath of the spike of adrenaline, my heart was pounding so hard I felt a bit dizzy.

Too dizzy.

I stumbled into the mantle, then slid sideways, crashing to the floor.

"Olympio!" Vass shouted, falling to her knees at my side. I looked up at her, her face blurry and distorted. "What's wrong?"

I couldn't move my lips to tell her. My tongue felt like it was glued to the roof of my mouth, and my limbs had gone stiff.

And the assassin laughed. And laughed. And laughed.

"Go!" Gryfian commanded. "Get Perla. Now!"

I heard a pair of feet rush from the room. His urgency was so… loud. I was beginning to feel foggy, like I was so exhausted after a long day I couldn't keep my eyes open, and I began to allow myself to drift off.

"Don't you fucking dare, Olympio!" I heard Vass's voice as though through water. "Stay with me."

Stay with her? Of course I would. I loved her. I tried to reach for her, but my limbs wouldn't obey.

99

It seemed like only seconds later a burning sensation started in my forearm, then began to radiate throughout my body, as though my very heart was pumping fire through my veins.

My lungs were stiff, but as the pain raged on, I found I could breathe easier, open my eyes, even speak.

"What happened?" I asked. As I focused on the room around me, I realized my head was in Vassenia's lap, and she was looking down at me with tears in her eyes. A glance toward my arm showed me Perla, phials and ampoules all around her as she mixed and poured them over an open wound in my arm, which was still glimmering with gold blood.

"You were attacked," Vass said, stroking my hair. Her hands felt so lovely. "They only got a scratch on you, but—"

"But the blade was poisoned," Perla said, wiping away some kind of paste with a cloth. The burning in my veins had somewhat subsided, but the still visible wound on my arm stung like salt had been poured onto it. "You're lucky to be alive, Your Highness. Lucky I was nearby. Five more minutes, and I wouldn't have been able to save you. As it is, I did the best I could, but…"

"But?" Vass said sharply as I finally managed to sit up.

Perla sighed and ran her fingers over the cut. I had yet to see a wound Perla couldn't fix in seconds, but the line of shiny gold remained on my arm. "But I could only remove the poison from his blood. I couldn't rid it from the wound as well. That… that scar will be there forever."

I held up my arm to the light, the shimmering streak like a tattoo reminding me of my hubris. Of my arrogance to think just because I

100

won the fight against the assassin, I was safe. Whoever she was, she was well prepared for any eventuality.

"Where did she go?" I asked, looking around. The last I remembered, Gryfian had her restrained.

"She's dead," Vass said. "She had some kind of capsule on her armor. She bit into it, and she was dead in seconds. Imagine if she'd gotten more of that into you… If one tiny scratch almost killed you, and an amount no larger than a fingernail can kill in seconds, then this is a potent poison. And we have no idea where she got it or who hired her."

I sat up, the day's events returning to me. Remembering the conversation Vass and I had been having before I was attacked, I put a bit of distance between us and watched her hand follow me for just a second before she dropped it back to her lap, defeated.

"Thank you, Perla," I said, standing up and stretching. I felt like I'd been unusually active and my muscles were sore from the effort, or like I was exceptionally hungover, but otherwise, I was rapidly returning to normal. She was a miracle worker. "I owe you my life."

She bowed and turned to take her leave, headed off to wherever she was before I was attacked. I turned around and saw Vass and I were alone except for Gryfian, who was still standing like a sentinel, watching over me.

"Gryfian," I said, addressing him, and he stood at attention. "No need, old friend. I wanted to thank you for your loyalty and service. I think I'm ready to be alone for a bit."

"Your Highness, after the attempted assassination, do you think that wise?"

"Don't worry," Vass said. "I'll stay with him."

"No," I said sharply, and Vass jumped like I'd scared her.

"No?" She crossed her arms and took a step back, a challenge in her eyes. But it was one I was more than ready to accept.

"No," I repeated. "Our conversation didn't change because I was attacked. Gabriel is still my soulmate, and if I need someone to keep watch, it will be one of my guards. Gryfian, please feel free to get comfortable once you've shown Lady Vassenia out. You will be staying in my chambers tonight."

"Olympio," Vass said with a small laugh, like she thought I was joking.

"Good night, Vassenia."

The look of betrayal on her face should have broken my heart, but all it did was make me angrier with her. I needed her support, her friendship, even her love as I tried to navigate the difficult task of winning over my soulmate, and she'd chosen to stand against that goal instead. If anyone had been betrayed, it was me.

Once Gryfian had escorted her out, he returned, taking a seat in one of the large armchairs, which he turned to face me.

"Thank you, Gryfian," I said, clapping him on the shoulder as I passed him, heading to my bed.

"Of course, Your Highness."

I crawled beneath my blankets, letting them block out everything that threatened to bring me under. I had to believe Vass would come around. She'd always been a perfect companion—she just needed time to get used to this new dynamic.

At some point, silent tears began to fall from my eyes, and I did nothing to stop them. And even when I let myself feel how overwhelmed I was, and my body began to shake with sobs, I didn't bother to stifle it.

I knew Gryfian would guard my secrets with the same care he'd always guarded me.

Chapter Thirteen
Gabe

I woke up to the sound of clattering metal and a headache that was starting to be as common as the summery, woody smell drifting in from the balcony. It had been a week since my kidnapping, and every time I resisted Ollie's powers, it burned something within me, always causing painful side effects. Headaches, nosebleeds, vomiting—just a few of the lovely gifts my "soulmate" had bestowed upon me so far.

I opened my eyes to see I was not alone—but that wasn't surprising. I rarely was. No, the surprise came in the form of exactly who was watching me.

A small, red man who looked like a cartoon devil on Nickelodeon was watching me warily from where he had bent to pick up the metal platter he had knocked.

Whatever expectations I might have had for the people of this place, I was surprised by how wrong I continued to be. Every time I thought I knew what to expect from their appearances, something new would pop up. And this man was no exception.

"Your... Your Royal... I mean, Your Honorable... I mean, Sir...
Future—"

"It's fine," I said, cringing at the way he was struggling to title me.
"Gabe is fine. As long as you never call me Gabriel, we're square."

"Yes, Gabe," he said with a little bow. "Though... it is an odd
name, is it not?"

I felt like I was in some kind of Game of Thrones alternative
universe every time this guy talked. "I dunno—I guess it's not where
I'm from. His Royal Pompousness has never said anything about it
being 'weird.' Though, now you mention it, he won't call me by it,
either..."

I didn't really have much time to think about the ramifications of
this realization before the little man scampered over, his forked tail
swishing as he walked, and presented me with a plate of something that
looked like a fresh apricot.

"You're supposed to eat," he said nervously.

"I'm supposed to do a lot of things," I replied, crossing my arms
but softening my tone. "Why don't we start with *your* name?"

"Tomos," he mumbled. "I-I'm your personal attendant."

I'd been aware of Tomos's presence for about thirty seconds, and I
already liked him more than Prince Douchebag. I reached down and
took the tray from him, seeing his smallish arms were struggling from
the weight of it.

"Well, Tomos," I said, walking to the wrought-iron table on the
balcony and setting the tray down. "I'm fucking starving, but I don't
want the prince to know I'm eating. Can you keep that a secret for me?"

I reached down to the tray and popped one of the odd little fruits into my mouth. My taste buds went wild as my body itself seemed to sigh from relief. It was like I'd been tuning out the hunger until the sweet juices met my tongue, and now I was ravenous.

Tomos paced back and forth, looking nervous. "I'm really not sure..."

"Oh, come on," I said, indicating to the seat across from me. "As long as you're doing your job, does it really matter if Prince Cockbreath knows?"

Tomos seemed to consider this revelation, then nodded firmly, his brow resolute. "I suppose as long as I'm doing my job." He hopped over and scrambled up into the seat, and I pushed the tray toward him.

"Have one," I offered.

"Oh, no, I really should—"

"Please. It would feel nice to share a meal with someone again."

Once again he paused, then grabbed for a fruit, giving me a chance to get a good look at his clawed little fingers.

Tomos bit into the fruit like it would save his life and let out a low hum of satisfaction, like a child who'd been given a cookie.

I couldn't blame him. I'd never had anything like it before. It was the color, size, and shape of an apricot, but instead of having the wrinkly, fuzzy skin of the fruit I knew, it was smooth. It smelled like some kind of berry, but with an almost vanilla-like undertone. Biting into it was weird, but incredible. There were two layers to the fruit inside—a firm, sweet pulp that tasted almost like a strawberry mixed with a watermelon, and a soft, almost gel-like center with little seeds like a kiwi. The tart flavor was citrusy and fresh, giving the weird fruit the most unique, complex, and delicious taste of any I'd ever had.

I felt a dribble of juice slide down my chin, and it was almost like life was normal for a minute. Like I was home with my parents, eating peaches in the summer heat.

"Those are my favorite," a clear, rich voice suddenly said from the corner of the room, making my heart pound.

How had I not noticed Ollie had come in? Had he been there the whole time?

I turned my head and saw him step away from the wall, and as he did, the very shadows behind him seemed to form into the ends of his rich copper hair.

I felt a noise rumble up from my throat, which, even by my own account, was extremely juvenile and dismissive.

"Were you spying on me?"

Ollie smiled as he stepped forward, but I could see something fighting against the expression, like he was hiding something. "I would prefer to think of it as observing rather than spying. How did you sleep?"

I don't know what it was about this guy that turned me into a preteen brat, but I shifted my body so my back was to him, putting the delicious fruit down and pretending I didn't hear him.

"So, why are you here, Tomos?" I said, engaging the nervous aid once more.

His head had been going back and forth like he was watching a tennis match, and if he really was my attendant, it was only polite to engage him.

I felt Tomos look to Ollie for instruction, and the prince moved to lean against the massive window frames.

"As I mentioned to you before," he said, "as my soulmate, you are going to be granted power and duties you will need to be ready for. You have never been in a position to learn combat skills, and you will need to learn Sefaeran customs and etiquette before you take your place at my side. Tomos is here to ensure you make it to your lessons and participate as expected of the future consort to the king."

I had to admit, there was a certain allure to the idea of being totally transformed. It was the kind of vibe that made reality makeover shows so interesting, right?

The part of my brain that had been raised by Hollywood executives could see the commercial for it now: "*Becoming a Prince: From Frat Boy to Consort.*"

But accepting anything Ollie was offering, even the shit that tasted good or sounded fun, was as good as giving my consent for what he had done to me—what he was going to do to me. And there was no way in hell I was going to condone the terror I felt at every waking moment, knowing I was at the mercy of someone who owned my body like some people owned cars. He could control my very atoms with his own desires. How long would it be before his "royal duties" included penetrating me?

I didn't turn to face him before very succinctly stating, "No, thank you."

The silence I was met with was almost as loud as if he'd yelled at me. It stretched on for what felt like minutes, maybe hours, before finally, he spoke.

"Gabriel," he said in a low, even voice. "You need to understand that I don't have any more of a choice in this than you do. The expectations and rules set forth for me were established thousands of years ago, and, as my soulmate, you are bound to them as well. And because I am the one whom the people of Sefaera look to for guidance and leadership, I cannot have the person destined to be by my side for eternity dissenting against me publicly. My throne is at risk every moment we are not on it—"

I stood up so fast I knocked the wrought-iron chair across the balcony's stone floor, and barreled toward him, ready to throw a punch. "Then fucking pick someone else! Anyone! Fuck Tomos for all I care. Just take me the fuck home."

From behind me, I heard Tomos make an uncomfortable squeaking noise, and I turned my head to look at him.

"Sorry," I said—he really didn't deserve to be in the middle of this.

Ollie stood, no longer leaning, forcing me to look up at him. His face was infuriatingly blank, as if my anger and fear had no impact on him.

"Gabriel," he said again, reaching for my wrist to prevent me from swinging. "If I could… I would have set you free already. I would have taken the throne with the person who was my confidant my entire life, knowing I would never love her the way I love you. But the soulmate bond isn't one that is chosen, and the throne will not accept a pair that isn't bonded. I need you, and my kingdom—*our* kingdom—needs you."

I pulled my wrist free and folded my arms across my body in a way I'd taken to doing and turned away, throwing myself back down onto my bed. If I was totally honest, the bed was the one thing I'd miss when

109

I went back to my regular life because they somehow made it feel like you were sleeping in a cloud—gravity-less.

I looked over at the fire, which roared with life twenty-four hours a day, but only gave off heat when the night grew cold. The cotton candy-colored flames danced in a mesmerizing tango that eased my mind momentarily. Until my thoughts drifted to another fiery situation…

My heart was already racing from trying to argue for my freedom, when all of a sudden, I was envisioning my parents' bodies burning in the plane crash. My mother screaming for my father, and my father trapped beneath rubble.

I swear I could feel the heat, hear their voices—

Suddenly I was convulsing, thrashing against the bed I had come to love so dearly, feeling like my skin was too tight for my body. I could hear my own whimpers and the scramble of those who were near me.

Still, my parents' voices rang in my ears, and I felt hot, burning tears expelled from me like I would never stop crying again.

Hands clutched my upper arms, holding me still, and suddenly I was pressed against a warm, firm surface, held in place by a pair of thick, strong arms.

"Gabriel," Ollie's voice crooned, cutting through the panic. "You are safe here. Whatever you're seeing, whatever you're feeling, you are safe from it."

"They're burning," I sobbed. "Make the fire stop. Please make the fire stop. It's too much…"

I heard Ollie suck in a sharp breath, then tighten his embrace. "Tomos," he said quickly. "Extinguish the fire. We will not light another unless the future consort requests it."

110

"I want my mom," I sobbed, knowing the absurdity of the statement. "Fuck... My mom is dead..."

Breathing became difficult quickly, and I grabbed for my hair, pulling at it, trying to eradicate the pressure sitting on my chest like a ton of bricks.

Ollie's grip on me loosened, but didn't vanish. I felt him breathing in a slow, steady rhythm, and something about it began to help my own breathing slow, and my hands to release my hair, coming to rest on his shoulders without even realizing it.

"I can't bring your mother back," Ollie said quietly. "But... perhaps I've been hasty in the way I went about bringing you here. You've lost so much, and now you've lost all familiarity from your previous life." He paused, and I felt his cheek rub against my hair. "Let me see what I can do."

He held onto me for a few more seconds, then let me go. He stood up from my bed, where he'd been laying at my side, and turned to Tomos.

"Gabriel will need some extra time getting ready today," he said. "Let Heriod know I have authorized any lateness to his lessons for the day."

He looked at me one more time, his gaze lingering in a way that made his longing all too obvious, then turned and left my room.

In my shaken state, I realized I felt something else. A weird, subtle little piece of me felt... *sad* when he left. Being held—even by *him*—had been so... comforting.

I looked over to Tomos, who appeared to have taken on some kind of military stance in an effort to not be jarred by my panic. "I'm hungry…" I murmured, not wanting Ollie to hear me yet.

The little man nodded, then marched for the door, presumably to fetch something else to sustain me.

I fell back against the bed, the pain in my chest an echo of what it had been. I felt grateful to the prince for his kindness—something I didn't know I could feel about the man who'd ripped away my entire reality. But it was enough to make me consider trying to see his side of things…

Maybe.

The fifteen foot high doors opened, and I sat up, ready to eat whatever Tomos had brought me, but it wasn't him. Ollie walked in, giving me a gentle smile, carrying a bundle of something in his arms, wrapped in paper and ribbon like a gift.

"I had hoped it was still here," he said as he approached me, setting the package on the bed beside me. "Thankfully, it was being kept to be put into a museum someday." He chuckled, like there was a joke I was supposed to be in on. "More will come, but for today, I thought you might be more comfortable with this."

I took the box and opened it, pulling aside some sort of material that reminded me of plastic but smelled like tree bark.

And there—tucked neatly in the box—were the clothes I had been wearing the night Ollie had dragged me to this place.

My jeans, my letterman jacket, my stupid Star Wars socks. All there, all perfectly preserved. And sitting on the very top…

"My dad's ring…" I said, choking up at the sight of it.

112

"You will still have to be in ceremonial dress for official events and appearances," he said, watching me closely. "But I see no reason why you can't wear your own things at other times."

I looked up at him and searched his eyes for the catch.

But I swear he shook his head, almost as if he knew what I was wondering and wanted me to know this was for real. He was bargaining—not as good as a concession—but it was still something.

"Thank you," I choked out.

Ollie's face relaxed, breaking into a relieved smile. "You're welcome," he said. "I know it's not the same as being back in your world. If I could give you everything you wanted and asked for, I would. But as limited as I am, I will do my best to help you be comfortable here, Gabriel. You have my word."

With that, he gave me a small bow, reaching out like he was going to touch my face and then changing his mind. Then he turned and left the room without a look back, and for the first time—I was considering playing ball. I'd never known someone who could read me that completely and attend to my emotional needs so thoroughly. Not even my parents.

And to be perfectly honest...

It was nice.

Chapter Fourteen
Olympio

I sat at the table in my chambers, poring over the dozens of papers and decrees produced in my long absence from the kingdom. The Council had taken care of most of them, but I needed to be aware of what had occurred so I could resume my role as ruler and, once the Consummation was complete, slip seamlessly into the role of king.

It was difficult to focus on any of it when I knew what was to come in just a few short hours.

I'd been informed by the Council, when I'd met with them earlier, they wanted the Consummation ceremony to occur as soon as possible to secure the throne, and they'd scheduled it for that very night. By the time I woke up the next day, my bond to Gabriel would be permanent and unbreakable, and the leadership of Sefaera would be protected.

My eyes were beginning to glaze over, all of the documents seeming to say the same thing, when a knock came at my door. I jumped up to answer it, expecting the delivery I'd commissioned of a full wardrobe of Gabriel's clothing from the human realm. But before I could even take a single step, the doors opened.

"Imagine being gone over a century and not even bothering to send for your sister upon your return," Ariadne said, giving me a teasing smile as she let the door shut behind her. "Disgraceful."

I quickly walked over to my sister, pulling her into an embrace.

"I was told you were on a diplomatic mission," I said, holding her tightly.

"I was," she said, patting my shoulder to indicate I should release her, but I held on a moment longer. "Moons and rivers, Olympio. I missed you, too, but you can let go."

I gave a chuckle thick with tears I was holding back before unwinding my arms from around her.

"I'm sorry," I said, feeling like the overbearing older brother I could be. Being away from home for so long had likely made me even more insufferable in that regard. She needed no convincing to step past me, flopping down onto a chaise near the sofa. With an indulgent shake of my head, I followed her. "Please... make yourself comfortable."

Ari smiled at me and kicked her feet up, lounging like this was her own room. I didn't mind. We'd always been close, which was why she was allowed unadulterated access to my living space.

"I take it you found them?" she said, cutting right to the chase. "I would assume so, since the word in court is you'll be having your ceremony tonight. I was barely back home for five minutes before I heard. A human, apparently. And I heard he's a male?" It wasn't unheard of for soulmates to be of the same gender, but it was less common. The last time it happened, Sefaera had enjoyed its longest reign of peace as two women sat on the thrones.

115

Ari had been the only person other than my mother who knew where I was going when I felt the bond form. And to be honest, I wouldn't have trusted almost anyone else with that knowledge.

"I did. His name is Gabriel. He's… struggling to adjust to his new life."

"Of course he is," she said, like it should have been obvious. "You were there for how long in their time?"

"Just shy of twenty years," I said.

"And did you acclimate right away?"

I paused, thinking about what she was asking. I hadn't had too hard of a time assimilating when I enrolled at Gabriel's school and joined his fraternity, but I'd spent nineteen years in that world, learning about customs and norms. And even then, I didn't always feel comfortable in situations with no parallel in my world.

"No," I admitted. "I suppose I didn't. I brought him some of his clothes to help him feel more comfortable. Do you think there's more I could do?"

Ari shook her head like I was stupid. No one else in Sefaera could get away with that but her. "How are you supposed to be king of our whole world when you can't even figure out how to take care of your soulmate?"

Her words stung, but I knew immediately she was right. I'd been so focused on trying to convince Gabriel to just accept his place here, I had ignored things that might make him feel like he belonged.

"What do you suggest?" I asked, open to whatever she might advise.

"Damned if I know," she said with a dry laugh. "I don't know him. But you do. So maybe pull your head out of your ass and use what you know about Gabriel to figure out what he needs."

Speaking with Ari was like breathing fresh air for me. I'd been trained, ever since my brother died, to speak a certain way, knowing I would take the throne one day. Ariadne never had that hanging over her head. As the royal Master of the Hunt, she was given the freedom to speak more bluntly and less refined, and I loved it, having missed that for myself.

"How do you always know exactly what I need to hear and what I need to do when I can't figure it out?"

"Because I'm the smart one," she said, grinning. "They wouldn't waste that on some royal figurehead. Leave the brains to those of us with real jobs."

I could always count on my sister to bring me back to my senses and make me laugh, even when laughing felt like a foreign concept. In fact, the relief I felt from just being able to let go was so great, I laughed far louder, harder, and longer than was called for.

But Ari didn't stop me. She waited for me to be finished, to center myself once more.

"Well," she said, rising to her feet. "I'd love to stay and catch up on the time you were gone, but I do believe you have a ceremony to prepare for." She paused, her usual jovial expression becoming serious. "I know how long you've waited for this. But Gabriel hasn't. And you know if the ceremony isn't completed with *both* of you fully invested and eager to seal your bond, it won't work. Don't put him through something if he isn't ready."

Her words took me by surprise.

"Why wouldn't he be ready?"

Ari shrugged, a small smile returning to her lips before she turned and walked to the door. "I don't know, Olympio. He's *your* soulmate. Maybe you should ask him."

Before I could respond, she opened the door and left me alone to prepare for the ceremony. And I could only hope Gabriel was actually prepared for this.

I took my time dressing in the ceremonial Consummation garb. Two panels of black silk were draped over my shoulders, creating a long "v" down my front to my hips, where a gold belt cinched the material, bringing it together to cover me from the hips to the floor. The slits created by the separate panels would be parted when the time came to…

I looked at the garment next to mine, hanging from the top of my four-poster bed, waiting to be taken to its owner. It was nearly identical, though while mine was black with gold accents, Gabriel's was gold with black accents, and the fabric of his was sheer except for the area covering his groin.

He was going to be stunning.

Ari's words rang through my head, sowing seeds of doubt within me. She was right. I'd been waiting for this for so long that, now that the time had come, all of my patience had evaporated. I would have waited years, decades, even, but now that the ceremony was upon us, I couldn't bear another moment without Gabriel at my side.

I grabbed his attire and quickly left my room, striding toward Gabriel's, passing members of the court who whispered behind their hands. There were over a hundred members of my court, but only the dozen members of the Council would be present for the ceremony. But that didn't mean what I was wearing went unnoticed.

I made it to Gabriel's room in record time, my eagerness propelling me forward. I stood outside the tall doors and took a deep breath. I needed to be calm, collected. I needed to show Gabriel there was nothing to fear, that I would make sure he was taken care of and comfortable.

I opened the door and stepped inside, hanging his clothing from a hook on the wall. The softness of the blue room suited Gabriel well. He was delicate, gentle, like the cascades of flowers all over his walls and the rosy quartz.

Gabriel wasn't back from his lessons yet, but I knew it was only moments before he was. I don't know when I'd ever been so anxious. I was about to share the news our bond would be consummated tonight.

And a part of me worried he'd refuse again.

I would never force him. Not in this regard. Even if I didn't find the very idea despicable, it wouldn't work if he had to be coerced or commanded to do it. And I wanted it to work. I wanted it to be real and permanent.

I wanted *my* Gabriel to truly be mine.

The door to the suite opened, and Tomos scampered in, chittering away, followed by Gabriel. My beautiful soulmate was laughing. It felt like it had been centuries since I'd seen him smile. It would never cease to amaze me how the very sight of him could take my breath away, how being in the same space as him made the bond hum and vibrate like the magic itself was delighted by our proximity.

"Hello, Gabriel," I said, keeping my voice even and clear. "How was your first day of lessons?"

His smile faded, and the laughter turned to an echoed memory. He didn't snarl at me like he'd been doing, but he certainly did not appear to be ready to share his warmth, either.

"Hello. Fine."

The tense, three syllable response sent another wave of anxiety through me that used every ounce of my willpower to hide.

"Wonderful," I said, as if he'd sat down and shared every little detail with me like I wished he would.

Gabriel moved to his bed, sat down, and unlaced his boots. A gift from me I'd had made the day he arrived from the finest leather in all of Sefaera. But I certainly wasn't about to tell him so. Not when seeing him wear them gave me a spark of hope.

"Did you need something?" he asked coolly.

It was now—the moment when I would share the news. But first, I looked to Tomos. "Can you please fetch Gabriel's attendants? All of them."

Tomos gave me a look of confusion, but did as he was told, glancing briefly at Gabriel before disappearing through the door.

Once we were alone, I turned back to Gabriel, but my throat seemed to be rebelling against me saying a damn thing. I knew what would help, what might take the edge off of my nerves, and walked to a cabinet in the corner. It had obviously not been explored by Gabriel yet, which was probably for the best.

"Is this about to be another speech?" he asked. "I don't think I can handle any more declarations of undying devotion from you this week. I actually had a nice day, riding horses and stuff. And there were these knives that—" He froze just as I reached in and grabbed a bottle of the same blue wine from our dinner with the court and poured us each a goblet full. "What are you doing? I'm too tired to get drunk."

I almost didn't want to answer. I wanted him to keep telling me about his day and about his life. I'd been there for it all, every moment. But hearing his voice speak to me with excitement about it was different. It calmed the storm raging in my chest, and I felt certain now he would be ready.

"A glass of wine won't get you drunk," I said with a chuckle. "I've seen the volume of liquor you can consume without becoming completely inebriated. But then again, you weren't exactly drinking Sefaeran wine at the frat house, were you?"

He shot me a scathing look that was vicious in the way it appeared, but clearly lacked conviction. He followed it up perfectly with a roll of his eyes.

"Okay… Dad."

I wasn't sure how to respond to that, so I continued to smile as I walked over to his bed and handed him the wine.

"I have to tell you something," I said, trying to convey excitement rather than nervousness, but I had no idea which came through.

Gabriel raised an eyebrow, but allowed me to sit on the corner of his bed. "Please tell me it's not some ceremony."

Damn.

My breath caught in my chest, but I took a sip of wine to cover it, letting the rich liquid soothe my shaking hands.

"It is," I said, once again trying to sound like this was a gift rather than something to worry about. "Tonight, you and I will have the Consummation ceremony to seal our bond."

Gabriel had just taken a drink of his wine, and in seconds it was all over him, and some on me as well. "Is that why you're dressed like a male stripper? Not happening," he said, wiping his chin and attempting—but failing—to lick it off his shirt.

I looked down at the small splatters on my garment, but the idea of heading into the ceremony with wine on my clothes paled in comparison to the idea of attending the ceremony without my soulmate to actually carry it out.

"Gabriel," I said in what I hoped was a soothing voice. I had to remember what Ariadne had said about Gabriel not being acclimated to his new life yet. He was still yearning for what he'd come from. Perhaps I could give him a bit of that by at least speaking to him on his level. "I know this is uncomfortable. I was so eager to have you here and have you ready to take on this new life that I can see now I took things too fast. You haven't had time to figure things out yet or to get used to your new role or your new home. Tonight is a single night—just like initiation back at the fraternity. The ceremony itself is an initiation in a way. And it has to be done so we can emerge on the other side as immortals together. Does that make sense? I want to get this one hurdle out of the way so we can have the time we deserve, and you can take things at your own pace."

Gabriel took a deep breath and held it in his chest for a moment, then exhaled very, very slowly. "So what do I have to do? This doesn't mean I'm agreeing to stay or anything, but—" He almost smiled at me. "I did pledge to be there for my big."

His words made my heart flutter with hope. Draining the rest of my goblet, I stood and showed him his own garment.

"First, your attendants will come and bathe you, dress you, and paint you," I said. "Once you're ready, we will go together to the Council chambers, which has been transformed for the ceremony. You and I will pledge ourselves to each other, affirming the soulmate bond, and then, under the observation of the Council, we will Consummate the bond."

Gabriel cocked his head to the side and furrowed his brow. "That means, like, eating something—right?"

It took me a moment to understand what he was asking, but when I did, I realized he truly had no idea what tonight would entail.

"I think you might be thinking of communion," I said. "Consummation is... well, it will be our bodies coming together in a union, sealing the bond between us."

Gabriel paused, and I could almost smell the smoke from the effort he was putting into understanding. "Wait..." he said slowly. "Do you mean... fucking?"

The bluntness was so unexpected, I actually choked out a laugh.

Gabriel slumped in relief and gave a chuckle himself. "Oh, thank god," he said with a snort. "I was definitely not down for some weird sex ritual."

Suddenly, my laughter was cut short. He truly hadn't understood, and I had to tell him.

"I don't know about weird," I said, trying to speak softly to ease the blow. "But… the Consummation *is* a ritual based around sex—around you and I giving our bodies to each other to symbolize the union of our souls."

"Fuck, no."

"Gabriel—"

"Fuck. No. Not happening. I would rather drink a bucket of Alex Kessinger's semen than have some weird public sex with you so you can be king. No fucking way."

The very use of Kessinger's name on the night of the ceremony, and particularly in the context it was used, set my blood boiling. I readied myself to use the bond to make Gabriel comply, at least until we got there. Once we were there, he would understand.

But I didn't. Even though I knew it might derail everything, I couldn't do that to him.

"It's not just so I can be king," I said, my patience wearing thin. "It is so you will be granted immortality, and *together*, we will secure the throne of Sefaera. And more than that… This bond has existed your entire life. I have been waiting your *entire life* for this, for our souls to truly become one." I reached out a hand, but withdrew it, not wanting to come on too strong, but needing him to be willing. "Please, Gabriel."

His face grew stony, unreadable. I watched as his posture changed and his shoulders squared and his lips became an impossibly thin line for such beautiful, normally plump flesh.

"Fine," he said quietly. "It's just another hook up, right? Why should I care? Not like I wasn't doing that before I got here."

I was torn between relief at his assent and devastation at what he said. A hook up? This wasn't some one time bathroom rendezvous in the frat house. This was a sensual experience that would transcend our bodies, calling forth deep, ancient magic to complete the ritual.

But for now, he was agreeing. I could explain everything to him later. I could win him over days, weeks, or years from now. Tonight... I just needed him to consent.

At that moment, Tomos and Gabriel's attendants came in, and they immediately rushed to his side, stripping him for a bath. My heart ached with every beat as I watched Gabriel do everything they asked of him, getting in the tub, standing, letting himself be dried, dressed, and painted with golden highlights on his cheekbones and eyelids. But he did all of it as though he had given up, like the soul I was bound to had left him, making him an empty shell.

Once he was ready, I walked up to him. He looked like an ethereal vision in the sheer gold silks and makeup. My soulmate was the most beautiful thing I'd ever seen, and as I took his arm and placed it in mine to walk to the chambers together, I had to use every ounce of willpower to keep from parting my silks ahead of time.

But then something happened. After we left Gabriel's room, every step seemed to cause butterflies to take flight in my stomach. I assumed it was just nerves and anticipation of what was to come, but by the time we walked into the room, where a large bed had been placed on a dais in the center, I could hardly breathe.

I glanced over at Gabriel as the high chairman of the Council, Typhir, stood to call us forward, and despite the fact that my feet felt leaden, I led Gabriel to the platform.

He looked like a shell of himself, like whatever life had been within him an hour ago when he was talking about riding had abandoned its host. He was treating this like something he had to "get through."

I had no idea what to do. We were in the chambers, positioned next to the bed to begin when Typhir sounded the bell. But my Gabriel—my soulmate—was somewhere else in his mind, because he couldn't be here.

I had no time to formulate a solution, because right when the bell rang, it was time.

I hadn't given him any kind of instruction, but Gabriel seemed to know what to do. He climbed onto the bed and lay there, perfectly still, waiting for me.

I wasn't sure how to begin. I'd pictured this so many times and so many ways, but in all of my imaginings, I didn't feel like I was carrying a massive weight on my shoulders. In my fantasies, this was sensual, erotic, beautiful. This felt... clinical. Even my cock seemed to think so, since the most beautiful creature I'd ever seen was laying right before me, ready and willing for our union, but I was completely flaccid.

I reached down, parting the panels and gripping my soft length, beginning to stroke it as I looked at Gabriel. There had been times when simply being near him could make me hard in an instant. But right now, when it was necessary for me to be, my member was taking its time growing to its full stiffness.

I looked at the planes of his body, trying to convince my own to cooperate. The curve where his shoulder met his neck, where I'd often imagined burying my face. The long lines of his legs, which I pictured wrapped around me. The soft swell of his lips, which I wanted to taste with my own. The bulge sitting between the silks, which I had longed to touch, to feel…

It took much longer than I expected, longer than it ever had. But eventually, I stood at the foot of the bed, my member as erect as it needed to be for the purpose.

Gabriel had not achieved the same goal. His cock was still soft, not even slightly stirring. Wanting this to be pleasurable for him, I climbed onto the bed and came to a stop, hovering over him.

"Just relax," I said, trying to show him it was okay. He didn't respond, so I ran my hand down his bare chest, my fingers grazing just inches away from—"It is not necessary for the consort to be aroused," said Typhir's slimy voice behind me. I glanced back at him, and he gave a motion as if to say, "*Go on.*"

So be it. This would be for me, as it was for Gabriel. A task to complete, something to get through.

I ran my hand over his thigh, sliding it between his legs. He may not have needed to be hard, but he would need to be prepared, so I didn't hurt him. Before I could even slip my finger into his cleft, I noticed my hands were shaking uncontrollably. And even as I had that realization, I suddenly found myself unable to breathe. My chest was tight, and every inhale felt like it was making its way through broken glass.

And a single glance at my soulmate's face told me everything I needed to know.

Gabriel was having a panic attack, and it was so severe I had taken it on without making a conscious effort to do so. I couldn't do this. I couldn't power through my own panic attack, and I wouldn't force him to power through his.

I had no idea what I was going to say to the Council about why I would be ending the ceremony, but I was spared coming up with a reason when Gabriel began to writhe beneath me. I moved so he could be free, and he leaned over the edge of the bed and vomited.

Thank Talaea.

"My friends," I said, rising to my feet, my length already going soft. "Clearly, the consort is unwell. The ceremony will need to be rescheduled."

"Do you not realize how important this is to the future of our kingdom?" one of them said as the others sighed in exasperation.

"I do," I said, my patience entirely used up. "And because of the importance of this event, I will not allow it to be treated as if it is a simple meeting. The ancient magic which the ceremony invokes will not be made a mockery of because the souls to be bonded were unable to be present and engaged. Now if you'll excuse us."

I turned to Gabriel, who looked up at me weakly.

"Come on," I said, lifting him into my arms. "I've got you."

And without a backward glance, I left the chamber to take Gabriel back to his room.

Chapter Fifteen
Gabe

I should have told him I was a virgin. I should have told him I'd never been inside anyone, and no one had ever been inside me.

As soon as I puked, it was over. I didn't like Ollie's style of romance, but he wasn't so much a scumbag that he was going to fuck me while I was sick.

He took me back to my room, carrying me like I was a child, and put me right in the tub. I sat shaking as he stripped me bare once more and cleaned my face of its adornments. I never knew what it felt like to wear makeup before then, but I wondered how women didn't scratch off their skin from the itch of it.

When Ollie was done bathing me, he put me in my bed, bringing me a sweatshirt and sweatpants. I didn't know where he'd gotten them, but I knew immediately they were mine.

Once I was dressed, I climbed into bed, ready for this whole horrible experience to be over. But I felt Ollie slide in behind me, and ease my head into his lap.

"I'm so sorry," he said, his voice thick with emotion.

I honestly wanted to respond to him, but nothing in me was working right. So instead, I nodded, allowing him to take my hand and hold it.

"I don't..." he began, but then shook his head. "I never would have pushed that on you if I'd known... if I'd listened."

"I'm a virgin," I blurted out. "I've never... Alex and I didn't..."

Ollie took a deep, shaky breath, then let it out in a huff.

"I know," he said. "It never occurred to me it would hinder your ability to..."

"What do you mean, you know?" I asked softly, with passive confusion. His body was warm against mine, and as much as I fought the feeling of comfort he was giving me, I doubted I'd be breathing without it.

His hands went to my hair, stroking it gently as he sat quiet for several seconds before saying, "Well... I thought I'd made it clear before, but... I... I've been watching over you."

I felt my heart begin to pound again, and I slowly moved away. "Watching me?" I asked.

Ollie tried to keep me in his lap, but I pulled away even harder. He lowered his head, looking down at the bed in what almost looked like shame.

"The day you were born, I felt the bond form, and I followed it," he said. "I found you that very night, not even a day old, but right then, I loved you with my entire being. And I swore to never let anything harm you. So I stayed close, and I watched, waiting for you to be ready for me to finally enter your life."

130

I felt like I might puke all over again, and I stumbled out of the bed and onto the balcony. "So, my parents… you could have done something… You could have saved them, and you didn't. For what?" I screamed so loudly my voice cracked. "You let them die so it would be easier for you to sweep me away to this godforsaken shithole?"

He jumped to his feet and followed me.

"I didn't know what was going to happen," he said. "I never wanted that kind of pain for you. Your agony is my agony. If I had the gift of foresight, I would have saved them. I had no knowledge of the crash before it happened, and no power to stop it if I did."

"Sure," I scoffed. "Sounds likely. Just like you had no idea we'd end up in the same fraternity."

Ollie actually blushed. "No. That… that was intentional. I needed you to meet me. I needed you to get to know me, to trust me so I could explain everything. But that bastard Kessinger backed me into a corner, and I had to rush things."

"So, the letter… the one you hand delivered me by my parents' graves pretending to be the son of their friend. The heartfelt letter from my parents…:"

"Gabriel…"

"*Dear Gabe*," I recited. "*If you're receiving this, it means we're gone, and you are going to have to navigate this difficult time in your life alone. This would never have been the way we wanted it, but since we cannot change what is, only what might be, let us leave you with these parting words.*"

Ollie looked panicked. He clearly hadn't expected me to have read it so many times that I memorized it.

"Be brave and be fearless. Those might sound like the same thing, but they're not. Only when you understand this, can you truly be your best. Take care of those around you and never let a moment pass that you don't cherish them. It could all be gone in an instant."

He looked like he was going to cry. "If you could just let me—"

"Lastly, a request. We have left you everything we've ever had. We hope that you will use those resources to get yourself an education and to build a life you love of your own. We love you so much, Gabe. Watching you grow up has been a joy and a pleasure. And, if the deliverance of this letter is any indication, we wish we'd had more time. Your parents, Martin and Elizabeth."

He didn't speak. He just… froze.

"Say something, you fucking coward. You wrote the letter, didn't you?"

I could barely hear him as he whispered, "Yes."

For one harrowing moment, I thought I might go into cardiac arrest. But the adrenaline transformed into rage like I'd never felt before.

I ran at him, fists swinging, making sure I got two hits to his face right away.

"You fucking sick bastard," I screamed, now aiming for his ribs. "You disgusting fuck."

Gold liquid burst from his nostrils and out of a split in his lip as I kept hitting him. He didn't even raise a hand to stop me. He just took it.

"You say you did this out of devotion," I screamed, shoving him before ramming into him with my shoulder, knocking him against the mantle. "But you sound like a stalker to me."

I took a few steps back, panting, tears streaming freely as I watched him attempt to limp forward.

"Don't touch me," I screamed, my voice straining. "I will never love you. Do you hear me? I will never want you. You can keep me here for the rest of my sad, pathetic mortal life, and I will never give you what you want."

I could feel my next words bubbling up from my guts before I even said them, and when they emerged, they were a snakelike whisper.

"I fucking hate you."

The look on his face was more hurt than it had been when I'd hit him. His shoulders slumped, and despite being several inches taller than me, he seemed small.

"I never meant to hurt you," he said, all life gone from his voice. "I knew it was time. I knew you were alone, and I had waited so long to be the one you took comfort in, and I did anything I could to help you get to me."

The anger which had previously been exploding inside me like a bomb now turned to a live wire of deadly venom. I took a few steps forward, closing the gap between us and leaning into his ear.

"You are nothing to me. And I will fuck anyone I can get my hands on. You said you feel what I feel? You'll feel every single second of it and know it's not you. Now get the fuck out."

I watched as Ollie lifted his head and set his jaw as if he was above whatever he was feeling, but the pain lingering in his eyes, which should have made me feel powerful, only succeeded in making whatever connection he and I had ache.

"Tomos will attend to you through the night," he said, his voice smooth despite how badly I knew I'd hurt him. Good. "And in the morning, he will escort you to your first archery lesson."

Without another word, he turned and walked halfway to the door, then seemed to give up on it and shifted into a living shadow, moving so quickly, I didn't even see it leave my room.

I dropped onto my bed, unable to conjure any more emotion for the day, and quickly fell into a deep, dreamless sleep I could not have been more grateful for.

I didn't leave my bed for the next two days, and I didn't leave my room for a week, refusing archery lessons day after day. I had returned to my previous plan of starving myself until he gave in and took me back, which hadn't had any success so far.

A week after the failed ceremony, I tried to make good on my promise by attempting to seduce one of my handmaids. She'd been particularly kind to me since I'd arrived, and I felt as close to her as anyone else.

Ollie had made it clear from the start that my staff—sans Tomos— were there to do anything I needed to be more comfortable.

Anything.

So when Faenia entered my chambers with my breakfast, I was ready with a plan.

I'd spent the half hour beforehand coaxing my own cock into working with the promise of freedom, which—surprisingly—didn't work very well.

"Good morning, future consort," she said as she opened the curtains to let the sunlight in. "I hope you slept well."

Frat boy mode activated.

"I did," I said with the croon I usually reserved for a Friday night keg party. "And I woke up with a little problem. I'm wondering if you can help me?"

She turned to me, approaching as I lay in bed, a feeble tenting occurring beneath my sheets. If she noticed, she didn't indicate, which, of course, made for an awkward transition.

"Anything you need, sir," she said with a curtsy that allowed me a nice glance at her cleavage.

Suddenly, a real performance was back on the table.

I indicated sheepishly to the now fine erection I was sporting, and I watched as her eyes got wide. A small, understanding smile graced her full, beautiful lips, and she nodded.

"I'd be more than happy, sir," she said, her voice suddenly sultry.

I gestured to her to join me in the bed, and it appeared she already knew the routine. In moments, she had the sheet pulled back and a firm grip on my cock.

Fuck's sake, I forgot how it felt when I was actually into it.

The door burst open, and a woman I didn't recognize marched in wearing what looked like fighting leathers, an ornate bow strapped to her back.

"Faenia," she said, crossing her arms at the foot of my bed. "Either finish him quickly or let him go. We have work to do."

I scrambled to cover myself, realizing this woman must have been someone of great importance if she could just burst in like that.

"I'm... I'm sorry," I muttered, looking at the familiar copper shade of her hair and yellow irises. "Are you... Are you Ollie's mom?"

135

Her mouth dropped open like she was in shock, but a smile tickled the corners of her lips, anyway.

"Two things," she said, holding up her hand and raising a finger. "Number one—I know we're immortal and, therefore, eternally youthful, but do I really look like his *mother*? Moons and rivers, I need to spend less time out in the woods." She held up a second finger. "Two— did you just say 'Ollie?'" She snorted a laugh on the name, like it was the most amusing thing she'd ever heard.

I felt dumbstruck and confused. "Oh, yeah, sorry. That's what Prince Dickhead told me his name was back in my world, so... old habits die hard, I guess."

Her laughter got even louder. "Fuck, I like you. I can't decide if Ollie or Prince Dickhead is a better name for my brother, but I'll keep them both in mind."

"Brother?" I said, with even more confusion than before. "Ollie never said anything—"

"Bet he didn't," she said, shaking her head with an indulgent smile. "He can be a little self-absorbed, don't you think?"

The way she spoke was so different from Ollie, almost like she was from my world, instead of this one.

"I think self-absorbed is putting it lightly," I scoffed. "But if you don't mind, as nice as it is to hear someone talk sense about that jackass, I'm trying to find a way home right now, and I don't think I can come with my 'soulmate's' sister watching me. So..."

She raised an eyebrow at me.

"Home, huh?" she said, then nodded like she was thinking. "Well, I don't have any ideas to help you with that, but I will wait outside for you to finish." She walked briskly toward the door, then ducked through it, leaving me alone with Faenia, who was still stroking my cock.

Goddammit.

I looked over at Faenia, who was trying to continue to appear enthusiastic, and I gave her a little wave to indicate she could cease her stroking on my very, *very* flaccid dick.

"Thanks for trying," I said.

She nodded, giving me a pitying smile, and then bowed before leaving the room.

I got to my feet and scrambled for some clothes, picking a pile of them up off the floor and giving them the ol' sniff test.

It was whiffy.

It would do.

I dressed as quickly as I could and went to the door, feeling actually curious for the first time in a week.

Ollie's sister gave me an amused look, like she knew exactly how it had gone down inside but didn't feel the need to say it.

"Well, then," she said, standing up from where she was leaning against the wall just like Ollie always did. "Shall we start where we should have a week ago?" She stepped forward and held out her hand. "I'm Ariadne, Royal Sefaeran Master of the Hunt and Keeper of the Sefaeran Wilds. You can call me Ari."

Strangely enough, Ari felt like a comfortable name, and it made me comfortable with her. Her air of ease and casual coolness was like what Ollie pretended to be and never had been.

"So, what am I supposed to do with you?" I asked.

"Well, obviously, I'm here to teach you how to fuck the Sefaeran way." My jaw dropped, and I was about to express my horror when she laughed and pulled the bow from her back to show it to me. "I'm going to teach you how to shoot, and I'm going to take you for a tour of the wilds."

"Really?" I said with genuine excitement. "Can you teach me to shoot well enough to nail *Olympio* in the face?"

I was eagerly anticipating the banter forming between us when someone interrupted.

"Well, you'd have plenty of targets to aim for, since the marks of our last encounter haven't quite healed."

We'd just stepped outside when the voice rang out from behind me, and I spun to look at the speaker, despite knowing full well who it was.

I felt my hands clench, ready to be on the defense if I needed to.

And yet…

I was experiencing some sort of internal pull, some kind of emotional conflict.

I hadn't seen Ollie's face once in a week and now, seeing him here, wearing the bruises I'd placed lovingly on his eye-socket and nose, I wanted to embrace him. It was like seeing a friend you didn't realize you missed until you saw them again.

But there was no way in hell I would be saying that out loud, regardless of whether he could feel it through the "bond."

"I suppose I owe you two hundred dromachs," he said, looking at Ari, who smirked and shrugged.

"You obviously lack my charisma," she said.

I looked between the two siblings, feeling as though I was purposely being left out. Was Ari in on making me miserable? Was she just here to help further Ollie's cause?

"And now, Prince Dickhead," Ari said, taking me by my upper arm as she winked at me, "we have shit to do. Go scamper off and do prince things, and *maybe* I'll bring him back later."

Ollie's expression was unreadable. It looked amused, but I could see the twitch in his jaw I'd gotten used to recognizing as a sign that he was anxious.

And I couldn't have given two shits. For the first time since I'd arrived. I felt I'd found a true ally.

"The rest of the hunt is waiting for us at the edge of the woods. You'll like them."

Something about Ari made me believe she was right. She didn't seem to buy into the pomp and circumstance every other asshole seemed to want from me.

"We like to keep our sticks in the woods and not in our asses like my dear brother." She guided me toward towering trees I could see across a large field. They were so tall, I didn't even realize how far away they were until we'd been walking for twenty minutes and still hadn't made it there.

"Is it much farther?" I asked, feeling the lack of food making me woozy.

Ari gave me an appraising look, then pointed. "Just there."

I looked to where she indicated and saw three forms standing near the treeline. As we got closer, I could see there was a man who looked like a human but with skin the color of onyx, a woman with glittering yellow skin and short magenta hair who was built like a mack truck, and a man who looked like he might have been as tall as Ollie, with tan skin, black hair, and horns.

As we approached, the man with the horns began to walk forward to meet us. His face slowly spread into a smile, and when he was right in front of us, he reached out, and Ari grabbed him by the front of his shirt, pulling him in for a long, deep kiss.

I was taken aback by the flagrant display of affection. Ollie was so stiff about every single thing he did, that his sister being so carefree was confusing.

I tried to picture Ollie and me like this, caring for each other. But it just made my blood begin to boil.

As if she sensed my confusion, Ari pulled away to introduce me.

"Gabriel, this is Liro. Liro, Gabriel. You know—the *future consort.*" She put a teasing emphasis on the words, like she thought it was as much of a joke as I did.

"Nice to meet you, future consort Gabriel," Liro said with a grin of his own, stepping away from Ari to shake my hand.

"Please," I said, shaking his hand back. "Please, just call me Gabe. It's my name, for fuck's sake, and no one seems willing to go against the prince so I can feel like myself."

Liro gave me an approving sort of look, and Ari seemed to be studying me.

"Gabe, it is," she said. "Come on. Let's introduce you to the rest of the hunt."

We walked over to the others, and she introduced me not only to Liro, who turned out to be her boyfriend/life partner, but also Keevan, the woman with the pink hair, and Dom, the man with the black as night skin.

They were all so welcoming, and not a single one called me Gabriel. We spent the day roaming the woods, shooting bows, and generally having a good time. I even ate a full meal for the first time since I'd arrived.

And for once, I didn't think for a second about going home.

At the end of the day, Ari took me to the highest lookout point in the woods and we broke clear of the trees. I could see hundreds of miles of land, all kissed by the sun and the oncoming dual moons. The dozens of rivers that seemed to canvas all crevices of the land sparkled in the sunset, make it look like the very land itself was magic.

"Wow…" I said, unable to keep my amazement inside. "I'm not really much of a nature guy, but… wow…"

Ari beamed with pride. "Incredible, isn't it?" she asked, nodding with her own approval and a hint of some kind of longing. "You know, 'Ollie' and I used to come up here a lot together. We'd spend our whole days just enjoying the wilds and each other's company. Of course, that was before our brother died and Olympio had to step in as the monarch."

I felt the majesty ebb a little, and I turned to look at her. "You're about to try and convince me to give him a chance, aren't you?"

I was certain she could hear the disappointment in my voice, and she stepped forward to put an arm around my shoulders.

"I'm not going to pretend Olympio isn't a huge prick sometimes. He doesn't even know his head from a boulder most days. But… he's not a bad guy. In fact, he's probably the best person you could hope to

141

have on your side if you're ever in danger. He's loyal to a fault, and he is really fucking in love with you, Gabe. I know you can't understand this, but every fiber of his being has spent the last twenty years feeling like it was on fire waiting for you, and that's not even counting the two and a half thousand years he's been alive, wondering if and when you would ever show up. And now that you're closer than ever to being together… it's a wonder my brother can even form words most of the time."

I dropped down to the edge of the cliffside, onto the mossy forest floor, and shook my head. "I dunno, Ari. I just feel so… invaded by the guy. Always have." I grabbed a stick and began to poke holes in the dirt. "Like it's weird enough he's been watching me since I was a baby, but the fact that he manipulated me into going to Columbia… It makes me want to puke."

Ari stepped up beside me, her toes so close to the edge they knocked little pebbles from the cliff, down into a purplish mist covering whatever lay a few hundred feet below.

"I'm going to be straight with you, Gabe," she said, pulling out her bow and aiming it as though she was going to shoot the moon rising beside the setting sun. "I have no idea what Columbia is or why he needed to manipulate you into going there, but I know my brother. He's a fucking idiot at times, but if he did something that hurt you, I can guarantee you he didn't mean to, and it's eating him up inside." She slung her bow across her back and folded her arms, her red hair glowing in the fading light, making the resemblance between her and Ollie glaringly obvious. "I can't tell you what to do or how to feel, but I can tell you if you just talk to him about it, you'll find he's a lot more receptive than you seem to think."

I scoffed without meaning to. Ari didn't really deserve to be in the middle of this. "I just can't wrap my head around the idea that I'm *meant* to be with this guy. I'm not even gay."

It was the same rhetoric I'd been vomiting since high school, and it wasn't entirely untrue. I wasn't gay—I was just... trying things out. Though if I was perfectly honest with myself, I did have a preference for men aesthetically. Girls were beautiful, but there was something about the rough way men kissed, the force, the animalism they put behind their desires... I liked the way that felt. Especially when I was the object of their attraction.

I had almost fallen for Alex, as much as I hated to admit it. I was never going to be happy being someone's rent boy, but Alex had a way of being tender when he wanted to.

I silently wondered if Ollie knew I was thinking about Alex right now. Maybe he'd always known.

"Look," Ari said, sitting down beside me and nudging me with her shoulder. "You didn't ask for any of this. I know it, you know it, and my daft brother knows it. He loves you and is in the unfortunate position of also needing you, which makes it hard for him to know where those lines are. But..." She took a deep breath and let it out. "I can talk to him if you want. Maybe you two can meet in the middle. Maybe... if you really, truly give being here a shot, if you're actually open to what Sefaera and Olympio can offer you, and you still don't feel connected to him or to this place... maybe he'd be willing to let you go home. I know he'd rather have you, to be able to spend your eternal lives together. But if that's never going to be in the cards for you, I don't think he would keep you prisoner forever."

143

"What an offer," I said flatly. "But I'll consider it."

Ari patted me on the back and gave me a sort of half-hug.

"You know," I said, taking the hand she offered and getting to my feet. "The prospect of having you for a sister is much more tempting than anything else he's offered me."

"Why do you think he saved the best for last?" she asked with a wink.

I couldn't help my laughter, and I gave her a proper hug. As someone who'd been an only child, these were the kind of moments I'd only ever dreamt about.

But was it worth it to give up everything I'd ever known for everything that *might* be?

Chapter Sixteen
Olympio

I had spent the day pacing, wondering what Gabriel and Ariadne might be discussing, when she came to me after escorting him back to his room after their hunt.

"I'm surprised you're in your room and not stalking your soulmate in his again," she said, moving to my couch to lay across it like a bed.

"Stalking?" I said. Gabriel had used that word too. I never thought of my following him and looking out for him as stalking. Had I been that ignorant of my own actions?

"You really *are* an idiot," she said, shaking her head but giving me a sympathetic smile. "It may not have felt weird to you, but for him, that was a huge violation of his privacy."

"I... I never thought about that," I admitted, sitting on the armrest near her feet.

"Of course you didn't," she said. "Because all you knew was that he was yours. You never thought about the parts of him that were supposed to be his to give. Maybe it's time you start."

She told me about her conversation with Gabriel, about how if he still wanted to go home after truly giving his all to feeling like he could belong here, I would let him. At first, I was furious, but I realized my sister was right. If weeks, months, even years went by without Gabriel being able to return my feelings, it was likely he never would, and nothing I did would matter.

Her words stayed with me throughout the following days, and, despite my need to see him, I stayed away from my soulmate, not even entering his room as a shadow.

I also avoided Vass during those days. Every time we'd had to interact in an official capacity, the warmth that had once sat between us had gone, leaving an emptiness in its wake. I hoped she would eventually come back around, but I was getting impatient while she held onto her anger.

Three days after the hunt, when I couldn't stand the separation any longer, I checked in on Gabriel. I kept to the shadows as he, Ari, and Tomos sat down to eat together, and for the first time since he'd arrived here, I got to see Gabriel smiling, laughing, eating. It was something so small, but each time Gabriel reached for an oulon and bit into it like it was the greatest thing he'd ever eaten, my heart skipped a beat. Seeing him enjoying a fruit native to my land, my favorite food, made me feel like perhaps he really could acclimate and grow to love it here.

After another two days, I joined Gabriel in his room as he was being bathed after a long day of training. He had mud caked in his hair and on his eyebrows, and more than one bright pink line on his skin that indicated he'd been cut and healed hastily. He didn't seem to be quite as nervous about his attendants washing him. There *was* still a

146

distinct element of discomfort—though that might have been because I was there. We still hadn't had a true conversation since he found out about my deception.

As I entered, his eyes met mine, and my heart began to pound.

"Oh. Hello," he said. "I was beginning to wonder if you still lived here, man."

It was the first words he'd said to me in days, and the first that weren't tinged with hatred in even longer. I moved over to the large doors leading out to the balcony and leaned against them, looking out at the twin moons for a moment before turning to face him.

"I've been a bit busy," I said, trying to seem nonchalant even though just the slight amount of peace between us had me wanting to jump into the bath and kiss him. "And I know you have been, too. Ari and Tomos tell me you've been doing well at your lessons. Apparently, you have an affinity for daggers?"

Gabriel smirked to himself. "Apparently so. Never pinned myself for a knife guy, but I've always had good hand-eye coordination, so I guess it makes sense. Helps when you have a very specific target in mind…"

He looked over at me and gave me an up and down to make it very clear exactly what target he was picturing.

It was then that one of his servants approached me, drawing me away from him to a corner of the room where she could report to me out of his earshot.

"Your Highness," she whispered. "He's been refusing his… manual stimulation. Should we not be ensuring our future consort possesses the capacity to—"

147

I put up a hand to silence her.

"I didn't order that," I said. I had been very specific after the disaster of a Consummation ceremony. No one was to touch Gabriel or even to suggest touching him in a sexual way unless or until he asked. I had planned on explaining the virility assessments and training to him once we were back on speaking terms.

"No, Your Highness," she whispered back. "But it is tradition—"

"And that tradition may recommence when and if I give the order, and not a second before," I said. She shrank a bit under my gaze, and I sighed before putting a hand on her shoulder to reassure her. "Gabriel requires a less orthodox approach than we are used to here. He will be ready in time, but we will not rush him."

She nodded and went over to the male attendant who was her partner. They whispered back and forth, then bowed to Gabriel and to me before leaving the room, their jobs not needed for today.

Gabriel looked up at me as they left. "What?" he said with a cutting tone. "Not gonna have them proposition me today?"

"No," I said, moving to his bed and laying down, kicking off my boots to cross my ankles in front of me as I put my hands behind my head. "They were attempting to carry out a long-standing tradition for the future consort, but they didn't realize my order to not put any kind of sexual pressure on you extended to their jobs, since they don't see it as having the same gravitas as you and I consummating our bond."

I saw Gabriel sneer at the water he was sitting in. "You've got a very... weird culture."

I chuckled. "I suppose to you, it would seem that way. You were raised in a society where sex and sexuality are treated as something

148

shameful. We don't have the same views, and so while there are certain aspects of sexuality we hold in high esteem for their intimacy or for the meaning they have or for the magic they invoke, like the Consummation, sex doesn't hold some taboo status from day to day. Personally, the idea of a society that is so rabidly aroused at all times, that advertises sex to children who haven't even come of age yet, and yet shames their people for daring to engage in or desire sex, seems very weird to me. But that's what is familiar to you."

Gabriel leaned back against the side of the stone tub, unknowingly giving me a full view of his body. It took all of my willpower to not show exactly how badly I wanted him, wanted to touch him and give him every part of me. He was the most beautiful thing I'd ever seen, and I could have stared at him for days, weeks without looking away.

"Your sister's cool," he said, changing the direction of the conversation.

I laughed and sat up on the edge of the bed, both to face him more directly and to hide the arousal I couldn't ignore.

"Please don't ever tell her that," I said with a smile. "Her ego needs no stroking, I assure you."

He chuckled, the corner of his mouth quirking up in the way it so often did. It was the most beautiful, genuine smile, and my stomach ached every time I thought about kissing those lips. "She is the only reason I'd consider staying, to be honest."

Consider staying. He'd actually indicated he might consider staying. That it would be for my sister, I didn't even care, because if he stayed, I would have time to earn his trust and love.

149

"Well," I said, smiling back at him, "I'm glad she's helping you to feel welcome." I looked down at my hands. My fingers were shaking slightly. I was dedicated to this calm, confident exterior I presented to Gabriel, but it was getting harder and harder to mask the uncertainty and fear I felt. "Anyway…" I stood up, my blossoming erection having calmed down. "I wanted to inform you ahead of time so you're not caught off guard like last week, there is a ball being thrown in two days' time. In our honor—yours and mine."

"A ball?" Gabriel asked. "Like… a Cinderella ball?"

The name rang a bell. I searched my memory and found a vacation he and his family took to a theme park when Gabriel was a small child, no older than seven. There was a fake castle in the middle of everything, and live actors portraying characters performed for the crowds. One of the shows involved this "Cinderella" and how she was going to go to a ball to meet a prince, complete with dancing and music.

"I suppose so," I said with a shrug. "It's fairly grand, with dignitaries and nobles coming together to discuss politics as they drink wine and attempt to swing their dicks around and one up each other both in conversation and in dancing."

Much to my surprise, Gabriel burst out laughing. His handsome fingers gripped the sides of the tub and he rocked back and forth as the beautiful sound echoed through his chambers.

"Swing their dicks around," he repeated. "Yeah, something like that." Then an even more surprising event occurred. Gabriel stood, with no shame or apprehension, fully nude before me. "Can you throw me a towel, man?"

150

I froze, willing my eyes to remain on his and not to travel down his body like some lecherous scum. Like Kessinger would have.

"Are you seriously having a moment over me standing here naked?" my soulmate giggled. "According to you, you've been watching me since I was a kid, like some kind of creep. Surely this isn't a new sight to you?"

My brain could hardly keep up with what he was saying, because while he was correct, this was the first time he'd ever been willing and looking me in the eyes as he stood bare before me.

"New or not," I said, forcing a cheeky grin to my face, "it's hard to maintain my composure when such incredible beauty is right in front of me. But I think I'll manage." I turned and grabbed a towel to hand to him, but when he reached for it, I playfully pulled it back before letting him have it on his second grab.

"Jerk," he said, still grinning. He went to wrap it around his waist but threw it over his shoulders instead. "Enjoy being tortured the way I've been since I met you."

Then he stepped out of the tub, his body moving gloriously as he walked past me, only his shoulders covered by the fabric. His eyes looked away from mine for just a second, allowing me the opportunity to glance down at his cock, which bounced slightly with each step.

Damn it. I was getting hard again.

"I think you and I have a very different definition of torture," I said, walking over to him and reaching for the towel, hoping he wouldn't notice the semi-erection beneath my clothes.

"Maybe," he said flippantly. "But…" He ran his fingers through his gorgeous chestnut hair and stretched in the sunlight that streamed onto

151

the balcony. "You're the one whose cock is pointed at me like a compass," he said, quoting something I'd said to him a month ago, back at the fraternity.

I couldn't help but laugh as I took the towel from his shoulders, hoping he wouldn't fight me. He raised an eyebrow at me, but released his hold on it. I started with his back, gently drying him off, taking in the scent of erula blossoms along with his own personal scent as I ran the towel across his shoulders and down his arms before moving to his legs. Still kneeling, I debated asking him to turn around right then, but I knew I would lose any and all will I had to resist taking him if I was eye level with his length.

Instead, I wrapped the towel around his legs to dry the fronts as well before standing.

"Turn around," I said, gently urging him to obey with my hands on his arms.

He hesitated for just a moment, then did, taking a small step closer to me.

I felt his heart rate spike through the bond, and my own wasn't far behind. He was close enough that I could lean down and kiss him if I wanted to. But I knew it wasn't the right time. I had rushed things so far. He needed to be able to trust me before I tried to take things any further. We'd nearly been friends back in his realm. Perhaps we could get back to that.

Well, as close as we could with me lovingly drying his body after a bath.

I ran the towel over his chest, where I could visibly see his breath coming in short bursts.

And then I felt it.

Gabriel's fingertips sliding beneath the fabric of the skirt of my garment and brushing the soft skin of my shaft. His eyes widened as though something about it surprised him, and they showed conflict within the radiant blue.

If I had been halfway to erect before, that slight touch from his fingers brought me to full stiffness, and I gasped, unable to restrain myself from leaning slightly forward into his touch, needing more.

Needing *him*.

"Gabriel…" I breathed.

"Yeah?" he breathed back, his lips inches from mine.

He closed his hand around me and began to stroke, watching my face, searching my eyes for something. He bit his lip, and I could feel his own hardness press into me. Consummation be damned—I wanted him right here, right now.

I placed a hand on his shoulder, right alongside his neck, then pressed my forehead to his as I began to move in time with his strokes, thrusting in and out of his fist.

And then suddenly, it was over. Gabriel pulled back, almost stumbling away as he grabbed the towel from me and frantically tucked it around himself. "I… I'm not…"

I smoothed down the front of my garment, though it did little to hide the bulge it draped around.

"I'm sorry," I said, mumbling the words to myself as much as to him. I turned, looking for something, anything to do to distract from the moment.

153

"Can you, um… Can you leave so I can get dressed? I'm just—I got confused. Uh… yeah. Get out. Please?"

I swallowed hard. I'd been so eager for this, for him, that I had allowed things to go farther than I intended, and now I might have lost all the progress I'd made with him, small as it was.

"Of course," I choked out, unable to decide what to do with my hands. After a few seconds, I settled for leaving them woodenly at my side as I left his chambers, hearing the door shut behind me, echoing through the hall.

"Are you alright, Your Highness?" Gryfian asked as I exited.

"Fine," I said, lying. He knew it, but also knew better than to press the issue.

Back in my own suite, I tore my clothes off, ripping the bottom and breaking the links of the chain around my waist. The small clinking as they scattered across the marble floor grated on my mind, and I threw myself into my bed, pulling the plush blanket up over my head.

No matter what I tried, I couldn't get my cock to soften, only using my willpower to make it happen.

It suddenly occurred to me I wasn't hard of my own volition. No, this was something different, something deeper.

This was the bond. This was Gabriel, and *his* arousal.

And I couldn't help but hope it was for me.

Chapter Seventeen
Gabe

As the door closed behind Ollie, I ran up to it and kicked it. How had he head-fucked me into wanting him? After all the defenses I'd put into place, he'd somehow managed to get under my skin.

And yet…

Somewhere in the back of my mind, I knew the difference between him controlling me and me wanting him. And if the raging hard-on was any indication, I wanted him.

I slid down the door, my tailbone hitting the stony floor with a thud, and I let the towel loosen and fall away from me. I looked down, and my cock was stiff with need, taunting me about the guy I said I would never want.

I closed my eyes and took a few deep breaths, and like a number connecting on a telephone, I suddenly could picture Ollie, clear as day, laying in his bed, cock in hand.

The fantasy felt so real, maybe a result of this supposed "soulmate bond," but I could practically hear the way he was breathing.

His fist was gripped tightly around his thick, throbbing length, and he stroked slowly, his eyes closed and his head leaned back. He let out a low moan, and then, even though he whispered it, it may as well have come through a megaphone when he said my name.

"Gabriel... *my* Gabriel..."

Well, that part wasn't as arousing as it could be, but at least the fantasy was realistic. I watched his movements and copied them, panting in tandem as he slowly moved his hand across his length.

Before I could stop myself, "Olympio..." slipped from my lips.

Ollie paused, his eyes opening. I wondered briefly if, somehow, he'd seen me, but he just smiled and began to move his grip faster along his hardness, his other hand pushing his hair back from his sweat-dampened forehead.

I suddenly realized how long it had been since I'd indulged in a little self pleasure, which was odd because I used to do it a lot. Embarrassingly a lot. I guess perhaps being kidnapped to a foreign land without wifi had killed the mood for me.

Now though, mood was all there was. I could feel every inch of my body tighten, all electrical impulses focused in one single place.

Ollie's fingers moved from his head down to his chest, feeling along the lines of his well-defined muscles I never knew he was hiding back at school. I'd seen them a lot since being here, since he wore those weird toga dress things that showed off his whole body, but shining with perspiration, he looked fucking ripped.

His touch drifted even further down until eventually he had one hand held in place, as he thrust up into it while the other tightly encircled the base with just his index finger and thumb. His breathing was heavy, and there was a ragged edge to it as he panted and groaned.

Fuck… I was getting close.

I tried to do everything possible to think of something else for when I blew my load, my brain first going to Alex.

But try as I might, Ollie kept popping back into my head, his lean, gorgeous body tantalizing me, making me wonder what it would feel like against me.

Knowing I could have it if I wanted.

The knowledge caused me to explode with a deep, guttural groan, and in my fantasy, I heard Ollie do the same, my name once again pouring out of his mouth, though now the word was less quiet and longing and more forceful and full of ecstasy.

I was left panting, breathless, the cool stone beneath me and the heavy wooden door against my back. I looked down to find I had made a significant mess, and I tried my best to clean it up with the towel I had before resigning. Some messes needed more intense care.

I stood and walked to the bed, flopping down on it and half-heartedly pulling on my clothes.

The hoodie and sweatpants were beginning to feel unfamiliar now, especially since Ari had bullied me into wearing what she deemed, "hunt-suitable clothing," and halfway through putting them on, I took them off again, tossing them to my floor and walking to my wardrobe.

I pulled it open to find a series of drapings I was nowhere near prepared to put on myself.

Maybe it was time for me to give him a chance. Clearly, my body wanted it, and I was enjoying Ari's company frequently. Sometimes I even enjoyed seeing Ollie.

But something in the pit of my stomach acknowledged that, if I tried, if I let myself relax into this experience and fully allow Ollie his chance, I would never see my world again.

And that terrified me.

Chapter Eighteen
Olympia

Whether Gabriel knew how deeply connected we were that night, I did not know, but I could feel the intensity of our shared climaxes like ripples of electricity across my skin. To my knowledge, it had been the first time the bond had been apparent to him, even if he did not recognize it for what it was.

I didn't visit him over the next day, choosing, instead, to spend my time creating something unique for my soulmate to wear to the ball. Something... special.

Something completely and utterly Gabriel.

It took nearly all day and the help of half a dozen seamstresses, but I was finally satisfied, and I was thrilled to be able to give it to him. The day of the ball, he'd been spared from his lessons, given the chance to rest and prepare for his impending public appearance. After his disastrous introduction and subsequent panic attack at the failed Consummation, it was easy for me to make a case for him to be afforded a bit of relaxation.

And yet, when I arrived at his chambers that evening, custom garment in hand, I found his room empty.

"Gabriel?" I said, calling for him into the echoing space. Worry flooded through me, but I hadn't felt the searing agony that would have indicated something had happened to him. And yet, he was certainly not here, where he should have been.

I focused my attention on the bond, urging it to tell me anything about his state or whereabouts, and I watched as it weaved its way from me, across the room, and through the closed balcony doors. I assumed that meant he was outside, since the balcony was enchanted to keep him safe.

I threw open the doors, but he was nowhere to be seen. The very idea, impossible as it may have been, that he might have fallen drew me to the edge. I knew if anything had happened to him, I would have felt it, but the line of the bond curled up and over the railing.

I rushed forward, and, much to my surprise, I did see Gabriel down below. But he wasn't hurt. On the contrary, he was down in the gardens with Ari, the pair of them sparring with daggers.

I smiled and sighed with relief, leaning forward on the railing to watch them for a bit. Gabriel was right—his innate skill and lithe frame had given him a natural gift for knife combat. Having spent thousands of years sparring with my sister, myself, I knew her technique as well as I knew my own. She was barely holding back for his benefit, and Gabriel—my Gabriel—was matching her, move for move.

Pride swelled within me as I observed them. Gabriel may have still been reluctant in his acceptance of his place here, but seeing his skills on such incredible display once more affirmed for me that this was exactly where he was always meant to be.

During a break where they caught their breath—or rather, Gabriel caught his breath and Ari juggled her daggers—she glanced up and saw me, offering what, at this distance, appeared to be a wink and a nod.

She and Gabriel got back into position. His form was flawless, and I leaned even further forward to see better.

"Go!" Ari shouted, and they began.

She spun, and it was clear she was no longer taking it easy on Gabriel. Her daggers sliced through the air, ready to bring the unscheduled training session to an end. But he held his own, fending her off for nearly a minute longer, making his skill even more apparent. Even with the expertise of two thousand years on her side, Gabriel was matching her better than I ever expected, especially at the end of a session, when exhaustion would have been a factor. But a natural gift still couldn't compete with Ari's long lifetime of training.

Gabriel lasted a whole minute, which was more than some of my best warriors would have done against Ariadne at her peak. But my sister, my Master of the Hunt, finally swept his feet out from under him and knelt on his chest, one dagger at his throat and the other at his diaphragm.

"I think that's enough for today," she said, and I was glad I was close enough to hear them.

Despite my joy, I felt a sudden pang of disappointment that I realized belonged to my soulmate, and my heart soared at the knowledge that there was at least one thing here in Sefaera that made him happy enough to be disappointed when it was over.

161

"One more?" he asked hopefully as Ari helped him to his feet.

"No, sir," Ari said, collecting the daggers made of the same obsidian as my sickle, and sheathing them at her side along with her own, making it look like she was wearing a skirt made of them. "You have a ball to get ready for."

I didn't wait for Gabriel's response, but as I walked back inside, I couldn't sense any anxiety or panic coming from him. Ecstatic he wasn't rejecting the idea of attending the ball with me, I quickly dismissed his attendants and got to work.

It took nearly ten minutes for him to return, and when he arrived, the sweet smell of erula blossoms, similar to the magnolias of the human world, drifted through the room. I'd filled his tub with warm, steamy water and added the flowers and some floral oil to it.

"Hello, Gabriel," I said smoothly, rising from the chair near one of the floor to ceiling windows.

"Have you ever read this?" he asked, pure excitement on his face. He dropped a book at my feet and flopped down on a chair. "The guy's a fucking genius when it comes to philosophy and political maneuvering."

It was the first time we'd been face to face since we'd had our hands on each other in the most sensual, intimate encounter I'd ever experienced. I'd been anxiously anticipating this moment since then, the question of whether or not he'd reject me playing through my mind on repeat.

I bent and picked up the tome, turning it over and feeling my chest swell. It was one of my old journals I'd written under another name to have it taken seriously. Nearly a thousand years ago, I'd finished it and

162

stuck it in the royal library, checking it weekly to see if anyone had taken interest in it.

Few had… until Gabriel.

I fought the manic grin trying to break free, not wanting to come on too strong. "A little different than your usual preference in literature. I know it has pictures—diagrams, really—but it's not exactly a comic book."

"Hilarious," Gabriel replied, his grin, for once, not breaking at the slightest prodding. "I read." He sounded insistent and offended, though the playful bite of his tongue told me differently. "How do you think I got into Columbia?"

"I suppose I thought that little donation and the paperwork *I* filled out for you were the main reasons." I knew it was a huge risk to make that joke, but it would be the true test of where we stood.

But my soulmate giggled and ruffled his own hair. "Oh, yeah…"

There was a moment where I wanted to continue. The conversation was going so well, I was worried any kind of transition would break the flow. But I knew we couldn't just banter like this all night, so I pointed beside me to the tub.

"I've drawn a bath for you. I wondered…" I took a deep breath, hoping my nerves weren't apparent. "I wondered if you'd do me the honor of allowing me to prepare you for your first ball myself?"

His eyes went wide, and my heart pounded against my ribcage like it wanted out.

But it wasn't anxiousness that had my blood racing through my veins. It was excitement.

Gabriel's excitement.

163

Suddenly, his face melted into a cool, unfettered expression, but he couldn't lie to me about what he felt. "Yeah," he said, as I felt the butterflies continue, betraying his attempt at aloofness. "If it means that much to you."

He was dressed in fighting leathers, which made him look like a true warrior, like a demi-god of his world's ancient civilizations.

I had never in my life been as nervous around another person as I was at that moment, and with as long as I'd been alive, that was saying a lot. Gabriel represented the promise of everything I held dear and the promise of both my future and the future of my people. Not only that, but in the time I'd known him, I had come to care for him, to love him, more than anything or anyone I'd ever known. I had done a relatively good job of remaining stoic so far against his resistance and rejections, but now, with him being willing and open, I was even more nervous than when he was fighting tooth and nail against me.

"Do you need help removing those?" I asked, somehow managing to keep my voice cool and even. "I know the lacing can be difficult if you're not used to it."

Much to my surprise, Gabriel's fingers moved with deft grace as he managed the clothing himself, shooting me a cheeky grin. "Super difficult."

I nearly melted when he directed that smile at me. He was beautiful. Perfect.

"Clearly, I underestimated you," I said, moving forward to collect the garments as he took them off. I could smell the sweat on him, the musky, sweet scent that made my head swim, and I wanted nothing more than to grab him. But I resisted, knowing I had to keep taking it slow with him. Had to give him room to come to me when he was ready. "I'll have to remember who I'm dealing with in the future."

Gabriel handed me each article as he removed them, then stood shyly, nearly bare. Only a single barrier existed between us in the form of cotton briefs. "So, uh… this isn't a sex thing. Right?"

I laughed and put the pile of leather in a basket at the foot of his bed for his attendants to collect and clean later.

"No," I said, turning to him with a warm smile. "This time, it's not. Tonight is for fun. Business, too," I clarified. "But since you haven't yet taken on the role of Justice, the only expectation on you will be to enjoy yourself and present yourself with dignity and grace. In other words, *not* with forties strapped to your hands."

Gabriel seemed to think for a moment, then nodded. "Think I can manage that. I used to go to a bunch of premieres with my parents."

"I know," I said before I realized what I was implying. He already knew, of course, but I felt like the reminder might be a poor idea, so I plowed forward. "But… you always seemed fairly miserable at those. I hope you'll find something enjoyable tonight."

Gabriel's eyes shifted like he went somewhere else—somewhere I couldn't follow. I was surprised at how much I longed to know what he was thinking every second, and how much agony it was when he wasn't accessible to me.

The silence hung heavy for a moment, but I wasn't about to let something we'd already covered ruin what had the potential to be a magical night.

"Well," I said, redirecting us back to the topic of the ball, "this won't be quite like that. There *will* be wine, which you already know is

165

highly potent for a human. Someday you will be more tolerant to its effects, but I just want to caution you so you don't get *totally wasted.*" I winked as I used the casual phrasing I learned back in his world.

Gabriel grinned at the prospect of getting drunk. "You would deny me the one thing I'm actually good at? Staying charming while wasted is a talent."

"Correct," I said, stepping forward to close the distance between us. "I have always found you to be charming beyond measure at any stage of inebriation. But endearing and dignified aren't always mutually inclusive, and I need you to refrain from vomiting in any of the topiaries." I put out a tentative hand near his lower back, waiting for permission to make contact.

To my surprise, Gabriel actually laughed, putting a hand on my shoulder like he'd done once upon a long time ago at the fraternity house. "Okay, okay. I'm a team player. So, what do I have to wear to this... event?"

I placed my hand on the small of his back, taking his initiative as permission. The feeling of having my hand on his bare skin was electric, like thousands of tiny bolts of lightning passing between us. I wondered if he could feel it, too.

"That..." I said slowly, "... is a surprise. Shall I help you into the tub?" The massive basin was sunk into the floor like a human hot tub, and I held out my free hand for Gabriel to take it. "You'll need to remove your underwear. If that's alright, of course."

I tried to take deep, steady breaths and not look too eager over the possibility of seeing him exposed once more.

166

But suddenly, he threw his arms up in the air and nodded at me with approval. "Go on, then."

He was allowing *me* to do it.

He was not only allowing me to touch him, he was happily willing to let me remove his undergarments.

I knelt down, trying not to make the gesture look lewd, though I'm certain I failed as I gripped the waistband and tugged them down, releasing his cock from the fabric confines. I could barely believe my eyes when I saw he was slightly hard, and it took all my willpower not to join him.

"Well," I said, still kneeling. "I suppose... I suppose you're ready for your bath, then."

Gabriel's grin widened. "What? I thought me popping a boner was what you were waiting for." He turned around and climbed into the bath, sighing with happiness at its warmth.

I blushed at the directness of his comment. I would have gladly taken him right then and there, but after the failed Consummation, I was loath to make the first move.

Yet.

I took a seat on the edge of the tub, placing my feet into the water on either side of him so I could reach him more easily. Then, with a cloth, I slowly and delicately began to wash him, starting with his down-soft hair, which had a lovely curl to it when wet.

Once he was clean, I dried him off with a towel, which he clutched around himself as I gathered the golden makeup and flakes. I dusted his face, highlighting his cheeks and lips before sprinkling the gold leaf into his hair.

"Close your eyes," I said, once he was ready except for getting dressed.

He gave me a suspicious look, but listened. I scurried away to the door to collect his garment, which I put on him before guiding him to the mirror.

"Open them," I said.

He did, and his eyes seemed to light up, which only served to make the moment even more wonderful for me.

The outfit he wore was glimmering gold, with a lace top beneath a silken toga that hung to the floor. The lace crept up his neck, nearly to his chin, and extended down to his wrists. The overall effect was a perfect blend of modern human fashion and the mode of Sefaera, and it gave him a look that, while vaguely feminine, somehow accented his masculinity as well.

"What do you think?"

Gabriel turned to look at all angles of himself, grinning. "I look like I could fit into ancient Greece," he said. "I'd fuck me."

The words, "*I would, too*," nearly toppled from my lips, but I held them back. Instead, I offered Gabriel my arm for him to wrap his own around.

"You look incredible," I said instead.

And he gave me a grateful smile that was so beautiful, I couldn't even breathe.

Chapter Nineteen
Gabe

"Are you alright?" Ollie asked me as we stood outside the ballroom, waiting to be announced.

"Yeah…" I said, my stomach lurching. "Just like pledging… right?" I reached out and grabbed his arm, giving it a little squeeze without thinking about it.

Ollie put a steadying hand on my waist and ducked his head to look in my eyes, but I saw him wince for some reason.

"What?" I asked.

"Nothing…" he said, looking away, but then he sighed and returned his eyes to mine. "Actually, it is something. I'm tired of keeping things from you, especially when it doesn't hurt you to know it. I've told you our bond gives me… access… to certain feelings you have. So when you feel nauseous, I do too. When you are having anxiety, I do too."

I knew exactly where this was going, and it felt like my ears burst into flame. "Does that mean when I…" My mind went back to this morning when my attendants had left the room, and I told myself I would touch my cock thinking about Ollie *one last time.*

"When you…" he said, giving me a sly grin that glowed like the turquoise moon I could see out a window behind him. "Have a craving for a steak? Yes, I also… crave a steak." His fingers flexed against me through the thin fabric, sending a jolt of electric energy through me.

I shivered against the contact and thought extremely hard about my parents dying in the plane crash. If he could feel everything I could… well, I was sure he didn't really mean what he said about steak.

"You can't touch me like that," I said, the heat moving from my ears to my cheeks.

He took a half step closer, his hand not moving, but I could see the sadness in his eyes. "Why not?"

I stumbled back just a little bit, his hands not letting me get too far. Were we… flirting? "Because it makes me feel like I don't hate you. And that's a problem for me."

Ollie's mouth tightened, and the grief in his eyes amplified. At that moment, I heard our names being called out from beyond the doorway. His hand dropped from my side as he held his arm out for me to take. "Well, we can't have that," he said. "Try to have fun. It's for you as much as it is for me."

I nodded. This would be my first real access to alcohol in this realm, and, even though Ollie wasn't my first choice for a party companion, at least he was popular—plus he came with a cool sister.

The minute the doors opened, I could see Ari snickering behind her hand, Liro at her side. The relief of seeing two of my—well, I'd almost call them friends—there, waiting to greet me was such a relief. I resisted the temptation to flip them off. It wouldn't be dignified in this setting, but I winked nonetheless.

We stood at the top of a grand staircase with gold painted railings and white marble steps. The floor of the entire ballroom below us was black marble with golden streaks in it, and everyone in the room was wearing white except for Ollie and me.

It looked like something out of a Disney movie, but no one was dancing. They were all staring at us, like the room itself was holding his breath, waiting for... what?

"Down the stairs," I heard Ollie say under his breath, with a glance in my direction. "Pause on the bottom one."

I gripped his arm like I'd fall without it, which I really may have, since we were a solid five feet from the railings on either side of us. I glanced sideways at Ollie, whose head was held high, making him actually look like a prince, much as it pained me to admit it. I tried to emulate him, but I had no idea if I succeeded.

On the bottom step, where we were nearly on the same level as everyone, I paused as I'd been instructed, and Ollie stopped beside me.

"Friends," he said. He wasn't shouting, but somehow, his voice filled the entire room. "Welcome. It is our absolute honor to be here with you tonight. My soulmate, as you may have heard, has had a bit of a difficult transition to our world. But tonight, I trust you will all help him to have a wonderful time, and to show him Sefaera adores him as much as I do."

If the words weren't enough, he turned to me and gave a deep bow, which everyone in the room copied.

I could have vomited. This all felt so weird and like something out of a fever dream. But I played along for Ollie's sake since he'd been so kind to me—so understanding.

Then the music started up, and everyone's stark posturing broke. Talking began, and Ollie looked at me with a grin. "And now we dance."

I did something halfway between a choke and a laugh. "Dance? I can't dance. You should know that. I mean…" I pulled away from him, keenly aware of Ari and Liro's eyes on me. "Unless you meant some of *this.*"

I put my hands on my knees, feet apart, and began to do something that likely looked like a rhino attempting to twerk. The look of horror on Ollie's face and the nearly instant laughter from Ari was enough to encourage me into a shopping cart, followed by a fishing pole where I attempted to "catch" Ollie.

I became very aware of the eyes of every single person in the room being on me, before they all looked to Ollie like they were asking him a silent question.

The war going on within him was as obvious as if his eyes projected it onto the wall. But with a glance over my shoulder at who I could only assume was Ari, he smiled and looked at me, then began to walk closer, letting my fishing do its job.

He looked so uncomfortable it was almost charming, and by the time he reached me, I found myself oddly breathless and wanting to kiss him.

So, I did what I did best in situations where I was dangerously close to being proved wrong, and I turned away. "Where are the drinks?" I asked. "I'm thirsty." I took a few steps towards Ari and Liro, trying to make it look like I was posing the question to them. Of course, it was all a ruse to hide the fact that if I'd looked at Ollie for ten seconds more, I was afraid I'd fall for him.

You'd never catch me telling him, but the pull to just gaze at him was strong. In his dress clothes, he looked like a teenage dream. He was alluring enough to make a thousand teen girls swoon... or one precariously bi-curious boy....

But suddenly, I felt his fingers close around my arms again, and he pulled me to him, turning me as he did.

"One dance," he said into my ear as he pulled me close. "Then I'll get you a glass of wine, myself. This is for optics. For the show. They all came for this moment. Please, Gabriel."

I then made the mistake of looking right into his eyes, and they flashed a glittering violet. Ollie, too, seemed taken aback. "What?" I asked softly, taking a step closer.

"Huh?" Ollie said in an uncharacteristically dense way. Then he cleared his throat and shook his head slightly. "Oh. That. Sometimes... When our connection is particularly strong, the bond becomes visible in your eyes. It makes them shimmer in a lovely purple color, which is what the bond looks like to me. Someday, once the Consummation happens, you'll see it, too."

I was confused. At this point, I was certain I understood what Consummation was, but I could already see the shift between yellow and violet.

"I just saw it," I said, a little confused. "I saw the purple."

Ollie's eyes lit up. "In my eyes?"

173

I nodded, and suddenly realized our hands were touching at our chests, our fingers unconsciously weaving in and out of each other's. I looked down at them for a moment, a warmth that had nothing to do with embarrassment rippling across my chest, and it suddenly felt like there were too many people around us. "Can we have that dance now?" I asked.

He took a deep breath, then nodded, moving his hand so it was held out to me as he turned to the side, looking at me over his shoulder. "Try to mirror my movements," he whispered. "It's not a difficult dance, but it's not exactly what we did back at the frat house."

I nodded, suddenly very eager to please Ollie.

I couldn't have told you what happened over the next few minutes, because all I noticed was the color of Ollie's eyes, the way he made it feel like we were the only two people in the room, and the fact that it didn't feel like we were nearly close enough. By the time the dance ended, I knew I needed to talk to him alone. The feelings this place was conjuring up in me were more dizzying than any booze had ever been.

As applause broke out from the guests—*our* guests—I leaned into him, whispering, "I'm a little hot. Can we find some air and a beverage?"

"A promise is a promise," he said, putting a hand on the small of my back before quickly pulling it away. "Sorry. It's just hard for me to fight against the innate need to touch you."

I felt actual physical pain as he withdrew, and I wondered if this was part of that bond he was always talking about. "Ollie," I said, clearly needing to be more direct. "I want to talk to you alone. I *want* to."

174

He blinked hard, the corner of his mouth slowly curling up in an excited grin.

"Yeah," he said in a much more casual way than he usually spoke. "Yeah. Here. This way."

He walked me over to a table of the same blue wine we'd had at my welcome dinner.

"Remember," he said, taking a sip of his, "it's a lot stronger than what you're used to. Go slow, alright?"

I nodded, taking a sip of the potent liquor.

"And now," he said, guiding me away from the drink table, "you said you needed air." He walked us over to a thirty foot tall glass door that led out onto a balcony. He glanced back into the room before opening the door, and I saw Ari raise her own glass and nod. She rushed over to the musicians to whisper something to them. Suddenly the music changed, and everyone began to do a more energetic dance.

And no one was looking at us.

"Come on," Ollie said, offering me his hand as he opened the door.

And somehow, I knew nothing would ever be the same.

Chapter Twenty
Olympia

My skin was tingling, my heart pounding as I led Gabriel out onto the balcony. It was the perfect time of night, with both moons hovering near the horizon, over the sea.

I motioned for Gabriel to go first, and when he did, I drained my glass of wine behind his back, setting it on a nearby ledge.

"Beautiful, isn't it?"

I could hardly believe how idiotic I sounded. Here I was with my soulmate who, for the first time, was *asking* to be alone with me, and I was making small talk about the moons.

Gabriel gaped as he looked out at them, breathing deep. "How have I never noticed this was the way it looked here at night?" He looked back at me, his eyes beckoning me forward. Then he reached his hand out for mine.

I couldn't help but notice it shaking with nerves. Or maybe that was the bond intuition, because my own weren't particularly steady themselves. But I moved forward and took his hand. He turned and pulled me against his back, and I placed my hands on the railing on either side of him.

"I don't know," I said, craning my neck around the side to look at him. "But it's better with you being a part of it."

Gabriel was shaking in my arms, and I wanted nothing more than to still him. But he wasn't pushing me away, and that was a start.

"I don't know what to do with these feelings, Ollie," he said in a meek tone I wouldn't have recognized as my Gabriel. "I want to hate you for forcing me to be here, but... all of a sudden, the idea of *not* being forced to be with you feels worse."

"I never wanted to force you," I said, hearing the most subtle crack in the words. "I did everything I could to earn your trust, but I got it wrong every time."

Gabriel turned in my arms to look at me. His eyes were so sad, and yet, the violet hue was burning brighter than it ever had. "I don't know how to deal with the fact that I'm scared to stay here, but I'm also scared to go home."

I watched as his eyes darted to my lips, and he subconsciously licked his own bottom one. I reached up with my thumb and brushed it gently across the spot he'd just moistened, not realizing I was leaning close to him until our faces were nearly touching.

"I don't want you to be scared," I breathed. "I want... I want to kiss you. Can I kiss you, Gabriel?"

He only half-nodded his head before he was on me, his arms snaking around my neck, pulling me down to his mouth. The impact of his lips on mine felt like fireworks going off in my soul, filling my body and beyond. I took his face in my hands, surrounding that incredible lower lip with my own, pressing my body against his so he was pinned between me and the railing.

My hands trailed down to his waist, and I dug my fingers into the soft flesh on either side of his spine, pulling him so no space remained between us. The proximity, the contact with my soulmate had me stiffening immediately, and I didn't even care. I no longer cared if he knew how I felt, because he'd not only consented to the kiss, but had been an eager participant in initiating it.

"Gabriel," I moaned as I took a break to catch my breath.

A small whimper left my soulmate's greedy mouth, and I watched as Gabriel's hand maddeningly dropped below his waist in an attempt to conceal his hardness.

"Don't," I begged, grabbing his hand away and pressing it against my own length. "Please, just let it be." In all honesty, I wasn't a fan of the desperation I could hear coming out of my own mouth, but Gabriel didn't even seem to notice.

"God, you're thick." He sounded like he was close to tears. "That thing is like a Coke can. Oh my god, Ollie," he said, pulling back. "I think I like guys."

I chuckled deep in my throat as I moved his hand along my stiffening member. "Hopefully not too many of them."

He wrapped his hands around my neck and pulled my lips back to his as if those ten seconds had been too long apart.

But this couldn't happen. Not here. Not like this.

"Gabriel," I said again, leaning back and grabbing him by the wrists.

His cheeks turned red, and he started to pull away, but I put my hand on his chin.

"Wouldn't you rather take this somewhere more private?" I nodded toward the windows, where my sister was making a big show of *not* looking at us.

He nodded, and that was all it took for me to consider it a binding agreement.

I grabbed his hand and the glass of wine he'd set on the railing, which I drank quickly, grinning at him. His jaw dropped in a combination of respect and indignance.

"You said—"

"I said it's strong for a *human*," I reminded him. "Someday, you'll be able to have a whole bottle of this without feeling it."

We went back inside, and I made my way around the room, avoiding as many gazes as I could. Thankfully, my mother caught my eye and smiled, recognizing the importance of this moment to me, and she pulled several dignitaries, including that snake Typhir, into a conversation, turning their backs to me.

We barely made it out without being stopped, but as soon as we did, I pressed him into the wall to kiss him again.

"May I come to your room?" I asked.

Gabriel nodded with vigor, and I could tell he thought this was going somewhere it absolutely could not. I hated to disappoint him, but that didn't mean it couldn't get... close.

With his hand in mine, I moved as fast as I could and still have it be considered walking until we made it to his room.

"Gryfian," I said to my guard when he caught up to us. "No one— *no one*—comes in."

He nodded, a slight smile playing on his face, and I pulled open the door, sealing Gabriel and myself inside.

The room still smelled of erula as I gripped Gabriel by the shoulders, pulling him in for yet another kiss as I walked him backward toward the bed.

"Are you sure this is okay?" I asked.

"Fuck, Ollie," he said with exasperation. "You've been trying to fuck me for months, and now you're getting shy?" He didn't stop, still moving to the bed, stripping off his clothes as he did.

I rushed forward, tearing at my own garments and throwing them to the side. Gabriel sat on the edge of the bed, and I stood before him, laying him back as my lips crashed down on his again. My fingers trailed down his front, stopping just short of the thatch of hair above his cock.

"I couldn't bear it if I ever touched you without you wanting it again," I said, thinking about the Consummation and how nauseating the very memory of it was.

"I want it. Jesus. I *want* it. Is that enough of a confirmation of consent for you?" He was giving me an adorably annoyed look that made me want to....

As much as I wanted him, this could only go so far tonight. And as much as I wanted to take him fully, I knew going from nothing to a full Consummation, after the way things started, would make for an ill start to our life together.

But that didn't mean I had to stop.

The soft skin of his length beneath my finger caused a hearty throb in my own as I ran just one from his base to his tip before slowly wrapping my hand around him. This was the moment. This was when I was touching my soulmate intimately, desperately, and it was because he wanted it. Because he begged for it.

My own hardness pressed against his thigh as I began to stroke him, my fist moving deliberately along his entire mass over and over. Gabriel let out a gasp, his arms sliding and tightening around my neck.

"Ollie," he panted as I stroked him slowly. "This is… nothing has ever felt like this before…"

As if he was being electrocuted, my Gabriel writhed against me, shining drips already falling on my hand and driving me crazy. I tried to resist but couldn't help myself as I brought my slick hand to my mouth and tasted him, leaving him whimpering as my warmth left his longing hardness.

The salty taste may as well have been honey for how sweet it was to me—for how any part of Gabriel felt. I needed him so badly, I felt a physical ache in my chest from resisting the bond, like muscle pains after difficult physical activity.

"I know," I said, bending forward to kiss his neck as I pumped him more, but it wasn't enough.

In a swift motion, I wrapped my arms around his waist and lifted him. I spun us around and sat down on the edge of the bed so he was sitting on top of me. I grabbed him by the backs of his thighs, spreading them, and yanked him forward, locking his hips against mine, our cocks pressed together between us.

"You feel incredible. The sounds you make are the most beautiful thing I've ever heard," I said as his jaw went slack at the feeling of me gripping him again.

Gabriel wrapped his arms around my neck once more, clinging to me like a tired child does to their parent, and the whimpering continued. He was melting beneath my touch, and my resolve was melting with him.

Suddenly, he pulled back and pressed his lips to my ear. "Can I... can we do this... together?"

I turned to look at him, tucking a finger beneath his chin to tip it up so I could see his face.

"Do what, Gabriel?"

I could feel the blush blossom across his cheeks as he hesitated. The boy who I frequently encountered sporting Alex Kessinger's fluids was... embarrassed.

"Can I make you feel good, too?" he asked, his fingernails scraping my chest slightly. "Or is there a special ritual for that?"

I froze for just a second before my face broke into a wide smile, and I pressed my lips to his in a desperate kiss. *This* was the Gabriel I'd watched and fallen for. The irreverent, witty humor I'd so missed was here, and it was for me.

"There's not," I said as I broke away. "But tonight... is for you."

Gabriel pulled back with a jerk, staring at me with confusion. "Wait? Really? I was being playful." He leaned back on his hands far enough for him to could see my face fully. "I'm confused, Ol. This is what you've been trying to get from me since we met—or at least, since I met you. Why the sudden pull back?"

My smile softened as I reached between us to wrap my fingers around his length once more. "This is far from a pull back," I assured him. "I have wanted you—all of you. And that means more than some

182

frat house bathroom hookup." I gave him a knowing look, though there was no malice or anger in it. "Being with you is something I've waited a very, very long life for. And right now, being with you—for me—means showing you how I want you to feel with me. Always."

I stroked him as I spoke, so I could feel him throbbing beneath my touch.

His breath hitched in his throat, and he put his arms around my neck once more. There was barely any space between us save for my active hand, and it felt almost like he and I had become one.

It didn't take long until Gabriel's whines became feral groans, and his hips took over in mindless thrusts against my hand.

"Ollie…" he groaned. "Oh, god, Olympio…"

The sound of my name, my true name, on his lips was ecstasy. I'd heard everything from Ollie to "creep" to Prince Cockbreath, but never my true name. And when he said it, the bond thrummed intensely. The warmth radiated out from my chest like a second heartbeat, filling my body and vibrating my soul with his. Suddenly, my own arousal was doubled as I felt Gabriel's as well as my own. The bond had taken my control and shredded it. It was such a strong feeling, it seemed like the bond took hold of my cock itself, and, before I could take a moment to calm myself, I was embarrassingly pulsing out my climax onto Gabriel's abdomen.

I froze, unsure what he would think. Had I ruined the moment?

Gabriel didn't move for a second, then reached down and touched where my warm fluids were splashed across his chest and own erection.

And then he giggled. "So that's how it is, is it? All I have to do is say your pompous royal name, and you're spilling all over me. Literally. I'll keep that in mind."

And then he took my hand, redirecting it back to his come covered cock and guiding me to use my ejaculate as lubrication for his own pleasure.

It was such a far cry from the angry, belligerent Gabriel I'd been dealing with for weeks that I let out a sigh of relief before taking control once more. I slid one hand up and down his stiffness as my other gripped him by the hip, holding him tightly against me, feeling like we couldn't get close enough to each other. Like there was no way for us to *ever* be close enough to each other.

I felt him begin to tense and writhe once more.

"Are you ready?" I asked.

Gabriel's response was a desperate sigh of need, his hips pressing in hungry thrusts against my hand. "I think maybe I've been ready for you all this time, Ollie," he said in earnest.

It was as if that statement made time itself stand still, the beauty of it falling onto us like blossoms off a tree in spring. I could tell him every day for the rest of eternity what those words meant to me and never be able to fully convey the depth of their impact.

"Let go, Gabriel. You're safe in my arms," I said in a soft, gentle voice. It wasn't a command, but a request. It was me asking for permission to share this moment with him, for him to trust me for the first time, and, hopefully, for all time.

Gabriel gasped for air, and a repetitive series of moans rode the silence of the palace like one of the rides at a human amusement park.

184

And like those bizarre thrill machines, the high was like no other. I didn't care if anyone heard him.

I wanted *everyone* to hear him.

There was a magic to the way his release caused his voice to echo off the walls of his chamber like a symphony of ecstasy. I felt him pulse in my hand, his body tensing as he spilled out onto me, covering my chest with his emission, mixing it with mine, before he collapsed onto me, shaking.

I wrapped my arms around him, holding him close.

"Thank you," I said, pressing my lips to his hair. "Thank you for sharing this with me. For sharing yourself."

I felt him get cold as the sweat on his body cooled, and he tucked his face into my neck, his lips parting slightly and pressing against my skin.

"I'm scared," he whispered.

I shook my head slightly, leaning my cheek against the top of his head. "Of what?"

Gabriel was silent for a moment, and even without the bond, I could feel that he was trying to decide whether to tell me or not. "I'm afraid I might actually need you," he said in the saddest whisper I could imagine.

I was conflicted. I needed him, and if he needed me, too, then things would be as the bond intended them. But the part of me that loved him for *him*, and not for what fate had decided for us, didn't want that for him. I wanted him to *want* me, not need me.

"Well," I said quietly. "You have time to figure it out."

And with that, I carried him to the bath and cleaned him, washing away the remnants of the ball and our rendezvous from him with gentle, caring strokes of the cloth, before drying him and carrying him back to bed. I turned to walk away, but his voice held me back.

"No…" he said, the word long and drawn out. "Don't go."

This time he was stone cold sober. This time, he actually meant it.

And since I would have given him both moons if he'd asked, I crawled into his bed and pulled him close.

And I fell asleep to the gentle sound of his snores, the sweetest sound I'd ever heard.

Chapter Twenty-One

Gabe

The room was one of the largest I'd ever been in, and as someone who grew up a billionaire, that's saying something. But it didn't matter. The walls felt way too close. The air was too hot. And too many eyes were on me.

"Your Grace?" said a voice to my right.

I turned to see the man Ollie called Typhir giving me a scrutinizing look, like he was judging me and didn't care much for what he saw.

I wasn't used to that title, since it hadn't been used before today. But apparently, "Your Grace" was the official address for my new role, even if I was still technically in training.

"Yes?" I asked, my throat so dry it was a wonder I could speak at all.

"You understand what to do, I assume?"

"Uh…" I looked down at myself. I was in a knee-length garment Ollie told me was "traditional" for the Justice to wear while passing judgment on people.

Which was what I was about to spend my day doing. Hearing stories of people who broke laws and deciding what their punishments should be. As if I had any clue what a "fair" punishment should be.

"They are waiting." Typhir's voice was brittle and scolding as he motioned toward the door on the other side of the throne room.

An actual fucking throne room, where I was sitting on an actual fucking throne like actual fucking royalty. None of the classes I'd had with Tomos could teach the way this would feel. The overwhelming desire to run wasn't mentioned either.

And I was going to be sentencing people, with Typhir looking over my shoulder and "guiding me." I didn't know what he meant by that, but when Ollie had given him a look of disgust as the day was explained to me earlier, I knew I was in for some bullshit.

"I'm ready." I nodded to Typhir, who motioned to the guards at the entrance.

They pulled open the doors, and at least a dozen people were marched in by more guards. They looked miserable—some looked like they'd been beaten. They were all dirty, like they hadn't bathed in weeks. Several cried out for mercy and forgiveness for whatever crime they were accused of.

"Do they usually... uh... look like this?" I whispered to Typhir, who stood behind my chair—throne—with his fingers gripping the back of it.

"Disgusting, isn't it?" He gave a nasty kind of laugh that wrinkled his nose and showed a line of sharpened, demonic teeth. "The filth and vermin of Sefaera. We wouldn't let them defile our halls if the Justice didn't see them here."

I started to feel sick. I was a trust fund baby. I had always had the best of everything and never had to set foot anywhere rundown or destitute.

But when I'd asked Typhir if this was normal, I hadn't been concerned because I was disgusted by them. I was disgusted by the way they had obviously been living, either outside these walls or as a result of being in them.

"Call forth the first." Typhir's voice was a snakelike hiss, which was fitting considering how much he reminded me of a serpent. Even his tongue seemed to dart within his condescending mouth, and a slight spray of spittle rained down over my half naked shoulder, like he was hungry for the potential retribution.

"Um, okay." I cleared my throat and said, loud as I could, "Whoever's first?"

Typhir snorted, and I wanted to turn around and punch him. This was my first time doing this, and I was doing it in a world where I knew next to nothing about the laws or customs. He'd been doing this job for a long time, apparently. Ollie had told me when his father, the last king, died, *his* soulmate, the queen, was technically no longer bound to the throne, and therefore was no longer tied to the role of Justice. So, until Ollie had his soulmate on the throne, the Council was responsible for passing these judgments.

A guy who'd been doing this for, like, two thousand years was mocking me for being nervous.

Well... fuck him. Didn't he know this was my first job?

The guards didn't seem to have any issue with the way I called for them, however. Two of them stepped out of the crowd, a young

189

looking woman between them. She barely moved her feet, forcing them to drag her, and her head hung down.

"What's wrong with her?" I asked, panic rising in my chest. I'd seen people who looked like this before at the "young Hollywood" parties I'd attended. That was typically the way their friends, or at least friendly acquaintances, dragged them out into the fresh air after they'd passed out from whatever their substance of choice was.

But this woman didn't look like she was on drugs. Rather like the very essence of hope had been pulled from her. Like death would have been a relief rather than a punishment.

What was Ollie allowing to happen to these people? How long had they been suffering like this? As the prince, I would have assumed it was his job to keep them clean and safe. But instead, it looked like his court had been more focused on keeping them in line.

"She's a criminal," Typhir said. "So it doesn't matter. Your job isn't to coddle the prisoners, but to sentence them."

I looked back down at her, and she finally looked up at me. It was hard to tell beneath the filth, but it looked like she had light pink skin, and her hair seemed to be gray—or maybe white when it was clean.

"What's your name?" I asked.

Typhir made a noise of protest, but I ignored him.

"Katinea." Her voice was a hoarse croak, and I watched as her lips oozed greenish blood from being so dry.

"Can someone get her some water?" I asked.

The guards looked confused, but one of the attendants stationed behind me poured a glass from the pitcher meant for me, then took it to her.

190

She gulped it down like it was the first water she'd had in years. To be fair, I had no idea how long it *had* been for her.

"Better?" I asked.

She nodded. "Yes, Your Grace."

Whispers rose up around the room, and my nerves started to build.

"So... uh... why are you here?"

The guard next to her spoke. "The prisoner has been accused of trespassing on royal grounds."

"How?" I asked.

"How?" he repeated, like he didn't understand the question.

"How was she trespassing on royal grounds?"

The guards looked at each other, and Typhir's voice was once again a hiss in my ear.

"It doesn't matter how. Sentence her. The usual punishment is five years in the labor fields."

"It matters to me," I said, loud enough for the guards to hear. "Because how else will *I* know what the sentence should be? And she hasn't even had a chance to give her side yet."

"Her side?"

I glanced back at Typhir, who looked like he was about to explode. Was this really the way the Council had been running things for two thousand years? It was horrifying. Without responding to him, I turned back to the guards, waiting for them to speak.

"The prisoner—"

"Katinea," I corrected. "She has a name."

Katinea looked at me with shock in her eyes and, what I thought was maybe a little bit of hope.

"Yes, Your Grace. Katinea was found lurking near the Royal Forest."

He said it like that should settle the matter, but it didn't for me.

"And how is that trespassing?"

"Citizens are not permitted in the Royal Forest. It's for use only by the royal family and those they permit."

"But wait," I said, frowning at him. "You said she was lurking *near* the forest. So she hadn't gone in?"

"We believe she may have gone in before we arrived or had the intention to, Your Grace."

I looked at Katinea. "Did you go in?"

"No," she said, her voice still a rasp.

"Were you *going* to go in?"

"No."

"Why were you there?" I asked.

She started to cry. "My pindore... Cerus... he ran away. I thought I saw him go into the woods. I was just trying to call him back, lure him with some food."

"And a pindore is a... a pet?"

"Yes, Your Grace," she said.

I turned my attention back to the guards. "So you arrested her because she was trying to find her lost pet, and she didn't even actually commit the crime you accused her of? And whose idea was it for a forest to be sequestered for the royal family? No one can own nature. That's ridiculous."

Silence fell on the entire room. It was obvious there had been no such thing as a fair trial under Typhir's command. But if I was going to do this job, even for just a short time until I could go home, I wasn't going to punish people just because I could. Never mind the training I'd had to be Justice of Sefaera, I'd had civics classes for at least four years in my education and the idea that anyone would be denied a fair trial, or wouldn't be innocent until proven guilty, made me sick. If this was the culture Sefaera was built on, I wasn't sure I wanted any part of it.

"Let her go," I said.

"What?" Typhir's whisper was furious. I was a little nervous because I didn't know what he could possibly do to me, either with magic or because he had more power than me. But I'd dealt with plenty of irritated tutors who couldn't get me to pay attention in chemistry, so I just tuned him out the same way.

I stood from my "throne" and walked down the carpeted runway to where Katinea was knelt. I extended her my hand and helped her to her feet before pulling her into a supportive embrace—the way my mom would have.

"On behalf of the entire royal family, please accept my apology for this wrongful detainment. We will do anything we can to help you find your... your..."

"Pindore?" she offered.

"Yes, pindore."

"Thank you, Your Grace," Katinea said, bursting into tears again.

The guards didn't seem to know what to do. Apparently, this was unheard of, and they were stumped.

"Take her home," I said. "She looks like she can barely walk. Get her there safe."

"Yes, Your Grace," one of them said, and with one last confused glance at me, they turned and left the throne room.

I spent the next several hours hearing case after case. Some of the prisoners were definitely guilty of serious crimes—one had murdered his neighbor and another had vandalized a competitor's shop. But most of them were like the first, people who had been arrested and were here to be sentenced with outrageous punishments. I didn't know what the labor fields were, but I wasn't going to send a man there for ten years for just stealing a loaf of bread because he was starving.

When the last prisoner was removed from the room, Typhir gave me one scathing look and said, "I will be discussing this with the rest of the Council." Then he turned, a dark red cape flowing behind him like some kind of supervillain.

I couldn't help but snort and roll my eyes. I'd known men like him my whole life, guys who threw their weight around, used to getting their way. Hollywood was plush with them. But men like that always had a weakness—it was just a matter of time before I figured out his.

I couldn't believe how much I was sweating as I stepped away from the throne and off into the curtained hallway. It was wild how much cooler I felt the second I stepped off that platform, like stepping out of a spotlight that wasn't really there. The pressure to get it right was exhausting.

As I felt the cool of the open hallway hit my face, I saw Olympio pacing. Clearly, his meeting had ended before I was done, and he was waiting for me. He looked up and saw me, his face breaking into a relieved smile as he strode over to me and opened his arms.

I happily leaned into them.

"Gabriel," he crooned softly as he stroked my hair. It was comforting, like being taken care of in a way I hadn't been since I was a child. "I was watching. You were incredible. I've seen the makings of a great Justice in you your entire life, but today… you surpassed my every expectation."

I shrugged, Typhir's face fresh in my mind. "Well, you're the only one who thought so."

The smell of Ollie soothed me, taking me from anxious to simply frustrated. I didn't know when my desire to get home had shifted into my desire to at least try my best while I was here, but the disapproval sat poorly on my shoulders. I was used to blind praise. I'd even say it was one of my major character flaws. When your parents were the ones who decided if a movie would get made or not and how much money the director would get, people tended to kiss your ass.

Ollie chuckled, pressing his lips to my forehead. "That old bastard doesn't think much of anything or anyone. I wouldn't put too much stock in his approval or disapproval." He sighed and gripped my shoulders to push me just far enough back to look at me. Sadness flashed on his face, and he looked down with a slight shake of his head.

"Well… thanks, then."

"Gabriel… *you* were perfect. I only wish I'd spent my time as ruler being half the man you are." He trailed off, his eyebrows furrowing as he frowned.

I don't know what compelled me to do it, but I went up on my toes, put my hand on his jaw, and pulled his lips to mine. It almost felt like if I could just kiss him, we would share the burden of what he was feeling.

195

And, out of nowhere, I gave a shit about how Ollie felt.

His hands drifted down my arms to rest on my waist as he returned the kiss, but there was a hesitation on his end, and he pulled away quickly.

"What's wrong?" I asked, a self-consciousness settling over me.

"Nothing," he said, one corner of his mouth curling up in a half-smile. "Come with me."

He reached out his hand for mine, and I took it without even thinking about it.

We walked through the palace to a hallway I hadn't seen yet. The light coming in through the windows was a little brighter, like we were slowly making our way outside.

When we finally made it to the door at the other end, Ollie turned to me with a gleeful expression.

"You're in for a treat," he said before flinging the door open.

As bright as the sun had been in the hallway, it was nothing to how it blinded me as soon as I stepped inside whatever this room was. It took a few seconds for my eyes to adjust, and when I did, my mouth fell open as I looked at what was inside.

Well, inside *and* outside.

We were standing at the top of a staircase in a massive glass dome with green vines covered in yellow and blue flowers crawling up the sides at random intervals. On the other side of the dome, a huge opening in the glass led to an outside area surrounded by a beautifully carved wooden fence.

Below me, within the dome, was neatly trimmed grass and dozens of small paddocks filled with purple hay, no bigger than a few feet on

196

each side and open, as if whatever they contained wasn't meant to be caged in. More of the vines and flowers wrapped around the wooden beams of the paddocks, and a smell like citrus and honey surrounded me as a comfortably cool breeze brushed over my face.

And there, in the very center of the dome, was a marble fountain that stood at least fifteen feet high, pouring out the same turquoise blue water that was always in my bathtub. Sitting on the edge of the fountain was a woman I'd only seen a handful of times—the queen. She held a bag of something, possibly seeds or grains of some kind, because surrounding her were dozens and dozens of—

"Meerads," Ollie said, pointing to them. "Babies. Only just born a few weeks ago. Right before you got here. My mother raises them here, in the nursery, until they're big enough to be let out into the fields to roam free."

The closest thing I could compare them to would be lambs, but, like everything else here, it was like someone had given a six year old creative reign to design their own kind of animal.

They were covered in wool, just like the ones back home, and their faces were really similar. But instead of being white or black, they were every pastel shade you could imagine, from sea green to sky blue, to lavender and pale yellow, and their feet ended in tiny, dainty little paws instead of cloven hooves.

"Woah..."

It was the only thing I could think of to describe how each of these encounters with a whole new world, one that was living, breathing, and thriving, felt to me.

Ollie was leaning over the railing, watching them, but he looked back at me with a wide smile, his eyebrows dancing playfully. "Would you like to see them up close?"

"Can we?"

I hadn't expected that, and I expected the butterflies that exploded in my chest as Ollie grabbed my hand and led me down the stairs even less.

Up close, the smell of the flowers was even stronger, and I took deep breath after deep breath, unable to get enough of it. I snatched one off the vine as we walked and held it up to my nose, only to be surprised they weren't the source of the scent. And it wasn't until we approached the fountain that I realized what I was smelling was actually the meerads.

"Hello, Mother," Ollie said as we got closer. At the sound of his voice, two dozen or more of the fluffy little creatures turned and started making a sound like some kind of songbird before bounding and jumping and running over to us.

Ollie dropped to his knees and began to pet each of them like a dog he hadn't seen in months.

"Hello, Olympio, darling," the queen said. "And Gabriel. It's so good to see you outside of an official function. From what Ariadne tells me about you, it's a crime we haven't been able to properly meet yet. I'm Parthenea."

I suddenly felt shy. No one—no one I was dating, at least—had ever introduced me to their parents before. "Nice to meet you."

"You'd think I never said a word to her about you at all," Ollie said, still with that smile that I was getting really used to... and swooning over.

"You're biased," the queen said, laughing, and reached out her closed fist to me. "You're not afraid of animals, are you?"

I shook my head and opened my hand for her, and she deposited a handful of whatever was in the bag, obviously some kind of food for the meerads.

There was something about the queen that simultaneously made me want to hug her and slightly fear her. You could feel her power in the space. It wasn't the kind of power that demanded attention, but one you couldn't help but be intrigued by. She reminded me of my own mom in that way—strong, beautiful, smart, but never one to say so.

She patted the edge of the fountain next to her, and I tentatively sat.

"So... to what do I owe this pleasure?" She looked back and forth between Ollie and me.

"I thought seeing your nursery might brighten Gabriel's spirits," he said, putting a hand on my shoulder and sending goosebumps down my arms. "He just spent the better part of the day with Typhir."

The slight shift in her expression told me everything I needed to know about how she felt about Typhir, and it was clear she didn't like him any more than I did.

"And what did *Lord* Typhir want with you?" She directed the question to me, pulling me into the conversation with them.

"It was my first day as Justice." One of the tiny meerads came over and nudged my hand, then proceeded to lick the seeds from it. I had always wanted a pet, but mom said it was unfair because we traveled so much.

"I see," she said, giving me a scrutinizing look before turning to Ollie. "Olympio, darling, I am absolutely ravenous. Could you go fetch an attendant to bring us a tray of fruits and breads, as well as water and some wine?"

Ollie tilted his head slightly as he regarded his mother, and I watched some kind of silent communication happen between them before he nodded, stood, and bent down to kiss me on the head.

"I'll be back shortly," he promised.

I watched him go, his strong frame the picture of masculine grace as he walked.

And, fuck, did his ass look good.

For a few minutes, we fed the meerads in silence. Then she turned to me.

"Tell me, Gabriel. What was your first day as Justice like?" Her tone was light, but there was something about her energy that made it perfectly clear her question went deeper than the words.

"Overwhelming. So many people were counting on me to make judgment calls I do not feel qualified to make. I haven't even finished college yet."

"College?" she asked.

"Higher education," I explained. "People go there to get qualified for… I don't know, life?"

"Ah, yes…" She smiled, a wistful sort of look crossing her face. "We had something like that when I was young. The Lyceum was the premier school for philosophy, though a particularly industrious man

200

called Plato founded another that was rather well respected. I wasn't able to go to either, as a woman, but my brother studied under the man himself."

The names of the school and the famous philosopher brought back memories of humanities and history classes, and I realized I might not be the only one from my world here.

"You lived in Ancient Greece?"

She laughed and touched my hand gently. "Is that what they call it? It was hardly ancient when I was there. It was the epicenter of intellect and progressivism in the world. But thank you, dear Gabriel, for making me feel old." Her eyes, which looked barely older than forty at the most, twinkled with delight, letting me know she wasn't actually upset.

"Oh, God, shit. I'm sorry."

First real conversation with my mother-in-law, and I fucked it up.

Mother-in-law.

Was I thinking about staying?

"No need to be sorry," she said, offering a handful of the feed to the meerads. "I am old. Many hundreds of times older than everyone I knew before I came here. Just like you. A human thrust into a world of demons and magic."

I perked up at that. "You're human? Or—you were?"

"Yes." She looked at me, and I noticed for the first time her eyes were the same violet I sometimes saw in Ollie's eyes. "And I don't know that I'm *not* human. But I am immortal now, and I do possess some of the gifts the royal family has. But having been here for over four thousand years, I would say, no matter what I started out as or what else I may still be, I am Sefaeran, through and through."

I felt my own chest swell with pride. "I hope I can live up to your expectations, or you will forgive me if I can't."

"And what expectations do you think I have for you?" The question was a challenge, but not an unfriendly one. It actually seemed like she was trying to help me out in a roundabout way.

"To stay in Sefaera and be a good Justice," I replied confidently.

She nodded like she was thinking about what I was saying, then remained quiet for several long moments, just feeding and petting the meerads. When she finally looked at me, there was an odd sort of sympathy in her expression.

"Is that what *you* want?"

"I—" I stumbled over my words, wanting to get it right, wanting to impress her. "I don't know yet."

"And I would imagine," she said, a knowing smile spreading across her face, "that my son, as well-intentioned as he may be, is being rather short-sighted to the fact that you feel that way."

I looked away. "Ollie is—"

"Ollie?" she asked, laughing. "Sounds less like the regal mountain he was named for and more like a drink garnish."

I felt my face get hot with embarrassment, and I gave the rest of my seeds to the nearest meerad. "I'm sorry."

"Don't be," she said. "The fact that someone would be close enough to my son to have their own little name for him is darling. Olympio rarely lets anyone that close."

Silence fell between us again before she looked away from the meerads to face me, her face serious for the first time.

"What is it like? The state of Justice under Typhir and the rest of the Council?"

"Barbaric. Five years for something someone *might* have done. I mean, your government ran the same way mine does, or at least mine pretends to. That isn't very democratic."

"Democracy…" she said, her eyes a million miles away. "Such a new concept back before I came here. My people at the time were creating a more civilized world, one where the government answered to the people, not the other way around." She looked down, frowning. "I did my best to instill those values in our government here while I was Justice, but when my soulmate died, the Council took over. I've been put out to pasture, so to speak. They tell me nothing. Everything I know about the way things happen now, I hear from Olympio. And even his knowledge is filtered through what Typhir wants him to know."

"Wait… so Ollie—Olympio—doesn't know what's going on in there? But isn't he the ruler or whatever?"

"In a sense," she said, shaking her head. "But he's not the king. While the throne isn't occupied by a bonded pair, the Council's power exceeds that of whoever is in line for the throne. Individually, the members don't have much power at all, but when unified, they can overrule Olympio whenever they choose. And Typhir has never failed to convince the others to fall in line."

I thought back to how upset it made me that Ollie might have been allowing people to be unjustly punished. "So, if Typhir is allowing people to be abused and wrongly sentenced, Ollie has no say?"

"Not until he's king," she said. "I had heard rumors of what Typhir was doing in there, but I didn't know for sure until speaking to you." She hung her head. "Olympio's father would have been devastated to see what Typhir has made of the Sefaeran Justice hearings."

"What was he like?" I asked, out of sheer curiosity.

"Who?"

"Your soulmate. Olympio's dad. And what happens after a 'soulmate' dies?"

Her eyes lit up, and I could almost feel their love radiating from her. "Truthfully... he was a lot like Olympio. Intelligent, cunning, and more than a little impulsive, but with a good heart and a powerful sense of duty to the kingdom. I can remember when he first came to me. I lived in a time and place where mythological creatures were spoken of like they were real, and when Kyerten showed up at my home, wreathed in shadows, I was terrified. I thought one of the dark creatures rejected by the gods had come to take me away, but he didn't. He stayed with me for several years, letting us get acquainted and teaching me about this world. He was... romantic and funny in a way most of the men I knew were not. He treated me as his equal rather than as a subservient woman, which, as progressive as my society was, was still mostly unheard of. It wasn't long before I had well and truly fallen in love with him and made the choice to leave my home for Sefaera."

She paused, putting a hand to her chest and smiling.

"His soul is bound to mine, and mine to his. His body has gone from this world, but his soul lives on within me. He doesn't have a true 'voice,' but I can still hear him and feel him. And when I depart this life for whatever comes next, either because I've chosen to move on or

204

because fate has intervened and brought my time to an end, our souls will leave this world as one."

Just then, a deep voice skated through the air.

"Allenda sent lymoc tea, oulon tarts, and her regards, Mother." Ollie came walking down the steps with a huge tray balanced on one hand, moving like a dancer in his grace. He was smiling broadly as he approached, setting the tray down between his mother and me. "Did I miss anything important?"

"Only Gabriel becoming the new favorite of my little darlings, here," she said, giving me a look that told me our conversation would remain between us as long as I wanted it to before taking one of the pastries and biting into it. "Oh, Gabriel, dear, you absolutely *must* try one. Allenda is the best baker in the entire kingdom—possibly in any kingdom."

I looked over at Ollie, who was studying me as his mother spoke, and I had the inexplicable urge to avert my eyes. He was so goddamn intense all the time.

"She's right, you know." He picked up one of the tarts and held it out to me, a cocky grin on his lips. "Here. I know you're hungry."

I nodded, taking the delicious pastry into my mouth and groaning as I slowly chewed and swallowed it. Ollie and the queen both laughed, nodding at each other as I took another.

And another…

The world was changing around me. It no longer felt like a prison, but more like a place of learning.

And yet…

Still not home.

Chapter Twenty-Two
Olympio

"Absolutely not."

"It is tradition," Typhir replied to me. He was already tired of dealing with me today, and it was entirely mutual.

"Fuck tradition," I replied, my temper failing me by the second as I stood before the Council, where Typhir had just given me an unacceptable directive.

"All due respect, *Your Highness*," he sneered in that infuriating way he always did. "Your soulmate must—I assume—possess some qualities that will *someday* make him a competent Justice. But that does not exempt him from the rites and rituals which have been passed down for generations."

His blatant disrespect would never cease to set my heart pounding in my ears. Sometimes I thought he was so patronizing just because he knew he could get away with it. His family descended from the same ancestor as mine, going back to the beginning of Sefaera. Over time, the lines diverged, with mine remaining on the throne while his was shuffled sideways into administrative positions, though both retained the gift of immortality.

But that didn't mean he'd lost all of his power. Oh, no, he'd made sure, thousands of years before I was even born, that the Council had nearly as much power as the king. And until I became king, the Council had at least some measure of authority over me. It was a system intended to ease the future monarch into their role, but in practice, it did little more than give undue influence to demons who should have made the journey to the afterlife eons ago.

As if I needed one more reason to want my bond consummated as soon as possible—something I was certain would be pushed even farther away if I agreed to this.

"I understand the importance of the Consummation," I said, my jaw tight in my attempts to remain civil. Regality wasn't inherent to me the way it had been to my brother, and Typhir knew better than anyone how to push me past my limits. "But this is a barbaric practice that has no place in civilized society, and certainly not in royal circles."

"That is where it is the most imperative," Typhir said with a condescending chuckle, glancing conspiratorially to the Councilors on either side of him, who shook their heads at me, their disdain apparent. "After the recent attempt on your life, I would think you would be begging for your soulmate to undergo this training."

"No one would want someone they love subjected to this," I spat.

"Both of my children and my niece have partaken in the ritual," he said, and the thought that Vass, another person I cared for, had dealt with this, made my blood boil. "It will take place at moonrise. You will be expected to escort him."

Moonrise. Barely more than an hour away. I could spend that time here, trying to argue Gabriel's way out of this, but I knew it would be futile, and if I wasn't there, he would be escorted without me. And there was no way I was letting him face this alone.

In fact…

"Fine," I said, slightly extending my arms in a show of surrender.

"We knew you would—"

"But I have a condition," I interrupted, my face hard.

A hush fell over the twelve faces before me, and they all exchanged confused glances.

"A condition?" Typhir echoed.

"Yes," I said. "I will be the one conducting the ritual."

If there had been silence before, there was now a void of sound as they all processed my demand.

"It's unheard of," said Orella from her seat beside Typhir. She wasn't as overt in her criticism as some of the others, but she was no more reasonable than they were when it came down to it.

"Either you will agree to my terms, or you will have to fetch us from the clouds," I said, crossing my arms.

Typhir's face turned a rather ugly, uneven shade of red as he looked up and down the row of Councilors, silently taking a poll. After several moments, he looked back at me, and the defeat in his eyes was absolutely fucking delicious.

"You may have your *terms*," he said, his voice constrained with the effort of conceding to me.

With a short nod, I turned and left the Council chambers, hearing Gryfian follow me as I passed him. My fury at Typhir forcing this ritual on Gabriel was overshadowed only by the anxiety that had my hands shaking. This was going to put his trust in me to the test in a way I worried was still too soon. We'd shared intimate moments, sexual and emotional, but this... This was something else entirely.

My heart fluttered against my ribs as the doors to Gabriel's chambers came into view. I knew there was little time to truly prepare him for this, but I knew by agreeing to do it myself, he'd be saved from the worst of it.

I stood outside the doors and reached out to open them, but I paused as I heard, to my surprise, Vass's voice inside, conversing with Gabriel. Suddenly, a vision entered my mind of a future where I didn't have to choose, where Vassenia and Gabriel had become close as well, and the three of us could live happily together—all three of us.

"Those are... interesting," I heard Vass say. "What are they called?"

There was a pause, then Gabriel replied, "Jeans?" He sounded far more confused than I expected.

"Oh," Vass said, and there was something about her tone that struck a familiar chord in me, and my enthusiasm began to fade, vanishing completely when she said, "So that's what commoners wear back in your world? They're so... well, they suit you."

"Oh, thanks," he replied with genuine happiness. "They're Gucci— or, well, I guess they're Gucci knock offs, technically. Ollie had them made for me."

"*Ollie* did, did he?" she said, and vindictive glee dripped from the words.

I knew what she was doing, but Gabriel had no idea. She was being condescending, and Gabriel was too pure to understand her words were

209

carefully curated to insult him. It was a skill she and I had perfected over the years so we could carry on at parties, but hearing her direct that cruelty toward Gabriel reignited the anger I'd felt just a few moments ago.

And it wasn't just at Vass. It was at myself as well, for having treated others like that. I had been conceited and arrogant. I still was, if I was truly honest with myself. But… Gabriel was better than that. Better than me. And he made me want to be better, too.

Having heard enough of Vassenia ridiculing my soulmate, I opened the door, and both of them turned to me.

The second our eyes met, Gabriel's turned the lightest shade of violet before flickering back to their normal whirlpool of various blues.

"Hey," he breathed. I watched in heart-aching frustration as he bit his lip at me. He didn't deserve any of this—least of all Vassenia's wrath.

"Hello, Gabriel," I said, offering him a gentle smile as I strode over to him. I bent down to kiss his cheek, trying not to let my face show the feeling of the sparks the bond set off in my heart. Only then did I turn my attention back to Vass, as if I'd only just noticed her there. If she was going to resort to passive aggressiveness, I could return it in spades. "Vassenia. Good to see you. To what do I owe the pleasure of my *soulmate* and my *friend* spending this time together?"

It was then I felt Gabriel touch my hand and wrap his fingers in mine. For just a moment, I truly did forget Vass was there. The feeling of Gabriel's hand in mine, not only because of the bond, but because this person I loved—truly loved—was offering me this small show of trust and affection, was all that mattered.

210

Things had been going so well between us. Every night for the last week, he'd fallen asleep in my arms. I'd come to his room after his training each day, and we… unwound together. It had been absolutely magical.

And it killed me because of what I came here to do.

"We're just talking about the differences in our worlds," Gabriel said earnestly. "It's so different." His attention went back to Vass. "In my world, you would have been so popular, though—especially in a sorority."

I'd only had a short amount of time to learn about sororities, but the girls in them who spent time in the fraternity house had this same vindictive streak I was only just noticing in Vassenia. And I didn't care for it from her any more than I cared for it from the human girls who thought they were better than others.

"You know," I said, smiling at Gabriel, "I think you're right. She would have fit right in." I knew she would have no point of reference, but I met her gaze with a hardness she would recognize from two and a half millennia of practice. She understood I was well aware of her games, and I was not going to tolerate them. "Well, I *hate* to throw you out, Vassenia, but I have something I need to discuss with Gabriel. You're dismissed."

Her mouth opened slightly as if to object, but she seemed to realize it would have been a poor choice, and instead, she bowed to me. "Your Highness," she said as she turned and left the room.

I watched her go, and I recalled thousands of times I did the same thing, enjoying the sight of her body swaying. But just then, all I could think about was how happy I was to see her leave.

211

I turned back to see Gabriel staring at me, trying to hide the adoration I was so grateful to see there. I would do anything to keep that look, to see his azure eyes swirling with the purple shimmer of the bond, looking at me like nothing would make him happier than to keep looking at me, a feeling I fully reciprocated.

"Alone at last," he giggled softly. "She was nice. Who is she again?"

I bristled at him calling her nice. Even before this, when I would have done anything for her, she was never *nice*. She was smart, and cunning, and sexy. But never *nice*.

"Vassenia?" I asked, as if I wasn't sure who he meant. "Oh, she's my lead advisor. She's also an old friend."

"A friend who had a *lot* of information about what you like during... sex." He gave me a suspicious look, challenging me without any aggression.

I hadn't expected that conversation to happen right this moment, but I was grateful for any excuse to delay the ritual. "Well, yes," I said, running a hand through my hair. "I've been alive for more than two thousand years, and she's been my closest confidante in that time. Sex isn't as taboo here as it is in your world. But it was never more than that—just two friends fooling around." I fought to keep my voice even, the pain of denying what I felt for her almost as hard as seeing her in a new light—one I hated. Gabriel had a little smirk on his face that confused me. "What?" I asked.

He pressed his lips together and shook his head.

"Gabriel..." I issued a warning I had no way of enforcing.

"Is it true that you…. finish in two seconds with a finger…" He took his pointer finger on one hand and made an "O" with his other hand, inserting the pointer through the hole.

My cheeks heated up until I couldn't even maintain eye contact. That wasn't exactly something I wanted him to find out second-hand, considering it was embarrassing enough without Vassenia trying to create awkward tension between Gabriel and me.

"I suppose…" I said, trying to smile as I looked back at him, "you'll have the chance to find out one day."

He gave a cheeky grin, then said, "*Damn,* you freak."

I assumed it was meant to be in a good way, but at that moment, I just wanted to escape the conversation. Thankfully, I had a horrible one to shift us to. "Regardless…" I said, taking both of his hands in mine and looking down at them. "There's something we need to discuss."

Gabriel stood from where he sat and walked over to the balcony to watch the moon rise. It was that beautiful part of the day when both the sun and one of the moons could be seen, and it was truly a sight to behold.

"Is it about how hot Vass is?"

There was no denying her beauty. She was voluptuous and confident, with raven hair, emerald eyes, and bronze skin. But for the first time in our lives, I had seen something ugly about her.

I followed him, leaning on the railing and following his gaze to watch with him. "Unfortunately, no." I took a deep breath. "You and I have… an obligation tonight. One I did everything I could to get us out of, but I was unsuccessful."

His smile fell, and he turned to face me. "The Consummation?" he asked nervously.

"No," I said. I actually wished it was. Even if it was disastrous again, it wouldn't be nearly as traumatic as what we were headed to. "It's... something else. Something I'm not letting you go through alone." I turned to look at Gabriel. He was just beginning to open up to me, to trust me. This could undo all of that. "As the future consort and Justice, until we *do* consummate the bond, you will be in danger of usurpers trying to hurt you to prevent my ascent."

"Shit," he drawled. "Really? Like, actual assassins?"

"Gabriel," I said, reaching out to put a finger under his chin. "I wanted to protect you from this. But on one of your first days here, there was an attempt on my life. In my own chambers."

His face fell, confusion dusting his expression. "Are you... okay?"

I looked down at my arm, at the shining golden scar, the reminder that until I took the throne, I wasn't safe, and neither was Gabriel. I held it up to him. "She left a souvenir for me. But otherwise, yes, I'm alright. But... there is a generations-old tradition for members of the royal family. Something the Council is insisting on, since the palace is clearly not as secure as it once was. You need to be..." I swallowed, not wanting to say any of this. "You need to be prepared for if someone comes after you. If they don't kill you outright, if you're taken... you could be tortured. For information or to hurt me, knowing it would destroy me to feel you in that kind of pain."

"Get to the point please, Ollie."

214

"You're being required to undergo… torture training," I said. "It's not something you will have to do more than once. But just once will be enough."

I felt Gabriel's panic through the bond. "Torture?"

I couldn't look him in the eyes anymore. "Yes. It's an ancient ritual where you will be prepared for what you might expect to experience if that were to ever happen."

"But… you're not gonna let them hurt me—right? You're not gonna let them do it?"

My lower lip shook. I wanted to tell him I was going to save him from this, but, until I took the throne, I was powerless to override the demands of the Council when they were unanimous in their decisions.

"You're not gonna let them do it," he said slowly. "Because you're gonna do it yourself. I can… feel it—I think."

I blinked, stunned by this revelation. "You feel it?" I asked. For him to be feeling much of anything was indicative of the bond between us growing stronger. But that thought, that determination, was so specific, we must have been so much more connected than I realized. I was thrilled, but terrified it would all end after tonight, and we'd be back to where we started.

Gabriel was silent, turning away from me, completely preventing me from seeing his face. But like him, I could feel his emotion through the bond, and he was contemplative. Not terrified.

Finally, he turned back to me and nodded. "Take me."

He extended his hand, and I could see it trembling.

I stepped closer to him and grabbed his hand, which I brought to my lips, kissing his palm, my eyes closed.

"I'm sorry." I finally opened my eyes into his. I couldn't say more, and there wasn't more to say, anyway. Leading him by the hand, we exited his chambers and began a quiet walk to the ritual chamber, the only sounds the scuffing of our feet and those of the guards on either side of us.

This room was used for only one thing, and it was in an otherwise abandoned wing of the palace. While every inch of the palace was opulent and luxurious, even the door to this room spoke of the darkness it contained. Gray stone in an unceremonious rectangle, closed with a wooden beam across it, thick enough to block out all sound. A matching beam was on the other side to allow us to lock ourselves in.

I nodded to the guards, who removed the beam, before reaching out and placing my hand on the stone. It felt unusually cool, like all warmth and goodness couldn't penetrate this place. With a push, it swung slowly open, revealing a dark chamber. It was only about ten feet by ten feet. The walls and floor were painted red with black trim. Hanging on hooks around the room were the tools I would be using, and in the center of the floor, five chains with restraints at the ends, and a small stone stool.

"Fuck…" Gabriel gasped. "This is like… for real." He fumbled for my hand, squeezing it once he'd found it.

I looked at the room in disgust. Our world had been civilized and sophisticated for thousands of years, and yet we were still resorting to brutish, abusive rituals in the name of tradition. It was enough to make me sick.

"I think…" I drew in a shaky breath and pointed to the restraints. "I think you need to be chained in."

He breathed in deeply, nodding and walking to where the chains emerged from the floor. He slowly kneeled and leaned over the stone stool, balancing himself and pulling off his shirt. He didn't look up at me. He didn't even shake. I could feel any fear he had was banished and turned to commitment. The first signs of his fate coming to fruition— of the Justice coming into his own.

I knelt in front of him, my hands gripping the shackles, but my eyes were on him. "I will make this as quick as I possibly can."

"Do what you have to do," my soulmate said with a grimace. "Can't be any worse than playing Edward Forty Hands at initiation."

He finally looked up at me and cracked a smile, and my heart broke, but I smiled back, fighting tears.

"That feels like a lifetime ago," I said. I was so proud of him, and so guilty over what we were here to do. Not to mention the guilt I still had over bringing him here before he was ready. I would never forgive myself for that. But he didn't need to see my tears. That wouldn't be fair with what he was about to go through.

"I trust you," he suddenly said, his nerves breaking through his steeled resolve once more. "I never thought I'd say that," he murmured. "But I do. Let's just get this over with. I'm sure you'll find a way to make it up to me later…"

I offered him a ghost of a laugh and nodded. He was right. There was no use delaying this any longer. I took the shackles for his feet, chaining them to the floor. Then his hands, stretching him over the stool. The fifth shackle was larger, and I realized it was for his neck, like a collar, one that would keep his head down. I let my fingers rest on the soft skin behind his ears before I stood and went to the wall, staring in horror at the array of torture tools.

One glance was all it took for me to be glad I had insisted on doing this myself. If I'd left it to Typhir, he would have chosen a sadist, one who would use one of the sharp, jagged metal instruments. My stomach churned at the idea of any of those things being used on my Gabriel.

It took several minutes, but I finally decided on a leather flogger. If he left here without a mark on him, the Council would absolutely demand it be redone with someone of their choosing doing the honors. This tool would hurt, which was required, but it wouldn't cause damage the way some of the others would.

And I planned to temper the pain anyway, so this would allow me to maintain my composure.

Taking my place behind Gabriel, where he was bent over in only his jeans and boots, I took one moment to take in his beauty, knowing that in a moment, his perfect, unblemished skin was about to be marred.

By me.

"Are you ready?" I asked.

"Yes."

It was just a single word, but it weighed more than almost any other he'd ever said to me. The trust in that one syllable was tangible, and with a knot in my chest, I drew back my arm and brought the flogger down on his right shoulder blade.

The scream that left his lungs quickly reminded me, from a lifetime of watching his every move, that he'd never felt anything worse than a broken arm—a broken arm heavily countered by pain medicine and me soothing him through the bond.

The cry was followed by a sob, and some spittle fell from his mouth.

But he quickly pulled himself together. "No," he said without even looking at me, clearly tapping into the bond once more. "I was just surprised. Keep going."

I raised the flogger again, but before I swung my arm, I reached along the bond like Gabriel had, but instead of trying to ascertain what he was feeling, I tried to take it from him.

But with the crack of the leather on his skin once more, I felt no pain, and I watched Gabriel's body jerk again, heard the whimpered breath that told me he'd felt every bit of the pain. I couldn't figure out why it wouldn't work, but then I remembered there were enchantments in place to keep anyone, any prisoners or enemies of the crown who were brought here, from using any kind of magic to temper their own pain. I had thought it might be different if I did it for him, if I used the bond, but I'd clearly overestimated my own capabilities.

Gabriel would have to endure this on his own.

Chapter Twenty-Three
Gabe

White-hot searing pain was only made worse by the fact that I was trying to hide my agony from Ollie. Trying to stifle every urge to scream or cry out.

I could feel the emotional torment rippling off of Ollie like waves of heat, and I didn't bother looking up, knowing already he was on the brink of tears.

The whip cracked over my back again. I'd lost count of how many times he'd swung it so far. He'd moved the impact around my body, never hitting the same spot twice in a row, keeping any one area from becoming too raw. Even so, with dozens of lashes, my entire back was burning, and parts had even gone numb.

What *wasn't* numb were my wrists, ankles, and neck. The shackles holding me in my kneeling position were leather, and despite their tightness, every time I moved, they rubbed against my flesh like sandpaper.

Suddenly, there was silence. No more slap of leather on skin. My eyes were shut tight, but I could hear Ollie's feet moving around me.

The feeling of something touching me at all caused me to jump, but I relaxed quickly when I realized it wasn't another tool of torture, but a hand wiping away tears I hadn't realized had been covering my cheeks.

I opened my eyes and saw him in front of me, kneeling down to my level, looking at me with concern. His fingers continued to dry my face until he laid his full hand on my cheek, the warmth of it seeping into my skin as I leaned into the touch.

"Allergies, right?" I said, unable to resist my own defense mechanism—making a joke.

"Gabriel…" he said quietly, the single word strained like he was in pain, too.

"It's not that bad, really." It was then I looked at my left wrist and saw the cuff covered in my own blood. "Barely worse than a scratch."

What was this? I suddenly couldn't stand to see him sad. When did this happen?

"You don't have to do that." He continued to touch my face, push my hair off my sweat covered forehead. "Not with me. I can feel what you do. I know how much it hurts."

"Yeah, but," I started, "I should be grateful, really. People pay big money in certain… circles…"

I tried to muster a lip bite, but the stinging of my raw skin likely left me looking a little odd instead.

Suddenly, he was gone, and I heard the clinking of glass and something being poured. Then he was back in front of me, holding a glass of that weird blue wine.

He looked at me, frowning, moving the glass side to side. There wasn't really an easy way for him to get it to my mouth without just pouring it over my head. But then the frown vanished, and he brought the wine to his own lips and took a long sip.

"Oh, okay," I said with a deranged laugh. "I can see this is really taxing for you. Please, don't resist on my account."

Without replying, he moved closer, until his lips pressed hard against mine. His tongue pushed forward, forcing my lips apart, and then I felt the rush of the wine from his mouth into mine. It wasn't much, but I knew by this point how strong that stuff was. It wouldn't be enough to get me drunk, but it would definitely help me deal with the pain.

Once I swallowed, Ollie pulled back, a sad smile on his face.

"They keep it in here so the torturers can have something to drink while they…" He shook his head and trailed off.

Just like last time, the effects were nearly instantaneous. A slight tingling began in my stomach and spread out all the way to my fingers and toes. There was a slight sense of almost relaxation when it reached my head, as it dulled the agony just a bit.

"Woah…" I groaned as the full effect kicked in. "I'll never get how you can drink so much of this stuff. Come on, then," I grumbled. "Let's get this over with."

Ollie touched my face one more time, then nodded and stood up, taking a long sip of the wine for himself, before moving behind me.

"I'm sorry," he said, and I knew he really was, even as he brought the flogger down on me again.

I braced myself for the pain and yet—it didn't come. Sure, I felt the sting of it, but it didn't feel quite so… torturous. In fact….

I kind of liked it.

I turned my head and strained to look at Ollie. "Is that all you've got?"

He froze, and I could see the look on his face. He tilted his head to the side and raised an eyebrow.

"I beg your pardon?"

"Yeah," I panted. "Alex Kessinger has spanked me harder than that."

The crack of the leather against my skin was instantaneous and sharp. That damn bond was so weird, because I could *feel* Ollie's irritation so strongly the words *"Fuck Kessinger"* played in my head.

"Damn," I coughed as a more vibrant wave of pain rippled across my jeans-clad ass. "Does he really bother you that much? He was always so good to me. Shit—I was so close to calling him Dad—"

The flogger struck me through my pants again, but then stopped as Ollie's hands were suddenly around my hips.

"Kinky," I giggled.

"Alex Kessinger can rot," he said gruffly as his hands fumbled at the button and zipper of my jeans, tearing them open and yanking them down so my ass was exposed to the cool air of the room. "And you will not mention his name again. Not to me. *Ever* again."

That had to be the fastest erection I'd ever gotten in my life, and I was so hard, I was embarrassed.

I was sure he would notice me going quiet, but all I wanted to feel right now was his retribution for clearly saying something that deeply affected him.

The leather lashed against my bare ass, causing my now rigid cock to bounce.

"Do you understand?" he said in a low, rough growl.

"Yes."

I tried to keep my tone even, but it crossed my lips as a half moan, and I knew I was moments from being discovered.

What was wrong with me? I was being tortured, for fuck's sake.

He paused again, and I heard his feet coming closer behind me.

"What's this?" he asked, his tone making it very clear my raging boner had finally caught his attention, and he knew exactly what "this" was.

Something touched the back of my thigh, and I jumped. But once again, it was Ollie's hand tracing one of the places he'd struck me.

I didn't have the boldness to admit the wine had been a turning point in the sensation for me. I wasn't drunk—far from it. But I felt bubbly, nice....

Horny.

"Shouldn't we finish this up?" I asked. "How long do we do this for, anyway?"

Part of me was hoping he'd say we were here for the duration of the night, and part of me was hoping I'd be dismissed to my room to take care of myself, or maybe, if I was lucky, with Ollie's help.

"Until the guards feel they've heard enough," he said, his hand still tracing lines from my lower back down my legs. His hand withdrew for a second, then came down hard against my ass. I barely had time to register the sting before he took a handful of the place he'd just spanked. All at the same time, I heard him make a low growling sound in his chest and felt his own arousal spike.

"Olympio…?" I breathed. What the fuck was happening here? Was this just what we were doing now?

"Gabriel…" he moaned, pressing up against my back, his hands gripping my hips and pulling me against him. He was hard, too, pressing into me through his toga. "*My… Gabriel…*"

Suddenly, I wanted to rip through my restraints and grab him. I was ravenous for Ollie—*Prince* Olympio.

"The guards…" I panted as his hands roved my body. "Aren't they gonna hear it's quiet?"

He bent over my body, pressing his chest against my aching back, then leaned into my ear to say, "Then you'd better not stay quiet."

The command itself hit every nerve in my body, but if the words swimming through my mind weren't enough, I could hear them through the "bond." It was like he was talking past me, directly to my body, and I moaned loudly.

"Well done," he said, and as if to reward me, his hand slid between us and reached to grab my cock and give it a long, slow stroke.

The muscles in my lower stomach clenched, and it took every ounce of willpower not to spill into his hand.

"Ollie…."

"Louder," he said, stroking me again.

"Shouldn't—" I panted. "Oh, god… Shouldn't you be 'torturing' me?"

I knew screaming his name over and over again, preferably while he filled any and all orifices, was what I would prefer, but his guards would probably get wise quickly.

I scanned the room, looking at the instruments placed around for the purpose of pain, and saw a single candle, unlit, with a device to light it.

"What's that for?" I asked.

Ollie was suddenly gone from my back, and the cool rush of air on my skin made the welts he'd left me with throb. He walked around me to pick up the candle and the instrument, lighting it.

"Let me show you," he said, a secretive smile playing on his face. "Don't forget to scream…"

He walked back over behind me, but didn't return to his position against me. Instead, I heard his feet stop slightly to my side, but I couldn't turn my head enough to see him before a burning hot drip of wax landed in the center of my back, rolling halfway down my side and solidifying again.

"Oh, fuck," I screamed, more out of surprise than anything. The instant the wax hit my back had been a flash of pain, especially against the raw skin Ollie had beaten before. But when it dripped and cooled, it left behind a tingling feeling of relief, and I wanted—needed—more. "Thank you," I whispered, panting.

Ollie responded by letting more wax fall onto my bare skin, slowly moving up and down my spine to cover my skin in a thin layer of candle wax. I thought that was maybe going to be it, but then, out of nowhere, I felt his hand spank me again, jolting my body against the stool.

I howled in a way I didn't know I had in me and felt a knot in my stomach from my arousal that I had no way of sating.

Whimpers escaped my lips, and I hung my head, waiting for another blow to befall me.

But it didn't.

Ollie moved around in front of me and knelt down again, his eyes searching mine. Then he set the candle on the floor beside him and reached out to undo the shackles on my wrists and neck.

It felt amazing to be released, but I was in such a state of desperate desire, I was worried we were "back to business."

I needed to come.

I needed Ollie to make it happen.

He ran his fingers lightly over the places where the shackles had cut into my skin, then moved around behind me to remove the restraints on my ankles. Then he pulled me to my feet.

"Are we... done?" I asked.

Ollie then made a sound I'd never heard from him before. It was deep, rich, and sensual in a way I had never experienced.

"Not even close."

Suddenly, he had pulled my jeans all the way off and had lifted me up and carried me to the wall, where a second set of shackles had been bolted in. Spreading my arms up and out to the sides, and my feet shoulder width apart, he strapped me in so I was just as immobilized as I'd been seconds before.

Ollie stood for a moment, studying my naked form, then turned around and pulled something from the collection of torture tools.

A riding crop.

I'd seen them used a million times when my parents would take me to visit horse races. Were we going to be riding? Surely he wasn't about to draw and quarter me.

"Ollie?" I questioned nervously.

He responded, not with words, but by stepping forward, so he was less than an inch away from me. The hand not holding the crop touched the spot just below my abdomen where soft curls gathered, then trailed up my chest, his palm firm against my skin as he gently wrapped his fingers around my throat before moving to my hair. He ran his fingers through it for a moment, then grabbed it firmly, tugging my head back, exposing my neck.

And then he kissed me. Hard. Passionately.

And there was nowhere I wanted to be more in that moment. You couldn't have tempted me back to my world right now with anything.

I was so hard it was painful, and I could feel a sticky wet patch on the inside of my thigh from all of the teasing.

But I didn't have to suffer long. Ollie's tongue was a warm, welcome presence on my own until he pulled away, his hand still coiled in my hair.

He looked at me, and then, with a smile I was beginning to associate with the feeling of being rock hard, he leaned forward to whisper against my ear. "I want you to scream my name. Over. And over. And you only come when I tell you to. Understand?"

I nodded, but he pulled my hair tighter.

"Say it."

"Ollie…" I whimpered. "You've been teasing me for thirty minutes, at least." I looked him in the eyes, pleading with him. "There's no way I'm gonna—"

Another tug at my hair, and Ollie's lips on my neck, kissing the places where the collar had left little scrapes. I could feel his own erection poking me in the hip.

And then it wasn't. Because Ollie was looking me directly in the eyes as he slowly sank to his knees in front of me.

"Ollie," I begged. "Olympio…please…"

I was alternating between pathetic whimpers and deep groans. There was something totally different about watching the ruler of an entire kingdom—an entire *world*—go to his knees…

For me.

My orgasm was fighting against every mechanism I was using to stifle it, but this was almost too much.

He put a hand on my thigh and slowly moved it to the place where my leg ended, stopping less than an inch from the base of my cock.

"Louder."

And then he was not only gripping my shaft, but he had opened his mouth and taken my tip between his lips, sucking gently as he began to pump my base.

"No…" I groaned, mostly to myself. "Oh, god, Ollie…"

I looked down to see a glimmer of something shiny drip down his chin.

"Ollie…."

There was a shock of cold air against wetness as his mouth had suddenly withdrawn. I didn't know why at first, but then I heard the

229

quiet whistle and the loud crack of the riding crop coming down hard on my thigh.

"I said… louder."

And without warning, he'd taken me so deep into his mouth that his lips pressed against my body.

And that was all it took for me to lose the battle I was fighting with myself. Like a monsoon at the end of a hot summer, my climax came in waves of pleasure. It was like nothing I'd ever felt before, and I couldn't stop my lungs from closing off and my eyes rolling in my head.

As if it wasn't enough for me to have the most intense orgasm of my life, I could feel that weird connection linking me to Ollie, and he was coming too, which only amplified the pleasure over and over.

It was like holding up a mirror to another mirror and that dizzying feeling you get when you realize the image never stops.

"I love you," I panted out.

And then the room went still, as it felt like time stopped entirely.

Had I really just said that? Did I actually feel it?

Ollie rose to his feet, his face flushed. His eyes bored into mine, and his hands rose to cup my cheeks.

The look on his face was like he'd just seen color for the first time. The tiniest smile curled the corners of his lips as he leaned in and gave me a gentle, lingering kiss before pulling back away and pressing his forehead to mine.

"And I love you."

I wasn't ready to decide whether the declaration was true or just orgasm nonsense. I was exhausted and covered in both our fluids.

Ollie released me from my shackles and dressed me in a simple wrap before pulling me onto his back and prying open the door to the room.

The guards looked at us and nodded to him, the horror on their faces clear, though what they were horrified about was *un*clear.

"You may report to the Council the ritual was completed and the future Justice performed admirably," he said, and one of the guards, who wore a slightly different uniform than the other two, turned and marched away. Then he looked at me over his shoulder. "Do you want to go to your own room? Or... would you like to come to mine?"

"Yours," I yawned, half asleep already. "Guess it's about time I see where I'll be sleeping after the—" Another yawn escaped me. "Consummation."

I could feel a ripple of joy at that, and even though I knew it was from him, I let it wash over me and through me, lulling me into a post-orgasm stupor as he carried me to the one place he had wanted me the most.

Chapter Twenty-Four
Olympia

The weight of Gabriel on my back, the feeling of his face resting on my shoulder, was as intimate or more than what we'd just done down in the torture chamber.

I carried him the entire way back to my room. I took him to the bed, where I set him down, gently waking him as I did.

"Gabriel," I said. "We're here."

He stirred, grumbling something about ten more minutes, grabbing my blankets and pulling them to his face. "Ollie…" he sighed as he breathed deeply into them.

Then he pulled them around himself and over his head, as if he was a teenager refusing to go to school.

I laughed. I'd watched him do this hundreds of times, but never before had I been able to reach out and pull the blankets away from his face to see the precious expression he wore in his sleepiness.

"You are wonderful," I said, crawling into the bed beside him and opening my arms, hoping he would move between them.

To my happiness, he didn't need to be told before he did just that, burying his face in my chest.

I could vaguely remember what it felt like to expend yourself sexually to that intensity—where you can barely keep your eyes open or care to do so.

But for Gabriel, this was a first.

A first of many, if I was lucky.

It wasn't long before his gentle snores rumbled my chest. My arms tightened around him, the bond practically singing with the intensity of our connection at that moment. Tears formed in my eyes and dripped down toward my pillow. I had never in my life felt happiness this great. Sadness, yes. Loss, anger, pain. But, just then, I realized I had never known *happiness* until Gabriel was against me, trusting me so fully, he would sleep in my arms.

I brushed his hair back from his face, wanting to see him. He'd been through so much in such a short lifetime. I had done what I could to protect him, but he'd had to face much of it on his own. His beautiful blue eyes were haunted, even in his happiest moments.

But just now, his face was completely relaxed, free of the troubles he'd gathered like shells by the shore throughout his life. It usually didn't matter if he was asleep. Nightmares would haunt him every night, furrowing his brow and turning down the corners of his mouth. But not tonight. Tonight, he was at peace.

And there was no greater gift I'd ever received than being part of that.

Chapter Twenty-Five
Gabe

I was dreaming.

I was warm, and all around me was a blanket of peace and protection—one that smelled like an expensive cologne and something else I couldn't have named if I tried.

Something that smelled like mine.

Like home.

I slowly opened my eyes to find my face pressed into a warm wall of skin that I quickly realized was Ollie. I tried not to move too much, hoping maybe I'd have time to decide what to do here before he realized I was awake.

"The bond tells me when you're awake," he said, his voice rustling the hair on my head. He leaned back just a bit so he could look at me. He was smiling—a bright, vibrant smile I hadn't seen before, with just a hint of laughter sparkling in his eyes. Or was that the purple swirls in his yellow irises? "Good morning."

"Damn," I said, a smile spreading across my lips without me intending to do it. "This relationship really is starting rough if I can't even get a white lie past you."

It hit me that I'd just referred to what Ollie and I had as a relationship, and it left an odd, hollow feeling in my stomach. Sort of like I was betraying my home world.

"What just happened?" he asked, putting a finger under my chin to tilt my face up to look at his. "You were happy, and then... something changed. What was it?"

"N-nothing," I stammered. "Just half asleep still." I made a big show of yawning before falling back onto the pillows. "This bed is *huge*."

Ollie's brow furrowed just a tiny bit, but he seemed to be willing to let it go for now. His face relaxed into another smile, though it was slightly less easy than before.

"Yes," he said, running his hands over the blankets. "I suppose it would seem that way, considering the size of the beds you have back in your world. It's like they actively want to discourage you from sharing the bed with even one person, let alone several."

I felt my ears heat. "Yeah... weird... Hey, why did saying Alex's name wind you up so bad back there?"

Any trace of happiness vanished from Ollie's face, and his jaw and eyes were suddenly hard.

"I hate that little pissant," he said.

It seemed like a rather brief answer for someone who'd spent so much time trying to keep us apart. "That's it?"

"Hating him isn't enough?"

235

"I mean… he isn't all *that* bad."

Ollie's eyes, which had always been either yellow or some combination of yellow and purple, suddenly looked like they were made of shadows, like that weird thing he could do where he moved really fast. It was… kind of scary.

"Alex Kessinger isn't just bad," he said, and I could *feel* the fury radiating off of him. "He is the worst kind of human—the worst kind of any being. He is selfish and careless, to the detriment and danger of others. He is arrogant but substandard, especially to someone like you. He takes advantage of people he sees as vulnerable because he knows he has nothing going for him, but if he can make himself feel stronger by making others seem weaker, then he can pretend he has some kind of worth. He is dishonest, underhanded, and has absolutely no sense of morality or humanity. He is attracted to men but hides it because he sees it as something shameful, and then uses other people's homosexual tendencies as fodder for belittling them. He has not a shred of decency, and he never once deserved you. I'm not even sure *I* do, but as your soulmate, I will strive every day to try to be worthy of someone as inherently good as you. Alex Fucking Kessinger would never, ever make that effort because he has already fooled himself into believing he's just fine the way he is, when he's about as far from fine as a person can be."

By the time he was done, he was breathing heavy, like he'd just done an intense workout, and I could feel the rage that was so much stronger than what he was showing outwardly, so much that I felt nauseous from it.

I'm not sure what made me do it, but I reached up and touched Ollie's face, and suddenly felt the "bond" grow still—almost peaceful. "Let's not talk about Alex anymore, okay?"

He closed his eyes and leaned into my touch for a moment before opening them, the fury gone. "I would very much like that."

We stayed that way for a moment, but something like self-consciousness crashed over me, and I suddenly pulled back, running my hands through my hair. "So," I started, plastering a cocky grin on my face. "Did I pass your torture test?"

Ollie let out an embarrassed sort of laugh and rolled onto his back, putting his hands behind his head. "With flying colors, I'd say. Though, even with you enjoying it as much as you did, I think I still would have preferred you not had to endure that."

I felt heat whip over me like the time we'd vacationed in Arizona. Like stepping out the front door and into an oven. That intensity of warmth filled my face as my stomach flipped with embarrassment. "I didn't... I mean, I... Okay, I loved it. Fuck you, dude," I said, laughing. "Should I not have?"

Ollie's cheeky smile told me everything I needed to know, which was good because, before he could say anything, the doors to my room opened and Vassenia walked in, her eyes finding us immediately.

I pulled the blanket up instinctively, even though I was still mostly covered. You'd think by that point I would have gotten used to people seeing me naked, but I guess good old American shame didn't vanish that easily.

Ollie, on the other hand, simply stretched his chest without moving his hands from the back of his head. "Good morning, Vass." He raised an eyebrow at her, and I was surprised to feel something… hard through the bond. They had been best friends—with benefits—for longer than the name Hoffstet even existed, and their faces were calm and pleasant, but I could feel the rumblings of something I couldn't see seething below the surface.

"Your Highness," she said in an easy tone with a slight bow. "I wasn't expecting *both* of you to be here." Every word was gentle, but somehow I could still sense something wasn't quite right here.

"And yet, here we are," Ollie said, throwing back the blanket and standing up, his entire form on full display. "Did you need something?"

Her eyes gave the tiniest flick downward, then over to me, and I couldn't help but remember what I'd learned yesterday about their… relationship before I came along. "I came to fetch you for the celebration," she said, her smile to me so saccharine sweet that I was starting to question whether she actually liked me or not.

"Celebration?" I asked, looking at Ollie. He hadn't mentioned anything, but then again, I'd been surprised by plenty of events so far.

Ollie just shrugged, however, and looked at Vassenia. "Care to explain?"

She walked over and sat down on the edge of the bed as if it were her own, her hand resting on my leg through the blanket. Something like a warning flared up inside of me, and I realized it was from Ollie. We'd had such a nice conversation the day before. Had I missed something happening between then and now?

"It's for you two, of course," she said, squeezing my thigh. "Well, for Gabriel, really. For surviving his… training."

Surviving? I looked to Ollie, whose face was still plastered with an easy smile.

"Funny, Vassenia," he said. "Thankfully, Gabriel is much stronger than you'd expect for a human. I daresay his fortitude would rival yours."

She giggled, and despite the warmth of the sound, I felt a chill in my spine.

"Wouldn't that be a fun challenge?" she said, directing her grin at me. I tried to return it, but I could feel it faltering. "Anyway… Uncle Typhir wanted to show his support by throwing a feast for breakfast. People are already arriving."

"Typhir's your uncle?" I asked, thinking back to the dickhead who made my first day as Justice miserable, and who had been so heartless during the disaster of a Consummation. So far Vassenia had seemed nice, but the tension I was feeling from Ollie and the new knowledge that Typhir was her uncle had me questioning my judgment about her.

"Of course!" she said, like it was the most obvious thing in the world. "He's been helping *Olympio* be a better ruler ever since he became the future king."

For the first time, Ollie's smile faltered. "That's a matter for debate. Thank you, Vass. I think Gabriel and I can get ourselves ready."

"I'm sure," she said. "Do you need me to send for some *jeans* so you two can match?"

"Not for today, but I think you may be onto something," Ollie said, crossing his arms and giving me a look that made me feel like he was planning something. There was a long moment of silence where they stared at each other, and then Ollie motioned to the door. "You are dismissed."

Vassenia's smile widened as she tapped my leg—or tried to. Her hand managed to come down, instead, on my cock, making me jolt with surprise and the instinct to protect it. She didn't seem to notice, however, as she stood and walked to the door, her hips swaying in a way that made it impossible to look away.

The door had barely closed when Ollie said, "If you let your mouth hang open like that for much longer, warnils are going to fly in."

I looked over and saw him looking at me with an expression I hadn't seen since we were back at the frat house and I was off to meet Alex. "What?" I asked, fully knowing what and hoping I could play it off as casual.

"Believe me," he said, walking around the bed to sit next to me. "Vassenia has entranced thousands, and will entrance thousands more. I'm well aware of how beautiful she is. But... let's not worry about her right now. It seems like we have a feast to get to." He looked at me with a mockingly concerned expression. "Do I need to worry about you throwing bread again?"

I giggled softly, remembering that day and realizing how irritatingly immature I had behaved. The same effect could have been achieved without acting like a toddler... I think. "I'm not gonna throw any bread." I leaned into him, searching his eyes, hoping he could tell I wanted a kiss.

And if the smile spreading across his face was any indicator, he knew exactly what I wanted.

He leaned forward, wrapping a hand around the back of my head, his fingers playing with the short hairs at the nape of my neck as he looked into my eyes for just a few seconds. Then, as though it was our first kiss all over again, he pressed his lips to mine, and it felt like my entire body lit up with fireworks, every single burst of which caused my need for him to grow until I could barely stand it.

When I finally pulled back, my head spun. "Whoa." Kissing Ollie felt like I'd never kissed anyone else before, and for the first time, I could have sworn I saw a purple glow surrounding us.

But as fast as I saw it, it was gone.

"Whoa, indeed," Ollie said, his jaw tight and his fingers, still on the back of my head, tense. It was like he was in agony, but it didn't take much to realize that pain wasn't the issue.

As Ollie leaned back, I could see the kiss had gotten him hard all over again, and I bit my lip, attempting not to stare.

"Fuck…"

The word slipped from my mouth without me meaning it to.

"I would like absolutely nothing more." He looked at me with yet another expression I remember from before we came here—the one that made me feel like I was a steak and he was starving, though now there was a smiling curl to his lips instead of a hard stare. "But if people are already arriving, I don't think I have the time to do it the way I'd like to, long, slow, intimately, and with the intention of making the first time everything it should be for you." He stood and took a few steps back, and I could feel a pull, like my heart was being tugged toward him. "So, for now, let's get ready for breakfast. I daresay we both could use a bath after last night."

"Wait." I reached for his hand and pulled him hard back onto the bed, the weight of him causing him to bounce as he hit the mattress. "I just... this is new," I said hesitantly. "I really like you... or I guess—" I nearly bit my tongue, stumbling over my words. "I love you. I don't know how to behave when I feel like that."

I stared down at him from where his head was nearly in my lap, and I'd be lying if I said that didn't make me feel certain stirring sensations as well.

"You know..." He took a deep, shaky breath. "This is the second time you've pulled me onto a bed with you. And I can honestly say having you say you love me is a much better addition than drunken punches." He chuckled, a breathy sound like it was taking all his control to remain calm. He reached up and touched my chin. "I love you, too, Gabriel."

The air around us seemed to still, and our eyes locked on to each other like they were always supposed to do so.

I leaned in, pressing a kiss to those glorious lips, sucking his tongue gently into my mouth and groaning as his hand wrapped around the back of my neck once more.

Without breaking the kiss, he shifted, so he was upright before pressing even further forward, laying me back on the bed. My blanket was still between us, the only barrier keeping our bodies from full contact. Even so, I could feel his hardness pressing against my thigh, and I reached down, needing to feel the warmth of him against my fingers.

He took a sharp breath in through his nose, then moaned against my mouth. The vibrations of the sound only spurred me on, and I began to stroke him.

"Gabriel…" he whispered, his lips still against mine. It was a warning, one that was clearly a struggle for him to offer. "You have to stop."

I pulled back, giving him an incredulous look. "You spend the better part of six months trying to make me fall for you and sleep with you, and now you're trying to stop me?"

I was teasing him, but there was definitely an element of trying to guilt trip him into spending the day here with me.

In bed.

"First of all," he said, rubbing his nose in a small circle on my cheek, then trailing his way across my jaw to kiss my neck, "I wasn't trying to get you to 'sleep with me.'" His hand gripped my chin, tilting my head to give him better access to the soft spot behind my ear. "That was obviously where I hoped it would lead, for many reasons you're well aware of." He slowly began to move his lips downward, toward my collarbone. "Second of all… I'm not trying to stop you. Just… delay you." He looked up at me, his eyes solid violet without a trace of yellow. "Because once I start, Gabriel, I don't know if I'll ever be able to stop."

A shiver cascaded the entirety of my skin, and I dug my nails into his back. "Then don't stop."

I arched my back, pressing my cock up against his stomach, trying to sway him in his seemingly firm decision not to have me right here, right now.

There was one small matter, though. "I've never had anything… inside me. Aside from my fingers, I mean. Do you know… I mean, like, I just don't know how to get that started."

I felt embarrassed my bravado didn't back up any real experience, but according to what seemed to be true about Ollie, he'd have some answers.

He pushed up just a bit so his weight was no longer on me and looked down into my eyes.

"When the time is right…" he said, his voice strained. "I will make sure things are not only started, but that you are well prepared and comfortable. When we cross that threshold, every step will be carried out completely before rushing you into the next." He sighed and looked down at his cock and the tented blankets over mine. "Which is why it can't be now. Because it's bad enough Typhir has to be present at the Consummation. I won't have him interrupting us in the sanctity of my own bedroom." He closed his eyes, and I could feel the effort it was taking him to pull back. But then I felt something like a release, a relaxation, and he opened his eyes again. "But since we need a bath anyway, and I know I won't be able to focus if I'm thinking about having you during the feast… we may as well have a little release to ease the tension. Don't you think?"

I nodded with desperate enthusiasm, pushing up off the bed and practically jogging to his tub. The water was a soft, milky color with flower petals floating in it and various other foliage. When I first arrived, the idea of having a bath in debris really put me off. But now, it felt like more of a luxury than an inconvenience. I sat down on the edge and watched as Ollie slid in before me, then quickly took my throbbing cock in his hand and dipped his head to pleasure me.

The slickness of his mouth around me again was as intense as the first time, and I found my hands twisting in his hair as he once again used his free hand to stroke himself beneath the perfectly warm water.

After a few seconds, however, he pulled away, and I let out a soft whine of protest, which drew a deep, throaty laugh from Ollie.

"Don't worry," he said, his hand still moving up and down my shaft. "I'm not anywhere near done with you. I would never pass up the chance to have my mouth stretched open by the most impressive cock I've ever seen."

I gaped at him. "Wait really? You're telling me you've seen dozens of *immortal* schlongs and mine is the one you consider most impressive? You're definitely full of shit."

He gave me a cocky grin, then dipped his head to run his tongue slowly up the underside of my length before pulling away again. "I've seen *thousands* of cocks," he said, correcting me. "But none of them has been immortal. Yours will be the first. And yes, it is the most impressive. Size is only part of that, though you certainly aren't lacking in that area." What the other parts that made a cock impressive were, I didn't get the chance to find out, because he took me all the way into his mouth, bobbing up and down slowly, and driving me abso-fuck-ing-lutely insane.

But right as I was nearing that edge, he stopped.

"What? Why? Again?"

He didn't answer. Instead, he stood up in the tub and moved between my legs so he could kiss me. As he did, I felt his own hardness against mine, and then he took my hand and guided it down, wrapping it around both of us as his did the same, so we were working both of our cocks in tandem.

In moments, I was spilling over us, my essence dripping copiously into the already opaque waters beneath. As I did, I leaned forward and sunk my teeth into Ollie's shoulder, feeling like it was impossible to get close enough to him, feeling like I'd never be satisfied until we were one person.

It wasn't until he released his grip that I realized it wasn't just me that had finished. He sighed against the side of my face and kissed my cheekbone before grabbing me by the waist and pulling me down into the water with him.

"Now…" he said, reaching for a cloth to wash me with. "Can you behave until after breakfast?"

"All I can promise is that I'll try." I was still panting and pressed a desperate kiss to his lips. "You are just so… damn irresistible to me. I can't even believe it, to be honest. Like a month ago, I was calling you a weirdo and dodging your calls."

He returned the kiss, then turned me around, so I was leaning against him as he reached over my shoulder to wash my chest.

"And now you understand why I was a weirdo whose calls you dodged," he said, kissing the side of my neck. "I've felt that way for a long time."

We exchanged a final kiss, then with double the speed of our intimate encounter, the prince and I scrubbed ourselves clean.

"Now the real question," Ollie began, striding to his wardrobe. "Is what will you wear to breakfast?"

I walked up behind him, peering inside and seeing it full of his typical apparel. "What about that?" I said, pointing to a gold fabric that looked heavy and was draped gracefully. "I'm supposed to wear gold or white, right?"

Ollie looked like Christmas had come a month early, and I saw as his fingers subtly curled around the edge of the wardrobe and squeezed, like he was trying to steady himself from his disbelief.

"That's right," he said, and I felt his elation through the bond as he pulled it out and held it up for me. The color was a rich gold, but without the metallic sheen. The fabric was gathered at one shoulder and hung to what looked like about knee length. It had a white belt on it, but Ollie pulled it off and grabbed a black one with gold embellishments to match the fabric. "And I think this would be perfect for you. It was one of my favorites when I was... younger."

The way he hesitated was strange, like he was going to say something else, but then changed his mind.

"Well, I figure I better start embracing the fashions now, right?"

I felt another jump of excitement through the bond from Ollie, but my stomach did an all too familiar guilty flip. The one I got every time I said something that indicated my choice had been made.

"At least until I go back," I said.

Now it felt like I'd been punched in the gut. Sadness hit me like a ton of bricks, and I noticed Ollie's fingers had frozen in their perusal of his clothes for something to wear himself.

"At least until you go back," he repeated.

We got dressed in silence after that, and now I realized I cared about the betrayal that was going to occur either way. Either to the world I knew and loved, or the man I was growing to love more every day.

Chapter Twenty-Six
Olympia

I couldn't have told you who was in attendance at breakfast other than Gabriel. He looked radiant in the silk garment, with just a hint of gold painted across his cheekbones to highlight them.

Every time I looked at him, between accepting congratulations from dignitaries and shaking hands with sycophants, he was smiling and greeting the guests with the warmth I knew him to offer everyone he met. It couldn't have been more obvious he was nearly as loved by the court as he was by me.

And it broke my heart, knowing he still couldn't see himself having a place here.

As we walked back to his chambers after the celebration was over, I wrapped my arm around his waist, needing to feel him there, as though a part of me was worried he'd vanish back to his world at any moment.

"You know…" I said, breaching the silence we'd been walking in. "I've spent the better part of fifteen hundred years trying to win over the Council. Some of them have been alive that long, while others have come and gone, but I've never had any of them warm to me the way Orella did to you today."

Gabriel giggled. "Well, I've always had a way with the ladies. It's my soft boy vibes." He did some odd gesture that looked like he was making guns with his fingers, and I couldn't help but laugh. Gabriel was joy incarnate; he was everything good and pure in the world—in any world.

"It's incredible." I pressed a soft kiss to the side of his head as we approached his doors. I opened them, allowing him to step inside first.

"Gabe," a voice said from the plush chairs near his fire. I glanced over to see Tomos rushing forward, a piece of parchment in his hand. "It's good you're back, just in time!" He looked down, his eyes scanning the page. "Your training for the day—"

"Will be canceled," I said in a gentle but clear voice, turning to Gabriel to smile at him.

Gabriel raised an eyebrow at me in question. "Yeah?"

I nodded once. I hadn't even planned for it. This was entirely a whim. If he was truly thinking he still wanted to leave Sefaera, he may as well see all of it before he did.

"Tomos, can you please go fetch two extra guards? Gabriel and I will be leaving the palace today, and after the attempt on my life recently, I don't want to take any chances."

Tomos looked confused but did as he was told. I heard him speaking to the guards just outside the room, and I stepped closer to Gabriel, wrapping an arm around his waist to pull him against me. I placed my hand on the side of his face and ran my thumb over his cheek.

250

"I want to show you my kingdom. Well, part of it. The city outside is just a small part of Sefaera, but you've been here for nearly a month, and I've been keeping you cooped up here. Except when you're with Ari, of course, but even then, you haven't really been exposed to the people you'll be presiding over." My stomach gave a small lurch as I said it, hoping he could still be convinced to take his place here.

Gabriel got an odd look on his face. "I never actually thought about the ruling part, making decisions for thousands of people, not just the few I've seen as Justice. I think I'd like that, thanks."

The joy I felt was so overwhelming that all I could do to express it was to pull his face to mine, to press a kiss to his lips.

"I think..." I said, releasing him and stepping back to look at him. "You'll probably be most comfortable in your own clothes. Besides, I want the people to see you as you are, not as some figurehead. What do you think?"

Gabriel seemed to consider my statement, then nodded. "I don't know that I'd be able to walk confidently around strangers while worrying my skirt was gonna fly up. It's not like you guys believe in underwear..." He gave me a challenging look.

It was true. The concept of undergarments seemed restrictive and honestly rather unsanitary. But nonetheless, Gabriel had insisted on wearing his briefs beneath the draping he'd sported at breakfast.

"Fair point." I walked over to the bed and sat down on the edge. "Well? Get changed, then."

He hesitated for a moment, then walked backwards as if he didn't want to take his eyes off me, turning only at the last second to retrieve clothing from his wardrobe. He pulled forth a bright blue t-shirt with

251

the Columbia logo on it, and what I had ascertained was his favorite pair of jeans.

He quickly got dressed, and I watched every glorious minute of it, practically pulsing from the realization that I would get to spend the rest of my life this way.

As he stood there in his casual, everyday human clothes, I couldn't help but stare. He was a vision in Sefaeran finery, but he was just as breathtaking in something as simple as a t-shirt and jeans.

I stood, walking over to him and taking his face in my hands.

"You look perfect." And then I pressed a soft, lingering kiss to his lips before taking his hand and walking with him to the door, where the guards were already gathered, waiting for us.

It took more than fifteen minutes to reach the palace gates, which were on the opposite side of the palace from the exit Gabriel was used to leaving through when he would go out with Ari. On this side, a tall stone wall and black and gold iron gates, as well as an enchantment that prevented the noise of the city from penetrating the palace, separated us from the people of Sefaera.

"Ready?" I asked, looking at Gabriel.

I could feel through the bond that he was nervous, and his eyes kept darting around like he wasn't sure. "This is, like, a whole other world. A real one."

I wanted to make a joke to ease the tension, but instead, I brought his hand to my lips and kissed the back of it.

"Yes," I said. "But so was Columbia at one point. You've always been able to adapt to any situation thrown at you, and I know you will continue to do so."

His hand squeezed mine, and he clung to it. I could have sworn my heart was moments from bursting for the happiness that came with each milestone for us.

"I'm ready," he said. "Let's go."

I nodded to the guards, who stepped apart and raised their swords toward the gates. Much like my chambers, the gates had been enchanted to only open under certain conditions. In this case, two palace guards needed to present their weapons, preventing them from being opened under duress.

The ornate gates swung open slowly, and the sounds of the city came rushing toward us.

"Whoa," Gabriel said. "It's, uh… it's loud."

I raised an eyebrow at him.

"I think you forget we both attended parties at the frat house," I said, walking forward, pulling him along with me. "I don't think my ears have been the same since."

He gave a nervous kind of giggle as he followed me through the gates and into the bustling city. Right outside the palace walls was a market with hundreds of stalls lining walkways, selling everything from produce and jewelry to pottery and toys.

Crowds parted as we walked along, with people bowing as they saw me, then whispering as they caught sight of Gabriel, who seemed torn between embarrassment at the way people were acting toward us and being enthralled by the selection of goods.

"Whoa!" he said, coming to a sudden stop. "What's that?"

I looked at the stall he was asking about. Several cages hung from the thatched roof, with even more stacked on the floor, lining every wall and surface. Inside was a veritable menagerie of domesticated Sefaeran creatures.

"It's a pet shop," I said, guiding him over to the stand.

The owner gave me a somewhat withering look as he sank into a bow. "Your Highness," he said, a slight bite to the words.

I sighed, disappointment flooding through me. I don't know why, but I think a part of me had hoped the people would have warmed to me over the last one and a half millennia. But it seemed the public still hadn't forgiven me for not being my brother.

"Look at this!" Gabriel said, pointing to a cage, blissfully unaware of the tense interaction. "What's this thing?"

The owner stood up to see what he was looking at and smiled, taking a tentative step toward Gabriel. He glanced at me, and I put out a hand to tell the guards to stay back, but to remain vigilant. Once the man knew he wouldn't be executed for approaching, he moved, so he was standing beside Gabriel.

"You've never seen a kormarrin before?" he asked, reaching to open the cage and drawing out the little creature to let Gabriel see it up close.

"Uh…" He looked at me. "Should I have?"

It was barely larger than the man's palm, with vibrant yellow-green fur, little velvety wings, and four soft paws with pads on the bottom and claws on the toes. Its little nose twitched, sniffing the air as the seller held it out to Gabriel.

"They don't have them where he comes from," I informed the man, who glanced at me with his bright red eyes.

"Right, of course," he said, looking back at Gabriel. "Well, they are highly loyal and affectionate pets, and easy to take care of. They only eat once per week, require very little hydration, and they will thrive even when left to their own devices."

"It kind of looks like a cat." Gabriel reached out to pet it, and it made a small trilling sound as it arched into his hand. "I had a cat when I was little. She got sick and my parents had to have her put down, and we never got another one. Didn't really make sense with all the traveling we did."

"Would you like to hold her?"

Gabriel looked up at the man in surprise. "Can I?"

"Of course," he replied before glancing at me, as though worried I would have something contrary to say.

Instead, I simply nodded and watched as the man handed the kormarrin to Gabriel, who cradled it in his arms. I could feel the thrum of happiness in him as he looked down at the little creature. It was the same feeling I'd had the first time I saw Gabriel as a small baby in his mother's arms. The instant, unconditional love and desire to care for and protect.

"Would you like to buy him?" I asked.

Gabriel looked at me with his mouth slightly open.

"You mean it?" He glanced down at the kormarrin. "Like… have my own pet?"

"If you want," I said, reaching out to pet its back, smiling when it trilled at me, too. If it made Gabriel happy, I'd buy him every single creature in the market.

And the fact that having a pet might be an anchor to Sefaera for him was just an added bonus.

"Yeah," he said, his grin as wide as I'd ever seen it as he held the creature close to his chest. "I do. I want her." He looked up at me, his eyes shining with tears that I could feel were based in gratitude. "Thanks, Ollie."

I kissed his head, then turned to the stall owner. "How much?"

He looked deeply uncomfortable and began wringing his hands. "His Highness certainly doesn't need to pay. You can simply demand—"

"How much?" I repeated, making it clear I had no intention of leaving the man without compensation.

He pulled a price tag off of the cage and handed it to me. With a slight chuckle, I handed it to one of the guards and said, "Pay him double."

The man looked stunned as my guard extracted a handful of dromachs and handed them over.

"His Highness is most generous," he said, curling his deep brown fingers around the gold pieces and looking back at Gabriel with a bow. "Your Grace, if I may…" He hesitated, once more glancing at me as if I was going to have him executed for simply speaking to Gabriel. "Your attire… it's very unusual."

Gabriel chuckled and nuzzled his nose into his pet's fur. "For here, it is, I guess. Back where I'm from, this is pretty normal."

"It suits you," the man said, and I wondered if he was being condescending like Vassenia had, but his expression was sincere.

He genuinely liked Gabriel.

With a glance around, I saw the rest of the market had gone still and somewhat quiet while we'd been talking. I hadn't noticed, having been so focused on Gabriel, but once I did, it was clear that, while the expressions of the people had been furtive and discontent toward me, the energy of the city had shifted. People were watching Gabriel with open curiosity, and many were smiling. Just like at breakfast, Gabriel had won over the people with a single interaction. Not by being their Justice or the future consort, but by simply being Gabriel.

With the man paid, Gabriel thanked him, and we continued our walk through the market, though now the atmosphere had changed. There was a fervent energy as stall owners called out to Gabriel, trying to get his attention.

"Your Grace! Try an oulon—the best in the kingdom!"

"These rings would look lovely on you!"

"Please, Your Grace, my bed linens are the softest you'll ever sleep on!"

Somehow, despite the overwhelming amount of people speaking to him, Gabriel was able to give each of them his attention like they were a personal friend, and every single person he spoke to left the conversation looking even more enthralled with him than before. When he'd laugh, it rang through the streets like a clear bell, and people seemed to gather even closer when they heard it.

"They love you," I said into his ear as we rounded a corner.

"Really?" he asked, looking at me. "I just thought they were being friendly."

I sighed and looked around. "They are," I said quietly. "That's how I know they adore you."

"What do you mean?"

It was now or never. I'd told him nearly everything, save for this. For the wound that still ached to this day, fifteen hundred years later.

I stopped walking and pulled him over into a quiet alley. A few faces followed us with their eyes, but the guards stood at the entrance, giving us a small measure of privacy.

"I don't know if you noticed when we first left the palace," I started, "but I'm not particularly popular with my people."

Gabriel looked confused, his brow furrowed as he stroked his kormarrin. "I guess I didn't. Why is that?"

"Because…" I let out a deep breath. "Because I wasn't always the future king, and before I was, I wasn't exactly someone the royal family was proud to be associated with."

Gabriel remained silent, waiting for me to continue, and a part of me wished he would have just accepted that as enough and let us move on. But I knew I owed him the truth—all of it.

"I wasn't the heir to the throne, not at first. My older brother, Vasileios, had that honor. I, on the other hand, had no expectations placed on me, and chose to use my power and influence to win people over, often resulting in sex. When I said earlier I've seen thousands of cocks, that's because I spent the first thousand years of my life without a single care in the world, and I treated the people who shared my bed as disposable—except for Vassenia. She was the only one I ever connected with, and even with her, it never matched what I feel with you."

"So what happened?" Gabriel asked. "How did you end up as the future king?"

My chest heaved with the breaths that came too hard. They say time heals all wounds, but it doesn't, really. It glosses them over until something rips them open again. And having to talk about what happened to my brother was the deepest wound of all.

"It was after the king died," I said. "Father fell ill, and no one could find a cure. We're immortal, but not invulnerable. We can die if someone or something makes it happen. Five hundred years after that, Vasileios found his soulmate." Gabriel opened his mouth like he had a question, but I held up a hand. If I stopped now, I may never have gotten the words out. "There was a party. Everyone was drinking and celebrating, because it would only be a few short years before she would come of age and join Vasileios on the throne."

The memory of that night was as strong as if it had only happened yesterday. Anytime I came close to forgetting, it would haunt my dreams. The flowing wine, the beautiful people Vassenia and I had chosen to join us for the night. A quiet moment alone with my brother, where he told me about having a soulmate, about what it felt like. And then more wine. And more.

When I woke the next day, I was brought a letter from Vasileios. He'd slept with Lyria, his own advisor, like Vassenia was mine. The reason I had pushed her away so strongly. I couldn't make the same mistake.

"He broke his bond," I said. "Once your soulmate is born, you cannot share your body with anyone else. If you do, the bond will break. I've told you what happens if a bonded pair doesn't take the throne. Out of shame and a hope that fate would be kind and grant me a soulmate of my own, even though I hadn't been born to rule, he took his own life."

"He… he's dead?"

Gabriel was clearly stunned, and I suddenly saw his eyes go vacant, a faint sweat developing on his brow. He was thinking about his own dead family, his own heartache that would never heal.

"Yes," I said, for once not trying to temper his pain. It was in equal measure to my own, and, in that moment, we were sharing that experience, that grief. "And since then, there was never a guarantee I would ever even have a soulmate. No one knew if becoming the heir after a soulmate had already been born for my predecessor would grant me that honor." I put my hands on either side of his neck, wrapping my fingers around the back to stroke his hair, and leaned my forehead to his. "I did my best to follow in my brother's footsteps, but my reputation preceded me, and I did little to change that perception. I would perform royal duties during the day and continue to spend my nights drowning in wine and beautiful people, numbing out the feelings of inadequacy and emptiness from knowing I would never be able to measure up to my brother—not in the eyes of the people nor in my own."

I took a long, slow breath, trying to keep myself composed. I didn't need to give the people peering at us from the alley's entrance one more reason to whisper about their weak future king.

"I acted, never knowing if you would even exist," I said quietly, returning my attention to Gabriel. "I never understood what it would feel like to have you in my life. I did my best to honor my brother's wishes, but I was selfish and petty and convinced all I had was all I'd ever have, and, someday, someone would realize I would never be king and take it away." I tilted my head up, kissing his forehead. "But now you're here, and now I have the chance to be the king my brother should have been, to show the people their ruler cares about this world. And... and I don't just want it because it means being king. I want to be someone you would be proud to rule alongside. You make me want to be a better ruler and a better man, someone who would be worthy of being yours. And I am, Gabriel. I'm yours."

I lingered there for a moment longer, then took a step back to look at him.

Gabriel had moisture clinging to his lashes, and I'd watched him long enough to know he was trying not to cry.

"That's really sad," he said with a sniffle, running a hand through his hair and then shoving it in his pocket.

His kormarrin trilled and rubbed its furry face against him, perching on his shoulder. He reached up with his free hand and patted it.

"Depends on how you look at it," I said, reaching up to pet the creature as well. "Parts of it are sad, yes. Parts of it left scars that will never fully heal. But..." I smiled at him. "I prefer to look at the hope of it all. You have given me reasons to change things, hopefully for the better. And if the people's immediate love of you is any indicator, your influence on me and on the way things are done can only make Sefaera better." I paused for a moment, just to truly look at him, to admire how beautiful and amazing he was. "I love you, Gabriel. Not only because you're my soulmate, but because of who you are, and who you make me want to be."

Gabriel shifted uncomfortably. He was still a little unsure of how to handle declarations of affection.

"I love you, too," he mumbled, his eyes darting to the guards. "Do they always have to be here?"

I glanced over at them and gave them a tilt of my head, indicating they should turn around and head back to the entrance of the alley and remain facing away. It wasn't the privacy I would have looked to offer him, but it would have to do for now.

Taking his face in my hands, I pulled him toward me to kiss him, pulling his lower lip between mine and letting my tongue roll over the smooth skin. I heard the slight whimper he let out as he leaned into me, and it took every ounce of willpower to pull away.

I looked down at my Gabriel, his kormarrin still perched on his shoulder, and smiled.

"I will always do my best to give us the privacy we deserve," I said. "But I once promised you, even if you never knew I did, I would always put your safety first and happiness second. Which means, because of how precious you are to me and to Sefaera, there will be guards close by at all times. But for now…" I took his hand in mine once more and nodded back toward the street. "Would you be willing to accompany the pariah prince on a walk through the city?"

He nodded, and I led him back out into the market, where his presence was once more met with enthusiasm and delight. And as we made our way through the rest of the city, I knew that to be here with him made me the luckiest man in the kingdom.

Chapter Twenty-Seven
Gabe

By the time we returned to the palace, my feet ached, and I was ready for a long nap. But as Ollie would have it, that wasn't in the cards.

He guided me back to his room, but before we went inside, he turned to me and said, "This room..." He sighed and looked up at the massive doors. "This room is enchanted to only open for the monarch of Sefaera. This panel—" he pointed to a flat surface on the otherwise ornate door "—will respond to my hand like a key. And just like with a key... I can give access to anyone I choose."

I must have looked confused, because he put an arm around my shoulders and turned me to face the door.

"Right now, it opens for me, of course. But it also opens for Ari, for my mother, and for Vass."

I grimaced at the name. After this morning, I wasn't sure what to think about her or the relationship she and Ollie had for so long. But he simply leaned his forehead against the side of my head.

"And now I want it to open for you, too," he whispered.

I turned to look at him.

"How?" I asked, wondering if there was going to have to be some kind of ritual like there seemed to be for everything here.

Ollie winked at me and pressed his hand to the panel, and I watched the gold begin to glow around his hand like it had been melted. He pulled away, and I could still see the outline of his handprint as he reached for my wrist and held my own hand up to the door.

"Touch it," he said, and if it wasn't for the soft, easy smile he was giving me, I would have been terrified of what was about to happen.

But I did as I was told and pressed my palm against the gold panel, and I was surprised to find it wasn't cold, but it wasn't hot like it looked like it would be after Ollie touched it, either. It was warm in a pleasant way, like bathwater without the wetness. Then, I felt a tingle spreading from my palm and fingertips up my arm—not an unpleasant feeling, just a weird one—that reached my heart and suddenly receded back into my hand before vanishing completely.

"There," Ollie said, grabbing my hand to lower it before pressing against the door, which swung open easily. "Now this room is open to you whenever you'd like."

We walked inside, and I looked around. I'd been so exhausted when we came in here the night before, I hadn't really paid much attention.

If my room was like someone made cotton candy an aesthetic choice, this one was like "being king" was the entire vibe. The floor was black and gold marble, while the walls were white and gold. The bed looked like it was made out of solid, brushed gold, giving it a matte finish, and black curtains hung around the frame. While my tub was made out of what looked like rose quartz, his looked like it was carved obsidian, like the sickle he carried with him everywhere, and gossamer gold curtains covered massive windows.

"I have another surprise for you," he said, interrupting my gawking and sitting me on the edge of the bed, then standing before me, my face in his hands. "And, unfortunately, we don't have that much time before we'll need to be ready for it. But I have been resisting you all day and can't for another second."

Before I knew what was happening, Ollie had tossed me onto the bed and was gnawing on my neck like a dog with a bone. "Ollie," I laughed, though I was hard in an instant.

"Gabriel," he replied, his voice barely more than a growl as his hands went everywhere, holding the back of my head to deepen our kiss, pulling my hips up to meet his so I could feel he was just as aroused as me.

One thing I had always liked about fooling around with boys was the fact that it felt more like an erotic wrestling match than an intimate event. Ollie was doing exactly that, and I wanted him to.

I'm not sure what exactly came over me, but I leaned up into his ear and whispered, "I'm so hard for you right now, Your Highness."

Ollie moaned loudly and ground his hips harder against mine. "Tell me what you want," he commanded in a low, throaty rumble.

"I want you to fuck me," I whined. But that seemed to be wrong, because he pulled back. "What? You didn't like that?"

Ollie gave a quiet laugh. "Oh, I liked that very much, Gabriel." He shook his head, his eyes still devouring me. "Every single fiber of my being wants nothing more than to give you exactly that. But I've told you, this is the first time I've cared about the connection between us more than the end goal of fucking someone. And since you've never actually had anyone inside of you, I want to build you up to that slowly, without rushing things. I want your first time—*our* first time—to be a positive experience." Suddenly, he smiled wickedly. "But that doesn't mean we can't start preparing you now."

The words hit my ears, and I realized what he was going to do a split second before he did it. He grabbed me behind the knees and flipped me over so I was face down on the bed. Slowly, he crawled on top of me, his hands snaking beneath me to fumble with my jeans. The motions of his touch had my cock throbbing as he pulled my pants and underwear completely off, leaving me in only my t-shirt.

"You have to promise me," he said as he walked away. I started to sit up to see where he was going, but he gave me a look that clearly said to stay put, and I did. "That you will be open, communicative, and honest about what you're feeling. If anything hurts or even feels slightly wrong, you will say so immediately." I heard him open a drawer, rustle around inside, and then close it before moving around behind me again. "Gabriel. Promise me."

It worried me slightly that there was a precursor to whatever he was intending, but I agreed anyway. "I promise."

"Good," he said, and I felt him move between my legs from behind. His hands ran up the backs of my thighs to grip my ass, squeezing before the warmth of his lips between his hands surprised me—though not as much as the teeth that nipped at me a second later.

"Ollie," I squeaked in shock.

"Too much?" he asked, pausing his movements.

I was panting, my fingers dug into the sheets below me. "No," I said honestly. "I was just surprised."

"Good," he said again, and his fingers began to dig into the soft skin of my backside, kneading and pulling me open. The cool air was a strange sensation in contrast to the warmth that part of me usually held onto.

The sound of a glass jar being opened startled me enough that I turned to look, finding Ollie dipping his fingers into a small container of some kind of clear, viscous liquid I guessed was lube.

I turned my head, pressing my face into the sheets again and waiting for the inevitable penetration, but it didn't come. Instead, I felt Ollie's fingers sliding over my entrance, slickening the whole area. He pressed gently on the tight little hole, but didn't breach that barrier yet. He just massaged and teased, helping me to relax against his touch as he used his other hand to stroke my rigid length where it lay between my legs.

I bit my lip, trying to stay cool about all this. This was the closest thing to trusting someone with my life I'd ever experienced, and Ollie was... something else.

This was something else.

"Fuck, that feels good." My words came in whispered sighs, filled with a euphoria I hoped I would never come down from.

"You said you've used your own fingers before," he said, moving to lay against my back, still working the lubricant all around my opening. "How often? And how many?"

I suddenly became extremely conscious of my own body, and my face heated with embarrassment. "Oh, uh... just one... just once..."

"Good to know," he said. "We'll start with just one, then, and when you feel like you want more, say so."

I nodded, thinking I would have no idea how I would know if I wanted more, but trusting that Ollie knew what he was talking about. Then, with an ease that must have come from thousands of years of experience, he pressed one finger gently forward so the very tip of it was wrapped in the tightness of my entrance.

It was an odd sensation, almost like a sleight of hand. He expedited his stroking just as he entered me, and it was like my brain couldn't figure out which sensation to focus on, blending the two together in an overwhelming wave of pleasure.

It was different than anything I'd ever experienced, and every tiny hair raised on my arms, like this was what I'd been missing.

I grabbed a handful of blanket and bit down on it.

"Too much?" he asked, his finger stilling inside of me. I could tell it wasn't very deep at all yet, and even with just that small penetration, I was writhing with ecstasy.

"No," I panted. "I'm just trying not to scream."

Ollie let out a breathy chuckle against my neck, and I nearly lost the battle for silence right then and there. But I kept my lips clenched together as I felt his finger go deeper before pulling back, then pressing forward again in slow, gentle thrusts that opened me up as he gave me more and more of him.

And then his finger curled in on a single spot inside of me, and I no longer had control of my vocal chords—or any part of me.

I felt like I was floating and falling all at once, and my breaths came exclusively in gasps. "Ollie... oh, fuck, Olympio..."

"Good boy, Gabriel," he murmured in my ear, his finger continuing to press against that magical little area that sent me into wave after wave of pleasure.

"More," I gasped, unsure what I even needed more of, but my body was calling the shots now.

Ollie shifted behind me, his finger pulling back so it was just barely inside of me anymore.

"Remember your promise," he said, pressing a kiss to the side of my neck as I felt the pressure at my opening increase.

I gasped, a throaty, guttural noise escaping me, and I swear to god my eyes rolled. This was ecstasy.

And I was so glad I hadn't given this to Alex Kessinger. In fact, I had practically forgotten he even existed, particularly at times like this, when Ollie had me so thoroughly under his spell.

"Good, Gabriel," he said as I began to whine and push back into him. "Take it slow, there is no rush."

But there was a rush. A rush I had no control over, and it was barreling toward me like a boulder in a goddamn action-adventure movie.

I buried my face into the blankets as I screamed over and over again, as wave after wave of my orgasm crashed into me.

My hips, which had been captive to Ollie's whims, began to thrust of their own accord, needing to empty myself into whatever part of him he was willing to surrender. I could feel my heartbeat in my cock, and my lips turned to deserts as I screamed Ollie's name into the sheets.

But the prince wouldn't allow me my silenced pleasure. No, he wanted everyone to know what he had.

As I was coming, he grabbed the back of my hair, wrenching my neck up from the pillow and forcing me to scream his name to the heavens, listening as it echoed off the walls.

"Good boy, Gabriel. Just like that." He released me as my screams turned into whines and began to stroke my head. "Just like that. Every time. That's how I want you to scream my name every time."

I was half-asleep in ecstasy, even as he pulled away and went to the nearby basin.

My brain went crazy with the implications of him doing so. "Everything... okay?"

Olympio held up his hands before dipping them into the basin, showing me they were perfectly clean, save for the copious lubricant. "I don't want to lubricate your hair when I run my fingers through it. But yes, everything is alright. Sometimes messes will happen, but it's nothing to be ashamed of. There's always soap."

He slid back into the bed with me and rolled me so we were facing each other.

"What about you? You never ask for anything, and I'm starting to get self-conscious after your talk about the 'thousands of cocks.'"

"You have nothing to prove to me, Gabriel," he said. "Being with you, pleasuring you, is greater than anything I've ever experienced."

I frowned, hoping he could sense this displeasure wasn't surface level. "Olympio, I want you. I want to touch you, to feel you..." I sighed in frustration. "To taste you." I folded my arms across my chest and looked away.

But his finger was there, directing my chin back toward him.

"Nothing would please me more," he said, smiling at me. "I just want to make sure you don't feel like this is transactional in any way. I know that your... previous experiences... weren't done with your pleasure in mind. But if you truly want that, not because you feel obligated in any way, then yes, please... taste me."

I felt my frown vanish as I processed his request. Then I pushed up onto my hands, sliding down the silken sheets, my eyes never leaving his.

I could smell his arousal, and I wasn't even one of these immortal fucks yet. It was sweet and sweaty, and I wanted it closer to my face.

It was a new experience giving a blowjob to a man who not only didn't wear underwear, but wore what essentially was a skirt, and his length poked right out of it, the fabric gathering around his hips. This allowed me to quickly take it into my hands and then, moments later, into my mouth.

"Fuck..." Ollie hissed, his hands immediately fisting in my hair. His grip was tight, but it wasn't aggressive the way I'd known other guys to be. "Gabriel... moons and rivers, I've needed you—this—for so damn long..."

And that was all I needed to motivate me to make this last as long as possible.

Chapter Twenty-Eight
Olympio

The touch of his hands was ecstasy.

The touch of his mouth was universe shattering.

Every warm, moist inch of his lips, his tongue, his cheeks, enveloped me, and I very nearly spilled into his mouth immediately. But after nearly twenty years of having no one, I wasn't about to let this end that fast. I wanted to savor the feeling of Gabriel, savor the agonizing pleasure that came with crossing that intimate threshold with him.

My fingers twisted in his soft hair as he began to slide up and down my length, taking me deeper than I expected.

And yet, I needed more. But I had seen the encounters Gabriel had experienced before this, and I wasn't going to repeat the behaviors I'd been so appalled with in... others.

Instead, I forced myself to loosen my grip on his hair, letting him take the reins with only small, involuntary thrusts on my part.

"Gabriel..." I moaned as his mouth stretched wide around my length, before he took me all the way into his throat, his lips meeting the small thatch of hair at my base.

And that was all it took.

Once again, I climaxed embarrassingly quickly, pulsing out my orgasm into his mouth. He closed his eyes and swallowed every drop like it was the sweetest thing he'd ever tasted. When he finally pulled away, I watched as a single drip escaped his mouth, sliding down his chin and onto his shirt.

"Come here," I said, reaching for him and pulling him toward me. He moved forward, so he was sitting astride my legs as I sat up and wrapped a hand around the back of his neck to bring him close. But instead of kissing him immediately, I dipped my head to the wet spot on his shirt and licked it away.

"Ew." Gabriel laughed, still panting from the effort. "That's disgusting."

"More disgusting than walking around a party with it on there?" I asked, giving him a playfully challenging look. "Besides, I've kissed you after you've finished in my mouth. What's so different about this?"

He paused to think. "I guess you're right." He leaned in and pressed his lips to mine, snaking his tongue into my mouth and biting my bottom lip. "Why was I resisting you for so long?"

"I'll never know," I said, running my hands through his hair. "I know the bond feels different for us, and on my end, there was never a chance of me resisting you. Then again," I said with a small laugh, "you were absolutely perfect, and I was an overbearing... what was the word you used? Weirdo. An overbearing weirdo who thought the bond would be enough to make you want me without taking into account that my own behavior might be a factor."

Gabriel threw back his head and laughed. My favorite sound in the world—in *any* world.

Well, my second favorite sound now.

"*I love you*" had taken first place.

Gabriel flopped back onto the bed and pulled up the blankets like he was contemplating a nap.

"I wouldn't get too comfortable there," I said. "We have somewhere to be fairly soon."

Now that we'd gotten things out of our system, I could think straight again, and my excitement for the event I'd surreptitiously enlisted Ari's help in putting on while Gabriel and I were out was thrumming in my chest.

Gabriel whined and pulled the blankets over his head. "But I'm tired. It's not every day you explore a whole new world *and* have mind blowing sex."

As if to corroborate his complaint, his kormarrin, who still remained nameless, jumped up on the bed and bristled her wings at him. He opened the blanket just long enough to let the little creature inside before pulling it tight over him once more.

"Gabriel…" I said sternly, trying not to laugh at how incredibly adorable he was being.

The covers were suddenly thrust back and Gabriel emerged, kormarrin in arms, sliding out of the bed in the odd, wet noodle type of way he liked to do. "Okay, okay…" he said.

I couldn't help myself. I walked over to him and pulled him into a deep kiss.

"What was that for?" he asked breathlessly when I released him.

"For showing me something worth, not just surviving, but actually *living for* after two and a half thousand years."

274

Gabriel blushed and smiled, and it was all I could do to not throw him back into the bed.

But I didn't. Instead, I turned to my wardrobe and grabbed the handles to pull it open. I knew I had the right garments for the event in there, but I had been hoping to surprise Gabriel when we arrived. If I got dressed now, the surprise would be ruined.

Going back to the nightstand drawer I'd pulled the lubricant out of before, I extracted a silk blindfold and held it up in front of him.

"I thought we had somewhere to be," he said with a giggle.

I looked at the blindfold with a grin, then back at Gabriel.

"We do," I said. "And given your reaction, when we get back here later, I think I'll make use of this again. But for now, this is so the surprise isn't spoiled before you get there."

He looked down at himself, wearing only a shirt that still bore the remnants of our encounter and nothing else.

"Is this what I'm going to be wearing, or do I need to borrow another toga?"

I laughed and took the kormarrin from his hands, setting her on the bed, and pulling his shirt off over his head. I stepped back to take one more look at him, marveling at the perfection before me, then turned to the wardrobe and pulled it open. I didn't take my own clothes out yet, but I pulled out a folded outfit that had been placed in here for Gabriel.

"I had some of your clothes brought to my room for you," I said, holding up the very outfit he'd worn when I brought him here, the one I'd given back to him to help him feel more at home.

"You're gonna let me wear that in front of people? Wait—" Gabriel froze, his eyes simultaneously filling with fear and joy. "Are you sending me home?"

I could feel the conflict inside of him, and it threatened to tear me in two, especially hearing him call the world he came from "home."

"No," I said, trying to keep my voice even. "But... I did make you a promise. If, once you've seen everything I can possibly show you to convince you to stay, you still want to go... home... I will take you back myself."

Gabriel shifted from one foot to the other, nervously playing with the skin on his fingers. "Promise?"

I stepped forward, handing him the bundle of clothes and leaning forward to press my lips to his forehead. I'd sworn many things to him since the day he was born, but this was by far the hardest, knowing I would keep it if it came to that, and what that would mean for Sefaera.

What it would mean for me.

"I promise."

Chapter Twenty-Nine
Gabe

My senses were a total mess as Ollie led me through the halls of the palace. All I could hear were his self-pleased chuckles and the scuffing of my sneakers.

"Okay, but seriously," I protested. "Where in the world are you taking me? I mean literally—where in the world?"

The rich, deep sound of his laughter rang through the stone hall, and his hand squeezed mine.

"We're still in the palace," he said. "And we're almost there."

I was equally nervous and excited for whatever lay on the other side of this blindfolded walk, but as much as I wanted to be fully present, I still couldn't help but think about what he'd said back in his room.

"I did make you a promise. If, once you've seen everything I can possibly show you to convince you to stay, you still want to go... home... I will take you back myself."

All I had to do was hold out a few more weeks, and I'd be back in my shitty bed at Columbia again.

But—did I want that anymore?

I felt a slight pang of sadness that didn't feel like mine, and I realized it was Ollie's. I didn't know for sure, but I could guess why. Guilt was added to the list of conflicting emotions I felt as Ollie finally came to a stop and turned me so I was presumably facing him.

"I meant what I said." He gripped both of my hands in his and raised them to his lips. "I will take you back if that's what you want. But for now, I wanted to bring just a bit of your world to ours."

I didn't know what he meant by that, but I didn't have to wonder for long. He reached up and untied the blindfold, then pulled it off me.

The late afternoon light was blinding after being in the dark for half an hour. I covered my eyes while they adjusted, and when they did, my jaw dropped.

The Ollie before me wasn't the "Prince Olympio" I'd gotten to know since coming here. The person before me was just… Ollie, in a black button down with the sleeves rolled up, matching black jeans, and some sleek leather boots—the outfit *he'd* been wearing the night he brought me here.

I felt tears well in my eyes and a million memories with *this* Ollie raced through me. The first time we'd met, the funeral where he'd given me the letter he fabricated, the night he'd come to my dorm and watched a movie with me.

I still don't think to this day he knows I know what he was doing behind me.

"Ol…"

I couldn't even finish the phrase. I was too choked with emotions.

I stumbled forward, wrapping my arms around his neck, burying my face against his skin in the special place that smelled like mine and kissed it.

His arms tightened around me, holding me close, like he was afraid to let me go. He rubbed his nose in a small circle on my cheek, then drew it back toward my neck, kissing me just below my ear. He'd taken to doing that often, and it was almost like a little ritual of our own—an "I love you" without the words.

The tears that had been collecting in my eyes leaked onto his shirt, and I pulled back.

"Ugh, sorry," I sniffed, wiping my eyes with the back of my hand. "I'm such a little bitch baby."

"There's no need to apologize," he said, reaching up to run his thumb across my cheek, catching a tear I'd missed. "But there will be if we keep everyone waiting any longer."

I leaned in and clung to his neck once more. "I love you."

"And I love you," he said quietly into my ear. "Come on. I think Ari is particularly excited to see you."

I snaked my hand into his, squeezing it for comfort.

Maybe I was born for Ollie...

But he was born for me, too.

With one last smile at me, he reached out a hand and pulled back the curtain separating us from whatever was inside.

Immediately, I saw Ari's coppery head bobbing up the stairs in front of me, and it felt like I was in some kind of weird dream as she approached, her signature smirk firmly in place as she struck a pose.

"Well?" she asked. "How did we do?"

Usually in some kind of leather hunting gear or a female version of the type of clothes Ollie wore here, Ari was now dressed in a hot pink sequined and mesh tunic over a pair of black leggings with some kind of high-heeled shoe.

"I…" I started, but I couldn't find the words.

Liro came up beside her, dressed in a white polo and khakis.

As I looked around the room, I realized every single person was in clothes from my own world. Some were slightly out of fashion, but they were all from at least the last twenty years. I saw everything from t-shirts to sweaters, bodycon dresses to cargo shorts.

"Well?" Ari said, grabbing my hands and looking around the room as well.

I was speechless. "I…" I looked up at Ollie, who was beaming. "It's like being back at the frat house," I laughed.

"But without the smell of weak beer and stale piss." His eyes sparkled with joy, and I wanted to throw my arms around him again, but Ari had my hands firmly in her grip, and she dragged me down the stairs.

"I hope we got the details right," she said, bringing me over to a table where there was a display of some of the most basic, fast food types of American food. Hamburgers, chicken nuggets, french fries… "We had to make do with ingredients we had here, since we don't have the same kind of game your world does, but our chefs are geniuses, and it tastes pretty good."

I liked the food here in Sefaera, but there was nothing like a goddamn french fry.

"This is amazing, you guys. Thank you." My smile was so big and unwavering that every word I spoke was tinged with laughter.

I hugged Ari and kissed her temple. She felt as much like my sister as anyone ever could, and I had a warm feeling thrumming gently in my chest. Something I hadn't felt in a while. Something that barely had a name.

Family.

"Alright, alright," she said, laughing as she pulled away and popped a nugget into her mouth, but the look in her eyes made it clear she felt the same. "Enough with the touchy-feely stuff. I barely want Liro touching me most of the time, and you and Olympio seem to be on a crusade of hugs lately. Enjoy the party. I'll be around."

With a wink, she all but vanished as she stepped away from me and into the crowd of people who seemed to want my opinion on the clothes they'd picked out.

One by one I gave them a ranking on the outfit they'd chosen, never dipping below an eight, of course. The effort alone practically made each one a ten out of ten.

I couldn't believe how easy it was to socialize with these people from a whole other life than mine, all appearing around my age, but it was only a guess. It was incredible to see the diverse ways people appeared, with no two even looking related, let alone the same.

None but the royals, that is.

"Having fun?"

Ollie's voice tickled my ear as he came up behind me. I turned to look at him, and he was as happy as I'd ever seen him.

I nodded, swells of emotion almost making me lose my cool and start bawling.

Because I knew what this was.

This was Ollie's Hail Mary. Ollie was realizing he was running out of time to convince me to stay.

And I realized it, too, my decision none the closer to being made.

I felt some panic rise in my chest as I allowed the thought that had been prodding me for weeks to cross my mind. The idea that if I loved Ollie, if I stayed, that meant I would likely never see the human world again.

No more cell phones or XBoxes. No more superhero movies, or airplane rides to huge celebrity parties. No more corner stores, no more Columbia.

No more visiting my parents' graves.

And it terrified me how close I was to still choosing that.

"Gabriel," he said, his hand firm on my waist. I felt a slight wave of calm hit me, and I realized this was that thing he did where he tried to help my panic attack. "Why don't we step out to the balcony for a minute?"

The offer came too late. I sank to my knees, struggling to catch my breath. Ari noticed me go down and took a few steps toward me, but Ollie held up a hand before bending to scoop me into his arms, where I buried my face in his chest.

He placed a gentle kiss on my forehead, the calming sensation like Xanax against my troubled mind, and rushed me out toward the fresh air in a way that was hurried but appeared casual. He didn't want to draw unnecessary attention.

We were nearly at the doors when suddenly Ollie came to a complete stop, jolting me a bit.

"Olympio! I've been looking all over the party for you."

Vassenia.

I turned my head to look at her, and I don't know why, but I was surprised to see she had come dressed in a clearly Sefaeran gown rather than the "human" clothes like everyone else. She was flanked by two burly looking guys with similar features—brothers, maybe.

"Not a good time, Vass," Ollie said in a clipped tone, taking a step to the side to move around her, but she moved, too, blocking our path.

"Then when is a good time?" she asked, her face and voice pleasant, but I could feel the rumble of anger from Ollie. "Because it seems like you can't be bothered to meet with your advisor lately."

"A good time would be when my soulmate isn't suffering," he said, his voice low and dangerous.

"It's a party," she said. "What does *he* have to suffer about?"

"Maybe it's to do with the fact that *his* soulmate's best friend couldn't even be bothered to come to his party in the requested attire," he snapped, trying once more to walk around her.

"I didn't think you were serious," she said with a laugh. "Surely you can't blame me for thinking it was a joke. I mean… look at yourself."

"Vassenia," he said, his voice rising. It might have been my imagination, but I thought it felt like he was rising up even higher than his already towering height, and maybe it was my panic, but I swear I saw horns form on his head from that shadow he seemed to turn into. "You knew full well it wasn't a joke, and you chose to make a statement by wearing that, the way your uncle made his statement by refusing to

283

come at all. And since you have made your position perfectly clear on being my ally in making Gabriel feel welcome and at home here, allow me to make mine clear. I have always seen the best in you, but ever since Gabriel got here, you have shown me the worst, and it's like washing a golden statue to find it was just painted, rotting wood. I cannot remove you from court because of your lineage, but I can assure you my days of being 'advised' by you are over. Now step aside so Gabriel and I can go outside."

My fingers dug into his chest, clinging to him—to my soulmate. I didn't care what "form" he took, I couldn't remember a time I'd ever felt safer than right now.

But I could also feel his anger, burning white-hot beneath a cool exterior, and I leaned up to tuck my face into his neck, pressing my lips to the delicate skin there.

And this seemed to be Vassenia's breaking point.

"No," Vassenia said, and I looked over to see her face filled with rage as, suddenly, her gown began to shimmer and shift, becoming thick leather armor. It only took about a second before the transformation was complete. Then she raised her hand overhead to bring it down on me. I braced myself for a hit, but as her hand moved, I saw a glint of silver as a sword materialized in her hand.

She was going to kill me.

I was still in Ollie's arms, so he was helpless to stop her. He tried to step back, but she moved forward, raising her hand to strike again.

But then a dark streak struck her wrist hard, and she released the sword, which clattered across the floor. Shimmering silver liquid dripped from her hand as she grabbed onto it, crying out in pain. It took me a second to realize the liquid was her blood, and in that second, another dark streak raced toward her, stopping right against her throat as she dropped to her knees.

It was a knife made entirely of the same kind of shadows that Ollie could change into. I looked in the direction they'd come from and saw Ari with a hand extended in front of her, a slight swirling of shadows around her fingertips that began to solidify into another shadow knife. Her eyes, which were normally the same yellow as Ollie's, had gone black as she walked forward.

"I think that's quite enough of that," she said, looking at Vassenia like she wanted nothing more than to let the knife finish the job.

Ollie turned to glance at Ari with a nod of thanks before returning his attention to Vassenia. The sound of pounding feet echoed through the now silent ballroom toward us, and within seconds, we were surrounded by guards, all of whom had their weapons trained on her. Her "bodyguards" didn't seem to be too interested in backing her up anymore, because they'd disappeared into the crowd at the first sign of trouble.

"Olympio…" she said, her eyes pleading with him, but he just continued to stare at her with radiating fury.

"You have committed treason against the future Justice of Sefaera, against the crown, and against me," he said, his voice cold.

"It was an impulsive mistake—"

"One that could have ended with the death of my soulmate." He shook his head, his lip curled in disgust. "And since I cannot trust someone who would make such a dangerous, irreversible 'mistake,' I am hereby banishing you."

"You can't," she said, desperation soaking her words. She reached out as if to beg Ollie, but the knife at her throat pressed down, making it clear she wasn't to move. "You said—"

"I said I couldn't remove you from court. But that was before you committed treason. You lost every right you had within these walls the moment you raised a hand to Gabriel."

"You're just going to toss me out into the city?" Her eyes were wide with fear.

"No," Ollie said. "You are not welcome within a hundred miles of the palace. And be glad I don't send you to live out a mortal existence in another realm."

"Olympio—"

"You will not address me," he said, nodding to the guards, who took her by the arms. "Ever again. Not by name, not even by my title, because this is the last time you will ever see me. Do you understand?" She didn't speak, but tears began to roll down her face. "I hope it was worth it, Vassenia. I'd wish you well, but I honestly can't say I do."

With a nod to the guards, Ollie signaled them that it was time for them to remove her. The crowd parted to allow them through, and the last thing I saw of Vassenia was her looking over her shoulder at Ollie, her eyes still begging him to reconsider.

Chapter Thirty
Olympio

"Put out the command that not a single person in Vassenia's family is to come anywhere near this room tonight. If Typhir tries to exert his authority, remind him his power is only granted by the full might of the Council, and without them, he has no right to overrule the monarch he *serves*."

Gryfian nodded from where he stood right inside my chamber door. "Understood, Your Highness." He glanced over my shoulder to where Gabriel was lying on the chaise before the fire with a warm cup of liramin tea to help calm his nerves, his kormarrin curled up on his lap. He had been hesitant to let me light the fire after the panic attack he'd had the last time, but he was shivering from shock.

"Thank you, Gryfian," I said, putting a hand on his shoulder, a gesture he returned, the camaraderie between us never more evident. He was my guard, my subject, but he'd been by my side, protecting me and those close to me for more than half of my life. He wasn't immortal, but his line still lived longer lives than most, and he'd given nearly two thousand years of that life to my service.

"I will personally be outside the door," he said, straightening up. "Are you certain I can't convince you to allow me to station myself and another guard in the room with you?"

"I'm certain," I said, looking at Gabriel, who was simply staring into the flames, absently petting the kormarrin. "He needs some space to cope with what just happened."

Gryfian nodded and turned, walking through the door and closing it behind him.

I stood there a moment longer, staring at the door, before turning back to Gabriel. He had been so close to feeling like he belonged here, and in one fell swoop, Vassenia had given him every reason to want to leave and never come back.

Steeling myself for what I knew I needed to say, I walked over to the chaise and knelt down by my soulmate's side. The purple shimmer that always swirled between us was nearly solid with the depth of our connection. I didn't doubt what was between us, but I knew loving each other was only one part of the equation. He needed to be as committed to Sefaera as he was to me, or the Consummation would never work.

And after tonight, I was certain it never would.

"Gabriel," I said quietly, reaching up to brush a lock of hair off his forehead as he looked at me. "I'm so sorry."

Gabriel nodded, not saying anything but breathing so shallowly his shoulders didn't even move. Like he was afraid if he breathed too hard, Vassenia might come back to finish the job.

"I should have seen that darkness in her sooner," I said, stroking his face gently. "I should have protected you better. I never thought someone I cared about that much would ever betray me like that. But you are far too precious to me for me to want to keep you here against your will any longer, not when there are dangers I never anticipated. Which is why…" With a deep, shaking breath, I continued. "Which is why I will take you home first thing in the morning. I would rather lose you and have you be safe and happy than force you into a life you never asked for, one that will never truly be yours. And I won't put you in danger for another second."

"No—" Gabriel said suddenly. "I don't want to… I…" He looked to the floor and swallowed hard, and I could hear my heart pumping my golden blood through every inch of my body. "I want to stay. I've never felt as safe and like I belonged as with you. I choose you, Olympio."

I replayed what he said in my head no less than three times before the words took hold. He wanted to stay. With me. He was choosing me, this life, *our* life, *our* kingdom. He was giving up everything he ever knew to stay with me, to be mine.

Forever.

I took his face in my hands and pressed a desperate, grateful kiss to his lips. The rush of joy had my blood pumping fervently, the bond demanding the connection be Consummated.

Gabriel kissed me back, gripping at my shirt like he was afraid I was going to leave. His kisses were desperate and wild, his hot breath panting against my lips.

And in a matter of seconds, he was in my arms, having practically leapt off the chaise, clinging to me with his legs.

I could feel the bond coalesce and throb in tandem with our kisses, like it had finally reached full capacity, and we were truly as connected as it was possible to be. The sheer feeling of it, of the connection, was better than any orgasm.

I stood up and carried him to the bed, where I laid him down and continued my exploration of his mouth with mine, letting my hands feel every inch of him, every single inch that was *mine*.

We could Consummate the bond right here. The ceremony was just that—an event where the Council could see the bond being solidified. But the Consummation itself was rooted in the ancient magic that protected Sefaera, in the union of my soulmate and me.

But a small voice in my head caused me to pull back. After what he'd been through, I didn't want to push Gabriel to make a decision that would bind him forever when he was still possibly in shock.

"Olympio," Gabriel panted, his eyes practically violet with the magic in them. "If you don't have me now, I swear to god—to *any* god—that I will go home and never look back. I'm yours, all yours, and I don't even remember the name of anyone I had feelings for before you. I need you now."

The words burst open a dam inside me, and every single bit of resistance I felt against what I wanted—what I needed—shattered. He was mine, and I was his. Completely and eternally, and if he was ready to make that leap, I would jump with him.

I ripped my shirt open, scattering the buttons across the room as I tore it from my body, pulling his own shirt off right after. I needed to feel his skin against my skin, his warmth seeping into me. I wrapped an arm around his waist, pulling him up against me tightly, my lips reclaiming his as my tongue swirled around his own.

I felt him whimper into my mouth, and I ended the kiss with a growl of need, moving my lips to the space where his neck and shoulder came together, before I buried my teeth into the soft skin there.

Gabriel, on the other hand, had dug his fingers so firmly into my back that, had his nails been any sharper, he would have drawn blood. He didn't try to hide his noises this time. He didn't try to hide anything. He truly gave himself to me.

Gave me the freckle just above his left nipple, gave me the tiny scar on his upper lip where he'd once fallen off his bike, gave me each beat of his heart and every throb of his arousal, pressed firmly into me.

The sounds he was making were driving me insane. Tiny whimpers in an octave higher than his speaking voice, which sent chills down my body and gave the sensation of wanting to tear him to pieces—to consume him.

I reached down between us to undo the button and zipper on his pants so I could reach inside, palming his length and moaning as the warm, velvety skin touched my fingers. I was suddenly glad we'd given him a taste of what was to come before the party, because I was desperate with need.

But I had no intention of neglecting what he needed in favor of what I wanted. Kissing further down his body, I closed my lips around one of his nipples, the hard little nub cold in the air, but warming under my tongue as I wrapped my fingers around his length.

His hips pressed up into my grip, and I could feel a layer of slick had already developed there. He was as desperate as I was, and yet, we both would rather boil in the sexual frustration, taking our time to enjoy each other, than give into the primal beast within each of us.

291

Gabriel tucked his fingers in my hair as my tongue flicked over his nipple, eliciting tiny squeaks from him with each pass of the flesh, and I couldn't help but to aggressively press my longing hardness against any part of him I could find friction from.

With a gentle bite, I released my hold of his nub and continued my journey down his body, pulling his pants down just enough that I could see the lines separating his abdomen from his hips, that glorious "v" that pointed directly to where his arousal throbbed in my hand.

Still stroking him inside his briefs, I let my tongue run over those lines, knowing how sensitive that spot was on my own body, and to my delight, he bucked up at the touch.

"Fuck…" he whimpered, and the sound only served to increase the need I had thought couldn't grow any more.

Using my free hand, I removed the barrier of my own jeans, glad to be rid of them. I'd always hated how restricting they were, and even with the underwear I wore beneath them still in place, their removal made my cock feel liberated. But it wasn't enough. I pulled the waistband down and kicked the constricting garment away, taking myself into my hand and stroking in time with my movements on Gabriel, my mouth still suckling on every sensitive inch of his body.

In seconds, Gabriel pushed my hand away from my length before pulling me back up by my hair, and took me into his own fist. We lay there, staring into each other's eyes and pleasuring each other the way we were always meant to.

Strangely enough, it barely took any effort to resist finishing too fast. The steady pulse of our bond seemed to be doing its part to keep us on track for the final goal—complete Consummation.

Gabriel shifted beneath me, turning his body one hundred and eighty degrees so his face was now between my knees, my cock resting on his face. He wasted no time licking me from base to tip and taking me deep into his throat as I watched the shine of precome ooze from his own opening.

I opened my mouth and caught the drip before it could fall, and in the same motion, I wrapped my hands around Gabriel's backside to hold him against my face as I slid my lips around his long, rigid member. I gripped the soft mounds, digging my fingers in and pulling them apart like I'd done earlier, already envisioning him opening for me.

As we lay entwined, a never-ending circle, I was lost to anything except the overwhelming pleasure. I had never felt anything this intense. Lesser unions had ended before the ecstasy could build this high, but with Gabriel, every moment put to shame any climax I'd ever had.

I allowed my fingers to move to his cleft, gently pressing on his opening. It was still pliant from earlier, ready to accept me, but I wanted to make sure he was well lubricated before I pushed forward. Instead, I simply teased and massaged the area, drawing moans that vibrated through my cock.

A shockwave rippled through my body as I felt Gabriel withdraw his mouth from my aching length, and a warm wetness pressed against my own opening.

Slowly, and with agonizing precision, he teased my hole with his tongue, his hand tight around my cock, keeping time with his oral prodding.

I released him from my mouth just long enough for me to moan, "Gabriel…" My entrance pulsed against his touch, and my heartbeat pounded between my legs.

I couldn't take it any longer. I reached out with my hand, fumbling for the jar I left out earlier. My fingers closed around it, and I flipped the lid off with my thumb, plunging my fingers inside to coat them in the slick liquid before returning them to Gabriel's ass. I spread it around, taking care to massage the whole area, relaxing the muscles to make everything smooth and pleasurable as we continued.

His tongue moved with such precision and skill that, if I didn't know better, I'd think he'd had years of practice. But I knew the depth of the bond was such that we were as in tune to each other's bodies as we were to our own in these moments. Indeed, when I finally slipped a finger inside of him, he pressed forward with his tongue at the same moment.

Gabriel whimpered, panting against my flesh, "Olympio…"

Enough. It was enough. Every single atom in my body was screaming for him, to have him now.

I moved, shifting off him so I could turn around. I laid my body over his, covering his lips, face, neck with kisses as I pressed a second finger inside of him, feeling how open he was for me.

"Are you ready?" I asked, knowing his body was, but needing to know this was the right moment to finally cross this threshold, to finally consummate our bond.

Gabriel bit his lip and nodded in a way that nearly made my mind explode with frenzied desire, and a tiny whimper accompanied it like harmony to the melody that was his own aching need.

I withdrew my fingers and pulled his legs up on either side of me, positioning myself between them.

"That promise from earlier still applies. If anything doesn't feel right, you tell me," I said, though I knew full well we were too connected for it to even be a question. At this moment, everything we felt was shared and amplified to a fever pitch.

Gabriel nodded again, and I reached down, taking my cock in my hand and lining it up with his entrance. I leaned forward, feeling the slight tension of his ring before it easily gave way, opening up for me and allowing me to slide inside.

The bond seemed to explode in a cascade of fireworks around us. I stilled, just barely in past the tip, my eyes locked onto Gabriel's as his warmth surrounded me. Every encounter I'd ever had seemed to fade into the background, this moment eclipsing any pleasure I'd ever felt with anyone else.

"I love you," I said, my hand caressing his face.

Gabriel simply nodded, pulling my forehead to his own, and kissing me like he never had before.

And as I pressed forward, filling him completely, my heart, the one Gabriel owned, was filled in equal measure.

Chapter Thirty-One
Gabriel

Ecstasy is the only word that could have come close—but really, there wasn't a single thing in the English language, probably in any language, that could describe the perfection of having Ollie inside me.

"Oh, god…" I moaned, my fingers gripping at the sheets in desperation.

He wasn't as long as I was, but he was thick and filled me thoroughly, and the moment his cock hit that spot he'd been priming, a thick drip pushed forth from my tip.

Ollie wasn't moving, just letting me adjust to the size of him as he reached down to take me in his hand, stroking me slowly as he finally began to pull back, then push forward again, over and over, starting with small movements but gradually lengthening the strokes and increasing the speed.

Each time he thrust in, striking that little point within me, my member throbbed and pulsed in his hand. It felt like coming nonstop, but I knew I hadn't yet. And if this was just the buildup, I couldn't even fathom what the climax would be like.

"You feel…" Ollie panted, pressing a kiss to my lips between thrusts. "Incredible. Perfect."

"You too," I breathed. "Fuck, I can't remember a single moment when my body didn't belong to you, Olympio."

Boldly, I pressed up into him, and I heard a deep, masculine sigh of delight. It gave me goosebumps to hear him respond like that, so I pulled forward, feeling him slide against the resistance inside me, and did it again.

"Yes," he moaned against the side of my neck, his teeth claiming me once more. "Don't stop, Gabriel. Ride me."

I was more than happy to oblige as I continued to move my hips in time with his thrusts, my legs around his waist giving me the leverage to deepen the penetration so he was slamming into me, sending me into fits of pleasure. My eyes clenched shut, but Ollie grabbed me by the chin and spoke with a smooth, commanding voice.

"Open your eyes. Look at me."

I forced them open, and for the first time, I saw not just the purple in his eyes, but what looked like a shimmering violet cloud around us, and through that, coming out on either side of Ollie, a pair of wispy wings made out of shadow itself.

"Oh, god, Daddy…" I moaned, the sight of him like porn to me.

Ollie laughed then, looking at me with nothing but unbridled adoration. "You know… I spent nineteen years in your world, learning as much as I could, but the appeal of that was one thing I never quite understood."

I laughed back, though neither of us stopped our passionate lovemaking.

I had once read an article that couples who had mind blowing sex lives only spent fifty percent of the event generating actual pleasure and fifty percent on socialization and laughing. I didn't know if that was true, but if it was, Ollie and I were well on our way.

"You know," I gasped, smiling an uncontrolled, playfully cocky frat boy grin, trying to pay homage to where we'd started. "This is kind of gay, bro."

Ollie returned the expression. "By definition," he said, dipping his head to lick my nipple again before looking up at me. "I hope you're not just realizing that now?"

I wrapped my arms around his neck as he thrust particularly deeply, and it nearly took my breath away. "I'm not... even gay," I panted, trying to force words from my lungs while also trying not to come and laughing. "Oh, fuck..."

"Yes, I remember you saying that." He reached down and grabbed my hip, pulling at me in time with his own movements, increasing the intensity. "I'll make sure to keep that in mind."

It was ironic this conversation was happening now, because Ollie hadn't even finished what he was saying before I was screaming his name the way he told me he liked, spilling myself all over his sheets—hands free.

"Oh, shit," I said as he slowed. "Sorry..."

"I'm not," Ollie breathed, kissing me with a need I felt just as strongly. "But don't think for one second we're done."

I loved the way he talked to me like that. Like he was reassuring and dominating all at once. I felt his lips on my neck, and his thrusting slowed to a teasing pump inside me.

"I bet," I whispered, "I don't even come close to some of the lovers you've had."

He stopped moving and pushed up on his hands to look down at me, his expression suddenly serious.

"You're right." I felt my heart begin to sink before he smiled. "You don't come close, but it's not because you can't measure up to them. It's because not one of them can hold a candle to you. Being with you is the greatest thing I've experienced in two and a half thousand years." He lowered himself so our chests were pressed together again, and he kissed my forehead as he began to thrust in and out of me again in those same tiny, slow motions.

I shuddered, then nudged him up off me, turning over so I was lying on my stomach and we could be even closer.

He kissed down my spine and across my lower back, before re-lubing himself and sliding back in.

And just like that, I was hard again.

The weight of him on my back was everything as his hands slid up my arms, over my head, to lace his fingers in mine. His breath, coming in short, hard bursts, rustled the hair next to my ear, raising goosebumps across my whole body.

"I will never tire of feeling you," he said, his body moving against mine in a wavelike motion, bringing me higher and higher. Just waiting to crash over again.

"The feeling is mutual," I sighed. "I love you, Olympio. I want all of you forever. And then when that's done, I want you again. I can't remember where I end and you begin now."

He chuckled slightly before pressing a kiss to the side of my neck. "I could show you where, but I'm a little busy in that area at the moment."

Suddenly, the energy of the moment shifted, and the air stilled around us. The sounds of our tandem panting were the only notes that filled the room, and a slow build began to warm my belly once more.

Ollie's movements became erratic, more desperate, and his grip on my hands tightened.

"You feel it, too," he said. "Don't you?"

"Yes." I turned my head and leaned up to kiss him. He met me, and it was like a circuit completed.

His lips were still on mine as he said, "I can't hold it back anymore."

"Then don't," I begged. "You've waited so, so long for this. And my heart has always been yours."

He pumped into me three, four more times, then, with a rugged groan, I felt him tense behind me.

"Olympio," I sighed, "I choose you. I forever choose you. I want *this*... forever."

The sounds he made as he came were ethereal. Tiny whimpers that sounded exactly like you would imagine almost twenty years of build up would sound like. And not just twenty years of waiting, but centuries, millennia of loneliness he didn't even know existed until he met...

Me.

The feeling of him releasing inside me brought me to a second climax as well, but I was utterly silent so as not to miss one delicious sound that crossed his lips. And the minute I felt him still, releasing a heavy, contented sigh, I began to weep silently. The moment was so beautiful, it felt like it rearranged the stars and wrote our names in history.

Olympio and Gabriel.

Forever.

Chapter Thirty-Two
Olympio

In my life, I'd had more orgasms than I could count. I'd felt that moment of completion so often, I thought there was no more to it than that—a finish to the event.

But when I reached that peak with Gabriel, when everything within us both spilled over, every part of me, body and soul, released. It was like I had been holding onto this unspecified emptiness inside of me for so long, I'd managed to forget it was even there. It wasn't until Gabriel and I crossed that line, felt the culmination of our connection, that I even could feel he was the missing piece. For the first time in two and a half millennia, I felt complete.

We hadn't moved. Our bodies were still pressed together, neither of us wanting to be the first. But as that incredible feeling of finally knowing I had found something I never knew I was missing crashed over me, my eyes welled with tears that began to spill over, dripping onto Gabriel's neck as soft sobs rocked my body.

"It's okay," he whispered from beneath me. "I'm here now. You'll never be alone again. You'll never have to grieve again."

I shifted to the side and tugged on his arm to roll him over so he was facing me. So he could see my smile.

"I know," I said, running my hand through his hair, brushing it away from his perfect face. "And that's why I'm so… happy. I've never felt joy like this before."

It was only then I saw the glisten of tears on his cheeks and felt the difference in our energies. This was the happiest moment of my life, but there was a sense of melancholy coming from Gabriel.

And then I noticed the bond still swirling in his eyes, the blue visible beneath it. The blue that would be gone once the consummation was complete.

It hadn't worked.

"Gabriel…" I reached up and wiped away his tears. "What's wrong? Was something not right for you? I didn't hurt you, did I?"

Gabriel shook his head, opening his mouth to speak, then closing it again and trying once more. "I just realized I've never wanted anything more in my life than to please you, than to be here for you, than to love you. I didn't care about Columbia, I didn't even care about being the popular billionaires' kid—I definitely didn't care about Alex Kessinger. But you… it's like you are every beat of my heart, and yet… something's missing."

I frowned, sliding down beside him and wrapping my arms around his waist so we were facing each other on our sides.

"What?" I asked. "What's missing?" I would scour every realm, every world, for whatever it took to give Gabriel what he needed. If there was something I still hadn't given him, I would never stop until he had it. But I already knew. It was the same unease I felt creeping in myself. It was that our connection felt as strong as it could possibly be.

And yet…

Not now, I decided. Not in this moment. Not when everything was so close to perfect. Tonight, we wouldn't worry about what was still to come. Tonight, we would celebrate what we already had.

"Come with me," I said, pressing a brief kiss to his lips before sliding out of the bed and reaching for his hand. He followed, of course. I'd been noticing it for a while that Gabriel quietly obeyed commands I gave now, and not because one ounce of me was forcing him to.

"What is it?" he asked, jumping up on my back with the agility of a gymnast.

I caught him just as easily, gripping his legs behind the knees as his arms looped around my neck. I turned to look at him and laughed as I started walking toward the other side of the room.

"It's this amazing creation," I said. "A Sefaeran wonder. Something that can cleanse the body and soothe the soul."

"Like a fountain of youth?" he asked in utter seriousness.

"Like a bath," I said with a wink, carrying him over to the sunken tub, stepping down into it until I was waist deep before letting Gabriel down into the warm, soft water.

Gabriel let out this little giggle that made my heart swell and splashed me in the face with some water the second he got the chance. "Oops," he said. "I didn't mean to."

I gasped in mock indignation and wiped away the droplets from my cheeks. I looked down like I couldn't believe it, then back up at Gabriel.

"Oops, indeed," I said, then waited a single beat before I lunged forward, wrapping my arms around Gabriel's waist and flipping him sideways to dunk him in the water.

His shrieks quickly drew in the guards, led by Gryfian, ready to attack. "Your Highness?"

I looked up at them, still laughing, as I wrapped my arms around Gabriel's head, holding him against my chest. "Everything's fine, Gryfian. Just letting off some steam."

Gryfian nodded, then turned to the other guards. With a nod, he directed them to leave and followed behind, closing the door once more.

I squeezed Gabriel tightly, then let go so I could look at him.

"This has been a... big day," I said, knowing I was greatly underscoring the vast chasm between the highs and lows we'd experienced since waking up that morning.

Then he asked me the thing I'd been dreading him bringing up. "Did it... work? Are we...?"

I sat down in the bath and pulled him into my lap, beginning to wash him with a soft cloth.

"No," I said after a long silence. "I don't know why it didn't, but that doesn't matter right now. Consummation or no, being with you was the single greatest moment of my life. And as long as you're by my side, we can figure it out together. But for now, I just want to enjoy the afterglow of making love to the person I love most in the entire world—any world. We can deal with anything else tomorrow, or the next day, or the next."

For the next several hours we lay in my bed, with Gabriel asking me questions about my life before him, and me answering.

Until we got to questions about the future rather than the past.

"So… if we're both men," Gabriel began. "How do we… carry on the line or whatever?"

"It's, uh…" I gave a soft laugh. "It's a little different than what you learned back in the human world. The royal line, my line, doesn't conceive and give birth the way others do. For us, it's a ritual."

"Do you all do anything without an audience?"

"Yes, in fact," I chuckled. "This isn't like the Consummation in the spectacle of it. When the royal pair decides they're ready, there are… places we can go. Places that aren't part of the human world or of Sefaera, but that lie somewhere in the ether between. They exist to be little pockets of paradise, where we can go to take a break from the pressures of ruling. When a bonded pair decides they want to procreate, they steal away to one of these outer worlds, where they make a commitment to each other. Then, they make love, meditate, laugh, cry, generally rile up the bond in any way they can, and the bond taps into the ancient magic that created it, and a child is created from that magic."

"That's…" Gabe rubbed his face on my chest. "Intense."

"It is." I kissed the top of his head. "Which is why the ritual has to be done. There's no such thing as an accidental pregnancy or an unexpected birth. For the royal line, it's a deliberate move where the couple must be fully committed, or it won't work."

Like the Consummation.

Which *hadn't* worked.

Gabriel said he was all in, all mine, but maybe... maybe there was more he wasn't saying, or possibly more he hadn't even realized, himself.

My thoughts threatened to fly off on their own, consuming me, so I forced myself back to the present, now, with Gabriel. Decidedly *not* thinking about the bond and what might have gone wrong. "Did, uh... did that explain it well?"

There was no response, and I looked down to find Gabriel asleep on my chest. I wondered how much he'd heard before he dozed off. It didn't matter, really. As long as we could figure out what was missing from the Consummation and fix it, we would have eternity for me to answer his questions as many times as I needed to.

I settled down onto my pillow, raising my hand, then lowering it to quench the fire, darkening the room. My arms wrapped around Gabriel, and I kissed his head, content for now in the knowledge he was mine.

And no ritual, no Consummation, failed or otherwise, would ever change that.

Chapter Thirty-Three
Gabriel

A shrill laughter cut through my deep and beautiful sleep, and I startled awake, nearly falling off the bed. Or I would have fallen off the bed if Ollie hadn't caught me.

"Ari," Ollie said as he helped me back onto the bed. "What are you doing here?"

Ah, yes. That was definitely Ari's playful cackle.

"Well," she said, walking over and sitting on the edge of the bed, "I went to fetch Gabriel from his chambers, but I was told he's been sleeping in here. I just didn't realize he was *not* sleeping in here, too."

I opened my eyes and saw her evaluating the state of the bed, making her own judgments about what was going on between us. "I would have thought me screaming your brother's name last night would have been your first hint, Ari."

I heard a sharp intake of air beside me as Ollie clearly tried not to laugh and squeezed my shoulder in approval.

Ari grinned wildly. "It's about time you grew some claws, Gabe. I was starting to think you'd be our little wallflower forever, but I think you may finally be worthy of joining my family. Congratulations."

I stuck my tongue out at her. "According to fate, I've always been worthy. Didn't you hear?"

She waved her hand like she was brushing away my words. "I do remember something like that…" She looked at Ollie, then back at me, her expression softening. "Sounds like you've decided, then?"

My stomach dropped, and I bit my lip. "Oh, um… yeah."

Ollie's grip around me tightened slightly, and I saw a narrowing of Ari's eyes as she looked between Ollie and me. But for once, she didn't have a comment.

"Well," she said, standing up. "It's a training day for Gabe. Hunting. And we want to get an early start, so I'm afraid I have to break up your little slumber party."

I looked up at Ollie, wondering if today he was going to let me go. "I guess I have to be going."

"I guess so," he said, but the smile on his face didn't seem to indicate he was as disappointed as I was. I started to get out of the bed, but he held on. "I guess we all do."

"What?"

He looked at Ari, who shrugged and stood up, smirking at Ollie. "As long as you don't slow us down, *Your Highness*. It's been, what, twenty years since you've been on a hunt? Your aim was terrible then. I can't imagine it's improved."

"Do you mind?" Ollie asked, looking at me.

I felt like I missed part of the conversation—again. "What?"

"He wants to tag along," Ari said.

It felt like a thousand butterflies exploded into my abdomen, and I saw the purple flash in Ollie's eyes as I met them. "Yeah?"

"As long as you're not worried I'll 'slow you down,'" he said, grabbing a pillow and throwing it at Ari, who caught it and threw it back, managing to hit both of us.

"Definitely not," I replied, my voice deepening as I slowly leaned forward to taste those delicious lips.

"None of that bullshit, either," Ari said, but her expression was kind. Despite her teasing, it was obvious she was happy for her brother.

And for me.

"We'll keep our hands to ourselves if you and Liro can do the same," I said. "I've seen the way you two are when you get a few trees around you."

"I like you more and more every day," she said, walking to the door. She opened it and was nearly through when she poked her head back in. "Twenty minutes. Outside. Anyone who's late becomes bait."

The door closed, leaving Ollie and me alone again.

In seconds, I was straddling him, my fingers in his hair and kissing him. "Does this hunger for you ever stop? No matter how much I touch you, nothing makes it go away."

His hands were insistent, gripping my hips as he devoured my lips. "We don't have time," he mumbled, but he didn't stop.

"No, we don't," I breathed into his mouth. "Not for you to do exactly what you did last night all over again. Because I won't accept any less. I'm your soulmate, after all."

310

"How dare you say such seductive, enticing things when we have obligations that are out of this bed?"

I kissed him more ravenously. "As much as I hate to…" I said, tugging his gorgeous red hair, "I think I can fix this in two seconds. Just let me get a few feet away first."

I moved off of him, kicking my feet over my head and rolling backward off the bed, backing up a few feet before whispering, "Alex Kessinger…"

I felt the familiar flare of anger from Ollie at the sound of the name, but I could tell it was less intense than before.

I backed up a few more steps and hissed again. "Alex… Kessinger…."

Ollie turned slowly so his feet were hanging off the edge of the bed, then stood and faced me. He took one step toward me, then another.

"What did I tell you about saying that name?" he asked, his foot moving forward again.

"Oh, Alex," I said in a higher pitch than usual. "Your muscles are *so* big. You're *so* handsome." I could barely say it without giggling and continued to move away from Ollie without turning my back to him.

My cock swung between my legs and my feet slapped against the stone floor as I jogged naked to cross the room.

Shadows swirled around me and coalesced into a solid shape, the last thing to disappear being those wings that vanished into thin air, before I was wrapped in a vise-like embrace—one arm around my waist, and his other shooting up to wrap long, strong fingers around my throat, just tight enough to set my pulse racing.

"What… did I tell you… about saying… that name?" he said, his voice low and rough, but I could feel his lips brushing my ear and knew he was just as much in the game as I was.

"He's just so hard to forget," I teased, and he squeezed my throat tighter, making my cock throb with hardness.

"Is that so?" he asked, reaching down to take me in his hand. "Doesn't feel like it, but maybe I need a closer look."

He walked forward, pressing me against the wall and dropping to his knees, taking me into his mouth in a swift motion.

I shuddered at the surprise and groaned as he gave me a noisy, wet, sloppy sucking. "You naughty prince," I moaned softly.

Ollie laughed, the vibrations making the sensation even more powerful. He took me deep, all the way into his throat, and I knew it wouldn't be long.

"God, you're fucking good at that." I watched as his eyes met mine, the purple in them vibrant.

His tongue flicked up the underside of my cock, and I felt a throb that meant I was getting close.

"I hope you wanted cream for breakfast," I said in the lowest, most macho voice I could muster, to comical effect.

"Oh, I do," Ollie said, pulling away and stroking me with his hand as he continued to stare at me. "And you're so close to giving it to me, aren't you?"

I made an exaggerated, high pitched porn star type of moan, pulling a dramatic face. "Yes, Daddy." I stretched the word out for several seconds, almost like a squeal.

This was, admittedly, as fun as it was arousing. Like having a best friend you wanted to live in one body with. Which sounded a lot weirder when I really thought it through.

Ollie's mouth was back on me, forward and back like his life depended on it, and my fingers gripped his hair tightly as I neared my climax.

"Oh, fuck, Ol—"

And suddenly, he pulled away and stood up, his face etched into the same smirk his sister always wore. With an evaluative glance down at my still hard length, he shook his head. "Damn. We're out of time."

Without another word, he turned around and went to his wardrobe, pulling out two sets of hunting leathers and tossing one onto the bed as he began to lace himself into the other.

I watched him, dumbfounded, as he moved around the room like nothing had just happened, smiling in a serene kind of way. He was dressed quickly and walked to the door, then turned and looked back at me with a playfully wicked grin.

"It's too bad Alex Kessinger isn't here to take care of that for you," he said, winking and stepping through the door.

I dropped onto the bed in shock. Did he really just do that?

Where had the stoic, serious, and wildly broody *Olympio* gone? Who was this cheeky fuck who knew how to give it as good as he got it?

I slowly got dressed, shaking my head in disbelief every few minutes. It was super fun trying to stuff my hard-on into the tight leather pants. Once I finally managed it, I followed where Ollie had disappeared and out to our morning hunt.

"Damn," Ari said as I approached. "Right on time. Another minute, and we'd have been tying you to a tree for a murix to chew on while we got a few good shots in."

Ollie was looking at me with a gleeful smirk.

"Would have been a lucky murix," he said.

I grabbed my bow from the ground and attached the sword to my belt. It was odd how comfortable getting geared up like this was now. "I'm going to pretend I know what the fuck a murix is." I chuckled as the siblings exchanged a look. "Good morning, Liro."

As I straightened up, I put my hand out for the tall, horned man to shake.

"Morning it is. Good—who knows? My sleep was deeply troubled as it seems the ghost of Vasileios has come back to haunt us. Hours of wailing and moaning echoing through the palace halls last night."

I looked at Ollie, worried the mention of his brother would reopen that grieving wound, but he just laughed and nudged Liro with his elbow. "Pity you weren't able to drown it out with some screams from your own room," he teased, and Ari rolled her eyes.

"Fuck's sake..." she mumbled, slinging her own bow over her shoulder.

"For some of us," Liro replied, snaking Ollie's bow out from between the prince's legs, "our lover having an orgasm doesn't have to come with a month of foreplay. When you make them come four times a—"

"Alright," Ari said loudly. "You boyfriends can all compare cocks later over drinks, but the day isn't going to stop moving along while we all wait for you." She winked at me and tossed me a leather bundle. "For you."

The leather was soft and fine, and I opened it to reveal the most beautiful knives I've ever seen in my life. A pair of daggers that had "Justice Gabriel" carved into the handle. The blades were the same obsidian Ollie favored in his own weapons, and they were sharp, even to the eye.

"Thank you," I said with true sentiment. I took a step forward and pulled her into a hug. "I always wanted a sister. Someone to protect. One out of two isn't bad."

Ari hugged me back, warmth radiating from her. "It's good to have you here." She let go and grinned at me. "And it's good you realize which of the two of us would need protecting."

"Absolutely," I said. "I can't even be trusted to make good choices in bathing schedules." I looked over at Ollie, grinning. "I thought we were gonna hunt."

He raised an eyebrow at me and reached out, snatching a hunting knife off of Liro's belt, throwing it in the air and catching it before giving it a twirl and sheathing it on his own belt. "That's why I'm here, but if you would all rather socialize…"

Ari, I had learned, had a very short amount of patience once she put her mind to something. So, when she hopped on her mount and rode off without us, I wasn't even a little surprised.

But Ari was the one person here I was maybe a little afraid of, so once she took off, I followed.

The "horses" here were slightly different from the ones back home. First of all, like most things in Sefaera, they came in a wide variety of vibrant colors. Liro had explained it was because most of the plants the animals fed from had really vibrant colorants in them. Kind of like plants being green because of chlorophyll.

I think. I *really* wasn't good at science.

The lymere (as it was properly called) I was currently riding was bubblegum pink with a sky blue mane and fuzzy yellow antlers, which were apparently used to carry equipment. At least that's what the royals did.

I loved riding through the forest, and not just because I was apparently good at it. It was the first thing I'd ever known that felt like true freedom.

Ollie was quick to catch up, coming up right behind me.

"You look like a natural," he said, looking like some kind of fairy tale prince, sitting tall and regal on his own lymere. His was electric purple with royal blue markings and green antlers.

"Thank you," I replied. "But for the record, you're not being sneaky. I can feel what you're doing."

The hearty laugh that came from behind me penetrated deep into my core, igniting that desire for him that never seemed to fully go away anymore.

"If you could see what I can, you wouldn't blame me," he said.

"We're not going to find anything if you don't stop talking about Gabe's ass," Ari shouted back at us.

Ollie suddenly appeared beside me, making a face. I could feel how insufferable we were being, but I couldn't muster the energy to care.

"Ariadne, darling," he called to her, "Gabriel's ass is so enticing, we shouldn't have to be quiet. It's perfect bait. No natural predator can resist a piece of juicy meat."

"Moons and rivers," she grumbled.

I felt my face get so hot, I could have been sporting a fever, and I made myself really busy pulling tiny brambles out of the lymere's mane.

"… And if that's not enough," he continued. "There's always the thick lure he's sporting between his—"

"For fuck's sake, Olympio," Ari growled at him so loudly it echoed. "Please, for the love of our eternal bloodline, *stop*."

Liro burst out laughing and circled back to where Ari had come to a full halt. "It seems like no one is interested in being quiet today." He slid his arm around the princess's waist, kissing her cheek. "So, why don't we go check on the orchards instead? We should be pretty close to perfect oulons."

"What do you think?" Ollie asked me, his eyes lit up with excitement. "You haven't mentioned seeing the orchards yet, and they're magnificent."

I nodded. "I like fruit."

I was still a little overwhelmed with this dynamic. Ollie was so multifaceted that when he acted like a dickhead older brother, it jarred me. Nonetheless, I was so grateful to have found this family. They were all such incredible people.

"Then you are in for quite the treat," he said, reaching out to squeeze my hand before gripping his reins again. "Oulons are delicious most of the time, but right off the tree? They may as well be magic."

I dug my heel into my mount's side, and she took off like she wanted nothing more than to run forever. It was only seconds before Ollie caught up to me, and without a word exchanged, a challenge was issued.

We darted left and right through the trees, the leaves every shade of the rainbow. The sun shining down through them made it look like we were living inside a kaleidoscope. Every so often, flying animals would swoop by overhead. They might have been birds or something else— they were too quick for me to tell.

Eventually, we broke past the tree line, Ollie beating me by several seconds. Our lymeres trotted out into the daylight, their coats gleaming and shining even more brightly. We came out of the woods into a large field with rolling hills, the grass green like it was back home, but glittering like emeralds.

"Where's the orchard?" I asked, looking around at the wide open space.

Ollie, Ari, and Liro all exchanged a knowing look.

"This way," Ollie said in a weird, loaded way, before riding his lymere forward about twenty feet.

Where he disappeared.

"What the…"

"It's fine," Liro said in his deep, gravelly voice. "It's hidden to prevent thieves and animal scavengers. Just go forward."

I took a deep breath and closed my eyes, nudging my lymere forward.

And then the air shifted to a cool breeze, and I peeked out into the sun.

As far as the eye could see, there were orange, pink, and blue trees of varying heights, with their leaves blowing in the wind. The smell was heavenly, like a wave of citrus and a little bit of vanilla, making it smell like someone was baking.

Ollie had tied his lymere to a post nearby and was leaning against a wooden fence. His arms were crossed, and one of his feet was in front of the other. His copper hair glowed in the sunlight as he smiled, his eyes devouring me as I approached. The black leather he wore, sleeveless and skintight, showed off every single one of his muscles, making him look like a god rather than a demon prince.

"Do you like it?" he asked, nodding to the orchard behind him, his eyes never leaving mine.

It was the most beautiful thing I'd ever seen—besides Ollie—and it strangely reminded me of California. "It's…" A tear fell, and I quickly wiped it away. Who was I turning into? Where had frat boy Gabe gone?

And why did it feel so much better to be Gabriel, future Justice of Sefaera?

Just like before, there was a punch in my gut that whispered "traitor" in my ear. The truth was there were so many people who deserved a chance like this over me. I'd always lived in luxury, an easy life with easy parents. Practically everyone I'd ever known had needed to work harder than I had, and yet…

Ollie stepped forward and took the reins from me, leading my mount over beside his. I started to dismount, but he caught me around the waist, holding me above the ground, my head above his so he was looking up at me.

The adoration in his eyes was a tangible thing, sending butterflies through my whole being. I wondered if that would ever fade. Right now, it didn't seem like it.

"Why are you crying?" he asked.

"Uh…" I wiped my nose, brushing away the feelings with a shake of my head. "Allergies."

"No," he said. "It's not. What is it?" He wasn't harsh, but it was clear he wasn't going to let me blow off the question.

Thankfully, at that moment, something flew at our heads.

Faster than I could even register, Ollie's hand went up, and his fingers closed around a fruit I'd never seen.

"How did you…?"

He just grinned, shrugged, and held up the fruit for me to see. "Just luck, I guess," he said, and I could tell he was holding back his answer until I gave mine. But he wasn't going to push it either. "Here. Try this. Raquin. Not as good as a fresh oulon, but delicious, nonetheless."

I opened my mouth for him, waiting for him to put it in there, but for a moment he just stared. "What?" I asked.

"No, no, no… Hang on a second. Open back up."

I did as I was told, confused as to what he was looking at.

That is, until he used his thumb to run across my bottom lip, biting his own.

"Yeah, that'll do."

"Ollie," I laughed. "They're gonna kill us." I nodded to where Ari and Liro were actively pulling fruit off trees.

"And if the last thing I see is those lips and that tongue, I will die a happy prince."

I took a step forward and kissed him sweetly before pulling back and biting into the fruit.

The incredible taste rushed my senses, and I groaned. He was definitely wrong—the raquin was my new favorite. It was like someone had taken apple cobbler, with the sugar and cinnamon and spices, and put that flavor back into a crisp, juicy apple.

Ollie's hand was still around my waist, and he pulled me even closer, like being pressed together wasn't close enough, which I totally felt, too. He slowly reached up and took the raquin from my hand, then leaned in like he was going to kiss me, but at the last second, shifted down to lick away a drop of raquin juice from my chin.

"Like I said…" he breathed, straightening to look in my eyes once more. "Delicious."

And… I was hard. Twenty feet away from his family.

"Ollie," I whined, gesturing to the unmistakable tent in my pants.

That same wild glint came into his eyes, just like it had earlier, and he kissed me, slowly, lovingly, before pulling away and saying, "Later… you will pay for what you did earlier."

"Have I not already suffered enough?" I begged. "Ari said we had a dinner after this. Are you gonna make me wait until after that?"

"I haven't decided," he said, shrugging, but then he laughed. "No. As long as you're a good boy the rest of the day, I'll make sure you get your spanking *before* dinner."

Fuck Olympio and his obsessive desire to get me to come in my pants. I shifted uncomfortably, tucking my hard cock up into my waistband and walking toward an oulon tree in the opposite direction of his sister.

321

We spent the rest of the afternoon eating fruit and laughing, and, mercifully, Ollie resisted the urge to torture me further.

Because if he'd kept it up, I wasn't sure I wouldn't have torn his clothes off right there.

Chapter Thirty-Four
Olympio

I could have stayed all day that way.

Lying in the orchard, leaning against a raquin tree with Gabriel's head in my lap. From here, I could reach up and pick one every so often, slicing it with my knife to feed it to him.

This was my idea of absolute paradise.

In moments like these, I could forget everything else. I could forget about the weariness that came from ruling a kingdom and the pressures to live up to a standard I was never meant to. I could forget about the heartbreak of being betrayed by the person I'd trusted most, someone I'd loved so deeply, for so long.

I could forget that, as perfect as things felt between Gabriel and me, something was getting in the way of us consummating the bond.

"Are you happy?" I asked. I could feel through the bond he was, but the smallest niggling of insecurity made me want to ask.

"What?"

I ran my hand through his hair and looked into his eyes, the purple shimmer that was so thick around and between us mirrored in his perfect blue irises. It occurred to me that, once the bond was consummated, they would never be blue again. Both of our eyes would permanently change to the shimmering violet of the bond, the physical manifestation of our union.

"Are you happy?" I repeated. "Right now. Here, like this, with me. Are you happy?"

"Very," he sighed. "Almost like I never had a perfect day 'til this one."

I cut another slice of raquin and held it to his lips, closing my eyes in ecstasy as they wrapped around my fingers.

"Perfect is exactly right," I said, letting my head fall back against the tree.

"If I walk around this tree and either or both of you are naked, I reserve the right to shoot you and take you home as trophy kills," Ari called from behind us.

"Guess you'll have to take that gamble." I laughed and winked at Gabriel, who shook his head with a grin and an indulgent roll of his eyes.

Ari's face came into view, her eyes scrutinizing us. "Hm… I guess you get to live. For now."

"How benevolent of you," I teased. She shot me a playfully scathing look, and I blew her a kiss.

"Don't praise me for that just yet," she said, reaching up to pick a piece of fruit, which she bit into. "We have to start heading back. Mother arranged this dinner herself to try to get to know Gabriel better, and I don't think showing up in filthy hunting gear will go over well."

I sighed, wishing that, for one day, Gabriel and I could just exist as ourselves without having to be prince and consort. That we could have one day where we could just be any other couple in love, able to spend a day together without having to worry about public appearances or political ramifications of our actions.

"You're right." I helped Gabriel up to a sitting position and climbed to my feet, offering him a hand. "All good things must come to an end, it seems."

As my gaze met Gabriel's, I could see and feel how melancholy he truly was. His eyes were wistful, and the way he surveyed the orchard was like he worried he'd never see it again.

"I'll bring you back here soon," I promised, pulling him to standing and kissing him softly.

He nodded slowly, turning away reluctantly with a furrow in his brow. "Yeah. Soon."

The way he said that left a pit in my stomach. I had given him almost everything I could to convince him to stay, had shown him the things he would get to experience forever, but it still wasn't enough. His heart still lay back in the human world, even if it belonged to me.

I wrapped my arms around him from behind and leaned my chin on his shoulder.

"I love you, Gabriel."

Tears formed in my eyes as I said the words. I knew if he went back, what we had would be over. He would be living a normal, mortal, human existence while I continued to be the immortal ruler of my world. I could visit, certainly, but it might be years between times I saw him. He would age, and I wouldn't. He would get lonely, and others would earn parts of his heart, parts I selfishly wanted to keep for myself. And one day, one not too far off, he would die, and I would have to live the rest of eternity knowing what we'd lost.

But I didn't let the tears fall. I wouldn't do that to him. I could feel how conflicted he was without adding my own selfish thoughts to his considerations. I held them back and held my soulmate for just a moment longer, choosing to treasure every moment, not knowing how many we might have together.

For the first time since we'd begun the conversation, Gabriel looked me straight in the eyes, and I saw more blue in them than I had for days. I was losing him already.

I saw Ari poke her head around a tree, her mouth already open to scold us for taking too long. But she must have realized the gravity of the moment we were sharing because she chose to remain silent and head back to the lymeres without us.

"Come on," I said, once I knew that, if I tried to keep him here any longer, I would begin to weep. "We should get going. They're waiting."

Gabriel nodded and plastered on a smile I knew was fake. "Great. I'm starving."

Then he reached for my hand, the saddest look I'd ever seen on his face.

"Ollie…" he started. "I have to tell you something…"

This was it. The moment where he would tell me it was over. The moment where he would tell me he wanted to go back. The moment he would cease to be the future Justice, future consort, future *anything* in Sefaera. The moment where I would go back to the emptiness I never knew I was living in before him. The moment *my* Gabriel would no

326

longer be mine. The moment where I would have to give up the one thing I knew I couldn't live without.

But as fate would have it, I wouldn't have to.

Because then... it was pain.

Not just in my heart and through the bond. It was a sharp, burning pain in my back, between my shoulder blades.

"Ollie!" Gabriel cried out.

I jerked forward and turned, trying to regain my footing, but I stumbled into Gabriel, knocking him to the ground. I heard the sound of footsteps rushing my way as I faced my attacker.

It was another assassin, dressed in the same lightweight armor, though this one was a male. He smiled victoriously, holding a short blade covered in golden blood.

My blood.

"Fuck, no," Gabriel growled.

I watched as my soulmate moved like his own version of a shadow. His technique was graceful but cutting, and I could hardly take in what was happening before the assassin was pinned against a tree with Gabriel's new knives. One in each shoulder—

Two in the throat.

The assassin choked, and his blue blood dripped down his chin as Gabriel approached and dealt the killing blow, a coup de grâce across the protruding vein in the assassin's neck.

The second the attacker stopped moving, Gabriel turned back to me, relief washing over his face, followed quickly by shock.

"I… I've never killed someone before." He looked down at his bloody daggers, then dropped them in the grass before walking back to me.

"You did what you had to," I said, opening my arms for him, but it took enormous effort. The scar on my arm had been a reminder of how deadly the assassin's poison was, and that was from just a scratch. I could feel the burning of the poison, buried in my back, already working its way through my body, but I forced myself to stand just a little longer.

He stepped into my embrace, and I was shocked by how warm he felt. I was already going cold, the toxin putting me into shock before it worked its deeper damage.

"Gabriel…"

My mouth felt like it was full of cotton, and my vision was already blurring. I pulled back from him, wanting to see his face, his eyes. I'd known this day might come soon, the last time I ever saw him, but I hadn't expected it *this* soon, and I hadn't thought it would be like this.

"I am…" My breath was like molasses as it tried to fill my lungs. "… so proud of you."

Gabriel looked at me, and his expression suddenly changed to one of horror.

"Ollie…?" he whimpered.

"It's okay," I panted, grabbing for any part of him my fingers could find purchase on. "Be… fearless."

"Olympio!" Ari's panicked voice broke through, but it sounded like she was underwater. I reached one hand up to touch Gabriel's face, and the last of my strength left me. I crumpled to the ground, my eyes open but unfocused as I heard the voices of my soulmate, my sister, and my

328

friend all around me, who was speaking becoming more and more unclear by the second.

"What's happening?"

"It's poisoned—the blade was poisoned!"

"Get him on a lymere! We have to get him back to the palace *now*!"

I was being moved, lifted and carried, and when I heard a voice in my ear, my mind couldn't discern who it was, but my heart knew. My eyes finally shut, and I used my last seconds of consciousness to listen to my soulmate's last words to me as he sobbed.

"I've made my choice, dammit. I choose you. I choose here." He let out a shuddering wail, pulling at my clothing. "But you have to live."

And if it had been my choice, I'd have given him anything he asked of me.

Even that.

Chapter Thirty-Five
Gabriel

When we brought him back to the palace, carried by Liro, Ari immediately called for help and began bossing the guards around.

"You!" she shouted, getting the attention of one of them. "I need you to get Perla, Her Royal Highness, and Gryfian. Bring them all to His Highness's room." The guard paused to salute her. "Stop. Don't waste time. Go!"

"Ollie," I moaned in agony. "Please. Don't die. We need you. *I* need you."

Liro and I rushed to Ollie's bedroom, and I opened the door as Liro carried him in and set him on the dining table, an easier place for Perla to work.

As soon as his body was settled there, Liro took a step back, allowing me to clutch Olympio's hand to my chest and look at my beautiful prince, who was barely breathing.

His hand was cold, like he was already gone, and if it wasn't for the rapid little rise and fall of his chest, I would have thought I'd lost him. A small pool of golden liquid—his blood—was seeping out from beneath him, even though Ari had done her best to stop it.

I looked down at myself and my soulmate. That blood, that shining, shimmering golden life force, was all over us. Both of us. His chest, arms, and face were covered in it. It was even dripping from his copper hair.

And it was all over me. From where I'd clung to him before Liro had gotten him on the lymere. From where I'd buried my face in his chest, needing to feel his heart beat against my cheek. From where my hands had touched any part of him I could, just hoping he'd feel me and hang on.

I leaned in and drew a small circle with my nose on his cheek, trailing beneath his ear—through the golden mess on his face—and placing a kiss on his neck. "I need you to open your eyes, Olympio," I whispered. "You told me, you *pledged* to me, you would never leave me. Not while your heart is still beating, *dammit!*"

I got to my feet, anger filling me, and I picked up a shining bowl filled with oulons, flinging it across the room. The clattering of the metal on marble seemed to reverberate for eons before I dropped to my knees beside the table, sobbing.

"Your heart is still beating, asshole! Open your fucking eyes."

But his eyes remained shut.

The door flew open, and Ari came in, followed by the same purple woman who'd healed my leg when I first woke up here.

"Over there," Ari said, pointing.

They rushed over, and Perla set down her big leather bag and immediately began digging through her collection of potions.

"Gabe," Ari said, reaching for my arm. "You're going to have to give Perla space to work if you want there to be any chance of her saving him."

I yanked my arm out of her grip, glaring at her. "You would *never* leave Liro's side if he was like this." Then I threw my arms around Ollie's chest and sobbed into it. "Wake the fuck up. Tell them they're being stupid. Tell them you can handle yourself. Goddammit, if you don't open your fucking eyes, I'll say the name. I swear to *every* god, Ollie, I will say the name."

And when even that failed to invoke his passion, I knew he was really gone.

I'm pretty sure I screamed, or at least someone did.

"Gryfian."

Ari's voice called out, and I heard him approach.

"I think His Grace might be more... comfortable... if he could rest. Can you please take him to his own chambers?"

"No," I screamed, as I felt Gryfian's hands close around my upper arms. "No, he wouldn't want this. You know he wouldn't want this, Ariadne." I tried to shove Gryfian, Ollie's friend, off me, but he was too strong. "Ollie..."

My body gave in and gave up, and Gryfian began to take me from the room. "I'm sorry, Your Grace."

"No," I said in panic. "Wait. Let me sit on the bed. I promise not to say a thing, just don't make me leave the room. I can't feel him. I can't feel the bond. I feel like I'm drowning. I've never been without him before."

Flashes of Ollie blinked through my mind like an old time projector, and all I could hear was the times I told him to go away. Ollie at the convenience store, Ollie at the cemetery, Ollie in my arms the night of the party when I'd been pretending to be a lot more drunk than I was.

Telling him I would never love him…

Gryfian seemed to think my proposition was fair and released my arm, allowing me the freedom to bury myself in Ollie's blankets, in his scent, in the place where we had almost finally been happy.

But nothing would ever be happy again if my soulmate didn't open his eyes. Because for the first time ever, I knew what alone truly felt like.

Chapter Thirty-Six
Olympio

My mother had always talked about how my father was still with her, his soul forever bound to hers. I had hoped when I died, I would be granted that same gift.

But I wasn't.

Gabriel and I never consummated our bond, which meant the magic binding us together was incomplete. Which meant, when I was poisoned, when I was killed, my soul was lost.

Darkness had always been my ally. I was one with the shadows, and they were one with me. It would always hide me and carry me where I needed to go.

But now, I was formless, floating in a void I couldn't see through, one that was ripping at me, tearing into my very soul.

It was agony. It was terrifying.

The only thing keeping me from allowing the darkness to have me completely was that I could still hear Gabriel's voice. As long as my soul remained here, I could still imagine him speaking to me. If I gave in, I had no idea what would come next, and I wasn't willing to risk losing even the memory of my Gabriel.

"You told me, you pledged to me, you would never leave me. Not while your heart is still beating, dammit!"

I did. I had made that pledge to him on the balcony at his first ball. And if my heart could still beat, I would never leave him. But I knew the poisoned blade worked quickly and effectively. There was no chance anyone had found a healer in time. I knew before I even closed my eyes that it was the end for me.

"Your heart is still beating, asshole!"

If I had the ability to chuckle, I would have. Even in this purgatorial state, I could still imagine exactly what he would say, down to the expletive he would certainly have directed at me if he thought there was any chance of me surviving.

"Goddammit, if you don't open your fucking eyes, I'll say the name. I swear to every god, Ollie, I will say the name."

Cheeky little bastard. He always knew exactly what to say to push my buttons.

An unbearable ripping happened then, and my soul was rent from the very fabric of reality. The little glimpses of my soulmate faded as the darkness pressed in on me, the feeling like suffocation even though I had no lungs here.

At least... at least my final thoughts were of him.

My Gabriel.

Chapter Thirty-Seven
Gabriel

I didn't even bother to hold back the tears that came easily as I paced the hall outside of Olympio's room. I'd been there for hours, almost a day even, and we still had no answers.

According to Perla, it could go one of two ways, but we wouldn't know until he woke up.

Or didn't.

The sound of several pairs of feet came up behind me, and I turned to see the queen approaching, flanked by guards.

"Hello, Gabriel," she said, walking over to me. She wore an almost detached expression.

I flung my arms around her, hugging her in what was probably not traditionally acceptable. But she held me, stroking my hair like Ollie often did, rocking my body a little.

"How are you doing? You look like you haven't slept at all."

"I haven't," I admitted. "How could I, when he's just laying there, and he doesn't know that... I..."

I crumpled, bursting into tears as my knees hit the floor.

Two guards started forward, but stopped suddenly. The queen dropped to the floor beside me and wrapped her arms around me again, pulling my head onto her shoulder.

"Gabriel…" She whispered my name as she stroked my hair. "He knows, darling. Even if he can't show you, he knows."

"But how?" I sobbed. "He thought I wanted to go home. But I could never be home again without him. I need him to—"

All of a sudden a bright purple shimmer surrounded me, and a gentle breeze rustled my hair. It was warm, comforting, and brighter than any of the magic I'd seen before.

I got to my feet and turned to find a sparkling purple trail that led right from where I stood, across the threshold and behind the closed doors to Ollie's room.

I didn't have to ask. I didn't even have to think.

I knew.

It was like my heart came back to life, and I ran for the double doors, pressing my palm to them and bursting through. I felt like I was halfway between coming and throwing up, but that didn't matter. All that mattered was Ollie was alive.

And conscious.

Not only conscious, but on his feet. He had climbed out of the bed and was standing, an arm wrapped around his middle like he was going to be sick, but still standing. He was paler than usual, his shining hair dull from the sweat and grease and blood that had gathered there over the last few days..

But he was alive.

He looked up as I walked in, and despite the agony on his face, he smiled at me.

Without hesitation, I flung myself at him full force, and he caught me as he fell back onto the bed, his bare skin warm again and his hands wrapped into my hair. He pulled me tightly against him, and I buried my face into his neck and sobbed.

"I thought I fucked it all up. I thought I lost you for good."

"I was fairly certain you were right," he said, kissing every inch of my head he could reach with me buried in that soft crook between his neck and shoulder. "I truly thought I was dead."

My lips went to his, and my fingers tucked gently into his red locks. He tasted like mine, he tasted like home.

"Never again," I gasped, kissing him as hard and as much as I could. "We're never that far apart ever again."

"Never." His fingers dug into my back, like he would pull me inside him if he could, just to be that much closer together.

We lay like that for long enough that I think I fell asleep, because when I looked up, I could see the moons over his balcony.

Ollie hadn't moved, his fingers still stroking my hair. I saw him gazing at me, a soft smile on his face.

"I want to Consummate the bond," I finally said. "I want it to be forever. I don't care what I'm giving up."

He put his hands on either side of my face and pulled me to him for a soft, loving kiss.

"If you're sure," he said once he released me. "Not that I would ever give up the chance to feel you beneath me, but as you know, the Consummation won't work if you're not completely sure."

I didn't even wait for him to finish before blurting out, "I'm sure. I don't care if we have to do that stupid ceremony. I hope Typhir watches and likes it. Or better yet, I hope he watches, and it gives him the ick."

Ollie chuckled, then winced, still in pain from whatever lingered from the poison's effects. Then he shook his head, smiling like he had a secret. "I don't want to."

"Consummate the bond?"

"There isn't a damn thing in the universe I want more than to Consummate the bond," he said. "What I don't want is for Typhir or any of the other idiots on the Council to be a part of it in any way."

"Then how—?"

"Alone," he said. "I had the idea the other night, when we finally made love. I realized that, once the bond is consummated, that's it. I'm king, and the Council's say in what I do or how I run the kingdom becomes little more than advice. Which means I can tell them to take their voyeuristic ritual and shove it up their asses."

I pressed my lips to his once more, moaning against his mouth. "It's kinda hot when you go all monarch."

Ollie kissed me back, but I felt him tense and pull away.

"What's wrong?"

He shook his head and kissed me. "Just a little pain. I'm healing quickly, thanks to you and Ari getting me to Perla so fast, but I think I'll still need a day or so before I'll fully be myself again."

"So, that means..." I was painfully hard already, but I didn't want to hurt him. I took his hand and guided it down to where I was at attention for him, pulling my garments aside so my length was in full view. "We need to wait, right?"

Ollie moaned softly and closed his eyes before forcing them back open. "It means that, as I always have, I need you like I need to breathe. But I don't think I would have the strength to do my part." Despite his words, he gripped me and began to slowly stroke. "But that doesn't mean I couldn't offer my soulmate some relief while he waits for me to be well."

With great difficulty, I shook my head, removing his hand. "I'm sure your mom will want to see you. Let me go change into my sleep pants, and I'll be back. We can cuddle, and I'll pretend not to have a boner."

"No… Don't go." For once, it was him saying it to me. "My mother understands the pull of the bond, and how much it hurts when it's in danger of breaking. I'll see her tomorrow. Please, Gabriel. Stay with me."

"I'll only be a minute. Close your eyes, and I'll be back before you know it."

I leaned in and kissed his forehead like he was a sick child. To be fair, he looked like one.

"Hurry back…" he said.

As soon as he closed his eyes, I headed for the door, feeling like a weight had been lifted from me. Ollie was going to live, I'd made a decision, and I was totally, completely, irreversibly his.

The soulmate to King Olympio of Sefaera.

I threw open the doors to my room and was amazed at how "not mine" it felt. This had been my only safe haven for months, and now it felt like it belonged to someone else.

To be fair, it did. That Gabriel had been a shitty little brat who didn't understand the bigger picture, who was scared of what he might find if he opened his heart.

It was over there, on my balcony that I'd tried to end my misery in such an epically comical way that I wasn't sure even now Ollie hadn't been laughing as he caught me.

And across the room, my wardrobe where I kept my clothes that I discovered Ollie had ordered for me in the style I was used to wearing.

And over there....

My bed.

The place where he'd first touched me in such a way that I truly felt like a part of him. Like a part of this world.

Suddenly there was a noise from behind me, and I turned, my knives impossibly far away.

"Who's there?"

A dark figure stepped out from behind the open door, and for a split second, I thought maybe it was Ollie in his shadow form. But when they spoke, I realized what a ridiculously wrong assumption that had been.

"The person you stole *everything* from."

Vassenia stepped into a beam of moonlight that filtered in through the curtains. She was in the same armor she'd magicked onto herself at the party, her usually lustrous hair tied up in a tight knot.

"I didn't steal anything, Vassenia. I was born to be his soulmate. Believe me, I spent plenty of time wishing I could be anything else. I would have killed to switch places with you at one point."

I tried to take a step back, towards my knives, but she was on me, so I put my hands up in surrender.

"Just go. This doesn't have to be an issue."

"Oh, don't worry," she said, stepping closer. Her hands were empty, balled into fists at her sides, though I knew from seeing it firsthand that she could conjure a sword faster than I could dodge it. "It won't be an issue at all. Once you're out of the way, Olympio will come back to his senses."

"Vassenia—"

Before I could reason with her, she opened her palms and blew some kind of dust in my eyes. It burned as if I'd rubbed them after eating chilis, and in seconds, I felt my vision growing dark.

"Olympio…" I managed to gasp.

"… won't even miss you for long…"

Chapter Thirty-Eight
Olympia

The agony was immeasurable.

I had thought I was past the worst of the poison's effects when I had awakened from the nightmare state I'd been in and was reunited with Gabriel.

But I was ripped from my sleep by a renewed wave of pain tearing through my chest. I opened my eyes into the darkness of my bedroom, clutching my heart.

"Gabriel!" My voice was a strangled cry. I couldn't feel him next to me, and I didn't give a single damn about seeming strong. The pain was blinding, and I wanted—needed—my soulmate.

But no reply came. I forced my eyes open and saw the room was empty but for me. Where was he? I remember he was going to change his clothes, but then he was coming back. By the brightening of the sky, it had been hours since then.

Where had he gone?

I forced myself to my feet and started for the door, and that was when I saw it.

The bond. The swirling purple magic that had been so vivid the last few days had become such a deep shade of red it was nearly black.

"No…"

Not again. Gabriel was in danger—grave danger, and I had no way of knowing why or how. I was weakened by the poison still, my usual strength coming only in short bursts. But I needed to find him.

Now.

"Gryfian!" I shouted, and within seconds, my door flew open and my trusted guard came rushing toward me.

"Your Highness?" Gryfian had an arm around my waist only seconds before I nearly collapsed.

"Gabriel… is in danger," I barely managed to say. "Did you see where he went?"

Gryfian frowned and shook his head. "The last I saw him was when he left your chamber hours ago. His guards accompanied him to his chambers."

"He never came back?"

"No, Your Highness."

I forced myself back to my feet, the throb of the bond growing by the second. I needed to act quickly, or I might be too late.

And I wasn't going to lose Gabriel now. Not after everything we'd overcome.

"Take me to his chambers."

Gryfian nodded and walked with me to the door, where the other guards stood at attention. Gryfian took his position out in front, and the others all followed behind me to Gabriel's room.

344

I didn't even have to go inside to see something had gone horribly wrong. The guards assigned to Gabriel lay dead in pools of blood outside the door, which was slightly open. Gryfian pushed it open with his sword, holding it at the ready as he entered first.

Not content to simply wait for Gryfian to decide it was safe, I followed him in, my eyes scanning the room for any sign of Gabriel.

But it was empty.

"Gabriel!"

I didn't need to search for him. The bond, though screaming to me about the deadly situation my soulmate was in, was still able to show me he wasn't here. I could see the path leading from the place on my chest that felt like it had been opened with another stab wound, and it went out to the balcony and over.

I could feel how far away he was. It was miles. And worse… I could feel he was in pain. Physical, emotional, agonizing pain.

"Gather the lymeres," I ordered Gryfian. "We're going after Gabriel. We need to find him before—"

My eye caught on something on the ground, and I bent down to pick it up.

It was a gold bracelet, a fairly simple bangle with an olive branch etched into the outside. I recognized it. It had been a gift to Vassenia during her thousandth year. I'd had it commissioned myself, wanting her to have something as unique and special as her.

She did this. She took Gabriel and was hurting him, and she was so confident in whatever she was planning that she'd left me a token to expose herself as the culprit.

345

I closed my fist around the metal circle, watching as black wisps began to curl around my fingers. I squeezed hard, and when I opened my hand, the bracelet had been crushed into a blackened lump.

"Highness?" Gryfian was still awaiting my order.

"Get the fastest lymeres we have," I commanded. "Follow me. Due north. I don't know how far, but just keep going until you reach me."

"Yes, Your Highness." He turned to go obey, but I grabbed him by the arm, stopping him.

"You've been a loyal guard to me all this time, and a true friend when I had no one else. If you arrive, and there is a choice between saving me and saving Gabriel—"

"Then I will find the third option," he said, the hint of a smile on his face.

"Gryfian…"

"I will make Gabriel's safety my top priority."

With his promise hanging between us, I nodded, and he turned to leave, but stopped and pulled his supply bag from his shoulder, slinging it over mine.

"Just in case, Your Highness."

I walked to the balcony that had been enchanted to keep Gabriel from falling or jumping when he first got here, and that enchantment remained in place even now.

Lucky for me, I wasn't bound by such rules. Not when I allowed my true demon form to emerge.

In the pre-dawn light, I opened my arms and allowed the shadows to converge around and in me, and I felt my body shift and change. I grew several inches taller, and my muscles expanded as well. I felt the

346

familiar tingle as horns emerged from my head, and the beautiful ache as black wings sprouted from my shoulder blades, and my teeth elongated into razor sharp points.

I perched on the edge of the balcony and roared into the abyss before I took flight, the shadows and my wings carrying me toward my soulmate faster than the wind. I was racing the sunrise, the light still dancing below the horizon.

I roared again and hoped Gabriel would hear me and know I was coming.

And even more… I hoped Vass would hear it, and she would know that I brought her death.

Chapter Thirty-Nine
Gabriel

Everything hurt, and I felt my eyes stinging again the second I opened them.

"Olym…pio…" I managed to cough out.

"He's not here just now."

I tried to turn my head to look at who had spoken, but my neck was so stiff that if you told me it was broken, I would have believed it. Panic rose inside me. What had she done?

"Vassenia?" I asked, hoping the answer wasn't the one I expected.

"Glad to see I left an impression," she said, walking around until she was in my line of sight, then leaning on the stone wall in front of where I was tied to a chair.

It was a filthy room no bigger than the torture chamber back at the palace. The walls were mismatched stone held together by masonry, and the "windows" were just square-ish holes in the wall. It was still before sunrise, but I could see we were high up, two or three stories, maybe, which accounted for the ladder and trapdoor in the corner. Outside, there was nothing but forest as far as I could see.

In Vassenia's hand was a dagger—one of *my* daggers that Ari gave me—and she was tossing it in the air and catching it, her eyes never leaving mine.

"Please, Vass—" I gasped. "Please. Ollie is your friend. I will talk to him. Make him see you made a mistake."

"I didn't make a mistake." She held the dagger tightly in her hand and took a couple steps forward. It was a small room, so just those few steps brought her close enough to touch me. She raised the blade and pointed it at my face, then lowered it to my throat. *"He* did. But I plan to fix that for him."

I tried not to even breathe. One wrong move was the end of me. "Vassenia, I'm just trying to go home, to my home, to the human world," I lied.

"That's not what you said earlier," she sneered. "And if you consummate your bond, it doesn't matter where you go—he will always be bound to you. Until one of you dies, he will never be able to give his heart to anyone else. But don't worry. I had his heart for thousands of years before you were even born. I'm sure I can put the pieces back together when you're gone." She lowered the dagger's tip even further, to my chest, then my abdomen. Then...

With a flick of the blade, she sliced off the button of my jeans and cut through the fabric along the zipper, opening the front of them.

"Why don't we see what has Olympio so enthralled that he would throw away everything he ever cared about?"

I was shaking by then, willing myself to burst through my bindings and make a run for it. But it was no use. The ropes were so tightly wound that even wiggling in my seat was drawing blood.

"Please…" I begged. "Don't hurt me…"

"I'm going to hurt you quite a lot, *Gabe*." Another swish of my dagger, and my boxers had been cut free, exposing my flaccidity to the cool air blowing through the stone-hewn windows. "I plan to hurt you as much as you've hurt me. But it's going to be slow. I don't want you bleeding out before I can really enjoy myself." She looked down. "Hm. Not very impressive."

She turned her back to me to reach for something, and I felt rage, mine or maybe even Ollie's, boil me from the inside. "That's certainly not what Olympio has said every time it's in his mouth."

She turned sharply back to me, dagger at the ready.

"You're a fucking liar," she snarled. "Your bond isn't consummated."

"No, it's not," I growled back at her. "That was just because he couldn't resist once he saw it. He says *none* of his former lovers could even hold a candle to me. And that's—as you said—*without* the consummation."

She moved quickly toward me, and I expected to feel the sting of the knife on my most sensitive area, but instead, she took me into her hand and began to work me, stroking gently, trying to bring me to arousal.

"The fuck are you doing?"

"Just trying to see if there's anything noteworthy about you. Because so far, I fail to see what everyone seems to think is so special." She continued to play with me as she spoke. "You're not exceptionally attractive. You lack even the brains of a meerad—simple creatures, both of you. You don't seem to possess any kind of skill that might make you

350

valuable. And you don't even have a cock that's impressive enough to make up for your failings in every other way."

Vassenia had always been ruthless, but this stung. A verbal confirmation of my worst fears.

I wasn't special enough for Ollie.

Finally, after trying for several minutes to get me hard and failing, she released my member, letting it flop back down into my lap.

"Forget impressive. You don't even have a cock that works." She gave me a look dripping with unbridled contempt. "So what is it? What is it he sees in you that could take him away from me?"

"I…" I stammered over my words, feeling violated and afraid. I switched tactics. She touched me less when I made her believe I didn't want him. Maybe that would still work. "I don't know. You're a much better match. I swear."

My head snapped to the side with a burst of pain as Vassenia slapped me hard, then grabbed my chin, forcing me to look at her.

"I don't need you to tell me what I already know." She all but threw me away from her, nearly causing the chair I was in to topple over backward. Then she pulled my shining black dagger out again and held it up in front of my face. "But as long as I've got you, let's see if Olympio will remember you as fondly when he finds your body, and your face no longer looks like yours."

I didn't even have time to figure out what she meant before she swiped the blade, opening a stinging cut across my cheek.

Okay. Not too bad. It didn't feel good, but it was no more painful than a fight on the playground.

"Please," I begged. "I'll do anything. Just let me go. *Anything.*"

351

She stood there, peering at me for what felt like an eternity. Then the anger that riddled her features transitioned into an unhinged glee.

"I'll let you go," she said, a cruel smile crossing her face. "I'll untie you now and set you free. On one condition."

A light suddenly appeared at the end of my emotional tunnel. "Anything."

"I'm going to hand you this dagger. And when Olympio walks in—which he surely will—you kill him. Because I want him to feel the sting of betrayal he showed me."

I felt like I was going to be sick all over again. "What? Vassenia, no. You can't possibly want that." Her eyes were cold as steel, and she appeared unmoved.

In that moment, I knew what I had to do.

Because I loved him, and nothing else would ever matter more to me than protecting that precious thing.

"Be brave and be fearless…."

Words I once thought drafted by my parents, now came to me long after I knew they had really been written by my soulmate.

The other half of who I was born to be. Who I had always been destined to become.

"Then," I said, taking a deep breath and speaking clearly. "You will have to kill me. Because I would never betray the man who was made for me, the way I was made for him."

I had thought a million times about what making a decision like this would feel like, and I always imagined closing my eyes and just hoping it was over quick. But instead, I looked around, taking in my last few moments of this life before staring her dead in the eyes.

"If you're brave enough to do it."

And she laughed in my face.

"All good things in time, *soulmate,*" she said, running the blade of the dagger along my collarbone. "I want Olympio to watch you take your last breath."

Quick as lightning, she sliced into me again, but this time it wasn't a surface wound.

I felt the cool stone of my own dagger go straight through my rib cage, and a second later, I found that breathing was hard.

Not just hard. Nearly impossible.

I coughed and tasted blood in my mouth—felt it dripping from my chin.

Oh, god, I was really dying. It pained me to accept I would never see Olympio again, but if this protected him, I would...

My thoughts were cut short as I noticed a glistening purple string leading from my chest out through the door. It was... singing?

First a low buzz, it gradually got louder, sounding more like one of those meditation bowls than raw electricity.

Ollie knew how to find me. Vassenia was right.

I coughed once more, and blood sprayed into Vassenia's hair but, she looked unbothered.

"I would stop now," I said. "Olympio is almost here, and he won't show you an ounce of mercy. We both know it's true."

She pulled out the dagger, then swiped it across my other cheek.

"You barely know him," she hissed. "Months. You've known him for months, compared to the millennia I've known him. He'll forgive me. He'll see I did this for him—for us."

Her describing them as an "us" filled me with a new kind of rage I hadn't experienced before. I jerked against my restraints, trying to free myself and subdue her now. But I only succeeded in forcing more blood from my insides.

The world was darkening around me as the ethereal song of our bond grew louder.

"Ollie," I exhaled, moments from unconsciousness.

Blinding light broke through the darkness as the sun peeked over the horizon and streamed in through the window. But it wasn't the brightness that caught my attention.

It was the dark shadow growing quickly, blocking out the sun's rays as it got closer... closer...

The stone room shook as a massive black beast made entirely of shadow crashed through the window, breaking part of the wall as it did. It roared with fury at Vassenia, then lunged, grabbing her and throwing her to the floor.

It knelt beside her, raising a hand with Ollie's sickle in it, ready to deal a killing blow.

"Olympio," I panted with the last of my strength. "No. If you do it like this, then you're no better than... than Typhir and the rest... of those wannabe tyrants."

My words fell off at the end, but I was pretty sure the beast heard me anyway, because it turned its head toward me.

There wasn't really a face, just shadows in the shape of a massive demon. Horns, wings, claws, the whole deal. But as I looked closer, I saw a hint of yellow and violet growing brighter in the middle of the face.

The whole transformation took seconds as the beast shrank and gained color, until Ollie was there, pinning Vass to the floor, sickle still in the air.

I couldn't have called out again, even if I wanted to, and I gave a final wheezing cough, telling myself that at least I'd see my parents soon. They'd be so proud of me.

Dad would probably be wearing Columbia alumni gear. Mom would hug me for hours.

"Gabriel," Ollie said, his eyes really taking me in. "No…"

He hit Vassenia with the butt of his sickle, knocking her unconscious, before rushing to my side. His fingers flew as they untied me.

"I've got you," he said, lifting me and carrying me to a rustic bed in the corner. "I'm here. I've got you, Gabriel."

"Ollie," I gasped. "I wouldn't let her… hurt you."

"Shh…" he whispered, holding me in his lap and brushing my hair away from my forehead. "You were so brave."

I couldn't speak, so I just stared at him, taking in every detail. The copper hair shining in the dawn light. The violet swirls in his eyes. The soft pink lips…

"Gabriel," he said.

"I love… you." I had to say it to his face, looking in those eyes one more time before I went.

"And I love you." His voice was strained as he held me tighter. "And you're going to be okay, Gabriel."

I knew that's what they always said to people right before they died. I was raised in Hollywood. Had I been any more lucid, I would have called him out on it.

But instead, I just reached up and touched his face.

He put his hand over mine, then turned to kiss my palm.

"Here," he said, rustling around at his waist and pulling out a small vial. "Drink this. A gift from Perla."

Ah, yes. The administration of morphine to ease my passing. Honestly, it's like he wasn't there for my entire life. Assuming he was telling the truth, he'd seen the same war movies I had.

"I didn't have it with me on our hunt, but there was no way I was leaving it…"

He kept talking as I drank from the bottle he tipped into my mouth. It didn't taste all that bad, much better than the swallows of blood I'd been consuming.

And just like that, I slipped into my eternal slumber. With Ollie prattling on about how he had been clever enough to bring a sedative.

It was fitting.

Chapter Forty
Olympio

"Thank you, Perla."

She nodded and packed up her bag, putting away the collection of empty and half-empty vials that had been spread out all over the nightstand.

"It's been a long time since I've been called upon this often," she said, giving me a sly sort of grin. "I do hope this isn't indicative of how your reign will proceed, because if so, I'll need to take on a few apprentices."

"Never a bad idea," I said, reaching out to shake her hand. But she slipped two small vials of that life-saving yellow potion into my palm.

"Neither is this," she said meaningfully. "Though I'm sure you know that by now. That's one for you, and one for His Grace." She turned to leave, then looked back at me. "Please don't forget to take it with you on your next hunt. You might not make it back to me next time."

With that, Perla swept from the room, leaving me alone with Gabriel and three guards, Gryfian among them. I didn't even know when the last time he slept was, but I was ever grateful for his presence and for the bag he'd made sure I had with me.

I walked over to him and held out my hand.

"I owe you his life," I said.

He glanced down, hesitating, but then took my hand. I didn't allow him to pull away quickly, like he seemed inclined to do. Instead, I tugged him to me, pulling him into an embrace.

"Thank you, Gryfian. Truly."

I released him, and he quickly resumed his stance with the other guards, the hint of a soft smile on his face as I moved to Gabriel's side.

I sat on the edge of the bed, reaching for the cloth and bowl of cool water on the bedside table, gently dabbing at my soulmate's forehead as he slept. Vass had done a number on him, puncturing a lung and nearly causing him to suffocate on his own blood. If I hadn't arrived when I did and given him the potion, Gabriel wouldn't have been here with me now.

Perla's treatment had fixed his lung and closed up the wounds on his cheeks, though they remained slightly pink. Perla had said the obsidian blades were made to be fatal. She'd put all her energy and supplies into saving his life, and if the cost of that was a pair of thin, straight scars beneath each eye, it was a small price to pay.

I started to hum a Sefaeran lullaby my mother sang to me when I was a child. It was a soothing melody, one that had always brought me a sense of peace, and I knew Gabriel would need all the peace he could get after what he'd just been through.

He stirred in his unconsciousness, and slowly his hand reached out.

In an instant, I had hold of it, gripping it tightly, leaning over him.

358

"Gabriel…" I said in the most soothing whisper I could manage when my nerves were this shot. I knew he was going to be alright, but after seeing him nearly dead by Vassenia's hand, I needed to see him open his eyes, hear him speak, to truly believe it.

As if he'd heard my thoughts, his gorgeous raven lashes fluttered and opened, staring up at me with that color of azure I knew I'd soon never see again. "Hi…" he breathed.

"Is that all you have to say after nearly getting yourself killed?" I couldn't even pretend to scold him properly because I couldn't stop smiling over the fact that he was here, alive, awake.

He attempted a laugh but failed, his thumb making lazy circles on mine. "I'm… sorry…"

I bent forward and kissed his cheeks, then his forehead. "You have nothing to apologize for. How do you feel? Take a deep breath—your lungs need to stretch back to their usual capacity."

He did as he was told but immediately clutched his chest. "Ow," he squeaked. "Fucking hell."

The pain he felt echoed in me, the bond allowing me to share it with him, to take some of that burden.

"I know," I said, my hands returning to stroking his hair. I couldn't stop touching him, any part of him. Twice in the last two days, I thought I was going to lose him—first by almost dying myself, and then by him nearly dying at the hands of someone I once thought I'd trust forever. "It'll get easier quickly. Perla is a genius. The potions she gave you will have you feeling better within the day."

He curled into me, the pain still radiating through him. I would never admit it to him when he was in this state, but I was spent as well.

I still hadn't fully recovered from my own attack, and flying that far as a shadow had left me exceptionally fatigued.

"Rest, Gabriel." I kissed his cheek, then moved him so he was lying on the bed beside me. My arms went around him, like they had been anxiously awaiting the time when they could be there again.

Thankfully, the connection between us allowed us both to feel the pull of sleep at the same time. Gabriel's kormarrin flew over and curled up on the pillow above his head, nuzzling him with a soft trill before closing its eyes.

Gabriel's own eyes were heavy, and I could see him trying to force them to remain open.

"Sleep," I said.

"What if you're not there when I wake up? Or what if I'm not?"

"That will never happen again." I leaned forward and kissed him. "The threat is over, and my guards are just outside. No one will hurt us."

He seemed to trust me, because he finally closed his eyes and laid his head on my chest, falling asleep within seconds.

And I followed quickly.

It must have been a full day later, because the sun was in the same spot in the sky when I awoke, but I could tell I'd been asleep for a long time.

I stretched, rousing Gabriel, who nuzzled into me. I pulled him into my lap, cradling him and kissing his face.

"I feel... better."

I hadn't noticed until he said it, but I did, too. All of the pain of the poison and the stabbing had gone, and I could feel Gabriel's recovery was the same.

We lay there in silence for a while. Then Gabriel spoke.

"I get it now," he whispered.

"Get what?" I pressed my nose against his cheek, making a small circle, before making the trail to kiss behind his ear.

"Why you were so worried about the Consummation. In two days, we were both in danger of dying. Ollie, what would have happened to your family if we had died?"

I took a deep breath and let it out slowly. "Hard to say. There's always a chance Ari would be given a soulmate, the way I was after Vasileios died, but I would never want that for her. She's happy."

"The way you and Vass once were?"

My words caught in my throat, and I closed my mouth, taking a moment to truly think about my answer. There were no more secrets between us, no more barriers, which meant I wanted to give him the truest response I could.

"No." I shook my head with a sad smile. "Liro is truly good, and he's good for Ari. They make each other better for being together. I thought I loved Vassenia and thought I always would. But she had a darkness in her I didn't see, one that held me back from being the best version of myself. From being the king Sefaera needed. It was only after I met you that I could truly see it."

Gabriel tilted his chin up to me, and his beautiful blue eyes with the ever more present violet swirls begging me for a kiss.

And I was more than happy to oblige.

361

Our lips met in a burst of electricity that filled my body. Every time I kissed Gabriel felt like the first time, and I was ever more desperate for him.

His hands wrapped around my neck, and I laid him back onto the pillow, my body half-hovering over him as I wrapped a hand around the back of his head. My tongue explored his mouth as my other hand grew greedy, feeling down his arm, then back up to his shoulder, before moving to his chest.

He whimpered beneath me, a sound I would never get tired of hearing, as he hooked his fingers into the skin of my back beneath my clothes.

A groan escaped my throat, and my hips pressed forward, needing more contact. I could feel my arousal quickly growing, pressing into his leg, and I put my arm around his waist to pull him up into me.

He responded to me, perfectly in sync with my movements, leaning in to lick the side of my neck. My soulmate was already completely hard, and I could feel his need with the way he was fighting to press into me.

But one of the best parts of the bond, I'd found, was even though I couldn't read his mind, I could read his feelings. "Slow, Gabriel," I murmured into his ear. "Believe me, I want you just as badly. But we will have eternity. Just enjoy every moment for what it is."

"Ollie..." he groaned. "Can't we just—"

"We can't 'just' anything at this point, Gabriel. You've made up your mind to stay and to be a part of this world—with me. If we 'just,' that's it. And while every part of my body is screaming to take you now, I've been waiting for this moment for nearly twenty years. Please... let me do this the way I always wanted to."

Gabriel stared at me like he forgot who I was, then softened his body in my arms. "I didn't know you felt so strongly about it," he admitted, wrapping a finger in my hair and playing with it. "If it's what you want…" He gave a small smile, though I noted how heavy his breathing still was. I couldn't believe he went from the defiant brat who wouldn't even eat because I had told him to, to this warm, adoring creature before me.

"It is," I said, forcing myself to pull away and stand up. "Come here."

I scooped him up into my arms and carried him over to the tub, where I set him on a nearby chair to undress him. I took my time, paying close attention to every single touch, every time my fingers grazed the warmth of his smooth skin, every breath that hitched when I neared a sensitive spot. I wanted to memorize this moment, this event.

When I knelt to remove his pants, I paused, meeting his eyes only briefly before pulling the waistband down and exposing him.

He was still mostly hard, his length standing just slightly above his lap. I reached out a hand to touch him gently, running a finger from the base to the tip. Gabriel shuddered, and I looked up to see a blush on his cheeks that made me weak.

I wanted nothing more than to worship his body, to show him what it meant to me that he shared himself with me so thoroughly. I wrapped my hand around his hardness and leaned forward, my tongue tracing the velvety skin of his shaft before circling the smooth, round tip. I'd been with my fair share of men in my long lifetime, and not a single one of them had a cock as pretty as Gabriel's. It was a perfect shade of pink and smooth, with just a slight curve upward when hard. It was

363

pleasantly thick, but not overly so, and it was impressive in its length, long enough that I could wrap both hands around it and still have room to stroke him.

I saw a clear drip forming at the tip and wrapped my lips around him to catch it before it fell. Gabriel whimpered in response, making me pulse with my own desire.

Every beat of my heart brought with it the renewed question of whether we truly needed to draw this out. Having him nestled between my lips and on my tongue, I could have easily forgotten my fantasy about this and taken him, sealing the bond forever.

But these would be the last moments Gabriel had as a mortal. The last moments when his blood ran red rather than the glimmering gold. The last moments I'd be able to stare into those cerulean eyes before we would both forever share the same violet irises. And as long as I could, I would. Even as my mouth began to move up and down along his shaft, my hand sliding at the base in tandem, my gaze held his.

When I felt him beginning to tremble, to shift his hips to meet me with more force, I pulled away. I wanted to spend the rest of the day and the entire night pleasuring him slowly, drawing out the experience into one neither of us would ever forget, which meant not racing to anyone's finish line.

I stood up, leaning over him with my hands on his face to kiss his soft, plush lips.

"Let me bathe you," I said, straightening up and offering him my hand to help him into the tub.

"Ollie—" Gabriel squeaked, clearing his throat. "Are you sure you shouldn't just… uh… finish it? The last time you left me like this, we both nearly died."

I could see his cock bounce as it pulsed, the orgasm that would never be.

I laughed and pulled him to his feet, wrapping my arms around his waist.

"I have absolutely no intention of 'leaving you like that,'" I assured him. "But you said we could do this my way. And, unfortunately for you, twenty five hundred years has given me time to learn patience—no matter how ravenous the bond is for this."

I kissed him one more time, then lifted him beneath the arms and set him in the tub, the erula blossom infused water coming up to his waist while standing.

Gabriel relaxed into the water, closing his eyes and smelling the air as he sat on a submerged ledge.

"You know," he smiled. "I used to think those smelled terrible when I first got here. But now, I really like them. They smell like home."

His eyes opened, tears lingering in the bottom crease of his eyelid. The blue was like an ocean, and for the first time, I noticed a yellow freckle there.

I walked around behind him and sat down on the edge of the bath, putting my feet into the water on either side of him. I used both hands to gently tip his face up so I could look down at him and kiss away the tears.

"You have no idea what you saying that means to me." I gently rubbed my nose on his cheek, making our special circle. "Because I have lived here my entire life, but it never truly felt like home until you were here with me."

It had been over a month since the ill-fated Consummation. At the time, I'd been so focused on the ceremony rather than on what it represented. I'd allowed Gabriel to be manhandled by attendants he didn't know and to nearly go through with it while so detached that he had barely been there at all.

This time, I was committed to making it right. To making this special and just for us.

I reached for a cloth and dipped it in the water before running it across Gabriel's skin, clearing away the remnants of Vassenia's betrayal. The dirt and dust, the blood, the tension that still lingered in his shoulders.

I washed every inch of his body, then filled a pitcher with the ever warm water and poured it over his head, watching his soft hair curl slightly in its dampness. I massaged his scalp with my fingers, moving in slow circles to help ease any negative thoughts or feelings he may still have been holding onto.

"That feels nice," he cooed.

The utter relaxation in his voice and in the bond filled me with a deep, visceral contentment, and I remained there, giving him that one little gesture he said felt nice, for long enough that my fingers began to tire.

I kissed his head and stood, grabbing a soft, plush towel off of the rack and bringing it over to him.

"Here," I said, holding out my hand to help him out of the bath. He took it and stepped into my arms as he emerged.

"You know," he said as he began to dry himself. "You have some of the most incredible eyes."

"Really?" I asked, pleased by the compliment, but surprised. I'd been complimented on many of my physical features in my lifetime, having made my looks my entire personality for a larger portion of it. But it was rarely my eyes people seemed to notice.

"Mm-hm," he replied in an off-hand manner. "It was one of the first things I ever noticed about you."

I smiled and reached out, wrapping the towel snugly around him and pulling his back against my chest, holding him tight.

"And will you still like them when they match yours?" As I spoke, I ran my hands along his sides and front, drying him and trying to slow my racing heart.

"As long as I get to spend the rest of my life looking at them, I wouldn't care what color they were."

"And what a long, wonderful life it will be," I said, burying my face in the side of his neck and kissing the soft skin there.

Gabriel looked at me over his shoulder like I was his savior and pulled my hand to his face, kissing my knuckles.

"And now...?"

The question was simple enough. What was next?

"Now..." I kissed him one last time before looking into his eyes. "I treat you like the royal you were born to be."

I sat Gabriel on the chaise, urging him to recline, wanting him to remain this relaxed. I stood in front of him and ran my hands down his arms, then quickly grabbed his wrists and held them over his head, on the backrest of the chaise as I looked down at him.

I could visibly see him swallow, and his breathing became more audible and shallow. "Ollie…"

I smiled and leaned forward to kiss him, feeling him arch up into me and exercising every ounce of control I'd had to rely on before we'd gotten to this point. Every bit of practiced restraint I'd forced upon myself back in the frat house and even here, before he'd opened up to me. Every modicum of self-control I'd ever had to learn so Gabriel could come to me in his own time.

Because this moment wasn't just about a physical release. This moment was about the formal, cosmic union of our souls, and both of us deserved to experience this for the monumental step it was.

Yet his lips seemed so desperate to consume my own that I couldn't have pulled away if I tried. Every lick, every bite, every whimper nudged me toward the inevitable.

"Gabriel…" I moaned, my teeth nipping at his lower lip. "Slow down. Please."

"I can't," he breathed into my ear. "I need you. I need you so bad it hurts in my chest."

I felt it, too. I had thought the pull was strong just being in the same room with him once. But with our bodies touching, ready to come together, every second that went by without giving in was agony in greater measure.

"Not much longer," I begged, my fingers tangling in his hair, holding him back from me by only a couple of inches. "Please. Just a bit more. Just give me a bit longer with you still exactly like this. Let me relish this process. We will only get this one time—one time in all of eternity."

Gabriel seemed to understand and relaxed back onto the chaise, his towel falling open and his eyes softening into a meditative consciousness. He was choosing to take this in, moment by moment, with me.

"Stay here." I kissed him once, then went to the table near the bath where toiletries had been laid out and arranged, including the golden paints and adornments his attendants dressed him in for parties. I stacked them onto a small tray and walked them back to Gabriel, setting it on a table nearby. "Just relax. Let me pamper you."

Gabriel nodded like a child who had been told to hold up his foot and have his laces tied, looking at me like he couldn't imagine a more beautiful thing if he tried.

We couldn't help but continue to exchange small glances, tiny smiles, and little bits of laughter when I dropped some of the gold dust everywhere as I tried to sprinkle it delicately on his head. I wished more than anything in the world that I could just freeze this moment in time, and live in this pure happiness with him for eternity.

The paintbrush swept across his cheekbones, just below the small pink scars, making his cheeks glow golden. Next came his eyes, the gilded pigment enhancing the rich blue and purple irises.

Then I set down the brushes, admiring my work, and reached for his hand.

"Are you ready?"

Chapter Forty-One
Gabriel

There had always been a pull.

I hadn't understood it at the time. That first time I ever saw Ollie, when he ran into me in that store, the day my parents died, I'd felt something but couldn't explain it even to myself. And like every person who encounters something beyond their point of reference, I'd brushed it off as my imagination.

But now that I had given myself over to all of this, to Ollie and to the fact that I was his soulmate and he was mine, it was like a floodgate had opened. Every milestone along the way had tightened that little string that connected my heart to his, and now, on the precipice of that final step where I would allow my soul to be forever joined with his, I could hardly stand even an inch of distance between us.

He pulled me to my feet, and I stepped into him, his embrace tight around my shoulders. I pressed my lips into his chest and breathed him in, then looked up into his yellow eyes, the color barely visible from all the purple in them. It was like the magic there knew.

He didn't break the eye contact between us as he moved his hands to my waist and began to walk forward, forcing me backward. In any other circumstance, I might have been afraid of tripping, but my trust in Ollie and in the connection of the bond was so absolute that I didn't even question it.

Eventually, the backs of my legs hit the edge of the bed, and Ollie stopped. We paused momentarily, then—our energy wholly synchronized—I jumped into his arms and he caught me around the back of my thighs. Our lips met once more, and the need that had simmered there exploded into a wildfire of passion.

"Gabriel…" he moaned into my mouth, his fingers digging into my skin. "My Gabriel…"

"Your Gabriel," I sighed against his lips. "Always."

His arousal was adamant, pressing up underneath me, a mirror to my own, as he laid me back on the bed. His lips remained a constant pressure and rhythm against my own, the warmth of his body surrounding me, even through the garment he still wore.

"Can you take that off?" I asked. "I want to feel your skin on mine."

The sound of ripping fabric was almost immediate as Ollie roughly pulled his clothes from his body, too impatient to wait long enough to remove them with care. Small metal links hit the marble as his belt broke into pieces, leaving his body bare against mine.

"I'm aching for you, Ollie," I whimpered, not wanting to speed through this momentous occasion, but I needed him to know what he did to me.

"Me, too," he moaned, claiming my lips again. His hands went to my hips, gripping them tightly and pulling me against him, causing our lengths to press together between us.

I looked down to see what I felt, and my eyes rolled at the mind blowing image of us there, hard, together. I looked back up at the prince—*my* prince—and reached for his hand, bringing it to my barely parted lips and kissing each one of his fingertips. I took the last finger, his thumb, into my mouth slightly and sucked on it, my eyes never straying from him.

Ollie's eyes fluttered closed, and a deep, primal groan sounded from his throat. He applied just a bit of pressure downward, opening my mouth slightly, his thumb still resting on my tongue.

"Promise me," he said, licking his own lips, "that, every day for the rest of our eternal lives, you will look at me like this—just like this."

I nodded slowly, the promise filling the energy that was beginning to manifest in tiny purple sparkles all around us.

Then Olympio hooked his hands beneath my thighs once more and turned his body so he not only ended up beneath me, but pulled me up onto his chest.

"Ollie?"

"Closer," he said, his hands gripping my ass, urging me toward his face.

I scooted forward, my painfully hard cock bouncing slightly as I did, until it rested on his face.

He turned his face to the side, rubbing his cheek against my length until his nose pressed into the sensitive tip, nudging it slightly. The tender sensations sent a shiver through me, and a pearly drop emerged that slid down Ollie's upper lip and into his waiting mouth.

His eyes closed for a moment as his face took on a look of pure contentment. When he opened them again, he kept his gaze locked on mine as he began to run his lips gently along the underside of my hardness, base to tip, slowly, over and over.

"God…" I moaned in agony. "Please…"

He changed the angle, so I was pressed against his lips, ready for him to take me in, but he held back.

"Put your hands on the headboard," he said, nodding behind his head. "Lean forward. Give yourself leverage."

It felt like every hair on my body stood on end at his command, and I gripped the stone slab behind his bed like it was going to keep me from floating away.

Maybe it would.

"Now…" Ollie said, smiling and planting little kisses around my shining tip. "I want you to lose yourself. Do what feels right. Just take pleasure in this."

And then he opened his mouth, allowing me to push forward.

Inside was hot and soft and wet, and his lips closed around my shaft as my length ventured further into Olympio another inch after inch. I could feel his tongue wrap around it and run along the ridge beneath the head, causing another two pulses of restrained desire to coat his tongue with my essence.

He moaned against me, and the vibrations echoed across my skin, all the way up to my base as I pulled back and then thrust once more into him.

He took me in with a gentle sucking motion, wordlessly giving me permission to go deeper. As I bent forward even further, he reached one hand up to caress my chest, and his other slid across my backside to my cleft, his fingers quickly finding my entrance and beginning to press and toy with it.

The sensation caused me to thrust forward, feeling my cock hit the back of his throat, but he didn't flinch. Instead, I watched as his eyes rolled and he nodded, a whimper echoing between us, conveying his desire for more.

"I don't want to hurt you," I softly breathed.

Unable to speak, he made his position perfectly clear when he took the hand that was behind me and tugged firmly forward, forcing me deeper, his head tilting back to allow me access.

It was too much. It was all too much.

I almost began to panic and squeaked out, "Ollie—" patting his arm to tell him to stop. "It's too much," I panted. "I'm gonna come if we don't stop."

He responded by beginning to suck harder, his cheeks and lips moving around me, even as I remained inside of him to the hilt.

What he wanted couldn't have been more obvious. He wanted to drink me down to the last drop.

It was only then that I allowed myself what he had asked for and shifted, so I was almost supporting my weight on my knees, thrusting into his mouth like it was built to take it. His moans reverberated off the chamber walls, and I actually pressed my forehead into the cool stone as I let my hips do all the work, penetrating the barrier of his mouth impossibly hard and fast.

Sounds I'd never heard myself make escaped me, tiny yelps accented by deep, guttural moans as I claimed the prince of Sefaera's mouth.

And then I was coming.

Enormous waves of pleasure rippled down my body, all headed to one small point that sat at the back of Olympio's throat. I was calling his name out loud like it was the only word I knew, pulsing my climax into him.

Ollie remained still, his eyes looking up at me with adoration and his mouth continuing to pull at me, demanding every last throb of my orgasm.

I finally shuddered to a halt, Olympio's fingers embedded in me up to his knuckles. I collapsed against the headboard, and my lover—my soulmate—removed his fingers from me and pulled me by the hips downward until our chests were pressed together once more.

My brow was covered in a dewy sheen, and he kissed it, looking like he was halfway between cheering and crying.

I was too depleted to do much of anything, but my body carried on shuddering incrementally without me. Ollie leaned over the side of the bed to wash his hands in the bedside basin before returning to hold me.

He held me close, his hands running up my back and down my arms as the tremors began to subside. Eventually, he tilted my chin up to him and kissed me, the taste of myself on his tongue as intoxicating as anything else I'd experienced so far. Then his nose trailed across my cheek to my jaw, where he pressed kiss after kiss until his breath was in my ear.

"I need you, Gabriel."

I pulled back to look him in the eyes and nodded. "Anything," I sighed in a desperate promise.

Then I slid down the silken sheets as I'd done once before, but this time I positioned myself between my prince's thighs, looking up his body and locking eyes with him. He parted his legs for me so I could comfortably nestle between them on my stomach before taking him into my hand.

Olympio may have been a relatively average length, but I couldn't close my hand around him, and after he was inside me last time, I could barely walk properly—in the most delicious way.

As I pulled his glorious and worship-worthy member aside, I pressed tiny kisses to his thighs, slowly edging my mouth closer to his opening.

His hands were in my hair, twisting and tugging, not to control, but just to express the depth of his pleasure. "Gabriel…" he moaned, his hips arching upward.

"Is this okay, Ollie? I want to taste you. I want to have my face buried into you."

The sound he made was unearthly, and he nodded. "Fuck… please. Yes."

I giggled just slightly, not wanting to break the spell that had not only metaphorically, but literally settled over us, with purple orbs dancing like candlelight. "I'm honestly surprised that with you being such a top, you like ass stuff so much."

He propped himself up on his elbows and looked at me in confusion, his cheeks still flushed.

"I don't understand why the two would be mutually exclusive."

Truthfully, I didn't know. So, instead of asking more stupid questions, I curled my tongue and pressed it firmly against his throbbing opening. His body tensed beneath my touch, and he emitted a sound I'd never heard him make before. It was like he'd been holding his breath for a very long time, and this had been the thing to undo him.

"You have no idea how incredible that feels," he said, and I felt a slight shift above me as he began to stroke himself.

"I'd like to," I panted before running my tongue in a circle around him.

"Noted," he breathed.

I pressed my wet flesh into him over and over again, becoming more enthralled with his reactions every time I would manage to draw out a new one. Then, eventually, I put a finger into my mouth and wet it.

"Can I?" I held it up where he could see it.

"I would honestly weep if you didn't at this point."

It was then that I noticed a pull in my lower stomach. I was getting hard again.

I nodded and fell back onto my chest, licking him three more torturous times before pushing my finger inside him, crooking it up slightly, then reapplying my tongue around his rim.

"Yes, Gabriel," he said, his voice strained, controlled. "Just like that…"

I could feel how intense his orgasm was building up to inside him. Everything was impossibly tight, and I felt my cock twitch at the idea of plunging into that tightness.

We would have eternity.

There were no limits on the things we could try.

"More," he gasped, his grip on my hair tightening as his legs began to tremble.

"Do you... want another finger?"

"Yes! Please, Gabriel..."

I gave him what he wanted, sliding in my middle finger beside my index and beginning to pump them slowly in and out, going deeper and deeper, until I felt that little raised spot inside. I pressed on it, and Ollie let out a primal cry, stroking himself faster.

"Is that right?" I asked, concerned I was about to mess this up. "Is that okay?"

"Don't stop," he begged. "Please. Keep going. It's perfect."

I rubbed my fingers over the spot again and Ollie's hips bucked up as I felt him tense and release, a guttural, stunted noise booming into the space. His moans came freely after that as his orgasm took him over, and I felt his essence drip from his cock onto my face.

His body eventually relaxed, and I withdrew my fingers, moving to the same basin to wash my hands before returning to his side and falling into his arms for the main event.

I immediately leaned in and kissed him, sucking on his bottom lip and relishing in the hazy outline of a pair of dark wings resting softly on the bed. I hadn't noticed them appear, but I must have done something right if they had.

"Hi," I whispered when he finally opened his eyes again.

He smiled and ran his thumb over my cheek before kissing my forehead. "Hi."

"I'm starving," I said in between kisses. "Do you want to get some fresh air with me and have some oulons?"

Ollie nodded and helped me roll to the side so we could both stand up. I reached for a robe, but he grabbed my wrist.

"Don't even think about it."

We walked out into the warm night air, the purple shimmer filled with orbs of violet light following us like fireflies. I'd never been outside naked before, and I went to the stone railing to look over. "Can anyone see us?"

"Lucky them, if they can—"

"Ollie."

"No," he laughed. "No one can see us."

I reached out for him and pulled him against me, kissing him as he bent to meet my lips.

His hands were on my waist then, holding me back from him slightly.

"You know the Consummation isn't complete yet," he said gently.

"Yes," I breathed. "I know."

He gave me a searching look and said, "If you're spent... if this isn't the right time—"

"It's the right time," I said, not wanting to allow him to go too far down that thought path. "I want you tonight. I want you every night. I told you, I'm ready for this. My mind and my heart are in agreement. This is my home. Whether I'm in the orchard with you and Ari, or listening to Tomos drone on forever about people I've never heard of..." I paused, laughing. "Or even watching you glare at Typhir from across the room when you don't realize you're doing it—"

379

"I don't do that," Ollie laughed.

"Yes, you do." I reached up and played with his hair a little. "You offered this to me, and I accept. If you wanted to send me back now, I'd rather die."

"It would take an army to take you from me now," he said, bracing my shoulders. "And even then, I would fight to my last breath against it."

I kissed him again, the millionth of the night, but only a fraction of the kisses we would share in years to come.

Suddenly, I could feel him get nervous—a feeling I'd rarely felt from my soulmate.

"Ollie?"

He looked at me with thinly veiled confusion, but then dropped the act. "I can't hide from you anymore. You know what I feel as well as I do."

"Even if I didn't," I began, grabbing one of his hands and holding it up in the moonlight. "I know you well enough to recognize the skin chewed off your fingers. You've been nervous about something all week. What's wrong?"

He took a breath like he was going to say something, but then exhaled, looking at me like it was the first time he'd ever seen me.

"Gabriel…" He put his hands on either side of my neck, and the expression on his face was somehow deadly serious and ecstatic at the same time. "I lived thousands of years without ever knowing you, without knowing someone would come into my life and change me in the ways you have. You've opened my eyes to the person I was and have shown me the person I want to be."

380

Suddenly, he released me and turned to walk back inside, but reappeared within a few moments, bearing a wooden box about as big around as the ones my mother's diamond necklaces in, but thicker and with my name engraved in gold. I looked up to see tears clinging to his eyelashes.

"What…?"

"We don't have marriage here the way you do in the human world," he said. "But I wanted to give you something. Every bonded pair to sit on the throne has something made just for them, unique from all the others. But for us, if you would be willing, I want this to represent more than our status within the kingdom. I want this to be a symbol of our undying devotion to each other. I want you to be mine forever, and not just because the bond chose us to be together, but because we choose each other."

He opened the box and inside was a crown shaped like a golden laurel, like they used to award Olympians.

Fitting.

I felt myself overcome with emotion, and I broke down, falling into his arms. "It's beautiful," I whimpered.

"And it's yours," he said, setting the box on the railing and holding the crown up for me to see. "Just like me. I choose you, Gabriel. Will you choose me? Will you… will you marry me?"

My heart was pounding. I had no idea if I wanted to laugh or cry or just take the headpiece and wear it as we made new memories right here on this railing.

But I did know this—

I belonged to him from day one. It only seemed fitting that he pledge his love to me in every way possible.

"Yes," I sniffled. "Yes, please."

The sheer glee on his face as he reached up and placed the crown on my head was overwhelming, and his own eyes began to swim with tears as he stepped back to look at me.

"You were born to wear that," he said.

"Forever?"

"Longer."

Chapter Forty-Two
Olympio

I couldn't get enough of the feeling of Gabriel reclining against me on the outdoor sofa as we looked out at the horizon, where the moons were hovering. His back on my chest, the weight of him, it felt like being complete in a way I hadn't realized I wasn't until then.

I reached for one of the oulons beside me on the tray that was placed there each morning and held it up to Gabriel's lips.

"Another?"

"I mean, it's no raquin but... yes." He bit into the fruit, sending the juices dripping down my fingers.

"And starting tomorrow, there will be raquins on this tray every day," I promised, putting the other half of the oulon into my own mouth before pressing my juice-covered fingers to Gabriel's lips.

They parted, taking each of my fingers, one at a time, and sucking them clean. He turned back to look at me, a fiery grin on his face. "Kinky," he said with a giggle.

I chuckled and leaned into his ear, wrapping my arms tightly around him. "I beat you to completion in the dungeon, and you think *this* is kinky?"

"Fair point," he said, shrugging and standing. He walked back to the railing and leaned on it, his nude body far more beautiful than any art I owned.

He was bent slightly forward, his arms supporting him, and my eyes were drawn to that perfect swell between his legs and back. The glow of the moonlight on his skin was magical, and nearly enough to distract me from the appendage visible between his thighs, even from behind.

Nearly.

I rose from where I sat and moved over to him, positioning myself behind him, hands on either side.

"Do you remember the first time we stood like this?" I asked, pressing my lips to the side of his neck.

He nodded, and I could see his skin rise in tiny bumps that cascaded the length of his arms.

"I never told you how nervous I was." It was a difficult admission, exposing an insecurity I had kept well hidden. "Knowing you and I were beginning to truly connect, and terrified that I would do or say something that would drive you away from me again."

"I have a hard time believing Prince Thousand-Cocks was nervous." He turned in my arms and looked up at me. The blue in his irises was barely visible anymore—we were so close.

"Not one of those thousand cocks actually mattered. They were never intended to stay more than a night, so it was never an issue if I did or said the wrong thing. But with you... I always knew this would be forever, as long as I could get my head out of my ass long enough to give you what you needed. And the thought that I would never figure it out kept me awake at night constantly."

Gabriel sighed, leaning in to kiss me. "But we're here now," he said. "And we will never have to be apart if we don't want to be."

"And we won't," I promised, bringing my lips to his and urging him back, pinning him to the railing. "Starting now."

I felt his heart rate spike through the bond, and Gabriel got hard against me.

"This is it," I told him. "This is your last chance to stop this."

Gabriel gestured to his length. "Does it look like I want to stop now? Please, Olympio," he said, rubbing himself against my bare thigh so I could feel a string of wetness connecting with the skin there. "Please take me the way you've been waiting for all this time."

And that was more than enough consent for me to spin him back around, my hands holding his onto the stone railing as I pressed against his cleft, my hardness already throbbing, aching for him.

"Olympio…" he sighed, his back arching into me.

"Don't move your hands from that railing," I told him. "Understand?"

"Yes," he whimpered.

I released his hands and kissed the side of his jaw, then moved my lips to the back of his neck, and slowly let the contact drift down until I was kneeling behind him, my hands gripping the soft flesh before me.

"I believe I made you a promise."

Gabriel trembled beneath my touch, panting. "Did you?"

Without further explanation, I moved my face forward, pulling his cheeks apart so I could press my lips against his tight little ring before allowing my tongue to poke through, moistening and prodding at his opening.

"Olympio…" he groaned, and the sound echoed off the surrounding stone. I had no doubt at least half of the palace would hear, and the thought made my cock throb and pulse.

My mouth was insistent, moving against him, demanding the relaxation and loosening I desired, that I needed. I let my tongue press harder, slightly opening him up, just a bit, before withdrawing and doing it again, and again.

I felt him twitch and pulse against me and knew this would likely be my moment. The magic was practically breathing, it had become so insistent, the ancient powers ready to be made whole again after being adrift for so long.

Just like my kingdom.

My desire burst inside of me like an explosion, and I could feel the familiar coalescing of the shadows around me, forming my wings, my horns, and swirling out from my skin like smoke. It wasn't a complete transformation, but it was evidence that not a single part of me or the magic that surrounded my line was willing to miss out on this.

I pulled back and stuck a finger in my mouth to moisten it, then pressed it to Gabriel's opening. Immediately, he relaxed into me, and I slid in easily.

My soulmate whimpered, pressing back against my touch, forcing me deeper. "Please," he begged. "Please, Olympio. I can't stand to wait anymore."

I stood behind him and held myself at his entrance, one arm going around his shoulders to hold him against me as I pressed forward, his body accepting mine the way it was always intended to.

I pushed just past the tight ring of muscle, which enveloped the thick, smooth head of my cock, holding onto it as I paused, just taking in the sensation of his warmth gripping me.

Gabriel trembled slightly and began to whimper, pushing back onto me, trying to deepen the contact. I could feel his need as strong as my own, and I pushed forward again, feeling the resistance as I slid in a couple more inches.

His knuckles went white on the banister, and he began to pant, his entire body pulsing against me.

Fully sheathed inside of him, our bodies fully connected. He was tight, warm around me, his skin electric on mine as I held him against me.

"You feel…" I couldn't even finish the thought, because every part of me was so tuned into the sensation of his soft insides clenching and tightening around me in a steady rhythm, in time with the pounding of his heart.

"Olympio…" His voice came out in a hoarse moan before he said it again, louder. "Olympio…"

I pulled back, feeling his opening grip my base for how tightly he was wrapped around me, before plunging back in, eliciting a whine and a gasp from Gabriel when I did.

"Are you alright?" I asked, forcing myself to wait before letting that carnal need take over.

"Olympio," he grunted, "my cock is literally dripping all over the balcony. I need this. Now."

Good. Because I couldn't hold back any longer. I moved my hands back to the railing, pulling hard, so he was pinned tightly against me as I began to pull in and out, slowly at first, then faster and faster, his body responding to mine by pressing back into me, his voice no longer coming out in tiny whimpers, but in cries of ecstasy.

"Fuck, Ollie," he shouted. "Yes, god, Ollie… yes!"

Every affirmation and repetition of my name was met with a powerful thrust from me. But it still wasn't enough. I wasn't close enough, deep enough.

I pulled his hands from the railing and wrapped both of our arms around his body, bending us both forward over the railing as I plunged harder into him, not an inch between any part of our bodies. My lips were a constant presence on his neck, where his pulse beat so strongly I could feel it.

"Gabriel…" I growled. "I—"

"Me, too," he gasped. "Oh, god, me, too."

I let go, losing all control and rising up to the precipice without hesitation.

In an explosion of light and sound and moans of ecstasy from both me and my soulmate, I felt Gabriel become immortal in my arms. The purple magic that had been swirling around us all night, that had joined us together from the day he was born, gathered in a singularity. As I poured out into him, I watched the ball of shimmering light divide and shrink to the size of a marble before making its way home, first in his chest, and then in mine. The bond, which had felt so solidified and permanent only moments before, had vanished, existing now within us, rather than without. We had simply become one being operating in two bodies.

Gabriel gasped, and the remnants of the magic swirled around as I held him. When it finally came to rest, the last shimmers and glows fading into nothing, he collapsed into my arms, and I lowered him to where he could comfortably catch his breath.

"Ollie…" Gabriel whimpered.

Then he looked up at me.

The shimmering bond that had been between us now existed only there, in his eyes. I reached up and gently ran my fingers across the scars on his cheek, no longer pink, but gold, the color of the blood that now ran in his veins like it did mine. His very skin seemed to glimmer as the shining liquid pulsed beneath the surface.

"Ollie," he breathed. "Your eyes are…"

"Violet?" I asked, knowing full well the answer.

"Yeah."

"Yours, too," I said, smiling at him.

Every moment thereafter was like a vignette of contentment as we moved back inside and got cleaned up. I couldn't keep my hands to myself, constantly grabbing him to kiss him, or even just to feel his skin, to remind myself that he was real, that *this* was real.

The blissful haze of our afterglow led us to collapse into my bed. But it wasn't five minutes before the quiet of the moment was broken as Gabriel's stomach let out an audible growl, and he looked up at me with a blush.

"What?" he asked with a laugh.

389

"Were you planning to tell me you were hungry again?" I asked with a gentle scolding tone. He shrugged and looked up at me without reply. "Shrugging isn't an answer."

"I guess not," he said sheepishly. "You've just done so much for me tonight. I didn't want to—"

"To help me take care of my eternal partner?" I cut in. "Don't be ridiculous. Let's get you something to eat." I rolled out of the bed and pulled on a robe, then looked back at Gabriel. "Come on."

He followed my lead, pulling on his robe as well and heading for the door.

But he stopped just short, something across the room catching his eye and causing him to grin devilishly.

"Can I wear my laurel or is it just for special occasions? It's so fucking cool, dude," he asked.

My heart pounded with happiness, hearing him so excited about this, knowing how difficult a road it was to get here.

I walked over to my wardrobe and opened it, finding the matching wooden box with my own name engraved in black and opening it.

I turned around, my own headpiece in my hands, to show it to him. It was identical to his in every way, except instead of gold, it was crafted out of the same obsidian as my sickle and his daggers.

"And what about our first night as king and consort doesn't constitute a special occasion?"

Gabriel grinned as he placed his on his head, the little pieces of hair gently curling up around the edges like it tended to do after he'd been sweating.

Then he looked at me in anticipation.

390

"Welcome to the royal family, Your Grace," I said, putting my own laurel on and pulling him to me for a deep kiss before opening the door and leading him out into the hallway.

The guards all stood at attention as we left my chambers, and Gryfian raised an eyebrow at me as we passed.

It would have been easy to have something brought to us, but the feeling of walking through the palace, hand in hand with the person who had chosen to rule by my side for eternity, without the pressure and expectations that would come when everyone found out, was too much of a thrill to pass up.

I couldn't stop staring at him. He was clearly tired, sweaty, maybe even a little grumpy from his lack of being fed, and yet, he was the most gorgeous thing I'd ever seen in my life. Looking at Gabriel was like seeing the stars for the first time.

"You're up late."

I turned and saw my sister coming out of her room, which we'd just walked past.

"Just off for a midnight snack," I said, spinning Gabriel around so we were both facing her.

"Something about the sounds I was hearing earlier tells me Gabe has had his daily fill of pro—"

Her mouth opened, the ever familiar smirk appearing as she prepared to speak, and then she froze just as quickly. Her eyes darted up to our heads, to the matching laurels we wore. "What are you...?" Her eyes went wide, and she stepped closer, grabbing my face and staring into my eyes. "You didn't!"

I answered only by putting my hands over hers and smiling.

"Typhir is going to shit a fucking brick…" She shook her head slowly, a quiet laugh punctuating the words.

"Typhir can fuck off," I said. "He doesn't have power over me anymore. I'm officially king, even if he doesn't know it yet."

Ari put her hands on her hips and rolled her eyes, then put on a mocking tone. "*I'm officially king.* Please, Olympio. You can barely find both of your boots on a good day."

"And if I rule the kingdom barefoot, so be it."

She stuck out her tongue at me, and then suddenly her expression changed. "Moons and Rivers," she said, as if she'd just remembered something important.

"What?" I asked, glancing at Gabriel, who looked just as confused as I was.

"No time," she said, grabbing Gabriel's hand. "Come with me."

Ari didn't really give him much of a choice as she dragged him into her suite, where, upon entering, we found Liro shirtless in her bed. I diverted my eyes so as not to make him feel uneasy.

"Ari…" he grumbled. "What in the absolute fuck?"

"This is incredibly important. Gabe, sit." She pointed to one of her upholstered chairs and my soulmate did. I wondered if he realized he didn't actually have to. He ranked higher than she did.

Ari dashed across the room, her bare feet squeaking on the marble floor. Then she flung open the doors to her liquor cabinet, pulled forth one of the largest bottles of the celebratory blue wine I'd ever seen, and marched over to Gabriel. She snagged two glasses off her table as she went, placing one down in front of herself and one in front of him.

"Forget something?" I asked, gesturing to where one should have been set for me.

"Shh—"

"Ariadne," I said, trying to pause her long enough to be reasoned with.

"In Mother's name, do you ever stop talking?"

"Not usually."

She then took to ignoring me altogether and faced Gabriel, pouring them each a glass. "Drink," she commanded.

My consort looked taken aback, and his eyes went to me. "Oh, I don't really think…"

"*Drink,*" she demanded again.

Now I truly was considering reminding them both that Gabriel outranked her, but he took the glass in his hand and downed it like he used to do at the frat house with that vile malt liquor.

"You do know wine is intended to be savored," I said warily, eyeing him for any immediate effects.

Gabriel's eyes closed, and he breathed in heavily. Then he opened them and looked at me. "That's your favorite drink?" he said with confused disgust.

I was stunned for all of a second before I burst out laughing and leaned forward, taking his face in my hands to kiss him once more.

"Please desist in my chambers," Ari said as she sipped her own wine.

"Jealous?" I teased, looking at her out of the corner of my eye.

"Hardly," she replied. "There's a reason Liro didn't enjoy your sudden intrusion. Before I found you, I had my mouth around his—"

"Well played, Ariadne," I said, cutting her words off. "But if it's all the same to you, I *would* like a glass of wine. For each of us." I put my hand on her shoulder. "I owe this to you in so many ways. If you hadn't knocked some sense into me and helped Gabriel feel comfortable here, I might have fucked it all up for good. Thank you."

Gabriel slid his glass over in front of me. "Have mine," he said. "I'd barf if I drank any more of that stuff."

Ari laughed and went back to the cabinet, pulling out a glass bottle filled with a vibrant pink liquor, which she poured into a tiny stemmed glass.

"Try this, then. It might be more your taste."

Irravel liquor—one of the sweetest and strongest spirits in all of Sefaera. I raised my eyebrow at Ari, who smirked and shrugged.

"Let the man decide for himself. He just became immortal, for fuck's sake."

Gabriel's eyes drifted to me. He was smiling but exhausted, and I still hadn't fed him.

"While we appreciate the offer, I think perhaps we should go after all," I said. "We will need to be able to walk if we want to make it to the kitchens or back to our chambers."

Our chambers. The phrase made my heart flutter.

"Boo," Ari said. "Well, Liro will be glad to be rid of you, anyway. We were talking babies before you arrived."

I glanced back and forth between them, chuckling at the way Liro's face went slightly red beneath his deep tan skin.

"And that would be our cue to leave, for certain," I said, rising to my feet and reaching for Gabriel's hand.

394

My soulmate followed my lead, yawning as he did. "Good night, everybody," he said sweetly.

"Good night… *Your Grace*," Ari said, smiling at both of us as we closed the door.

Out in the hall, I pressed him against the wall for one more deep kiss before I pulled away, staring into those vibrant purple eyes.

"Come on," I said, pulling him behind me as I started off down the hall again. "I'm not going to make you wait any longer for me to feed you."

"Hey, Ollie," he said softly with another yawn.

"Yes?" I said, stopping to face him.

"I love it here. I love them, and I love Sefaera, and I love you. Moons and rivers, I love you."

Hearing him use that phrase was second only to the joy that hearing him declare his love for me, my family, and my world brought me.

But he knew. I had no reason to tell him, because he could feel it.

With a small smile, I patted my shoulder and gestured for him to climb on my back. He barely needed me to tell him, because he was already halfway there. Our connection was absolutely unreal in its capacity to synchronize our desires.

"I know I had to break my promise in order to get you here, but I'm grateful every day that I did. And now, I will make you a new one— well, an old one made new," I said as I began to walk toward the kitchens. "What you're up against won't be easy, and almost certainly it will hurt. But you will not face this alone. I will be with you. I will always be with you. Until my heart no longer beats."

395

Chapter Forty-Three
Gabriel

The morning of the trial for Vassenia, I couldn't eat. The past week had been a walking daydream, but this… this would be a nightmare. Not only would I have to come face to face with the woman who tried to kill me, but I would have to look at her with justice and thoughtful consideration.

I would never say it out loud, but Olympio was driving me insane. He wouldn't stop trying to baby me the last two days, and when he wasn't doing that, he was pacing. Just… pacing.

"Can you please sit down?" I said from the table on the balcony where our breakfast was getting cold.

He stopped and looked at me like he'd only just remembered I was there. With a slight shake of his head, he came over and sat down across from me. "I'm sorry," he said, running a hand over his face. "You're struggling with this enough without me adding my own concerns to what you're feeling."

I resisted the urge to roll my eyes. "When did big, bad, Alex Kessinger-hating Ollie turn into such a simpering mess? Honestly… I thought after what we did last night…" I wiggled my eyebrows at him, referring to some particularly filthy things he did in his utter domination of me.

He grinned and leaned back, and I could feel the little pulse of arousal from him as he remembered it. "We've talked about that name," he said, a dark look entering his eyes. "And we don't have time for me to take you back to the dungeon and remind you of that rule."

I bit my lip and tried to take a bite of my breakfast, failing the same as before.

We sat in silence for a few minutes, Ollie looking out over the glimmering sea. But finally, I broke it when my thoughts came tumbling out before I could stop them. "Ollie, I'm scared."

He looked at me, then held out his hand, urging me to join him, and I obeyed. The second he had me in his arms, he turned us so we were facing out together.

"What has you scared?" he said in a low, quiet voice, his lips right beside my ear.

"I have to make a judgment on the life of someone you once loved. Not only that, but my judgment… it could result in…" I didn't have to say it. He knew.

I heard the slow, measured breath he took, and I could feel the twist in my gut of the lingering sadness he felt about her.

"You have always been an advocate for things being fair, for the right thing, even in times when it wasn't in your favor. I remember watching you turn down a spot on the baseball team in high school when you knew you'd only gotten the spot because the coach wanted to be an actor and was hoping you'd be a connection for him. You insisted another boy, who'd outperformed you, take the spot." His arms tightened around me. "Vassenia made choices. She's not a child. She's nearly as old as I am, and has had all that time to choose to do things right. She didn't. And I trust you to oversee and conduct her trial with the same fairness you've always strived for."

I had been half hoping he would tell me I didn't have to do it, but I knew that wouldn't be the case, especially with this.

Still—

It was nice to hear him remember all the good things I'd done, the judgment calls I'd made along the way, never knowing they were all leading me to my destiny.

An hour later, we sat in the throne room, side by side. It was dead silent as Vassenia was brought forth in shackles. She looked terrible. Like a dying raven who'd lost all the sheen from its feathers.

She looked up at me briefly, then fixed her eyes on Olympio.

I glanced over at him, where he sat on the throne beside mine, but he didn't look back. I could feel the slightest pulse of the bond, Ollie reassuring me he was here with me, supporting me.

I opened my mouth to start the proceedings, but I was interrupted by the sound of a door slamming open, and every head in the room turned to see Typhir striding in from the side chamber where the Council held their meetings.

"I believe my invitation failed to be delivered," he sneered, looking up at Ollie and me.

"It was never sent, Typhir," Ollie said in a flat, matter-of-fact tone. "Your presence is not required at this hearing."

"I have served as Justice for—"

"Far too long," Ollie said, cutting him off. "And you cannot be impartial in this case, regardless."

Typhir's snakelike face turned a dull purple color as he went apoplectic with rage.

"Guards," Ollie called. "Can you please remove Lord Typhir—"

"You will not!" he spat at Ollie, then looked at me. "How dare you presume to pass judgment on a royal advisor, when you—?"

"Your Grace," I said calmly.

"Excuse me?"

"Excuse me, *Your Grace*. That's the proper address for the Justice and consort to the king. And as *our* subject, you are expected to conduct yourself with respect."

I could feel Ollie nearly explode with pride beside me, and even though my hands were sweating, I held Typhir's stare.

Eventually, his brain seemed to stop melting in his skull, because he sank into a low bow, though the disdain never left his face.

"*Your Grace*," he hissed. "And *Your Majesty*. Will you grant me the privilege of being present for the trial of my own blood?"

I heard Ollie take a breath to answer, but I beat him to it.

"No."

"No?" Typhir echoed incredulously.

"No," I repeated. "Your entrance has already derailed this trial, and you have proven you cannot be trusted to remain silent and impartial. You will leave the throne room of your own accord, or the guards will remove you."

Typhir's mouth fell open as a pair of guards approached him. One put a hand on his arm, and he jerked it away. With a final, withering glare at Ollie and me, he turned and left, not back to the Council chambers, but to somewhere else in the palace.

And he didn't look at Vassenia once.

She watched him go, then turned back to face us, her expression even more hopeless than before. It was clear she thought her uncle would be her golden ticket to a pardon or something.

For just a moment, the briefest instant, I felt pity for her. For this person who'd lost everything, and now had to face those she hurt in her worst moments.

But I lifted a hand to my cheek, feeling the raised skin where I would forever wear streaks of gold from her vicious attack, remembering the feeling of drowning in my own blood. Of watching her bring a sword down toward me at the party.

"Vassenia," I said, carefully leaving off the title she'd lost. "You stand before Justice, having made several attempts on the life of both the king and myself. You abducted me, tortured me, and inflicted a wound that would have been fatal if the king hadn't arrived in time." I took a deep breath. "But there's something I don't understand. You clearly wanted me out of the way so you could carry on with the way things were before I got here, and yet, the first two assassination attempts were directed at Oly—His Majesty. Why? Why try to have him killed if you just wanted him for yourself?"

Her mouth was a thin, hard line as she looked down at the floor. Silence stretched on for a long time until I was certain she had no intention of answering.

"This is your last chance to say anything to convince me there's something redeemable about you," I said.

400

She straightened up to look me right in the eyes.

"Everything I did, I did for love. Love for my kingdom, and love for Olympio."

I had been hoping for more, for better. For something that made logical sense, that would give us something to work with. But if there was one thing I knew, it was if someone was willing to commit a crime of passion, and do it multiple times, they could never be trusted. She had proven she would not be constrained by banishment, and she was cunning enough to move through a palace where she should have been apprehended many times over before reaching my chambers.

I couldn't send her away, because she would come back. I couldn't lock her up, because she would escape. And I couldn't just release her with a warning, because she'd already undermined the sentence Ollie had passed on her once before.

My chest was tight, and I could feel Ollie trying to soothe me, but I lifted my hand slightly to tell him not to. This was my burden, my decision. One I had to make on my own, ignoring my personal stake in the matter.

But I reversed my position with my soulmate's. If it had been him taken and tortured rather than me, I knew without a doubt what the sentence would be.

And it was the one I knew was right, even though I knew it would hurt the person I loved.

"Vassenia," I said, forcing the words out, despite my throat wanting to close around them. I did my best to keep my eyes forward, to pretend Ollie wasn't there for this, but, as always, I could feel him even without seeing him. "You have broken laws. You have hired assassins.

You have attempted assassinations with your own hand. You have put the throne in danger because of your recklessness and vindictiveness. And you have shown a disregard for the repercussions of your actions." I swallowed and stood. "You are hereby sentenced to death."

Her face fell in shock, and the slightest pang of sadness echoed through me as Olympio accepted what he likely had known was coming.

"For what it's worth..." I said, lowering my gaze. "I actually liked you. I wanted to be your friend. But you chose a path that could have led to the destruction of an entire world. I'm sorry you hurt that much. But I have to protect this world and the people I love in it. Do you have any last words for this court before you are taken to have your sentence carried out?"

She looked around the room wildly, like she was unable to fully comprehend what was happening. Finally, her eyes fixed once more on Ollie, her hands shaking, making the shackles clank.

"Olympio... please..."

I looked at her square on, though her desperate gaze never left *him*, my soulmate. "I accept your final words, and they shall be recorded. You are hereby dismissed, and may you have a purer heart in whatever comes after."

The ritualistic words still felt uneasy on my tongue, but I knew them all the same.

Then I broke any and all decorum and subtly grabbed for Ollie's hand, unable to breathe as I watched them drag her away. I would face the king's wrath later if that's what he chose for acting outside of the typically emotionless and sterile trials—but I doubted he would bring it up again.

Particularly when he pulled me into a tight embrace. I held onto him just as hard.

"It's over," he whispered into my hair. "Let's go."

I let Olympio lead me out, and once we were out of sight, he kissed me. Tears fell quickly, and I began to shake as the full weight of what I'd done came over me.

"I'm so sorry," I whimpered. "If you'd never found me… if I hadn't appeared…"

"Then my life would have continued to be empty, and I would have still been putting my trust into people who didn't deserve it," he said.

I looked up into his violet eyes and nodded. "All the same… I am sorry you lost your friend."

He looked down for just a second, but then met my gaze again. "She was never my friend. I know that now."

I tugged on his hand, and we began to walk side by side in the direction of our chambers.

"If it's any consolation," I said, trying and failing to keep my voice even, "if you get really lonely, we could always go back to Columbia and fetch…" I jogged a few steps ahead. "Alex… Kessinger."

Ollie's mouth dropped open in mock indignation.

"You're going to pay for that."

"I really fucking hope so," I laughed.

And with that, I took off running as fast as I could, with not one ounce of decorum or regality. Just a heart bursting with love for the man who had saved me, mind, body, and soul.

Chapter Forty-Four
Ollie

After a month of royal life, I was certain we would reach a point where Gabriel was tired of parties, but that time never came. The night before our departure on our Consummation Adjournment, he was flitting about our chambers, as wound up as I'd once seen him at frat parties.

"Aren't you pumped?" my soulmate said with a glittering excitement that had nothing to with his eyes.

"For what?" I asked. "What makes this party any different than the one two nights ago?"

"Because," he said as he dropped to the floor, shirtless, and started doing pushups. "It's the last time we will see our friends before we... you know..."

I smiled, looking his body up and down as his muscles flexed. But Gabriel didn't even glance up as he said, "Oh, really?"

"Don't," I warned.

"Don't what?" he asked playfully.

"We don't have time."

"Well, perhaps you shouldn't have ogled me."

"Perhaps *you* should have refrained from showing me exactly what I could have been having fun with instead of going to the fifteenth party in the last thirty days."

Finally, he stopped, dropping to his knees, panting and looking up at me with a smile. "You know, I hear stories about party boy *Olympio,* and I'm starting to wonder if you're even him."

I raised an eyebrow without saying a thing.

"All I'm saying," he continued, "is you seem to go to bed before dawn an awful lot."

"Imagine that," I replied. "A king who spends twelve hours a day addressing other people's problems is tired by the time the moon rises." I stood and walked to where he was still kneeling. "Unheard of."

I smiled, so he knew I was mostly teasing and cupped his chin, looking down at him. It never failed to take my breath away, how gorgeous he was, and Sefaera had caused his beauty to grow tenfold. He really did belong here.

It was then I noticed Gabriel's eyes trained to a spot below my waistline, and I groaned in frustration. "Once again, Justice, I don't believe we have the time for this, and if you keep playing around, it won't be a game anymore." I turned to walk back to where I'd been sitting before.

"Oh, I'm counting on it," he laughed.

"Is that so?" I turned back quickly, grabbing his chin between my fingers once more and tugging it hard. "That's how you want it?"

Gabriel nodded, parting his lips ever so slightly.

405

"Fine then," I growled, pulling my length forth and presenting it to him. "Don't say I didn't warn you."

My soulmate's eyes lit up, and the glittering whirl within them spun as he took me in his hands, guiding me to his mouth. "Do your worst, *Your Majesty.*"

I felt the head of my cock cross the threshold of his lips and threw my head back, groaning, at the exact same time the door swung open and Ari walked in. She was greeted with the sight of me scrambling to tuck away my length and Gabriel fighting me to keep it out.

"Oh, fuck," she said when she realized what she had walked in on. "This is the last time I enter without knocking." She crossed her arms as if she was rather put out.

"Please," I begged desperately. "Better yet, send a letter first. No, send a letter and then—Gabriel!" I grabbed my soulmate's wrist as it had snaked beneath my tunic once more and was attempting to arouse me as I fought with Ari.

"Gabe!" Ari also scolded.

He sunk back onto his heels, a slight pout on his face.

"Anyway," Ari continued with a dead panned look at our noble Justice. "I heard Typhir is going to show his face tonight. Maybe you skip this one."

I looked down at Gabriel, plans for a sensual night under the stars suddenly becoming a possibility in my mind once more.

But he looked disappointed, and Gabriel's disappointment happened to be my one weakness.

"Thank you, Ari—well, sort of. Moons and rivers, fucking knock next time." I watched my sister as she left and was grateful to have her, even if she needed to learn to respect personal boundaries better. Then I turned back to my Gabriel and crouched before him. "How about this?" I proposed. "We go to the party, and once Typhir shows his ugly face, we leave."

"Really?" asked my soulmate, his face significantly brightening.

"Really."

I suddenly found myself back-down on the floor as Gabriel threw his entire body weight at me. He began to kiss me deeply, and I finally gave in, wrapping my arms around him and holding him tight.

"You really are something," I managed to get out between kisses.

He sat up, looking down at me. "Something good, I hope."

"Something wonderful."

We were only a few minutes late after taking the time to ensure we were both fully sated—for now. It was like every other party in the last month, but it made Gabriel happy, and so I put on my biggest smile and wrapped my arm around him as we moved through the room.

It wasn't long before I was leaning against a column, listening to Gabriel explain the concept of beer pong to a collection of nobles "our" age.

"Olympio."

I heard a few snapping noises near my ears, and I startled, my eyes opening.

"For fuck's sake, Ollie. We got here fifteen minutes ago."

I looked around and saw the group he'd been conversing with had dispersed.

"If you don't want to come to these, I can come on my own." He didn't sound angry, but rather matter of fact.

407

I reached for his face, stroking his cheek. "As long as I'm alive, you will never go *anywhere* alone."

The corners of his mouth turned up in a natural and sweet smile, and he stepped forward to press his face into my chest. "Okay."

"I see the slumbering king has awakened." I turned to smile at my sister as she approached. "Nice to see you. It's much more pleasant to look at you without Gabe attached to your cock."

"Knocking would solve that problem, Ariadne," I reminded her.

"Knocking *and* waiting for an invitation to enter," Gabriel added.

She shrugged. "Guess I'll have to weigh the risks on a case by case basis."

"I'd rather you not," I groaned.

She then reached into her dress and pulled out a small piece of parchment. "I came across this today when Liro spilled a bottle of perfume on my vanity. It's addressed to you, if I remember correctly."

She handed it to me and, indeed, despite the ink running from where the perfume had soaked in, it was my name it bore, written in Vasileios's handwriting.

The letter my brother wrote to me before he took his own life.

My fingers trembled slightly as they closed on it, taking it from her.

"How did you get this?" I asked. It had been in the very back of a drawer, out of sight as much as possible, but still accessible for when I needed the reminder that he actually existed.

"When you left to find Gabe, I knew there was a chance that was the last I would ever see of you. I had no idea who or what was on the other side of that portal. So, I went and raided your room for anything sentimental and put it in a box along with some of the stuff I still had

408

from Vasileios. I looked at it all once or twice over the sixty years you were gone."

She watched me marvel at it, trying to keep my emotions in check.

"But I figured," she said slowly. "It was about time it was returned to its rightful owner. The King of Sefaera."

I opened the letter, looking at the words that had broken me an entire lifetime ago. My brother's final words, his trust in me that I would make things right.

"*I never wanted this for you. It is a hard road, one that will require you to become someone new. I wish I could somehow spare you from ascending so that you could remain free. But our family… our kingdom needs you now.*"

It had felt like a curse, like my life was over. The Olympio that had received this letter was lost, unprepared for the responsibilities he would have to take on. But in my brokenness, I had found Gabriel, who put together the pieces I didn't even know were still scattered within me.

I could hear Gabriel and Ari talking, but my eyes drifted down to the words I'd memorized, the ones I'd gifted to Gabriel when he needed them the most, and the ones I would continue to live by.

"*Be brave and be fearless. Those might sound like the same thing but they're not. Only when you understand this, can you truly be your best.*

"*Take care of those around you and never let a moment pass that you don't cherish them. It could all be gone in an instant.*"

I looked up from the letter at Gabriel, who was every bit a vision, laughing with my sister, truly happy.

I had nearly lost him. Many times. Lost him to the dangers of his world, lost him to another, lost him to my own hubris, and to the hand of my trusted friend. I knew I would obey my brother's advice, and I would cherish him, every moment we had together.

"Moons and rivers," Ari grumbled. "I think it's time for your exit. I can't believe that bastard really showed. What does he want to be at a party for?"

I watched as she gestured to Liro across the room, who stepped in front of Typhir, taking his hand and shaking it.

"Damn, he's sexy," Ari sighed.

Gabriel laughed and put his hand on her shoulder. "We owe you one. Same for Liro." Ari nodded and then Gabriel looked to me. "Ollie?"

I nodded as well, taking his hand. But instead of moving toward the exit, I pulled him deeper into the room to the balcony doors.

"That's not where our bedroom is, Olympio. Are you losing your mind along with your sense of fun?" He was giggling, but I could still hear the confusion in his voice.

I raised an eyebrow and grinned at him. "I lose my mind every time I look at you, but this isn't that."

I pulled him out into the fresh air, closing the door behind us to give us a bit of privacy. It was just before moonrise, the sun still lingering on the horizon and casting a golden glow over the land.

"I've been waiting to show you this," I said, barely able to contain my excitement. "But as we're about to leave on a long trip, I didn't want to wait until we got back."

"Okay…" he said apprehensively. "What is it?"

I walked over to the edge of the balcony, where a small, low hanging cloud sat just above the railing.

410

"Have you ever noticed how the clouds drift around down here, rather than keeping their distance like they did where you came from?"

"Not really."

I laughed. "I figured. Well, this is really going to blow your mind."

I stepped up onto the railing of the balcony, balancing for a moment and looking back at Gabriel...

Before taking a big step forward.

I heard my soulmate scream and realized I might have wanted to think that introduction through a little better.

"What?" I asked, spinning back toward him, my feet firmly planted on the cloud I'd pointed out to him before. "It's fine. Look."

"Listen, Ol..." He took a step forward, looking over the edge and shuddering. "I don't know what I'm on, but I don't have the greatest history with psychedelics. So, whatever I've taken to make me have this hallucination, please don't let me actually do it."

I reached out my hand to him, continuing to give him a reassuring smile. "You're not on anything. Come here. I promise you won't fall."

"That's exactly the kind of thing a hallucination would say." He looked terrified, but stepped toward me, anyway. "You know, there was a time when you tried to keep me *away* from balconies."

"And if I had even the slightest concern you were going to jump, I would maintain that position."

He took a deep breath and stepped forward, eyes closed, and fell into my chest.

"Am I dead?"

I laughed and kissed the top of his head. "You tell me."

I watched as Gabriel slowly peeked open his eyes and made the absolute first-timer mistake of looking down. He quickly clung to me.

"Ollie, I never thought I'd say this, but I hope you're not expecting me to get hard up here. I'm not sure if I've ever told you, but I'm not so fond of heights."

"You have nothing to be afraid of," I told him, taking his hand in mine and making a tiny leap to the next cloud, which sat just a bit higher than the first, and turned back to him. "Come on. It's so much better from the top."

"Top?" Gabriel squeaked. "There's a top?"

"One I have wanted to show you since the day you were born." I moved back to the first cloud. "It's a gift of my line, and my line alone. We can walk on the clouds like they're solid. As my bonded soulmate, that gift extends to you. But until you feel comfortable doing it yourself, I can carry you."

I turned around and offered him my back to ride on.

I heard him inhale and breathe out slowly before climbing on my back. "I'm your soulmate, right? And you only get one, right? And if you kill me, you lose the throne, right?"

"Yes, you're my soulmate. Yes, I only get one. No, I wouldn't lose the throne, but I would lose *you*, and that's so much worse."

"Well, there goes my insurance," he sighed. "Just do it."

I laughed, turning my head to kiss his cheek where it sat on my shoulder.

"As I believe they say in the human world, 'No guts, no glory.'"

And without any further ado, I began to leap and hop, climbing through the clouds like they were simply steps leading up to where they

412

grew larger and denser. Finally, we reached the uppermost cloud, and when we emerged from beneath it, I looked up, feeling Gabriel's gaze matching mine.

"Is that…?"

"Yes," I said, setting him down on the plush surface. Hanging in the air before us was a mountain, one that sat above the clouds, out of sight of the world below.

"Do you ever go up there?" he asked with the wonder of a child.

I smiled at him. "The last time I went up there was exactly twenty years ago."

"What was twenty years ago?"

"You."

Gabriel's eyes widened in sudden realization, and he smiled. "It's my birthday," he stated, happiness lacing every syllable.

"Yes," I said. "Twenty years ago to the day, I felt you. The bond came out of nowhere and changed me forever."

Gabriel went quiet as he looked around, taking in the new view of his world. "Do you ever wish I'd been someone else? Maybe someone more…" He paused to think. "Worthy?"

I shook my head and stepped forward, dropping to my knees in front of him and taking his hands. "No one, in any world, has ever been more worthy."

Gabriel went silent for a bit longer, a single tear falling from his beautiful lashes before he cleared his throat and looked away. "So, what exactly happens on a 'Consummation Adjournment?'" he asked.

413

"Well…" I stood once more, pulling him into my arms. "I assume you mean besides the obvious? Besides the endless hours and days and nights we'll be spending finding new ways to pleasure each other?"

"There's things besides that?"

"Fortunately…" I took a deep breath. "Not really. You and I will be secluded in a world all our own for a year."

"A year?" he said in shock. "Won't they need us here?"

"And that's where the magic comes into play. Time there moves differently. We'll only be gone a week here."

"Oh," he replied, leaning his full body weight against me. "So, how do we get there?"

I pointed to the top of the mountain. "The same way I came to you. We open a portal."

Gabriel looked up at me and bit his lip. He was nervous. "And what happens when we come back?"

I bent forward to kiss him slowly, letting my love for him infuse the moment.

"When we come back… eternity begins."

Gabriel leaned his head back into me, and I clung to him, watching the mountain bob ever so slightly in the moonlight.

"Will you always…?" he began. "Nevermind."

"What?" I asked, tipping his chin up to look at me. "Will I always do what?"

He sighed. "Will you always love me this much?"

I didn't even have to think. "I have loved you a little more every single day since I first saw you, and I will continue to love you more each day for the rest of our lives. I maintain what I said, what I have

414

always said. Gabriel, I will love you with all I am. Until my heart no longer beats."

And with that, I pulled Gabriel's lips to mine and gave him a taste of just what forever would feel like.

The Prequels

Pledged to the Kingdom

Eleanor Rose

Chapter One

"If I was sworn by fate to one person for all eternity like my brother, I think I would prefer to remove my own cock."

My words were flippant but had a definitive element of truth to them. It wasn't uncommon for me to ramble nonsense for entertainment, but this time I meant it. Knowing it would amuse was simply a bonus.

And being amusing was practically my defining feature.

I had timed my brazen statement to slither into the ears of Vasileios, my elder brother, like a snake sent to needle him. I needed him to know, in the most fraternal way possible, that I was enjoying his fate far more than he was.

He caught my eye as he walked past and shook his head, entirely aware of my intention to bait him. He was far too wise to be hooked, but attempting to wind him up was my right as his little brother.

"Don't sulk, Vasileios," I said in a mockingly parental tone. "In eighteen short years, give or take, you will have a forever bedmate. Just one. For the rest of eternity. Aren't you thrilled?"

I looked around at my audience, "yes men" and lovers. Beneath each arm, I had a beautiful companion to entertain. Against me to my right was Pyrine, the daughter of one of my brother's advisors. I pressed

v

a kiss to her neck as Raior, a Councilor's son, ran his hand down my thigh.

"I mean, I wouldn't be," I continued, with an exaggerated glance at those beside me before returning my gaze to my brother, daring him to defy his fate. "But aren't *you*?"

I awaited what was sure to be a well-curated answer, the way they taught my brother to respond. He had spent more than a thousand years learning how to never give a contrary reply.

I reached for Pyrine's goblet and drank down the full glass of my favorite blue wine, enjoying the irritation I could see in my brother's well-trained expression. It was like he was halfway between laughing and challenging me to a duel. The two revelers touching me, and even the cluster of tightly wound Councilors and royal advisors eyeing me with their usual disdain, waited for his reply.

"It's probably for the best you won't have to deal with having a soulmate," Vasileios said, grabbing us both another goblet as an attendant walked past with a tray of them. His eyes flicked to my left and right, to Pyrine and Raior, then back to mine with amusement as he handed me a drink. "It's not a responsibility to be taken lightly, brother, and I know how much it pains you to be serious."

"Why take things seriously when the future king provides such opportunities to expand my repertoire of debauchery through his many successes and the parties to follow?" I asked.

Vasileios laughed, patting me gently on the shoulder as though he was dealing with a precocious child. I made eye contact with Vassenia across the room, where she had garnered the attention of a stunning young man with white blonde hair that fell in gentle waves over his shoulders and a physique that could almost rival my own. Her gown of midnight blue with bronze colored wing embellishments at the shoulders hung sensually across her frame, catching the eye of more than just me and the man on her arm. She raised an eyebrow, covertly asking me if her choice was to my liking.

With a subtle nod to show my approval, I turned my attention back to Vasileios.

"The ball is to celebrate my soulmate being born, Olympio," he said with a beaming smile that showed just how pleased he was, despite my antics. "I can think of no greater cause to celebrate to the fullest, which you seem to have wasted no time in doing."

"I don't do anything small, brother," I said, swallowing down another mouthful of the smooth libation.

"Yes," he replied. "I have been unfortunate enough to walk past a group of governors' daughters while they discussed that."

"Jealous?" I asked, running my hand down Pyrine's backside to grip her curves. Her sharp intake of breath told me all I needed to know about whether I would add her to my nightly routine, and it was looking favorable.

"As much as I ever am," Vasileios said, ruffling my hair with a laugh. He'd always been more reserved than I had regarding sex, choosing to keep the company of one paramour rather than enjoying the benefits that came with being beautiful and royal. He and his advisor Lyria had been lovers almost as long as Vassenia and me, though my pairing often extended to include any others we felt inclined to. "Walk with me."

The ball was an intimate affair, with only members of court in attendance. Tomorrow would be the kingdom-wide celebration, with my brother on display for all to gawk at, but for tonight, he could enjoy the festivities—as much as a future king was allowed to, at least. They were for him, after all.

I gently pulled away from my selected companions, holding up a single finger to indicate that I would be back. I had no intention of passing up the opportunity they presented, but I would never deny Vasileios anything he asked of me. He was the only one who didn't see me as being a disappointment to the royal family, who treated me as an equal, even if I knew I could never measure up to him.

As if to prove my point, Typhir, one of the highest members of the Council, called out to him.

"Your Highness!"

Technically, the address was proper for both of us, but if we were together, it always was directed at my brother. He was the heir, and I was just the spare, whom most of the Council would ignore permanently if they could.

Vasileios nodded in his direction, indicating I should follow. A group of nobles, who all wore expressions of the greatest smugness, surrounded Typhir, as if having the ability to summon the future king made them superior somehow. I hated every single one of them, and the feeling was mutual.

"Talaea's glow to you all," my brother said to them, and they all echoed his toast, raising their glasses.

"I wanted to offer my sincerest congratulations at the birth of your soulmate," Typhir said, his voice as slimy as his hair. The rest of the group, including his insufferable son, was quick to jump on board, offering their own congratulations, throwing themselves at my brother like doing so would grant them power or influence they didn't already have. Outside of taking the throne themselves, they had as much power as they or anyone else would ever have in Sefaera.

"Thank you, all of you," Vasileios said. "Having you here tonight is the highest honor I could imagine. Every one of you is paramount to the prosperity of this kingdom."

He spoke in the quietest voice of all of them, yet they hung on his every word as if he'd shouted them. It was impossible not to listen to him when he spoke.

I, on the other hand, did not possess his patience for these leeches. My eyes glazed over with the boredom of having to be *"the prince,"* and my mind wandered to tiny details that I'd spent over a thousand years looking at.

The ceiling of the grand chamber towered five stories high, with openings that moved by magic to outline the moons as they made their ways across the sky, showing the stars when they would shimmer like fireworks. Glimmering glass doors almost as high as the ceiling lined the walls on one side, leading out to the balcony overlooking the sea, while they had adorned the other wall with gossamer curtains over white marble which contrasted with the floor. Nearly everything was detailed in the royal colors of black accented with gold.

A glance toward one side of the domed ceiling revealed the twin moons Talaea and Coricas as one rose and the other set. When we were younger, before he had to take on the mantle of future king, Vasileios and I would sneak into this ballroom at night just for the delight of watching the moons and stars for hours. I recall one night, after a memorably hard day when I was still little more than a boy, Vasileios, who had just come of age, had come to my chambers, pulled me out of bed, and dragged me here. The stars often sparkled and burst like they were raining fireworks, and on that night, some sort of cosmic event had taken place, which had caused every single one of them to shimmer and cascade for hours.

"For all that we are, and all that we will be someday," he said to me, his words full of wisdom even at a young age, "we will never outlive those stars. They've been witness to every king and queen and Justice, every prince and princess, every citizen of Sefaera so far, and they will be witness to every single one of our descendants until such time that our world ceases to exist. And maybe even longer. We see ourselves as important, but compared to the stars, we are fleeting. Temporary." He looked at me with a smile. "So the next time Typhir gets on your case about some mistake you've made, just remember that he is no more significant in the grand scheme than anyone else, no matter how inflated his ego is."

A soft smile spread across my face at the memory. Sometimes Vasileios was so convincingly pleasant with the Council that even I almost believed he actually liked them.

When my reverie ended and my eyes found their focus again, I saw that Vass and the paramour she'd chosen had made their way over to Raior and Pyrine. They'd all moved to a cluster of plush sofas in the corner, where the lighting was lower, provided only by a couple of braziers that cast their pink and blue glow across their beautiful faces.

We rarely used this space, since it was reserved for only the most important of events, and tonight we were celebrating the greatest joy of the last five hundred years—the birth of the future consort to the king, future Justice, and my brother's fate-chosen soulmate.

Even thinking of the pomp and circumstance of it nearly made me vomit up every drop of the blue wine.

And that really would have been a pity.

"How do you not feel like your life is ending?" I asked him as we moved away from the sycophants, a part of me believing that he was putting on an act for the sake of those who expected him to fall into the role they planned for him.

"Because it's only just beginning," he said, and for the first time, I could see the determination that this new chapter in his life had given him. "Everything before feels… less important. Like my life was shades of gray, and I can only just see color for the first time."

Even as he spoke, I watched as his eyes scanned the room. I knew who he was looking for. He was trying to see if his lover of a thousand years, Lyria, had attended the celebration. He was doing a good job of pretending he'd forgotten she even existed, but I knew better. I knew that Vasileios would have been content if his soulmate had never been born at all. Now that she was here, he was prepared to do his duty, and, if the stories were true, felt the pain of being even five feet away from his soulmate. But he had loved Lyria since they were children. The memories didn't just disappear because another connection had formed.

He led us out to the balcony, where we could find some fresh air away from everyone else, just the two of us. Vasileios and I had spent many long days and nights like this, just talking or enjoying comfortable silence between us. On balconies looking out at the rising and setting moons, in the woods when we were supposed to be hunting, out at sea on one of our best ships as the salt spray dampened our hair, causing it to fall into our eyes in dark copper waves.

He was the one person who never asked me to be anything I wasn't, who never put expectations on me I wasn't ready for. Even when he disagreed with the way I lived my life, he never shamed me for it. My mother and sister came close, but even they grew tired of my inability to be serious, as my brother had so kindly pointed out before.

I stood just outside the doorway and watched Vasileios walk to the balcony railing, holding his goblet in both hands as he looked up at the moons and stars. I approached him and saw the melancholy smile gracing his lips, the gentle intake of breath as the breeze brought the smell of seawater to our noses. My brother had always had a much calmer demeanor than I, but this...

He had anticipated this since he came of age, and it had been even more important since the death of our father half a millennium ago. With the king dead, the throne was no longer protected by the ancient magic that surrounded our line. Unless the heir to the throne was bonded with their soulmate, and that bond consummated, he could not be crowned king, and the threat of a coup was an ever present possibility.

But Vasileios didn't seem to be relieved at the security the bond would provide. There was a quiet energy to him. A bittersweet acceptance, like I could see the chapter turn before my eyes and knew that my brother was changing. It was like seeing Vasileios for the first time, and I wasn't sure what that meant for him, for us, moving forward from here.

"I've seen her, you know," he said, his quiet voice having the same effect on me as it had on the nobles inside.

My mouth fell open, and I nearly dropped my wine.

"You've seen her?" I asked. It had been mere hours since he'd told me the bond had formed. It was incredible to think that he'd already found her and paid her a visit.

He looked back at me and chuckled at my surprise, then nodded.

"I had to," he said, a far off, dreamy look in his eyes. "It was like being pulled by my heart itself to her side."

I'd never seen my brother like this, so... resolved. The assurance he felt radiated from him, like a puzzle piece had fallen into place for him.

Vasileios, our younger sister Ariadne, and I were as close as any siblings we'd ever known. But while I saw Ari as my equal, I'd always looked up to Vasileios, even if I didn't always understand him. As the heir, he had been raised with certain expectations. He acted with a decorum I could never hope to emulate. But I was the spare, which meant that eyes were only ever on me in relation to my brother. He was taller, handsomer, and much more well loved by our people. I knew what they said about the playboy younger brother of the future king.

Not that I cared much. Most of it was true, anyway.

But a part of me... a part of me wished I could be more like him. I'd tried when I was younger. For several hundred years, I tried to walk in his footsteps, to command attention with the same ease he did, just by his presence. To convince people to do as I say, not because they had to, but because they trusted my judgment. To be so confident in myself that I didn't feel like I always had something to prove.

"But... she was just born," I said, confusion coloring my words. "You can't possibly be in love with an infant."

He draped an arm around my shoulder and pulled me close, both of us facing the shimmering reflections of the aquamarine and rose-colored moons on the sea. I could tell he was trying to decide how to say what he wanted to.

"It's not love like anything I've ever felt before," he explained after a long moment. "It's like she's a part of me, a part I didn't know was missing until now. I feel protective of her, like I would go through hell and back to keep her safe, to give her the best life I can. The way Father told it, when she comes of age, I will finally be able to touch her, but not a day before. Things will be different after that, and when that happens, my body will follow what my heart and mind have already decided."

"You mean..." I made an obscene gesture with my hands, a grin lightening the feel of the conversation.

Vasileios rolled his eyes and sighed. "Yes, you heathen. That."

"And what about Lyria?" I asked. "Do you still love her?"

Vasileios frowned for the first time all night, looking over my shoulder back toward the party.

"Lyria will always be my closest friend and most trusted advisor," he said wistfully before shifting his eyes to me, a forced smile returning to his lips. "But the part of our lives where we were lovers is over. It has to be."

I couldn't imagine a time coming when I could be so at ease with the idea of Vassenia and me leaving behind that connection. We were not officially an item. We'd always seen ourselves as friends first, lovers second, and never felt the need to define our relationship beyond that. It wasn't as if declaring ourselves as a pair or even getting married would change anything. We would still be a spare and his advisor, a title she was given at a young age, thanks to Typhir, her uncle, pulling strings.

"Well, brother," I said, reaching out to put a hand on his shoulder as he often did to me, "I won't claim to understand, but if there's one thing I do better than anyone else in all of Sefaera, it's celebrating, and I don't intend to let the single most important moment of your life go by without doing exactly that."

He laughed, pulling me into a tight embrace before motioning to the door.

"Lead the way, master of celebrations," he said.

We strode the length of the balcony back to the massive doors. Once inside, I grabbed us each a goblet from a passing servant, draining one completely and watching my brother do the same, matching me drop for drop.

"I expect that to be an official title once you're king," I said to him as I turned away and toward Vass and the young woman and two men surrounding her, taking and emptying a second glass, feeling the heady rush beginning. If I had my way, no one, least of all my brother, was going to wake up tomorrow without having lived this night to the fullest.

Chapter Two

"How in the absolute fuck?" I whispered to myself as I stared down at my cock. The little bastard had the nerve to be hard even though he'd seen plenty of action the night before. It was particularly inconvenient because, at the moment, all the alcohol I had consumed the night before was weighing on my bladder.

Not to mention, I was trapped in the center of my bed by Vassenia and the three other revelers from last night's ball, all of whom were stark naked and sleeping, draped across the plush mattress like they'd fallen in battle.

As the first awake, I sat up slowly and admired the scene. Vass and I almost always ended up back here together, but it was a rare special occasion we invited others to take part. Last night, we'd enjoyed hours of ecstasy with those members of court who'd been gracious enough to join us.

After weaving my way through the bodies, I slipped from the bed, the slick fabric allowing me to slide easily from the surface. I walked over to the small bar on the other side of the room, where I poured myself a glass of the finest Sefaeran wine to take the edge off of the hangover I was trying to pretend didn't exist.

"I swore to myself that I would wake up before you, Olympio. I've never gotten to see what you look like sleeping."

The rising sun streamed in through the two-story tall windows, caressing the supple golden curves of a breathtakingly beautiful woman. Her dark, cascading tresses, like a raven's wings, fell loosely around her face and over her shoulders as she rolled over to look at me. Her emerald eyes, so bright they practically glowed, glinted with delight as they found mine, and I returned the smile she gave me.

"And if I have my way," I whispered, not wanting to wake the others yet, "you never will. How else will I make sure you don't kill me in my sleep?"

Vass laughed and rolled out of the bed to join me. I served her a glass of wine as well, then wrapped my hand around her bare waist to pull her against me.

She looked up at me, the way she always did, like her breath was bated for my next command. A deep, visceral urge to throw her on the bed and have her amidst the other bodies was overwhelming. But there would be plenty of time for that.

Eternity, even.

Instead, I leaned down and pressed my lips to the edge of her jaw, moving them along the planes of her neck to her collarbone, teasing her slightly, just to see what she would do.

A ripple of bumps cascaded across her skin, and I was not unaware of the way her nipples hardened at my touch.

"You can't do that right now," she breathed with a giggle. "We have responsibilities and commitments, and… stuff."

I chuckled low in my throat, but then sighed and pulled away. She was right. Today, the entire royal family would be put on display as we paraded through the streets, announcing the joyful event of the birth of my brother's soulmate to the entire kingdom. It wasn't often that I was required to attend official pompous events, so it was even more important for my brother that I show up as requested when I was.

And if it had been anyone other than my brother, I might have told them to fuck off. He was one of the few people in this world I respected, and the only one I could honestly say I looked up to, even after fifteen hundred years.

"I suppose we should wake the others," I said, glancing at my full bed. "I imagine Pyrine's father will expect her home before the parade, and…" I hesitated, unable to remember the names of the two young men whom I'd shared some deeply intimate moments with the night before.

"Axio and Raior…" Vass said slowly, like she thought I was an idiot. Truth be told, she did, and told me so often.

"Yes, those two," I said, smiling at her as she grinned back. "I believe they're supposed to be working as royal guards, so we should probably send them on their way as well."

Vass giggled, or at least her version of a giggle. She was much too refined to do something so immature and girlish.

I watched as she turned away and walked out to the balcony where a fresh bowl of oulons sat beside a pitcher of what was likely water. Her hips swayed with each step, and I was certain that nothing would ever please me more than watching Vassenia walk away from me like that.

I leaned on the bar for a moment, sipping my wine. Her skin was a gorgeous shade of golden bronze, one that reminded me of the way the setting sun shone on the sea the times she and I had gone sailing for days, weeks at a time, visiting other kingdoms telling no one where we'd gone, knowing it would have been forbidden for us to go without a veritable army of guards. Her hair billowed in the light breeze coming in over the railing, bringing the scent of erula blossoms into my chambers.

Having given my eyes their feast, I set down my glass and took a step toward her. What difference could another hour make?

Quite a bit, actually, because at that moment, Raior—or was it Axio?—rolled off of the bed with a loud thud that caused the other two to startle awake.

"Good morning, Your Highness," Pyrine said, climbing out of the bed. She walked toward me, but whichever of the others hadn't fallen from the bed jumped to his feet and wrapped an arm around her waist, pulling her close.

It was adorable, the way he held onto her like I couldn't have had her to myself if I wanted. I hadn't known that there was something between them, and a small part of me got a thrill at the idea of inviting her to stay with Vass and me.

But I knew it wouldn't be more than a passing whim, so I let her suitor help her gather her clothing, and within just a few minutes, the three of them filed out of my room, the door closing behind them.

At which point, I turned back to my most trusted friend and followed her out onto the balcony.

She was sitting, still nude, on the railing, looking out to the river and across the kingdom. If ever I was to have a ship commissioned, I would want the figurehead to look precisely the way Vass looked right now.

She must have heard the room go silent, because she looked over to me with a coy smile. "Alone again, are we? I suppose that means we should go over your plans for the day, Your Highness."

She slipped down off the railing and pretended like she was heading for her clothes, knowing full well I would stop her.

Which I did.

"My plans," I said, grabbing her around the waist and hoisting her into my arms, sitting her back on the railing with me positioned between her strong thighs, "don't begin for another hour at least. Which means I have time for an additional appointment. Do you have time for an audience with the prince, Lady Vassenia?"

Vass pretended to think to herself. "Well, I am terribly busy, what with the future king having found his soulmate and all. I really don't know—"

Her words were cut off with a gasp as I slipped my fingers between her legs and toyed with her. She was already wet for me, making it easy for me to slide one, then a second inside of her.

"You don't know what?" I asked, smirking, knowing exactly how to undo her over and over.

"I don't know," she sighed, a tiny whimper slipping through her lips, "how I'm going to get all my tasks done today when I've just cleared the next three hours to feed the prince his breakfast."

With a slight growl, I dropped to my knees as Vass balanced herself on the railing, wrapping her legs around my head. The scent of her drove me wild every single time, and I knew I'd never tire of this, want nothing as badly as I wanted to please her.

My fingers resumed their pressure inside of her as my tongue slowly ran along her crease, then slipped between her lips to find the sensitive spot, coated in her sweet juices, waiting for me to tease it, to make her cry out my name.

Her fingers went to my hair, pulling it hard the way she knew I liked, directing the pressure of my tongue where she wanted it. Vass and I had tired of being delicate with each other a long time ago, hundreds of years, if not more, and now we were like two feral animals feasting on each other's flesh, living to elicit the other's screams of pleasure.

The fingers of my free hand reached up to take her breast in my palm, her tight nub of a nipple fitting between two of my fingers so that I could squeeze them together, dragging forward a wild cry from her lips and a rush of wetness across my tongue.

I felt her clench around my fingers, tightening as she climaxed for the first time. But we were no children. We knew all too well how best to please each other, a familiar dance practiced over the last thousand and a half years.

I looked up at her as she panted, coming down from her orgasm.

"All done, then?" I asked with a mischievous grin.

"Hardly," she said, echoing my expression and pulling my head back to her center. "Until I beg you to stop, you don't, Olympio. And even then, you give me one more."

"As you wish," I said, standing up and grabbing her to carry her inside to the bed, where I threw her onto it before burying my face between her legs once more.

At some point, Vassenia decided she was temporarily sated of my tongue and shifted so that she was sitting astride my chest, pinning me to the bed. There was no one in the world I'd ever let get me in a position this compromising.

No one but Vassenia.

Vass snapped twice and pointed to my pillows, signaling me to move up the bed so that she had room to work.

I moved with a haste highly unbefitting a prince of an entire realm, knowing where such a command from her usually led and desperate to get there as quickly as possible.

As I expected, she slid down the bed, gliding over the silken sheets, and positioned herself between my own legs, her face gazing at me from behind my stiff length.

Having enjoyed the company of more than my fair share of men and women, I was well aware of the fact that I was longer than many and thicker than most. It stood straight and rigid, pointed at the canopy overhead, the pink tip pulsing with need.

Vass studied it, almost like she was confused. Then she sighed and pronounced, "Good. But I think we can do better."

I watched as she made a show of sucking on her own fingers before sliding them down my thigh.

There was the slightest bit of resistance as she probed my opening, feeling to make sure that it would allow her to enter. Thankfully, after a full night of enjoyment, I was already loosened up and ready for her to slip her fingers inside me, grazing the spot that sent a delicious throb through my cock.

"Trying to end things quickly?" I asked with a laugh. She knew just how sensitive I was to this kind of pleasure.

"Please," she said, withdrawing, then plunging deep once more. "If that's all it takes to undo the prince and our Master of the Hunt, then our beloved Sefaera is troubled indeed."

She took that moment to cover the end of my cock with her warm, inviting lips, and I knew if I didn't pull myself together, I would prove her right.

"Fuck," I moaned, knowing she was doing her best to challenge me. "Well... I suppose every royal needs to stand up to... extreme interrogation techniques, don't we?"

Vass almost choked for laughing with my member sliding deep into her throat, and the vibrations were driving me even closer to that edge.

But then, I felt a third finger shove past my entrance, and I sat up with a start.

"Vass," I gasped, reaching toward her. "Too much."

She grinned, pulling her lips in with a look that showed she knew exactly what she'd been doing. Knowing Vass the way I did, surprising me with a bit of unexpected discomfort was her idea of keeping our sex life fresh.

"My apologies, Your Highness," she said. "I simply thought His Royal Highness might wish to know precisely what it feels like when he 'accidentally' enters a hole unprepared for him. Like you did mine last night."

She was giving me a scolding look, but I knew it was all jest.

I was about to respond, but just then, a loud knock sounded at my door. I opened my mouth to tell them to wait just a moment so that Vass and I could get dressed, but she had other plans.

While I was distracted just for that moment, she dipped her head, quickly taking all of me into her mouth—or as much as was possible—and rubbing the spot she'd been teasing inside me.

I felt the familiar clench in my lower abdomen as she used the techniques she'd spent most of our lives perfecting, knowing she could make me come in seconds when she wanted to, and right then, that's just what she did.

I emptied myself into her mouth, watching her eyes flutter shut as she drank me down. There was nothing more perfect than watching my essence spill down her chin once she could hold no more inside those delicious lips.

Once her mouth was clear, she climbed up and kissed me. "Good little prince," she whispered in my ear, biting on my lobe as she did.

I whipped my head in her direction, a smirk forming on my face, but before I could say a word in response to her teasing patronization, the door to my chambers opened, and my sister walked in.

Anyone else might have been embarrassed, but I felt like, if Ari was bold enough to enter unannounced, she only had herself to blame for what she walked in on.

"Talaea's glow," I said with a shit-eating grin in her direction. "To what do I owe…"

My words trailed off as I looked, really looked, at my sister. Normally, she would have walked in and thrown herself onto my couch, poking fun at me for the compromising position she'd found me in.

She'd have helped herself to any food or drinks I had available, and stared me down in a silent battle of wills as I attempted to either compose myself or complete my task.

Not today.

Today, Ariadne stood just inside my door as it shut behind her with a slam that didn't even faze her. Her copper hair, usually pulled up high on her head with a tail that swung down over her shoulder, was loose, lank, and unkempt. And her face… her perpetually amused expression was gone, replaced with red splotches across her cheeks and around her red-rimmed eyes.

She looked lost. Broken.

"What's wrong?" I said, my heart pounding as I jumped out of bed and pulled on my robe.

Vass seemed to realize something was wrong, too, because she was on her feet as well, putting back on her gown from the night before.

Ari simply stared at me, which is when I noticed she was carrying a sheet of folded parchment.

"Ari…" I said, approaching her slowly, like she was an animal who might spook easily. "What's wrong?"

For the first time since our father died, I watched my younger sister's lower lip quiver as she held out the parchment to me. It had my name on it in my brother's hand, and my heart pounded even harder than it had begun to at the sight of my strong, unflappable sister so distraught.

The last time I'd been given a letter like this, it was my brother telling me our father would not recover from his illness, and we should gather to say our goodbyes. That was hundreds of years ago, but the pit in my stomach that moment left me with seemed to reopen, creating a gaping maw in my chest that threatened to swallow me whole.

My fingers shook as I opened the letter, dreading what might be inside. My mother ill? A declaration of war from another world, possibly even the human world rising up after all these centuries?

I wish it had been one of those. Any of them could have been fixed. Any of them could have been dealt with and made better. What was contained in the letter… was permanent and could not be undone.

"Vasileios…" Ari finally said, even before I could even read what was written. She swallowed, and her voice cracked as she spoke, the words like daggers in her throat. "Olympio… Vasileios is dead."

Chapter Three

The parchment was stained with tears; the ink running where my brother had cried as he wrote.

"*Olympio,*

I wish I did not have to write this. I wish I had made a better choice. I wish I'd had an ounce of sense about me, but I didn't. Brother, if you're reading this, I'm dead."

My heart seemed to stop, and the world went silent to my ears. I was adrift, undone. My body felt unreal, and my eyes lost their focus as I looked away from the letter and back at Ari, whose lip quivered as she watched me reading.

"Dead?" I choked out, my voice even tighter and hoarser than hers.

Her desolate wail, a sound I'd only heard once before in our lives, was answer enough. I leaned against the wall for support, but my legs gave up, and I sank to the floor, letting the parchment fall before me.

My hands wouldn't work, but my eyes were desperate to know what Vasileios would have sent me, and how he would have known his life was at risk.

And that was when I learned the worst news I ever had.

"You know that Lyria and I have long been lovers, much like yourself and Vass. I was so stupid, Olympio. I didn't even think before I did it. Before I took Lyria back to my chambers. Before I broke the bond with Kynthea."

Broke the bond.

He'd slept with Lyria after his soulmate was born.

Only the royal family were granted soulmates by the ancient magic that safeguarded our claim to the throne, so most never knew the intricate details that surrounded them. But for those of us who'd grown up learning about the way they worked, it was common knowledge that, once your soulmate was brought into the world, your sexual adventures came to an end with anyone other than the person fate chose for you. Otherwise, you would break the bond between you, and the throne would remain unprotected. The magic that made us immortal, the magic that gave us our right to rule, was solidified through a single act of consummation after our soulmate was born, allowing the magic to enter them as well.

And my brother had put our lineage at risk with a single drunken mistake.

His writing grew shaky as the letter continued, as if he was struggling to write the rest.

"I cannot face tomorrow, Brother. I cannot show my face to the kingdom, to the council, to you and mother and Ariadne, knowing that I have destroyed everything. I only hope that fate will be kind. That, even as the second born, once you take my place, you will one day be granted a soulmate of your own and will be granted the chance I squandered for myself.

"I never wanted this for you. It is a hard road, one that will require you to become someone new. I wish I could somehow spare you from ascending so that you

could remain free. But our family… our kingdom needs you now. By the time you receive this letter, it will be too late. I will have taken my life so perhaps you can do what I failed to.

"This would never have been the way I wanted it, but since I cannot change what is, only what might be, let me leave you with these parting words.

"Be brave and be fearless. Those might sound like the same thing, but they're not. Only when you understand this can you truly be your best.

"Take care of those around you and never let a moment pass that you don't cherish them. It could all be gone in an instant.

"Goodbye, my dear brother. The future of Sefaera belongs to you, and it is precious. Treat it as such, Honor my sacrifice.

Love in eternity,

Vasileios"

It felt like it had to be a joke, or a misunderstanding. Perhaps Vasileios was fine, and Ari only *thought* he was dead.

There was only one way to find out.

The sounds of Ari and Vass calling my name faded into the background as easily as I faded into the shadows, becoming one with them. I rushed through the palace, unseen, moving fifty times as fast as I could on my feet.

I came to a stop outside of my mother's chambers, knocking, the letter still in my hand. There was no answer. I looked frantically around, but no one else seemed to realize that anything was amiss. In fact, the entire palace seemed to bustle, getting ready for the parade as if their future king wasn't… as if he was still…

I could only think of one other place to look for my mother. I dreaded going, not knowing what I would find and fearing the worst. Fearing that my sister was right.

Vasileios…

I shifted into shadows once more, startling a small man with bright red skin and horns. It took me seconds to reach the massive doors with no handles. I took a deep breath, steeling myself, and placed my hand on the metal panel where a knob should have been.

It grew warm beneath my touch, like a living thing, and I pushed, feeling it easily give way. I stepped inside, looking around the space that made my room look like a storage closet.

This was Vasileios's room, the chambers of the monarch. I'd been in here countless times, lounging with my brother before his fire with cups of strong liquor; whiling away sleepless hours together; sitting at his table as he tried to explain some of the political dealings he was working on, ones I never took the time to understand beyond knowing that my brother was a genius at those kinds of things; gathering on his balcony to watch the stars rain to ring in the new year.

But not today. Today, when I entered, I saw only my mother kneeling at my brother's bedside; the curtains drawn around his bed. A broader glance revealed several of Vasileios's attendants and a handful of Councilors gathered around his table, their eyes averted.

"Mother?" I asked, my voice small, like a scared child.

She looked up, and her expression was even more hopeless than my sister's had been. She hadn't even looked this devastated at my father's passing, something she'd attributed to the knowledge that, someday, she would be rejoined with her soulmate in the afterlife.

xxx

"Olympio…" she croaked, her voice hoarse from crying.

I rushed to her side, throwing my arms around her.

"It's true?" I asked in a hollow voice. Everything so far had been clear, but I still struggled to believe. "Vasileios is…"

I felt my mother shift, and I followed her gaze over my shoulder. There, in the center of his bed, lay my brother, still, unbreathing.

Dead.

"No…" I whimpered, and my mother's arms returned my embrace, holding me as I succumbed to tears of my own.

My body trembled and heaved and ached as my voice rent the air with the wails I couldn't contain. My brother… Vasileios… the future king and the hope for our line…

Was dead.

"Olympio… Olympio…" My mother's voice did its best to soothe the raw agony, but there was no salve for this pain.

A knock came, and the sound of footsteps behind me let me know that one of the attendants had gone to open the door.

"I'm sorry, Lady Vassenia," the attendant said, her voice quiet but firm. "Only family and those of us who served His Highness may enter."

I heard her argue, but the attendant was firm, and after the sound of the door closing, I felt a slender hand on my shoulder. I glanced up to see my sister as she dropped to her knees beside Mother and me, and we all held onto each other as though our arms could shield us from the knowledge that Vasileios was gone.

"Your Highness," I heard Typhir say in a greasy voice. I hadn't even realized he was here. It felt wrong for someone so underhanded to be here, in this intimate moment, as my family grieved, but it wasn't like I had any say in it.

None of us moved for several seconds until my mother nudged me.

I looked at her in confusion, then she looked at Typhir with her swollen, tear-stained eyes, and back to me.

"He's speaking to you," she said.

It took me a moment to realize what she meant. In a room full of the royal family, if the words, "Your highness," were uttered, Vasileios would have been the subject unless otherwise indicated. In his absence, it would have been my mother. It would only refer to me if the only ones present were Ari and me.

But now, among all that remained of our family, the title was mine.

And I didn't understand why yet.

"What?" I asked bluntly, and, except for my mother and sister, everyone bristled like I'd offended them. Not that it was difficult to do. The Councilors, at least, cared little for me.

"The kingdom is expecting the festival," Typhir said, his voice lacking any kind of empathy. "How do you intend to handle that?"

"What do you mean?" I said, still confused. This wasn't my job. This was Vasileios's job, or my mother's, or even Typhir's own.

"Your Highness," he said, biting down on the words like it pained him to use them regarding me. "The *future king* needs to make an announcement of the tragedy."

"In case you hadn't noticed," I said, my voice laced with even more venom than his, "the future king is dead."

There was a heavy silence as implications settled amongst those present. With Vasileios dead, only those who had a claim to the throne could open the door. My mother was the matriarch, and therefore granted access to all places within the palace.

But me… I was only granted access to this room before because Vasileios had made it so. With him dead, I shouldn't have had access to these chambers…

Unless…

"No," I said, standing up suddenly, looking for some kind of escape, but my mother's hand gripped mine.

"Olympio," she breathed, pulling me back down beside her. My hand trembled in hers, and my throat felt like it was closing in on itself.

"No," I repeated, my voice cracking.

Ari's fingers closed around the ones my mother wasn't occupying, and my eyes met hers. There was a determination in them that I wish I felt in myself.

Why me? Why not her? The kingdom already adored her, unlike me. I was little more than a source of gossip. I wasn't…

I wasn't my brother.

And I never would be.

Chapter Four

"Olympio."

I closed the door to my quarters behind me, still in a daze, simultaneously unsure of what I was supposed to do, yet bound to a definitive path, one that never should have been mine to walk.

Vassenia had clearly been pacing my room, waiting for me to return. She wasted not a second from the time I entered before rushing to me and taking my hands in hers.

"Is it true?" she asked, though the drop in her voice was enough to tell me she knew it was.

Moving on their own because of centuries of practice, my arms slid around Vass's shoulders, holding her against me like her presence could fix everything. Like if my embrace was tight enough, it could save me from the fate that was never meant to be mine. Like if she just stayed close, it could be like this forever, that I wouldn't be the future king.

That Vasileios would still be alive.

She stayed still, holding me as tightly as I held her, the two of us remaining in silence until I finally slid to my knees, pressing my face into the softness of her waist.

"He's gone," I said, my voice hollow, the words sounding wrong even to my own ears, as if the truth they held had emptied me out.

"What does that mean?" she asked, her voice constrained.

I shook my head, still not releasing her. I knew what it meant in the broadest sense, but there were so many other questions that couldn't be answered.

Suddenly, the air in my room was too close, too thick. I stood, startling Vass, and looked around. This room had been mine my entire life, for centuries, but it wasn't mine anymore. My room was the one I'd just left, the one designated for the monarch of Sefaera.

"Come on," I said, grabbing Vass by the hand and dragging her out to the balcony.

She didn't ask where we were going. One of the wonderful things about Vassenia was that she knew me, knew my patterns well enough to not need to.

At the edge of the balcony, in the bright light of the sun, I looked out at what was now mine. The view of this room was mostly facing the forests and the river. My new room, the one I was expected to occupy by that very night, had a wraparound balcony that could see everything this one could, but also the sea and the entire village around the castle, where most of the people of Sefaera lived.

Where *my* people lived.

Without missing a beat, Vass wrapped her arms around my neck, and I scooped her into my arms. Our eyes met, and I could see the same emotions I felt mirrored in her eyes.

"Up we go?" she said, quieter and without the usual playful demand that would have colored the words.

Today, she was asking what I wanted. What I needed.

"Up we go," I confirmed, stepping up onto the railing of the balcony with Vass safely in my arms, I took a little jump to a small, nearby cloud, landing on it as if it was as solid as a plush mattress.

With well-practiced movements, I strode and hopped my way through the clouds, moving higher and higher. The little tufts, barely big enough to stand on, gave way to larger and larger ones, until they were big enough that ten people could have lain on them comfortably.

If they could, which no one but my family could have. The ability to walk on clouds was a gift exclusive to my lineage. Not even Vass could set foot on the clouds without falling through, which was why I always carried her when we did this.

After about ten minutes of traveling upward, we came to a cloud high enough that, from the ground, we would be such small specks that no one could tell there were even people up here.

Being careful not to let Vass down, not wanting her to plummet to her death, I sat down on the cloud, holding her in my lap before laying back, allowing her to use me as a solid surface. For the first time since Ari entered my room, something felt normal. Being here with Vass, like this, I could almost imagine that everything I'd ever known hadn't ended, that I would not have to relearn how to live my life.

Because this didn't need to be relearned. Holding Vass was as familiar as my reflection. And as we lay there in silence, I shut out everything else.

Until she voiced everything I was trying not to think about.

"You're going to be the king."

There was a carefully measured quality to the words, like she wanted to gauge my reaction before she revealed her own feelings about it.

"Maybe," I said, bitterness coloring my tone, and I did not know if the reason was because I might or because I might not.

"What do you mean?" she asked, propping up on her elbows which rested on my shoulder. She looked down at me, concern gracing her gorgeous eyes.

I reached up and brushed her hair back from her face, wanting to see it fully, to memorize every inch—just in case.

"I mean, they don't know if I'll be king," I admitted. "It has never happened that a monarch has died after their soulmate was born, but before their consummation, and certainly not after that bond was broken. No one knows if I'll ever get a soulmate. If I don't, then I'll never be king. The throne will remain at risk, possibly forever, because even if I have children, if I provide an heir, there's no telling if Vasileios broke the line when he broke his bond."

Vass hung on my every word, her face remaining, to my relief, neutral. My fingers traced designs on her back, reveling in the feeling of her skin. I would never, ever get enough of her skin.

"I was never supposed to be king, or future king, or in a position of genuine power," I said, hearing the desperate plea in my voice and not caring because the only one around to witness it was Vassenia. "I don't know the first thing about ruling. My expertise is in seduction and fucking, not politics and diplomacy."

"Who says you can't combine the two?" she teased, pressing a finger to my chin. Both the words and the gesture felt hollow, but I appreciated the effort. I grabbed the finger and pressed it to my lips, holding it there for several seconds before releasing her and shaking my head.

"Believe me," I said with a dry laugh. "I would if I could. Typhir couldn't even wait for my brother's body to go cold before he had me dragged into the Council chambers to discuss 'my behavior' and how the new power dynamics could harm the kingdom."

Vassenia cocked her head to the side, her mouth tightening. That was her uncle who'd been so heartless, after all. "What does that mean?"

"It means," I said, unable to keep the frustrated sneer from my voice, "that if the kingdom or any of our rival worlds perceives that the monarchy is being led by an arrogant, immature playboy, and that playboy has not secured the throne by consummating a soulmate bond, we might be seen as weak or vulnerable." I closed my eyes tightly against the flood of expectations.

"And are you okay with this all falling on your shoulders now?"

"No," I said, looking at her once more. "But I don't have a choice."

"Technically you do," she said, sitting up to look down at me with a serious expression, her legs astride my hips. "Technically, you don't have to do any of this. We could get on a ship, or you could open a portal, or—"

"I wish I could," I said, cutting her off, my voice suddenly firm. "But Vasileios left this to me. He believed I could do it. He…" My voice cracked, tears running from the corners of my eyes. "If I don't do this, if I don't get it right, if I don't become the king *he* could have been, it was all for nothing. He gave his own life to give the kingdom and the royal line a chance to do it right. What kind of brother, what kind of son, what kind of person would I be if I didn't honor his sacrifice?"

Vass frowned, dropping her gaze.

"I didn't mean to offend," she said. "I will, of course, support you however you need."

"I need you at my side," I said, reaching for her hands. "I need my most trusted advisor to help me. You've always been smarter than me. I need your help to figure out these new rules I'm supposed to follow and roles I'm supposed to fill." I brought one of her hands to my face, pressing it against my cheek. "Help make me a king."

She stroked my face, but tilted her head, smiling sadly.

"Olympio…" She took a deep breath. "I will stand by your side and help you however I can. But we both know I can't make you a king. There's only one way for that to happen."

"It may never happen," I reminded her. "And even if it does…"

"You'll break your bond like your brother did?" she asked, knowing the answer without me saying it.

I fell silent. There was no agreeable solution here. Vassenia and I had never defined our relationship, had never needed to, and now, any options we might have had were stripped away. We could be lovers, but there was an expiration date on that, and we didn't know when that was, or if it would ever come at all.

"Vassenia," I said, sitting up to wrap my arms around her waist. She put hers around my neck, searching my face. "You have always been my closest friend and most trusted advisor. I'm asking you to be that forever. Everything else…" I squeezed my arms around her.

"Everything else will be up to fate. Can you live with that? Knowing that we may have forever, but we also may not?"

I saw her jaw tense as she swallowed hard. Her lips were a straight line as she leaned forward and pressed a long, sensual kiss to my lips before pulling away, leaving her forehead on mine.

"I don't know. But we can try."

I knew it was the best that I could hope for, so I didn't convince her to make promises she didn't know if she could keep. I kissed her again, then shifted. I put her arms around my neck again so that I could stand, lifting her into my arms.

"It's getting late," I said, looking at the sun, which had moved in its arc, signaling that the afternoon was making way for evening. "I'm supposed to address the kingdom." I began the descent through the clouds, my deft steps bouncing on the soft surfaces. "I have to tell our entire world that my brother is dead, and that I, the prince they see as little more than a punchline or a lecher, will take his place."

"It's not that bad," she said, but we both knew she was lying. I'd bedded enough daughters, sons, even wives and husbands to have made a less than kind reputation for myself among my people.

"I suppose we'll find out."

We arrived back at the palace, on the balcony of my room. Well, former room. Even without walking inside, it was obvious it had been stripped bare, my belongings moved to my new chambers.

I walked forward, my legs all but numb, and stood in the center of the cavernous space. Despite it looking bigger because of its emptiness, it felt smaller, like the shell of a numire that it had outgrown.

But I didn't feel like I'd outgrown this. I had accomplished nothing to have earned this. Not even close.

I turned to Vass and pulled her in for one more kiss, holding her like I'd never let go… until I did. I took her hand in mine as we exited the room that had been mine for over fifteen hundred years and kept my grip on her through the hallways until we got to the door that concealed my new living quarters.

I paused. Earlier, I'd entered this room without realizing the implication.

Now, I understood.

My hand felt heavy as I raised it to the metal panel, feeling the familiar warmth spread through my fingers and across my palm before the door swung easily open.

My brother's body had been moved, along with all of his things. The room had been decorated with my own furnishings, and my chest heaved at the sight. Everything felt unreal, like I was stuck in a nightmare I'd never wake from.

I gripped Vass's hand, needing her to steady me as I looked around. This place was mine, but it had been invaded by everyone who felt they had a right to be here.

Typhir gave Vass and me a look from where he leaned against the wall. His expression, with one eyebrow raised at his niece, clearly showed that he had thoughts about what he saw but wouldn't say.

My mother and Ari approached me first, their arms finding their way around me while allowing me to keep a hold of my lifeline, of Vassenia.

"You're so brave," my mother said, her eyes full of tears. "To take this on, and to have to face it so soon after…"

Be brave and be fearless. Those might sound like the same thing, but they're not.

"You'll… figure it out. Eventually." My sister's playful grin, weighed down by grief, brought the first smile to my face in what felt like forever.

I would have stayed right there with them, with the people who could truly understand my pain, if not the burden I now had to face, for the rest of the night. Perhaps the rest of the week or month. But that cock Typhir was quick to break up the moment.

"Your *Highness*," he said, his voice an ugly sneer. "The kingdom awaits their future ruler."

I looked to the balcony, where attendants lined the doorways, but didn't cross the threshold. I would be out there alone, facing my kingdom, giving them the terrible news and hoping they would give me grace as I claimed my new title.

I released Vassenia's hand, not looking at her. If I did, I might change my mind about being brave, even if I couldn't be fearless.

But a small man, the one I'd startled earlier that day, with the red skin and horns, stepped in front of me.

"Apologies, Your Highness," he squeaked. "But… you can't go out there like that."

I looked at him in bewilderment. I had no idea what he meant.

"You're wearing white."

I looked down at my garment, white silk gathered at my shoulders and waist, hanging down to just above my knees. It took a second to understand what he was saying.

As the monarch, even if he'd had yet to officially take the throne, Vasileios was always dressed in the royal crest colors of black with golden adornments. He was the only one in the palace permitted to wear black, so that he would stand out.

And now, I would tell the people before I even opened my mouth, simply by the color I would wear, that I was their new ruler. That their beloved Vasileios was no longer the future king.

I stood in silence, my body numb as they stripped me bare and redressed me in something I recognized as mine, but that had been dyed black. The garment gathered at one shoulder with a golden cape hanging down from that spot. The fabric was cut on a diagonal so that it dipped down on the other side to my hip. A golden belt wrapped around the black silk, bringing it in at my hips. My shoes were replaced with golden sandals with straps that wrapped up to my knees, and several golden chains were hung around my neck.

I made the mistake of glancing in the mirror once they finished. I thought, in that instant, that I could see my brother in my reflection. In the black garment I wore, in the copper hair my siblings and I all shared, in the similarities in our faces.

Be brave...

I took a deep breath. I *wasn't* Vasileios, but he was a part of me and always would be. He had walked this road his entire life and knew the hardships I would face, but he had still chosen to leave it to me. I had always known I could never measure up to my brother, but here I was, forced to stand in his shoes.

The attendants parted, allowing my mother one more embrace, which I only returned halfheartedly, my mind and body feeling disconnected. Then, with my path clear, I walked toward the balcony.

Toward the future I never wanted, never planned for, but was resolved, from that moment, to put my heart and soul into it to make my brother proud, even if he wasn't there to see it.

Toward the future I knew would change me for good, and, I hoped... for the better.

The First Pledge

Eleanor Rose

Chapter One

Olympio

"Did you forget how to aim?"

I lowered my bow at the sound of Ari's voice. I'd just shot with—admittedly—terrible accuracy at an antlered drane, which had now been spooked and run off into the forest.

"Hello?"

I tried to ignore my sister's needling, but she was never one to be dissuaded that easily.

"Or are you just too hungover to see straight?" she said, her mind and focus clearly not on the hunt, since she was speaking far too loud and often, something she was too smart and skilled to do if she was taking this seriously. My sister was an excellent hunter, far better than me, even. It was probably for the best that I'd passed on the title of Master of the Hunt to her fifteen hundred years earlier.

Not that I'd ever tell her. Her ego was already nearly as big as mine.

"The future king doesn't have the luxury of being hungover," I finally said. That was only part of the problem, though. The truth was, I feeling even less enthused about my potential future title than usual after the meeting this morning where the Council had spent the better part of three hours criticizing me.

"Oh," she said with a gleeful expression. "You *did* hear me. I was worried that Vassenia or any of the other ladies of court you were seen cavorting with last night had burst your eardrums with their theatrical screaming. Honestly, it's like they're competing for who can be heard the furthest from your chambers."

Only Ariadne could earn a smile from me with a comment like that. I reached down and grabbed a handful of leaves to throw at her. She laughed and dodged out of the way, her dexterity unmatched within our entire kingdom.

This was how the hunts we went on together usually went. Teasing and taunting, and, sometimes, if we were lucky, we might end up with a kill to bring home.

"I'd *forget* how to hear you, if I could," I said with a grin.

"Impossible," she said, raising her own bow. "I'm completely unforgettable, unlike some members of the royal family."

"I'll be sure to tell Mother you think she's forgettable."

Without warning, Ari suddenly loosed her arrow—eyes never leaving mine—into the trees, and the sound of it striking something echoed through the forest. Watching her hunt was truly as magic as any of the powers our line possessed. She was made for this.

Unlike me, who seemed to be made for nothing.

My jaw tensed briefly as the memory of that morning's appearance before the Council played over in my mind, Typhir's disdainful voice reminding me that I was never meant to rule. I still hadn't garnered the respect my brother had when he was alive.

And part of me knew I never would.

Suddenly, I fell to my knees, gasping for breath, clutching my chest, my eyes clenched shut against a pain that struck me out of nowhere.

This wasn't the familiar lingering grief that hit me frequently and without warning over the loss of my brother. That was a wound that was ripped open every time I spoke of him and was reminded of what could have been.

This was something new.

"Olympio?" my sister said, quickly kneeling at my side, a hand on my back. But I couldn't answer.

It felt like my heart had been skewered on a hook, and I was being tugged by my very soul toward some unknown destination. The longer I resisted, the more agonizing that sensation grew, but it wasn't until I was able to open my eyes that I understood.

Emanating from my chest, from the center of my being, was a shimmering, glowing purple river of magic. I'd heard of this before, but had never seen it. How could I have? There was no guarantee I would ever see it. But I did. I saw it, and I felt it, and I knew, beyond a shadow of a doubt what had happened.

My soulmate had come into the world.

I'd been wondering if this day would ever come, ever since Vasileios broke his bond. No one knew if fate would grant me a soulmate after my brother died and left the future of Sefaera in my hands. We'd managed to keep that uncertainty quiet, known only to the royal family, our advisors, and the Council. The promise of my soulmate being born one day was all that kept the throne safe from those who might overthrow my family. I couldn't be crowned king without a consummated soulmate bond, and until I was, the throne was unprotected by the ancient magic that prevented a coup.

But now it was here, and I had never been so afraid of this moment. I knew all I had to do was to follow it to find the one who was destined to be mine for the rest of eternity and yet…

I knew what I would be giving up—*who* I would be giving up.

And despite that, I smiled. I hadn't understood when Vasileios had tried to explain it to me, but now I did. Somewhere out there was someone who had been born *for me*, and I could feel them. Without ever seeing them, without ever meeting them, I loved them with my entire being.

I looked up at my sister, who was often unfazed by anything, to find her looking at me with an unmatched level of concern.

"What's wrong?" she asked, and I could hear the quiver in her voice. I couldn't blame her. If I saw her collapse like that, I'd have been using every power I had to get her to a healer.

"Nothing," I said, feeling the smile spread even further across my face despite the pain and uncertainty. "Nothing's wrong."

Ari looked at me like I was out of my mind, but I didn't care.

"If you say so," she said slowly, motioning for our guards to come closer.

"There's no need—"

"His Highness may have been bitten by a cacolea," she said to them. "He's exhibiting signs of euphoria and delirium—"

"It's not a cacolea," I told her as I stood. "It's… it's *them*."

She looked confused for a moment, but the expression on my face must have been enough for her to understand.

1

"It's them?" she said. "*Them*, them?"

I nodded and pulled her into an embrace. "It's finally happened."

She froze for a moment, then wrapped her arms around me and pressed her face into my chest. I knew this moment was bittersweet for us both. We'd been through this once before, and it had ended in the greatest tragedy of our lives.

"This is wonderful, Olympio. Are you going to follow?" Ari asked. It wasn't really a question. She knew what I had to do.

"Yes," I told her, laying my cheek against her head.

Our verbal jabs were forgotten for the silly jests they were in light of fate smiling upon me. This was the first time since receiving the letter containing my brother's last words that I felt like, just maybe, I wasn't doomed to fail. If I'd been granted a soulmate, it meant that fate, that the deep, ancient magic that governed our land and the throne, felt I was fit to be king.

A thought that terrified me nearly as much as if this had never happened.

"How long will you be gone?" she asked, and my heart broke a bit.

"I don't know," I said. "Until they're ready." A soulmate bond could not be consummated until they had come of age, something that was not based on an arbitrary number, but on something in their life transforming them from a child into an adult—one who could rule at my side as Justice. "I won't put myself in the same position as…"

Ariadne pulled away from me and nodded as my words died in my throat. I thought perhaps I saw her wipe away a tear, but it wouldn't do to draw attention to it. If she was hiding it, she might shoot me if I asked just to make a point.

"Better get going, then," she said, turning away and nodding toward the palace. "You should tell Mother before you go."

"I will," I said, kissing her once on the cheek before turning to my home and taking off as fast as I could, becoming one with the shadows to exit the forest swiftly. Every second that went by was another that I was yet without my soulmate, and I would stop at nothing until I met them.

At the edge of the woods, like a graceful dance that only we royals could master, I let my body solidify once more and leaped into the air, landing on a small, low cloud, and continuing my journey upward that way. I jumped from cloud to cloud, the white fluff as solid as any stair for me. This would, of course, one day extend to my soulmate, but for now, it was just my mother, sister, and me.

"Olympio," my mother said, smiling softly as I arrived on the balcony outside her room. She seemed to be just leaving it, looking as elegant as ever in a sea green gown with her coppery colored hair—the same hair that Ari and I had—tucked and twirled into a coif on top of her head. "I thought you'd be out hunting with Ari."

"I was," I said, wiping sweat from my brow with the back of my hand. "I was. But…"

She suddenly frowned and grabbed my chin, tilting my head side to side and looking at my eyes. After a moment, her expression of concern transformed into one of wonder.

"You feel the bond," she said, a hint of awe lacing each of her words.

"Yes," I said. I looked down and saw the shimmering pathway undulating as though in a breeze. "It's beautiful and painful all at once."

She nodded and hugged me. "As it should be. Love is beauty and pain in its purest form."

I shifted, trying to understand. "Will it always hurt so much?"

She nodded with an empathetic yet melancholy smile. "And you must follow it."

I looked at her, feeling a lump in my throat. I hadn't been away from my family, from my kingdom, since my brother died. But I needed my soulmate—not only for myself, but for the future of my entire kingdom, which had been waiting far too long for this day.

"Will you tell Vassenia?" she asked.

My breath caught in my chest. I'd been avoiding so much as thinking about this topic. It was a difficult one for many reasons, not the least of which was the fact that I knew, based on the past, the danger seeing her now would present.

I shook my head, wanting nothing more than to tell my oldest and best friend what had happened and why I would be leaving, and why I would be gone for an unknown number of years. We'd spent our entire lives as lovers, but with the birth of my soulmate, to be with her in that way would break the bond. My brother hadn't lasted a single day after his bond had formed in the presence of Lyria, his own paramour, without giving into the temptation she had presented.

I knew I would need to remain away until my soulmate was ready to return with me, when the love I felt for them had grown beyond what I felt for Vassenia, or anyone else. When temptation wouldn't put the throne at risk again. My brother had trusted me with this. With his death, he had given me the chance to do what he could not, and I would do everything in my power to honor that sacrifice.

Even cut myself off from someone I loved.

"I can't," I said to my mother, who gave me a sad smile. She knew what was at stake and why I would choose this. "I can't stay here while…"

"I understand. You need to protect them. Protect the bond."

I nodded. "Mother… I'm going to do this right," I promised. "But I need your help. Please, don't tell anyone what's happened or where I went. I don't want… *anyone*… coming after me. I need to do this alone."

"Go," she said gently, pulling me to her to kiss each side of my face. "I'll take care of things here." She sighed. "I always believed in you. Vasileios believed in you, and clearly fate did, too. I can't wait to meet them, Olympio."

"Neither can I," I said, touching the radiant place on my chest that would point my way. The truth of those words surprised me.

She bowed, and I took my leave, turning and running through the palace toward the high tower, where I continued my ascent, up through the clouds to the floating mountains. The euphoria of closing the distance between my soulmate and me was unlike any I'd ever felt before, the pull being sated with every step I took.

At the peak of the highest mountain, I felt my magic urging me to move, to travel along the bond to another realm. I could suddenly see my destination in my mind, and I knew where the bond was leading me. I came to a skidding halt, horrified at the revelation I'd just had.

A human?

My soulmate was a human?

I'd seen the world at the end of this path by magical means, but had never been, myself. Not that I'd ever had cause to. My people hadn't had a problem with the human world since before I was even born. From what I understand, it's not even told in their history. But we'd been at peace with them since then—if being hidden from them to prevent their greed from tempting them again constitutes peace.

But I couldn't fathom why a human would be the one who was made for me, to be by my side for eternity. No human had crossed our borders in millennia. Why now?

The bond pulled at me, and I jerked forward, unable to resist.

A human it is, then, I thought as I allowed myself to become shadow, incorporeal and able to traverse the planes between. It was like being pulled apart by wind, not a journey for the faint of heart or those unsure of their purpose. I was neither, and I pushed my way through, knowing what awaited me on the other side.

It was night when I arrived, and within moments, I was nearly run down by one of their vehicles of transportation as I rushed across a street toward a house where I could see the end of the magic bond.

There.

Right there.

I shifted into shadow once more, the darkness itself forming wispy wings on my back as I bounced from corner to corner, invisible to the human eye. I had no idea who else might be inside or what they might do to a stranger, especially one claiming that their eternal partner was inside. So I used my own magic to traverse the outside wall, making my way up to the window where the bond led me. Then I slipped inside, unseen by the woman sitting in the chair, rocking back and forth.

The bond pointed to the chair. So this was her. This woman. She wasn't as young as I expected. I'd thought the bond would manifest earlier, at their birth, but I really had no other knowledge of how this all worked other than knowing it would lead me to them.

I approached her slowly, not making myself known, but wanting to see her. I was nearly close enough to step around and see her face when she suddenly stood, and I stepped backward into a dark corner to hide myself better.

And that was when I saw him.

"Goodnight, Gabriel," she said, kissing a small, sleeping baby on the head and laying him in a crib I hadn't noticed at first. She gazed upon him for a minute before she turned and left the room. A part of me expected the bond to follow her, but I knew it wouldn't. It led not to her, but to the child, who was surrounded with the shimmering purple magic that only I could see.

His little eyes were closed, and I stood over him, looking down at him. He was mine, and I was his, from that moment on.

I wanted to take him with me right then and there, to grow up where he belonged in Sefaera. But when I reached for him, I felt myself unable to touch him.

"The way Father told it," I remembered my brother telling me about his soulmate when she'd been born, before he'd broken their bond, *"when she comes of age, I will finally be able to touch her, but not a day before. Things will be different after that, and when that happens, my body will follow what my heart and mind have already decided."*

I looked down at the sleeping babe and smiled. His eyes fluttered open, and I worried he would cry and summon his mother.

I wasn't ready to look away from him. I had known they could be male, but I hadn't expected it. And yet, looking down at him, it felt right. He was perfect in every way.

But he didn't cry. He simply looked at me with his unfocused infant's eyes, and I could see the purple shimmer in his blue irises—the true indicator that he was the one. No one but me would see that shimmer until he was immortal like me. It was another gift of my line— the royal line of Sefaera. When our soulmates came into being, we would feel the pull and know that we'd found them by the magic between us and shining in their eyes for only us to see.

I shifted out of the shadow and gripped the edge of the crib. His eyes closed once more, and his breathing evened out. I knew then he'd fallen back asleep.

I couldn't take him with me. I couldn't even touch him. He was mine, though, and that meant he was mine to protect from anything that might cause him pain or harm.

"Gabriel," I whispered, leaning over him. "I cannot take you away yet. But I can remain by your side until you are ready to join me. You were made for me, and I for you. And by the bond we share, I pledge my eternal service to you, my soulmate. Your safety will always be my first priority, and your happiness my second. And when you're finally of age, I promise you that you will know me before I take you away from here to where you belong."

Years would go by from that night, with me intervening less than I expected, but more than I might have hoped. Using the power of our bond to share his pain when he'd fall and scrape his knee so that it didn't hurt so much. Slipping between him and the bully, who took a swing at him to redirect the blow so Gabriel could gain the upper hand. Urging him away from the water when he wandered from his parents and nearly fell in at the beach, well before he could swim. Drawing the effects of toxic substances from him and into myself when he nearly overdosed.

I'd made a promise, a pledge, and I would never break that promise. No matter what might happen.

Chapter Two

Gabe

Is there anything like a party hookup? You're feeling looser and more confident than any other time in your life, and, assuming you're not out to get over a breakup, it's the perfect time to fuck around with a stranger.

I had no clue what her name was, and likely the only thing she knew about me was that I was playboy/party boy Gabriel Hoffstet, son of Martin and Elizabeth Hoffstet, two major Hollywood producers.

Currently, I was kissing and dry humping some movie star wannabe who said her name was Cindy—or Candy. Something like that. I was really not too concerned about her identity as much as I was nearly coming in my pants over the idea of her botox injected lips around my cock.

"Let me blow you," she said, and it struck me how entirely unsexy it sounded when said out loud.

"Uh... okay," I said, my voice breaking with nerves. This was the first time for me, and I had a feeling it wouldn't be a very lengthy one.

"Just don't come in my hair."

She reached for the zipper on my acid washed distressed jeans, and I felt a weird wave of pressure radiate through my hips and down below my balls. I moaned softly, still fresh to the sex scene and she seemed to like it.

Cindy—or Candy?—started rubbing the front of my jeans over my dick, which had been hard for at least thirty minutes now, and I felt my cheeks get hot as the muscles tightened from my belly button down.

Oh, no.

"You're the producer's kid, right?" she asked me like she hadn't just waited through thirty minutes of virginal gyration to ask. She slid her hand down the front of my underwear, and the tug happened again. The feeling of an oncoming and unstoppable climax.

I'd never been touched flesh to flesh before, and I was about to be remembered for an entirely different reason than my parents' job.

"I—"

I was going to say yes, hoping that talking about my parents would slow my jets. Unfortunately, the rocket had already launched.

With a shudder and what I can only assume was an unintentional squeal from Cindy—or Candy—I felt a hot, wet ejaculation spill down the inside of my jeans.

Fuck.

"Did you just come in your pants?" she asked, looking more horrified than I felt was reasonable.

"Well..."

"Ew," she said, getting to her feet and nearly falling off her heels. "This is why I don't fuck kids."

lx

She walked around me like I was someone's vomit on the floor, like she hadn't been the one to lead me to this bedroom and initiate the… situation.

"I'm nineteen," I called after her. "That's not a kid."

Granted, she had looked about twenty three, so maybe to her I was.

I pulled down my jeans and underwear far enough to evaluate the damage and realized there wasn't going to be an easy clean up to all this. I needed to find a bathroom as soon as humanly possible.

I pulled open the door to the bedroom, which Candy had slammed shut behind her, and dipped into the hall. The hope was that I could sneak to a bathroom without being seen. Unfortunately for me, it looked like I'd either pissed my pants or done exactly what I did.

"Looking for something?" said a deep voice from behind me.

I turned to find myself uncomfortably close to a guy who looked about twenty-two with eyes that were so pale green they looked yellow. He was about six inches taller than me and had this red hair the color of a sunset.

"Uh…" I fumbled for my words, trying to make up an excuse that sounded reasonable. "Yeah, I'm looking for a bathroom. Spilled a drink on myself."

It definitely did not look like I had spilled a drink on myself.

"Party foul, huh? The bathroom is that way." He pointed down the hall not too far, and I nodded my head in thanks, still trying to casually keep my sticky clothes off my body without drawing more attention to the spot.

I practically ran for the bathroom, and, after I'd cleaned off the mess, waited a few minutes so that maybe people would think I was doing something—anything—else.

I hadn't long emerged when my best friend Aiden called to me from across the living room. "Gabe. Come do shots."

I gave him a look like I was less than interested.

"Unless you're a little bitch, of course." He smirked at me, knowing a threat of that nature would always get me to save face by doing whatever he wanted.

"Not a chance," I said, and rushed to down as much tequila as I possibly could.

As it usually did, once there was more alcohol than blood in my system, the night moved at a supersonic pace. The bass felt louder, the drinks went down smoother, and the boundaries between friend and lover were blurred.

I had been trying things out, and I still wasn't sure where I stood in terms of my sexuality. I found that kissing boys was just as nice as kissing girls, though I wasn't sure about sleeping with them.

That was until about four in the morning when I found myself knelt in the grass behind the house, sucking Aiden off like my life depended on it.

I liked the way his fingers gripped my hair and the sounds he made. I liked the feeling of his soft hardness rubbing against my tongue, and the way that I controlled him for those five minutes, even though it was him who was being pleasured.

I even enjoyed the finish. Salty and sweet all at once, in one warm swallow that I washed down with another shot of tequila.

It was my thirteenth of the night.

Which is how I ended up laying on my bedroom floor at home, listening to my parents get ready for our trip through the floor.

We were supposed to go to Los Angeles today via our personal jet to attend a movie premier of a film my parents produced. It was some heartwarming film about a rabbit and a boy or something, and right now, I would have rather died than get up off the floor to go anywhere.

A knock came on my door, and it opened with my mom peeking her head in.

"Gabe? You ready to go? What are you doing on the floor?"

"Sick… food poisoning…" I managed to groan, and her expression changed from confusion to one of sympathy.

"Aw… love. Do you still want to go on the trip with Daddy and me?"

I knew she wanted me to say yes, but I shook my head no. I wasn't moving from here for at least twelve hours, and, therefore, it would be hard to board a plane.

"Okay, sweetheart," she said, coming over to me and petting my hair. "You stay here, then. We won't be but a few days."

I nodded, my face pressed into the cool wood of the floor, and she rubbed my back.

"Feel better, baby," she said with a kiss on my head.

If I had known that was the last time I'd see her, I would have at least watched her go. Sometimes I nearly get sick over realizing I could have asked her to stay.

I did indeed lay on the floor until five pm, at which time I got to my feet to seek water and food. I also realized that my room smelled like old booze and farts, so I popped open the window and decided to walk to the shop around the corner from our upper east side penthouse.

The night was cool in the way late August nights tended to be, and for the most part, people were inside eating dinner, which made for a very relaxing walk. Particularly because I had put on my noise canceling headphones and was jamming to Taylor Swift while I pretended to be the main character or something.

When I reached the corner shop, I winced at the volume of the door chime as I entered. In all fairness, it probably wasn't very loud—I was just very hungover.

I walked through the aisles, looking at the bags of chips and candy, and nothing looked appetizing, but I grabbed a bunch of it, anyway. I also got some pain relievers because I had no idea where my mom kept stuff like that.

God, my head was pounding. This was definitely the last time I let Aiden talk me into shots.

I walked up to the register and dumped all the snacks onto the counter, then remembered I wanted to get one of those giant fountain sodas. "Hang on a second," I said to the cashier. I turned and dashed to the machine, filling the biggest cup available.

But as I turned around, I collided with someone else in my hurry to get paid up and back to my dark bedroom.

"Oops, sorry, I—"

My words stopped short as I realized I had run into the guy I'd seen the night before at the party.

"Hey," I said with a pained grin.

"Hey, yourself," he said, looking unimpressed. "You look like shit."

I recoiled at the insult and nodded at the guy, already moving to pass him. "Thanks, man. Good to see you again."

I pulled out my card as I approached the counter once again and handed it to the cashier. I watched him in a half-daze as he rang everything up, thinking about how rude that guy was. Who the hell was he to comment on my appearance? I didn't even know his name.

My phone started ringing, interrupting my line of thought, and I picked it up with a gestured apology at the clerk. I hated drawing attention like that. Sudden noises always freaked me out.

"Hello?" I said, not recognizing the number.

"Is this Gabriel Hoffstet?" the voice on the other side of the line asked.

I quickly hung up and looked back at the cashier. The only people who ever asked for me by my full name were telemarketers. "Sorry about that."

My phone started ringing again, and I groaned in annoyance.

"Hello?" I said with a little less patience.

"Gabriel Hoffstet? This is—"

"Look," I said in a shitty tone. "I'm not gonna buy your subscription or sign up for your card or whatever. Give it—"

"Mr. Hoffstet. I'm calling on behalf of the emergency services of East Hampton. I am afraid I have to tell you that your parents, Martin and Elizabeth, have perished in a plane accident."

My ears suddenly felt like they were stuffed with cotton, and my vision blurred. My heart stopped, and I swear I didn't breathe for an entire minute. I felt like I slipped out of my body and was watching the scene unfold before me like a movie, one I wanted to turn off but couldn't look away from.

"What?" I asked, even though I had fully heard what he said.

"Elizabeth and Martin have passed. Their plane went down about ten hours ago, and we couldn't identify them until just now. You are listed as their emergency contact."

I pitched forward, dropping my phone, and puked all over the floor.

My parents.

Dead.

The cashier came out from behind the counter and said something to me, but I couldn't hear him. I was floating, drifting, existing outside of myself in a reality where this was all a dream.

But the problem was, this wasn't a dream.

It was just the beginning of my nightmare.

Chapter Three

Olympio

I could hardly stand it.

It was the first time I'd touched him. The first time I'd come into contact with my soulmate. I'd been watching over him for eighteen years at a distance, unable to even brush his hand, and now I'd had a full body collision with him, letting me know in no uncertain terms that something had happened that had caused him to come of age.

And it was agony.

That first instant where our skin met, it was like lightning filled my entire being, and the pull, which I thought might be sated when I finally got to touch him, was stronger than ever and drove me nearly mad with need. With the desire to take him, to have him, a feeling that came upon me all at once and with the force of a hurricane.

Such was the power of the bond, that it would pull harder and harder now that he had come of age, though I didn't know at that moment what had changed. Before that moment, my love for him had never crossed the line into sexual or romantic interest. It had been protective, caring, nurturing. But now that my body knew what it was like to touch his, it was all I could do to resist. It took every ounce of willpower in every fiber of my being to not just grab him and take him with me then and there.

But I remembered my promise, my pledge—that I wouldn't bring him with me until he knew me.

And so I forced myself to simply walk away. To slip back into obscurity until the time was right. I already had a plan, one I would enact soon. I simply needed to put it all into place.

But then I watched as my soulmate staggered, and I felt a wave of pain emanating from him as he bent over and vomited. I knew, without a doubt, that it had nothing to do with the hangover I'd enhanced earlier. I'd had a feeling something horrible would happen, and I knew, beyond a shadow of a doubt, that whatever it was had transpired.

Because I knew that grief. I'd felt it myself when my brother had died. It was an unmatched pain, something unique in its violence.

And he needed me.

I tried to go to him, but an employee from the store got in the way, and I couldn't reach him. I couldn't comfort him, so I did the only thing I knew how to do.

I focused in on a feeling of calm, of serenity, and I sent it along the shimmering purple stream. The violent agony he felt dimmed slightly, but it wasn't enough. He was screaming inside, and it made me want to scream out loud for how much his pain affected me.

It wasn't until later that day, when I followed him home, that I even knew what exactly had happened. A plane crash. An accident that happened to a plane he was supposed to be on.

The realization that I might have lost him hit me like a wave, taking me under and throwing me about. Gabriel—*my* Gabriel—might have died before I'd ever even touched him. Our bond might have been broken, not by a mistake I might make, but by fate itself.

I knew then that I was being tested. After Vasileios had proven unworthy of his bond, I needed to prove my loyalty to my soulmate and my kingdom. I needed to prove I was worthy of this gift and of becoming king.

That was the beginning of the end, as they say, of my silent, hidden presence in his life. I needed to be where he went, at his side, with him knowing I was there for him. But I knew I couldn't just walk up to him and introduce myself as Prince Olympio of Sefaera, his soulmate. He was young and a bit naïve, but with a keen wit I knew would never allow him to accept something like that so easily. Trust would need to be built first.

And I knew exactly how to do that.

From watching him over the last nineteen years, I'd learned everything about him and his family and their plans for him. They wanted him to matriculate at Columbia University, a school of prestige in his world. There, he would be joining a fraternity—a brotherhood organization—that his father was a part of, and his father before him, and his father before him. These things had been decided for him, and I'd already taken some of the steps necessary to insert myself into his life. I only needed to make sure he was on the proper path to align with the one I'd put in place for us.

He left the store that day, and I remained in the shadows, watching over him and sending him waves of calming energy to keep him from spiraling into a darkness I'd never pull him out of. But at night, while he slept, I ensured that the paperwork was ready so that I could join him at university.

Up until the night before the funeral.

Gabriel had gone out to a party, with the same friends he'd been drinking with barely a week before, including the boy who had dared to put his cock in Gabriel's mouth, as though he was nothing.

Tonight, that boy was enjoying himself, surrounded by girls who seemed desperate to be noticed by someone of his status. Meanwhile, Gabriel sat in a corner, drinking heavily and keeping to himself, watching the rest of his so-called friends, not a single one of whom had even called to check on him, with a surly expression. I wanted to go to him, but I knew I needed to bide my time. Too many run-ins would be suspicious, and he likely wouldn't be as receptive if he thought I was stalking him for some reason.

It was a gamble, a risk, but I chose to be seen at this party. I didn't blend into the shadows—I walked in the front door in my corporeal form and began to socialize.

I was used to being fawned over. Up until the day I felt the bond, I had been well known for my promiscuity. Vassenia and I frequently invited others to join our nightly rendezvouses, and they rarely, if ever, occurred without an excess of libations. It was a frequent topic in meetings with the Council, but if I had to follow every strict rule they laid down all day, every day, then I needed a... release... every night.

Tonight, I was speaking to a girl who, even by demon standards, was beautiful, but the conversation was little more than a cover for me to keep an eye on Gabriel.

"I haven't seen you here before," she shouted over the music, leaning in close to me in a way that left no doubt as to her intentions.

"I just moved here," I lied, enjoying the way her eyes moved over my body.

"Well, New Guy," she said, coming even closer. "Do you need someone to give you a proper welcome?" She reached out and put a hand on my chest, closing her fist slightly, like she was preparing to pull me to her by my shirt.

I grinned and leaned in to kiss her, but stopped. This would lead nowhere good if I gave in to temptation. I took a step back as calmly as I could.

I'd spent most of the last nineteen years as a shadow, simply watching over Gabriel, unseen, not being a part of his world. This was the first time someone had touched me with the intention of engaging me in some kind of sexual contact in this world. I'd spent millennia enjoying lovers of all genders, having almost anyone I wanted because of my status, but now, a single tryst would bring everything crashing down. Not only would I lose Gabriel, but I would put my entire kingdom at risk.

The girl looked confused and angry at my silent rejection, and she looked me up and down. "Not worth it." She turned and walked away into the crowd, right at the exact moment that someone bumped into me from behind, and I felt that spark once more.

Gabriel.

I turned quickly and saw him pouring himself a drink at the table behind me, and it only took one second of focus to realize he was far too drunk. He seemed to have felt something, too, because he turned to me sharply and tried to focus his eyes on me.

"Hey," he said. "You were the guy from the store."

Shit. He wasn't supposed to remember me. But maybe it was better this way. Maybe familiarity was the way in. Not like I had much of a choice at this point.

"Oh, yeah," I said, like I didn't know anything about him. "You looked like you were having a bad day."

"You have no fucking idea," he said, downing one shot, and then another in quick succession.

"Hey, there," I said, reaching for his hand, worried that he was getting to a point of putting himself into real danger. "You might wanna take it easy."

"Easy," he scoffed. "Yeah, real easy being the Bruce Wayne of Long Island, only without the cool Batman shit."

Every stab of pain he felt echoed in me, and I could barely breathe for how badly it hurt. Even as drunk as he was, as much as I was trying to give him peace, he was still drowning.

"Gabriel…" I said before I could stop myself.

"Yeah?" he replied, not finding anything odd about a stranger knowing his name. Well, I suppose that was one benefit of the liquor he was poisoning his blood with.

I reached down and took his hand, and the bond exploded in a cascade which tingled and electrified every inch of me. The desire I had for him surged through me in a way that made me feral. I had to remind myself it would mean nothing if it was done like this, without him fully giving himself over to our connection and to his future with me.

But it wasn't time for that. Not yet.

Right now, Gabriel needed someone, and I was the only one here who seemed to give a damn.

His eyes went wide as our fingers met, and I knew he felt it, too.

"Whoa," he said, gripping me more tightly and leaning into me in a way I'd only dreamed of. "That feels fucking weird."

He wasn't wrong, but I didn't want to draw more attention to things he wasn't ready for.

I pulled him back into the corner he'd been sitting in before and stood him against the wall. He was unsteady, but leaning seemed to help him retain his balance.

"Gabriel," I repeated. "You are in pain."

"Nah," he said, holding up a drink I hadn't seen him grab. "I'm fine." He tipped his head back to drink it, but I pulled it from his grip and set it on a table nearby.

"You're not," I said, putting a finger under his chin and tipping his face up to look at me. He was tall, but I still stood several inches higher than him. Looking down at him, my desire to protect and care for him grew even more than I knew it possibly could. "And that's okay, Gabriel."

"Everyone calls me Gabe," he said, his eyes half-shut in his stupor. He was going to black out soon, and I knew my time to talk to him was running out. As it was, I doubted he would remember a thing that happened here, anyway.

"Gabriel," I said firmly, unable to get enough of saying my soulmate's name aloud. "It's okay to not be okay right now. Just know you aren't alone, even when it feels like you are. You're never alone, because someone is looking out for you."

"Who, God?" he said with a sarcastic sneer. "Heard that one before."

"Hardly," I said with a dry laugh. "Someone closer. Closer than you think."

Gabriel looked up at me again, and his eyes softened as they gazed into mine. Those brilliant blue eyes that sparkled with the purple magic of our bond, locked on in wonder, and I knew, even in his drunken state, he felt the pull of our bond as my hand wrapped around his waist.

"Who are you?" he asked, his words slurring.

I bent down, put my lips beside his ear, and whispered, "Someone close."

And that was when Gabriel turned his head to the side and pressed *his* lips against mine.

And the entire world stopped around us.

Because my soulmate was kissing me, and I was kissing him back. I wrapped a hand around the back of his head and pulled him against me, deepening the kiss. His tongue slipped into my mouth, tasting sweet and bitter, like the liquor he'd been drinking, but I didn't care. In that moment, we were one for the first time, and I knew, beyond any doubt, that I would stop at nothing until we could be one again.

It didn't last long, however, because only seconds later, Gabriel collapsed in my arms, passing out as I knew he would. I held him up, unsure what to do at first, but no one else even seemed to notice us—notice him, the boy they'd all been fawning over the week before.

I carried him outside and used his phone to summon a ride home, where I took him inside and put him into bed.

I sat at the edge of his bed, watching over him as he slept. I wiped his brow when it was covered in sweat as his body tried to eliminate the poison in his veins, and I gave him the constitution he needed to make it to the bathroom to vomit instead of expelling it onto his bed. I was his sentinel, his guardian.

As promised.

As he slept, I touched my lips, feeling the place where his had met mine. I knew now what my brother had meant when he said my body would follow. The love I felt for him had grown and taken on new life. Now, I not only wanted to protect and care for him, I wanted him. All of him. More than I'd ever wanted anyone.

Morning dawned, the day of his parents' funeral, and I could feel the rippling pain coming off of him. I did my best to temper it, but even with my heightened tolerance, it nearly crippled me to take it on for him.

And it couldn't have been clearer he didn't remember our kiss from the night before.

But that was fine. It wasn't like I didn't have time, and there was still my plan.

The funeral was a strange affair. Everyone was dressed in black to mourn someone's passing, but most of the people in attendance treated it like a social event rather than what it was. The only person who seemed to care, who seemed to have any connection to the event at all, was my Gabriel, who I tried my best to comfort from afar.

It was over more quickly than I'd expected, and everyone began to congregate in small clusters while Gabriel spoke to no one. He simply walked through the cemetery to the car waiting for him, and I nearly missed him for the crowd that separated us as he was leaving. But I still managed to get the envelope I'd carefully prepared through forgery and magic into his hands.

And then… all I had to do was wait.

Chapter Four

Gabe

I'd finally figured out what sucked about being a teenager but still a legal adult, and I found it out in the worst possible way. Turns out when you're over eighteen, no one has to check on you if your parents die in a horrible and nationally televised way.

Twenty four hours a day for three days straight, every news channel was covering it, and I couldn't escape it online either. Everywhere I looked, people were posting conspiracy theories about how their plane went down and why the pilot was found half a mile away.

Eventually, I turned it off, spending all my time asleep or answering calls from their lawyers about funeral arrangements. For someone who was newly an adult, there was a lot of stuff I didn't know how to answer.

Our closest relatives lived in Virginia and called only once to find out when the funeral would be. They didn't bother to ask how I was doing, only if there would be a church service and luncheon after the burial.

The night before the funeral, I did what I do best and went out to forget my troubles in a vat of alcohol. I immediately found a change in the way people reacted to my presence. I had gone from "son of fame" to "heir of new money" overnight, and people's typically warm receptions had gone cold.

I ended up drinking in a corner, watching Aiden do shots with three girls who looked like they could have been Victoria's Secret models. And in either an act of love or indifference, he didn't ask me to join.

It was bizarre to watch these people go about their lives like nothing was wrong, like I wasn't an orphan. Not that they should care—but it was all I could think about.

The alcohol didn't seem to hit fast enough, no matter how much I drank, and I have no idea how I got home. Likely, Aiden eventually took pity on me and put me in an Uber or something.

But either way, when I woke up, I was home and in my own bed, hangover free by some miracle.

I rolled out of my warm, safe cocoon and trudged to the bathroom to shower. I'm pretty sure people would have understood if I hadn't bathed, but my parents would be mortified, and this was about them after all.

The feeling of the hot water rushing over my skin conjured memories of being a kid and having my mom wash my back.

She would never do it again.

I dropped to my knees, a shock of pain rippling up my legs, and clutched my chest.

I couldn't breathe.

Fuck, I couldn't breathe.

I felt like I was dying, too. I felt like nothing would ever slow down and be good or peaceful again. I began to sob with such intensity that I didn't even make a sound, my whole body shaking.

The water suddenly went cold, and I shrieked with surprise, tumbling out of the shower and nearly hitting my head on the toilet. As unpleasant as it was, the freezing deluge had shaken me free of my panic attack, and that was a relief.

I leaned back into the icy cold and rinsed the shampoo from my hair, then wrapped a towel around myself before staring at my face in the mirror. Strong like my dad and pretty like my mom. I was a perfect combination of the two of them, and I alone would carry their faces with me until I joined them in death.

Dressing myself was pretty simple. I adorned the exact same outfit I'd worn six months ago to my grandfather's funeral. It was bizarre how different these two occasions felt, and not in the way you would expect.

When my grandfather died, I couldn't stop sobbing. I loved him dearly, and it was unfathomable that he would be gone. But right now, and every other moment outside of my shower, I'd been oddly numb. And not in the "I can't bear the pain" type of numbness. No, this was more of a lack of ability to get my brain fully in the space to believe they were gone.

It became more real when I stood beside their twin coffins, my dress shoes sinking into the wet mud that surrounded their graves. The air smelled like rain on pavement, and if I *hadn't* been so numb, it would have been kind of beautiful.

The way the grass was so green from the amount of rain we'd had lately. The way that hundreds of people had shown up to say goodbye, even the way everyone's eyes kept flicking to my face, waiting for an elusive tear.

"Gabriel," the minister said, looking up at me. "Do you want to say a few words?"

Shit. I was hoping this wouldn't happen and yet, here we were.

"Uh… no… that's okay."

The minister nodded and said another prayer, signaled for them to lower my parents into the ground, then beckoned my uncles to come forward and begin shoveling dirt on top. It was odd to see them here, let alone such active participants in this ceremony, since we hadn't heard from a single one of them in years.

The rain dripped off my hair as I watched, once again dissociating from my surroundings and almost feeling warm with disconnect.

The minute the ceremony ended, I walked away, not looking back once. It's not like they were there. It's not like I could get back that last interaction with Mom. The ceremony was for everyone else, not me. It was a who's who of Hollywood and finance alike, and I didn't fall into either of those categories.

I was just their son.

Just their son.

I walked up to my car, unlocking it through my phone, and was about to climb in when I felt a hand on my shoulder.

I was sure that it was one of my uncles wanting to know if my parents left them anything, or a lawyer trying to meet up for a review of the will. But instead, I turned around to find the tall ginger with golden eyes from the party looking down at me like he wasn't sure what to do with me.

"This is for you," he said, handing me an envelope. "Your parents wanted me to give it to you."

"How the—"

"I'm sorry for your loss."

He released the envelope into my fingers, but because I wasn't expecting it, I dropped it into a puddle on the ground.

"Shit," I said softly, grabbing it as quickly as I could and wiping it off on my jacket. "Sorry about that, I—"

But as I stood to speak to this guy once more, I realized he was gone. And not just like he was walking away, he had vanished.

I stared at the envelope in my hands, looking at the rigid print of my father's handwriting, and felt a single tear drip over my lower lashes. How the fuck did this guy know my parents? Why was he elected to give me my parents' last words?

I slid my thumb under the golden seal of the envelope and pried it open, the crisp tearing sound of the adhesive coming loose from the paper, louder to my ears than it should have been. Inside there was a delicate white note card with their initials embossed on the heading, and I pulled it free with ease.

I had never received anything from my parents before, and looking at their stationery, I could see why people were so enamored with them. They were glamor for real. Not the kind of shit you see in tabloids—two very classy, well paid individuals who now rotted in the ground.

"Dear Gabe,

If you're receiving this, it means we're gone and you are going to have to navigate this difficult time in your life alone. This would never have been the way we wanted it, but since we cannot change what is, only what might be, let us leave you with these parting words.

Be brave and be fearless. Those might sound like the same thing, but they're not. Only when you understand this, can you truly be your best.

Take care of those around you and never let a moment pass that you don't cherish them. It could all be gone in an instant.

Lastly, a request. We have left you everything we've ever had. We hope that you will use those resources to get yourself an education and to build a life you love of your own."

How very my parents to work in a Columbia plug as part of their last words. It made me laugh, which in turn caused a few tears to come loose and drip down my cheeks, strained from my teary grin.

I had been planning to ditch university altogether and use the money until it ran out. But, of course, they would make sure I felt just guilty enough not to let that happen. Not guilty enough to be bad parents, but enough to ensure their life savings didn't go to strippers and champagne.

"We love you so much, Gabe. Watching you grow up has been a joy and a pleasure. And, if the deliverance of this letter is any indication, we wish we'd had more time.

Your parents, Martin and Elizabeth"

The feeling of wanting to vomit through my unhinged little chuckles returned to me, and I crouched low to the ground to get my breathing steady. I was sure this was about to be the most painful experience of my life, and as long as I could endure and stay on the path my parents had planned for me, I was guaranteed a simple, relaxing life.

I stood once I felt right and got in my car, placing the envelope on the dashboard. I stared at it for a minute, then pulled away as I saw one of my actual uncles start walking toward me. I wasn't waiting around long enough that they had a chance to ask about money.

As the cemetery disappeared in my rearview mirror, I felt a weight lift off my chest like I was getting my first fresh breath of air after a lifetime beneath the waves. I had no idea whether my parents could have ever fathomed that this would be their fate, but they sure planned for it in case.

And their words were going to drive me to be brave.

Lead me to be fearless.

Chapter Five

Olympio

It was weeks later, and Gabriel had been settling into school nicely. Well, mostly. He was still partying heavily, and the only saving grace for my plan was that the place he'd chosen to go for his nightly fix of debauchery was the very fraternity I'd managed to join. It was much easier than I expected to "transfer" from another university into both the school and the brotherhood, and once I was in, I could keep close watch over Gabriel.

Of course, that meant watching as he began to use his newly found sexuality for things like favors. One upperclassman seemed to have taken a liking to Gabriel and his skills at fellatio and was willing to pay for the act in expensive gifts and favors.

I didn't like it. It wouldn't break the bond for him to be with someone else—only for me. But that didn't make me any less furious at someone using him. But for now, I simply had to sit in my displeasure, which, occasionally, was hard to stomach.

It was fairly obvious that Gabriel was going to be getting a bid, and Alex Kessinger, the upperclassman Gabriel had been cavorting with, wanted to be the one to deliver it, but I grabbed the envelope first, acting like it was random. Alex asked me to trade, but when I asked why, he didn't seem to have an answer. I suppose in his world, having any type of homosexual relationship could be considered shameful. He didn't want to be associated with that. No, he was the type to treat sex with men like it was his premarital right before committing to a life of heterosexuality, in full denial of his actual preferences.

Good. At least that was a small win.

I arrived at Gabriel's dorm room in midafternoon, which, in late September, was just starting to offer a chill in the air. Sefaera was temperate year round, though there were places you could go to enjoy a warm day by the sea or time in the snow. But here, in New York City, a light chill could become bitter as the wind whipped between buildings.

I pulled my hood up against the cold. I could have moved by shadow, but this felt like a moment that deserved me to walk on my own two feet. This was the moment where my plan would reach its apex. When I would confirm that Gabriel was joining the fraternity and would be under my watch day and night.

I knocked on his door and waited, but it only took a second for him to say, "One minute!" I heard a clanking of bottles through the door, and, after about the requested minute, he opened the door wearing pajama pants and a flannel shirt.

"Oh," he said. "Hey. You're not the RA."

I raised an eyebrow at him. "No," I said. "I'm not."

"You look familiar, though…" His eyes lit up. "You gave me the envelope from my parents."

He remembered. I thought he might have been too disoriented with grief, but he'd remembered my face.

"Oh," I said, rubbing the back of my head sheepishly, like I was embarrassed. "Yeah... Sorry about that. My dad was a brother with your dad when they went here. Apparently, your dad gave him the envelope, and he asked me to give it to you since he was busy talking to people at the funeral."

Gabriel gave me a skeptical look, but ultimately seemed to accept the story, which was good. It offered some level of trust.

"Okay," he said. "So... did you need something?"

I smiled in a way I've been told could bring any potential lover to their knees with weakness, but something about it made Gabriel uneasy. I could feel it in him—he knew there was something more here. Perhaps he was even remembering the kiss. I certainly couldn't forget it—not even for a moment. It had been all I could do to not have him every time I laid eyes on him and had resulted in many long sessions of solo engagement.

Even now, we weren't touching, but just his sheer proximity had my mind racing with thoughts of what I wanted—needed—to do to him. It was a pure animal need, driven by a primal kind of magic, which was why I knew I had to resist it. I was no animal, and I possessed the ability to care for him beyond what my body needed from his.

But I was also weak.

"Yes," I said, drawing myself up to my full height, which was nearly tall enough for me to hit my head on the doorframe. "Congratulations, Gabriel. You've been extended a bid."

"Awesome!" he said, but the excitement didn't meet his eyes, and I could feel the melancholy radiating from him. It was what his father had always wanted, but he wasn't around to see it.

"Are you okay?" I asked, putting my hands in my pockets and ducking my head a bit to seem less imposing.

"I'm good," he said with a bluster of false bravado, but I could see the cry for help behind his eyes.

"Okay," I said, not wanting to force him to talk if he didn't want to. We'd have plenty of time for that. I nodded over his shoulder toward the tv in his otherwise dark room, which was playing a fairly recently released action movie. "I love that movie." I'd never actually seen it, but it didn't seem like it required much attention to understand.

He turned and looked. "Oh," he said. "Yeah, me too. You could, uh... you could come in and watch with me. If you wanted to."

The longing he felt to be close to someone, and likely it was specifically me because of the soulmate bond, was overwhelming, and even if I'd had the mind to say no, I wouldn't have.

"That sounds great," I said. "I'm Ollie."

"Gabe."

"I know," I said with a smile as I walked inside. He closed the door, and I saw several empty beer bottles behind it, in addition to some full or half full ones.

He smiled sheepishly and pointed to them. "Did you want one?" he asked, grabbing one of the half full ones and taking a sip.

"Sure," I said, having no intention of drinking the foul substance. He handed me one and motioned to the bed.

"You can sit there, if you want. I'll take the chair," he said, going to sit in an oversized computer chair that likely cost as much as the top of the line laptop on his desk.

"Sounds good." I sat on the bed as Gabriel began to watch the movie, but my eyes never strayed to the tv. They were exclusively on Gabriel, on the back of his neck, which I could just see around the headrest of his chair, his eyes blocked from my view. I wanted to bury my face in the crook there, to suck and nibble on the supple skin until he moaned my name. I wanted to take that hand, which rested on the armrest and guide it down my front, into my trousers…

For the first time since we'd touched, I lost control and was completely hard in his presence. And it wasn't something I could ignore and hope it went away. Every minute that went by, it only grew more intense. I knew something would have to happen soon, and I didn't think walking out of here when it was clear he needed someone so badly would be the best idea.

So I did the only thing I could.

With Gabriel's back still turned, I slowly unbuttoned my pants, then pulled down the zipper. My throbbing hardness was straining against the thin fabric of my underwear, pressing upward toward my abdomen. I ran my hand over it and had to stifle the moan that nearly escaped me. I'd done this so many times thinking about Gabriel, but never in his presence, with him close enough that the bond was buzzing throughout my entire being, urging me on.

I slid the band of my underwear down, keeping my eyes on my soulmate to make sure he didn't turn around, and freed my length, which I grabbed firmly by the base and gave one slow, deliberate stroke.

I had no idea what the proximity of Gabriel would do to me, but it made every sensation more forceful just for him being there. I thought I might die simply from how intense the pleasure was, and I was only touching myself. I couldn't begin to imagine how euphoric it would be to have him against me, around me...

I slowly ran my fist up and down my member, bringing pulsing wave of pleasure after pulsing wave. It was shameful, I know, to be doing this while his back was turned, to sit on his bed and pleasure myself because of that pull the bond engendered. I stared at Gabriel, imagining his eyes on me, his body against mine as I kept up my slow motions, careful not to draw his gaze away from the television. It was unbearable, the need to have him, to—

I forced myself to remain silent as I came, wanting nothing more than to shout his name at the top of my lungs, but knowing I couldn't. I took a deep, shuddering breath, which, thankfully, was covered by an explosion in the movie.

I quickly pulled down my hoodie to cover up the mess and tucked my softening length back into my pants, zipping and buttoning them just in time, since the movie ended, and Gabriel turned around.

"Thanks for hanging with me," he said with a heartbreakingly sad smile. He downed the rest of his beer, then tossed the bottle into a garbage can beneath his desk. "I'd say you're welcome to stay, but I actually have some homework to do, so..."

It was then that I noticed the clear signs of arousal in my soulmate as well, and it took all my effort not to stare or to grin with glee. Clearly, the bond had worked its magic on him as much as it had on me, and he wanted some time alone to deal with it.

"No worries," I said, standing up and smiling at him. "Happy bid day. And congratulations. You're officially a pledge."

I turned and left his room, walking quickly until I got back to the frat house, where I stripped off my damp, sticky shirts and went for a shower, thinking about Gabriel and how it felt to be that close to him, to nearly have him to myself.

And no matter how many times I replayed the events in my head, the rumble of excitement lingered in my chest, rather than arousing me once more. The animal within me seemed to be sated, at least for now, and I was free to picture a life with me and Gabriel. My soulmate.

Forever.

Acknowledgements

This book is extremely close to my heart because, just like Gabriel (and Ollie, though he'd never admit it), I have had to "Taylor Swift" my career more times than I can count. I've had to learn that not all who are friendly are friends, and that the loves of your life can sometimes come in very unexpected packages. The inspiration for Olympio and Gabe came from the best real life couple I've ever known, Chase and August, and I would be remiss if I didn't thank them first. My brother-in-law has been instrumental in helping me to fully understand the kind of intimacy I was trying to portray (a far cry from the fanfiction I was writing in 2006.) They are my proof that true love—soulmates, even— exist.

Next, I want to thank some folks who made this book possible, whether they intended to or not.

Mal, you have been the "Gollie" number one fan since day one. Sharing this with you has been a pleasure. Oliver, you have done an incredible job of bringing my characters to life with your art. It means the world to have you understand my vision and make it happen. To the musicians whose music this book couldn't have been written without: Taylor Swift, Voilà, Imagine Dragons, Harry Styles.

Also, the authors who have directly inspired my writing style and character development, Mackenzi Lee and Scott Westerfeld.

Next, I'd like to thank my family. Mom and Dad, if you weren't exactly the parents you were, I'd have never become the person I am. Also my sister—who only convinced me to watch the Lord of the Rings movies once I'd been thoroughly convinced Sam and Frodo were gay.

Also to thank are my people:

Nay, you are the one who made me the fantasy nerd I am today. I am glad we can wander worlds together.

3BSK: There's too many of you to really give a good thanks, but you know what we've been through.

TKSC: Every single one of you has changed my life, filling in pieces of my puzzle I didn't even know were missing. Thank you.

My best friend like… ever, Rowan. You are the definition of besties for the resties.

Lastly, I'd like to thank all the other queer fantasy lovers who know that love is love, and the penultimate representation of that doesn't have to be reproduction. You are my people.
Well… you and cats.

All my love, enjoy the journey,

Eleanor Rose

About the Author

Eleanor Rose is a vibrant voice in the fantasy genre, often weaving tales that highlight queer couples. Passionate about representation, she is a staunch advocate for accurate portrayals of transgender individuals and those living with CPTSD. Eleanor's debut fantasy novel, *Pledge*, is set for an exciting release this October, following the success of her previous work, *Drinking With Cupid*.

An ardent traveler, Eleanor frequently journeys across Europe, drawing inspiration from its diverse cultures and landscapes. Closer to home, she cherishes the warmth and comfort of her cozy casita situated in the Southwest. Eleanor's adoration for cats is unparalleled, often weaving them into her tales or sharing stories of her own feline companions.

Her personal experiences deeply inform her work. Living with dissociative identity disorder, Eleanor is gearing up to release a self-informed speculative fiction on the subject next year, aiming to shed light on the complexities of the condition. This commitment to authenticity, combined with her unique storytelling, cements Eleanor as an author to watch in the literary world.

Made in the USA
Las Vegas, NV
17 January 2024